NHI

NON-HUMAN INTELLIGENCE

ISAAC HOOKE

To my Dad
My most devoted fan

CONTENTS

PROLOGUE

The dark void of the sky loomed above the even blacker void of the ocean, an eerie peace that was abruptly interrupted by a flashing glow from the annunciator panel.

Captain Lucas Morrison glanced down. A warning message appeared on the Engine Indicating and Crew Alerting System (EICAS) display, accompanied by the Boeing 777's aural fire bell.

FIRE CARGO FWD.

On cue, the faint, noxious smell of something burning hit the captain's nostrils.

He glanced at his copilot. Anton was staring at him urgently.

The repeated chime of the aural bell was getting under Lucas' skin... he hit the reset switch and the aural bell ceased. The warning message remained on the EICAS, while the light on the annunciator continued to glow bright red.

Anton began to read the non-normal checklist from the EICAS.

"Forward cargo fire arm switch," Anton said.

Lucas reached up and found the prerequisite switch in the flight compartment overhead panel. This would de-energize the recirculation fan and close the air vents in the forward cargo compartment in an effort to minimize the amount of smoke entering the cabin.

He flipped it. "Armed."

"Cargo fire discharge switch," Anton continued.

Lucas pushed and held the switch for one second, discharging the Halon stored in the two fire extinguisher bottles located in the forward cargo compartment.

"Activated," Lucas said.

"LDG ALT selector, set to 8000," Anton read.

Lucas pulled the Landing Altitude selector to the on position and then turned it to eight thousand. Normally this was used to set the expected landing altitude for the arrival at the destination airport. In addition to calculating the approach and landing speeds, it would also make the necessary adjustments to cabin pressure, in this case decreasing it—the goal being to minimize Halon leakage from the cargo compartment, where the pressure was currently somewhat less than that of the cabin.

"Engaged." Lucas hit the intercom button. "This is the captain, cabin crew to your stations."

"Issuing mayday." Anton was flipping through his tablet with his index finger. "The closest airport is Veer Savarkar, Andaman Island." Anton activated his headset. "Lufthansa 778, mayday mayday mayday. Cargo fire. We intend to divert to Veer Savarkar. Confirm."

Lucas changed course, making for the designated airport.

Without warning all the indicators on the instrument panel went out. As did the cockpit and running lights. The cabin was plunged into darkness.

"Why aren't the emergency lights kicking in?" Anton asked.

"I don't know," Lucas responded.

"Lufthansa 778, mayday mayday mayday," Anton tried again. "We intend to divert to Veer Savarkar. Confirm."

Lucas reached for his phone, intending to activate the flashlight feature. But before he could fish it out of his pocket his gaze latched on to something outside.

What…?

"Mayday mayday mayday," Anton was saying.

"Anton," Lucas interrupted. "We have another problem."

EVAN FISCHER OPENED HIS EYES. It took a moment for him to get his bearings. It was pitch black. The last he remembered, he was aboard Lufthansa 778 en route to Singapore from Frankfort. It felt like he was indeed still in a Lufthansa cabin, replete with the awkward economy seat that unnaturally contorted the lower back, inflicting a pain that would take days to walk off. So unless he was having one of those confused moments where one woke up in a hotel room bed or recliner and momentarily mistook it for one's own bed, then he still aboard the flight.

If so, something was wrong. There was no illumination in the cabin at all. No nighttime lighting of the aisle and cabin edges, and all the seat-back displays were off.

And then there was the smell. Smoky. Like burning electronics. Or worse.

With both arms he reached out in the dark and felt the armrests beside him, and then the itchy fabric of the sweater worn by the person in the seat next to his, confirming that he was indeed still aboard the Boeing 777.

His next thought was of the cargo. Was it safe? Had there been an accident? A leak?

He had the window seat, so he slid his fingers along the smooth surface of the wall beside him until he found the window screen and slid it upward so he could look outside. A bright, flashing light forced him to shield his eyes.

"Hey—" someone shouted. But the person's voice cut off, or rather choked off, as if they couldn't breath.

Evan felt like he was choking as well. Had the cabin depressurized? If so, why hadn't the oxygen masks dropped? He heard other people coughing.

He looked away from the flashing light and reached up, groping around the gasper vent nozzle above him, hoping to find some sort of manual release for the oxygen mask. He couldn't remember from the in-flight video if there was such a thing. He never paid attention to those safety briefings. He regretted that now.

The flashing light from outside illuminated the console above him at intervals, but there weren't any obvious release switches. He fumbled with the gasper nozzle, twisting it open. Nothing. Earlier one of the flight attendants had told him there was something wrong with the ventilation system. Indeed.

He crinkled his nose. The sharp redolence of smoke was only getting stronger. He tried closing the nozzle but it didn't affect the smell. The cabin was becoming uncomfortably hot. Or maybe that was simply the sense of impending doom that was kicking in, elevating his core temperature.

He tried to get up, but as soon as he pushed himself upward he suddenly felt dizzy and collapsed into his seat.

The light continued flashing outside... oddly, he was reminded of the raves he'd attended in his youth. Monstrous gatherings of teens replete with strobing lights and booming music. Those lights often gave the illusion of time slowing down and distorting, which was only amplified by the drugs he had been taking at the time.

Strange that he would remember something like that now, of all times.

He was tugged back to the present moment by his failing body... he felt so weak, a tunnel of stars spreading across his vision.

There were still a few people coughing somewhere in the cabin. They sounded so distant. Wait. That was *him* coughing.

He gazed one last time at the bright, flashing strobe light outside. He realized it wasn't a light, but a craft of some kind, orbiting the plane. No, two craft. Three.

He smiled sadly. These were not airplanes. Nor drones.

How did they know?

The tunnel of stars quickly overcame his vision and he lost consciousness.

———

DEREK BLACKWELL STARED at the paused footage

from Spy Satellite USA-229. It depicted a Boeing 777, Lufthansa 778 en route to Singapore from Frankfort. According to the logs provided by Lufthansa, the original Boeing 747 reserved for that particular flight had been grounded due to unscheduled maintenance. He wasn't sure if the aircraft substitution played a part in what he was seeing now.

Had Jackson Kane or other hostile actors been involved? Perhaps Jackson or his agents had smuggled something aboard the Boeing 777 and forced a last minute substitution that allowed the breach to escape detection by airport security. Blackwell had heard chatter that Jackson and his cabal were planning something big…

Blackwell had ordered an MQ-1C Gray Eagle drone sent out to scout the area of the disappearance for debris, but so far it had found nothing. Blackwell knew the only thing it would find was open ocean, but he would be remiss if he didn't at least look for signs of the flight.

He replayed the color-corrected spy satellite footage from the beginning. The plane appeared a bright white against the dark blue of the ocean. Shortly, the aircraft changed course. This would be after the pilots detected the cargo hold fire and issued the distress call before diverting toward Andaman Island.

And then, as if from nowhere, he saw them. Three orbs. Metallic, beautiful, yet terrible things. They were so much smaller than the plane, each of them roughly ten feet in diameter. They accompanied the Boeing 777 at first, and then begin to orbit it in a clockwise fashion. They maintained their spacing, remaining equidistant from one another and the plane. Their orbital speeds seemed to increase slightly, and they closed in with the plane, while still remaining equidistant from one another. And then, just like that, the plane and the orbs were gone.

He replayed the final section again, slowing it down and zooming in. It appeared as if the plane and orbs were sucked into some sort of central point. Like a black hole.

Or a wormhole.

He restarted the video again and stared closely at the footage. Was that…? He paused it and zoomed in once more. Yes, that was definitely an orb, following in the wake of the plane about two hundred feet behind it. He panned the zoomed footage around until he found the second sphere, and the third.

The objects had been following the plane for quite some time then. It was possible they had started the cargo fire. Either that, or the fire was the impetus for them to act, as if they had known it was coming.

He wasn't sure whether to be pissed off or terrified.

His channelers had told him there was a convergence coming in the time stream. He just hadn't expected it so soon. Then again, it was possible that this event was meant to obscure the real convergence.

With shaking hands he dismissed the footage from his augmented reality glasses and his gaze drifted to the tapestry on the wall that he had hung several years ago. One of the few decorations in his office, it depicted a lone man standing at the top of a rock pile, grasping a glowing jewel, single-handedly holding back the darkness all around him. Long, sinewy fingers stretched out from that darkness, reaching toward him, held back only by the bright light of the jewel in hand. If the light from that jewel ever went out, the darkness would swallow the man.

Blackwell grunted softly. *It wouldn't swallow just the man, but the entire world.*

The tapestry was given to him by his granddaughter. An amazing young woman, she was. Thinking of her calmed him a bit, and his hands stopped shaking at least.

As he continued to stare at the tapestry, he thought he could see the individual threads making up the fabric. A delicate weave. It had taken much patience and effort to put together.

All of the threads were related to one another in some small way. If even one thread was torn or went astray, the whole tapestry would eventually unravel.

Strands upon strands, all intertwined.

A knock came at the door to his office.

"Enter," Blackwell ordered.

Lieutenant Marcus Mitchell stepped inside, shutting the door behind him. Like Blackwell, he wore a pair of augmented reality glasses, which appeared similar to regular prescription glasses save for the light blue tint on both lenses. If one looked carefully, one could see the tiny outlines of purple-blue light on the surface of the lenses, comprising the heads-up-display Marcus had configured on the glasses.

"Any news from the MQ-1?" Blackwell asked.

"Negative," the lieutenant replied.

Blackwell nodded. "There won't be."

"Have you decided how you'd like to explain this one to the public?" Mitchell leaned forward inquisitively. "Boeing 777s carrying over three hundred passengers don't just vanish over the middle of the ocean."

"No," Blackwell agreed. If news of this ever got out and people actually believed it, the delicate aviation economy could very easily crash, bringing along everything else tied to it. So many strings.

Strands upon strands, all intertwined.

A lesser person might be tempted to short a few airline stocks before letting the news run wild.

But not Blackwell. *He* had principles.

"Get some debris out there," Blackwell ordered. "Make sure it washes up on the nearby shores."

"I'll get it done," the lieutenant promised.

"And plant something incriminating in the pilot's home," Blackwell added. "A suicide note would work."

Mitchell tapped his lips, pondering. "In it, he admits to killing himself and everyone else aboard…"

Blackwell nodded. Yes, he had principles.

To a degree.

"Also leak the satellite video," Blackwell said. "Via the usual disinformation agents. And have them come up with three or four competing conspiracy theories."

The lieutenant bowed his head. "I'll see that it gets done."

People would believe anything online, especially if it seemed like a consensus had formed in the tribe they were a part of. Controlling consensus reality was something his disinformation team had gotten very good at when it came to the online conversation.

When and if the truth ever came out, no one would believe it.

"That is all," Blackwell said.

Mitchell remained motionless in front of Blackwell.

"Well?" Blackwell raised an eyebrow. "What else, then? Out with it."

Was he going to ask the unspoken question? *What do we do if this happens again? And then again?*

But the lieutenant cleared his throat. "There is another matter. This one is unrelated, but still important."

So the question remained unspoken, and unanswered. For now. Good. Because Blackwell didn't *have* an answer.

Mitchell held out an empty palm, then made a sliding motion with his index finger followed by a tapping gesture.

A share request promptly popped up on Blackwell's augmented reality glasses.

He accepted and scrolled through a series of what appeared to be intercepted messages. At first he was relieved that the contents had nothing to do with vanishing planes, but as he further skimmed the contents, his eyes widened in alarm.

He quickly dismissed the display, clearing his vision, then explained in detail what he wanted Mitchell to do about this latest problem.

When the lieutenant confirmed that everything would be done according to his specifications, Blackwell asked: "Anything else?"

Mitchell smiled wanly. "That was it. For now."

Blackwell exhaled in barely concealed relief. "Good. Always putting out fires."

"That's what we do," Mitchell agreed.

Blackwell smiled patiently. "That will be all."

"Thank you, General." Mitchell turned to go.

General, he thought to himself vaguely. *They still call me General.* He had retired from the army years ago. His men called him by his former rank only to honor him.

Actually, *retired* perhaps wasn't the best term. You could never leave the army, not really. He smiled sadly. Once a general, always a general.

Even so, to the rest of the world his official job title was 'Managing Director.'

As he watched Mitchel go, Blackwell's thoughts returned to the plane. The original question, though unspoken, still burned inside him.

What do *we do if this happens again?*

When Mitchell had gone, Blackwell navigated to his virtual inbox with his augmented reality glasses and sent a message to his channeler team lead:

Ask our friends why we're having our civilian planes attacked now, and whether or not we should expect more such incidents. Also, was that the coming convergence you spoke of?

He dismissed the virtual inbox and sat back. With a sigh, he lay his hands on his desk and intertwined his fingers.

Even if the channelers were able to make contact and get an actual response to the question, and that was a big if, it would be impossible to tell whether the answer was truth or falsehood.

Blackwell wasn't the only one staging a disinformation campaign.

He stared at the tapestry.

Strands upon strands, all intertwined.

1

G arrett stared into the burning flames.

He was seated on his patio, the fire table situated about six feet in front of him. The clear stones glistened beneath the flames, the air above distorting with heat. Beyond the shelter of his canopy, the rainfall had diminished to a mere sprinkle.

A Glock sat on the armrest beside him. He glanced at it, smiled sadly. It was time.

He picked it up and confirmed it was loaded. He wrapped his finger around the trigger and held the tip to his temple.

His mind instantly cleared and his senses sharpened. He heard the subtle, deep hiss of flowing propane and crackling flames occasionally punctuated by a nearby songbird or the drip of the recent rainfall pouring from the canopy. He smelled rain, wet soil, grass, pine, and hints of a wet animal, like a dog, or a wolf. Resinous, teeming, dusky, and fertile.

Goodbye, world.

Unbidden, Isabel Lockwood's face filled his mind.

One of his oldest friends. He hadn't seen her in quite a while. They had grown apart. It was long past time to catch up. And yet it was too late for that now wasn't it?

He imagined her falling to her knees and crying when she found out he had died from a self-inflicted gunshot wound.

He immediately lowered the Glock.

He smiled grimly. No, it was a pleasant fiction he was telling himself, that she would shed even one tear for him when she learned of his demise. Likely, she would take the news without batting an eye, maybe expressing a moment of pity for what had happened to him, but then immediately moving on with her life, like the rest of the world.

Beyond the protection of the canopy, the rain picked up.

Hardened, he held the Glock to his temple once more, his resolve renewed. His finger tightened over the trigger, preparing to squeeze…

SHE NEEDS YOU.

It was not Garret's thought. The words veritably rattled his skull.

Stunned, he blinked and lowered the weapon. "Who said that?"

In answer, he heard only the subtle hiss of propane-fed flames and the pitter-patter of the rain.

He wasn't sure if he had imagined the words. And yet, that was the only explanation.

Or was it?

He set down the Glock and, on a whim, retrieved his phone and found Isabel in the contact list. He was almost surprised to find her still on the list, but then again he hadn't changed his phone in a long time.

He held his thumb over the call icon and hesitated for what seemed minutes, but in actuality was little more than a few seconds.

Finally he pressed the button.

As the call dialed, his heart began to beat frantically. He had been in a hundred battles, killed countless insurgents. He had survived Nasiriyah, Fallujah, Ramadi.

And yet he was terrified about talking to some little girl.

Not just any girl, he reminded himself.

The phone went directly to voice mail: "Hey, it's Isabel. I'm not available at the moment because I'm busy doing important things... like trying to teach my cat how to play air guitar. Leave a message and maybe I'll let him rock out for you later. Oh wait, I don't have a cat."

He smiled, shaking his head, and tried again.

Same thing. No ringing, just direct to voice mail.

He furrowed his brow. Why was he suddenly worried about her? Because of some imaginary voice he'd heard? There was a thing called sleep paralysis, a semi-conscious state he was somewhat familiar with— he occasionally experienced it and its associated hallucinations while waking up.

And yet he hadn't been asleep or waking up. Far from it. When he had held that gun to his head, he had been more attuned and more focused than he had ever been. Something about putting your life on the line does that.

He felt certain something terrible was going to happen to her, or was happening right now.

He got up and shoved his Glock into the waistband of his pants at the small of his back and went inside to pull on a jacket.

If he was wrong, and Isabel was merely watching

a movie somewhere and had set her phone to airplane mode—or her battery had died—then they could laugh off his visit for years to come.

Assuming he allowed himself to live that long.

ISABEL SAT on two yoga blocks on the floor, her hands resting on folded knees, her eyes closed. The sound of ocean waves lapping against the seashore filled her hearing, punctuated by the rhythmic pulsing of binaural beats. She tried to clear her mind and envisioned gold light flowing into her, but the nagging, everyday issues of life kept seeping in.

She imagined an iron box and visualized shoving her problems inside, a technique that sometimes helped when unwanted thoughts intruded, but it didn't work, not today. She couldn't help but feel she was wasting her time meditating when she should be looking for a job, and yet she'd already spent all morning submitting her resume. At this point she was so desperate she'd even applied to a few local coffee shops, deleting everything related to molecular biology from her resume.

She sighed and opened her eyes.

I should've just shut up and did what they wanted.

She took off her headphones. Before she could set them down, she heard the front door open. James, her brother, was home. She didn't like imposing on him like this, but it was a temporary thing, at least until she could get back on her feet.

It was an odd feeling, giving up everything for one's career—moving away from friends and loved ones, missing out on starting a family and living a normal life—only to be summarily dismissed for trying to do the right thing. The lawyers fees from the resulting lawsuits drained her to the core, not just financially, but mentally too. She had bet everything on those lawsuits.

And lost.

She stretched, stood up wearily, and walked to the kitchen.

James was putting something back into an overhead cupboard and he glanced at her with a cracker hanging from between his lips. He bit it in half and shoved the remaining portion into his mouth a moment later.

"How are you feeling, sis?" He was still chewing, but sounded uncharacteristically excited.

She raised an eyebrow. "Someone's happy. Especially after spending half his Saturday on campus."

At least I have a job, she half expected him to taunt.

"It worked," he said with a grin.

She folded her arms. "That mysterious experiment of yours?"

"That would be the one." His smile deepened cryptically.

"Details or it didn't happen," she stated.

"I don't want to jinx it just yet." He downed another cracker. "I still have some final tests to perform before I'm ready to share my discovery with the world."

She arched an eyebrow. "I see how it is."

He gave her a wry grin as he plugged in a blender. "Don't worry. You'll know soon enough." His expression softened, as if only now remembering her dismal life situation. "How about you? Any job offers today?"

The kitchen countertop was cluttered with jars

and canisters. He ran his gaze across them, selecting one particular container out of the bunch. He twisted it open and from it scooped some powder into the blender.

"Nada," she replied. "Who would have thought that nobody would want to hire a disloyal whistle-blower who sued their previous employer for wrongful dismissal and reprisal. Guess I should have thought of that before."

"You certainly won't find a job at any defense contractor," James agreed. To the blender he added a cluster of frozen blueberries, along with a handful of spinach leaves from the fridge. "Why not go back to university. Pursue academia?"

She laughed. "Like you? Not for me. I'd rather work at Starbucks."

"You'll get your wish." He added a generous scoop of Greek yogurt to the blender.

"I'm not so sure," she replied. "I applied to a few coffee shops already. No bites."

"You're overqualified." James put the yogurt, spinach bag, and frozen blueberries back in the fridge.

She smiled disdainfully. "They don't know that. I gave them the slimmed down version of my resume."

"I can tell you hate doing that," he said.

"Yeah," she agreed. "When you spend all that time and money on a degree, you kinda want to use it, you know?"

James activated the blender and a deafening, choppy buzz assaulted her ears, sounding like a cross between an angry drone and a bee. After some moments he pressed the stop button. In the blender, the different layers of food had merged into a purplish-green goop, which he promptly poured into a measuring cup.

"Want some?" He held up the cup.

She shook her head and mouthed emphatically, "no." She'd already eaten, and the last thing she needed now was problems with her weight.

James shrugged, then took a sip from the cup, leaving behind a purple-green mustache on his upper lip.

"So you've been submitting your resume non-stop all day?" he pressed.

She sighed. "Basically. Up until an hour ago, anyway. I needed a break. I downloaded—"

"A new dating app?" He wore a wry expression, eyes twinkling with amusement.

She smiled dryly. "Sorry to disappoint you, big bro, but no. Only some new binaural beats."

"Oh," he said with a frown. "Meditation. I don't know how you can stand the stuff. Always puts me to sleep."

"You're the one who should download a dating app," Isabel commented. "A relationship might do you good."

He shrugged. "I don't have time for dating. Especially not now." He took another sip of his protein goo and stared off into the distance.

She thought that was a sign the conversation was done, and she turned to go.

Unprompted he said: "A tridekeract contains more than three-hundred and fifty thousand tesseracts, did you know that?"

She gave him a curious glance. "What are you going on about?"

"A tridekeract." His eyes were defocused, as if he was mentally visualizing. "A thirteen-dimensional hypercube. Twenty-six dodekeracts act as facets, with thirteen touching per vertex. Hence the thirteen dimensions. You add in a time dimension and you get fourteen dimensions total."

She frowned. "I have trouble visualizing any dimensions past three..."

His eyes seemed to glow and he spoke as if more to himself than to Isabel. "The tridekeract was the key. I almost can't believe it. But the math, it's irrefutable. And the results... everything is going to change, sis. Everything."

"Because of math?" she pressed.

Her words seemed to bring him back from whatever far away place his mind had gone, and he met her gaze steadily. "Physics will change, anyway. Well, it will need to be updated."

"Good thing I chose molecular biology as my specialty then," she quipped.

"That will change, too, you'll see," he promised.

She wasn't sure she believed him. Whatever he had discovered, there would always be bills to pay, food to put on the table. Neither science nor physics could ever change that. It was how the world worked.

Still, sometimes she thought he was too smart for his own good. She had to give him credit. He had a brilliant mind: not everyone could be a physics professor, after all, a polymath in his fields of choice who understood materials science just as well as high energy physics and differential geometry. Then again she wasn't so shabby herself. Molecular biology was in no way, shape, or form "easy." Even so, compared to the brilliance of her brother, she sometimes felt like a light bulb against the sun.

Just the same, to Isabel he would always be James. Her big brother.

She chuckled quietly and shook her head. "A *tridekeract*. What a silly name."

Before he could counter, the doorbell rang, followed by a knock at the front door.

She gave James a curious glance. "Expecting anyone?"

"Nope." He was already heading toward the door.

G arrett sped through the streets in his jeep like a madman, slowing down only when he was a few blocks away from the James Lockwood residence.

When he'd found Isabel's home unoccupied, he'd talked to her neighbor, who had informed him that she'd sold her house to pay legal fees of some kind. Apparently she was staying at her brother's, whose address the neighbor happily provided. This was why Garrett rarely told neighbors his new address—they were usually far too loose with their lips.

In any case he'd visited her brother's home a few times in the past when he was closer to Isabel, so he had a vague recollection of the location anyway. It was situated in one of the more expensive areas of town, next to a golf course—not the easiest place to forget.

So unless she or her brother had since moved, he'd soon be laughing with her over a beer and letting her chide him over how silly he'd been for ever thinking she was in danger.

And then he could go home.

My Glock and I, we have unfinished business.

The pistol sat patiently on the passenger seat, ready for him when he needed it.

He slowly drove past the house, not stopping. Nothing seemed out of the ordinary. The windows were intact. The front door was closed, as was the garage. There were no cars outside or on the road in front. There were a few vehicles parked against the curb further down the street, but they were inconspicuous, not the kind anyone would use if they were staging an ambush or running surveillance. Then again, maybe the tradecraft had changed since his heyday…

He shook his head.

Listen to yourself. Now you're imagining an ambush. When I knock on the door, Isabel is going to answer and give me a hug. She's completely fine.

When her brother's house was behind him, he considered simply leaving the neighborhood right then and there.

But then he sighed. "Might as well check up on her. Came all this way." He glanced at his Glock. "Our little date will have to wait a bit longer."

He made a U-turn and returned to the house, parking on the road directly in front of the driveway so that he blocked the entrance.

He grabbed the Uber Eats delivery bag he sometimes used for side income and shoved the Glock inside, then zipped the bag half closed.

He raised the collar of his polo shirt and grabbed the cap he'd stowed next to the delivery bag. He pulled it low over his head and glanced at himself in the rear view mirror. The cap worked nicely with his big sunglasses to conceal his features.

Bag in hand, he got out and made his way to the front door. He kept his head bowed, shielding his face behind the rim of his cap and his raised collar.

He slung the strap of the delivery bag over one shoulder so that the pistol was more readily accessible. Out of the corner of his eye he could see the metallic glint of the weapon beneath the half-zipped cover.

He instinctively scoped out his surroundings as he advanced, trying not to make it obvious he was scanning what could become a potential battlefield. That bushy, trim scotch pine next to the garage, perfect for an ambush. The steepled roof of the house and garage, good for snipers to pick him off. That long, raised brick garden bed next to the front steps, ideal for taking cover or making an egress to the side of the house.

His survey complete, he reached the main steps and ascended to the front door, doing his best the whole time to convey calmness and ease of mind in his manner, when he felt anything but.

He rang the doorbell and knocked.

———

Isabel stared at the goopy measuring cup James had set down on the kitchen counter. She was kind of hungry…

I wonder what it tastes like?

She pursed her lips in consideration, then shrugged, grabbing the half-full container. She wouldn't gain weight from one little bite. And she'd be done well before he returned from answering the front door.

She gave it a whiff. Smelled good anyway. Like blueberries.

She lifted it but before she could take a tentative sip, something was shoved into her face from behind. A rag of some kind.

Her first thought was that it was a prank James was playing, as all brothers liked to do, but she quickly dismissed that possibility when the gloved hand continued to roughly press the rag against her mouth and nose, very hard. Meanwhile another arm mercilessly wrapped around her upper body and pinned her to an unyielding chest, locking her arms to her sides and lifting her legs right off the floor. She dropped the measuring cup in shock.

The rag had a bitter yet sweet smell, cloyingly so. Almost fruity.

She immediately held her breath and struggled against her unseen captor. She tried to free her pinned arms, but it was like fighting against an iron vise. She kicked her legs into the air, hoping to push off the wall or the fridge, but she was too far away from either.

She would have to take a breath of air soon. The rag had to be some combination of sevoflurane mixed with nitrous oxide, like anesthetists used. That meant she would have to breath it in for at least ten to fifteen seconds to lose consciousness, if not a lot longer. Unless, of course, her assailant had adjusted the sevoflurane and nitrous oxides contents to dangerous levels.

She risked a quick inhale and then held her breath once more. Good. Her eyesight still seemed mostly normal: there were some stars swimming in her vision, but that was likely from from holding her breath.

She kicked at the air and fought against her captor with renewed effort. The hand only squeezed against her mouth all the more tightly.

She felt a prick on the side of her neck. There must have been someone else present, because the hands that held her hadn't loosened. The prick subsided and she immediately felt sleepy. Despite her best efforts, she began to inhale once again, but it was already too late by then. The stars crisscrossing her vision were spreading.

Her captor set her down, and as her knees buckled, calmness filled her. Now that the fight or flight mechanism had subsided, she could think again, at least for a few seconds. She wondered just what sort of trouble she had gotten herself into now. No doubt her former employer had decided to make good on all the threats they'd made.

The stars completely filled her vision now; sight began to uniformly fade so that all she saw was gray. Her eyes closed, and her only regret before the darkness took her was that she had dragged her brother into all of this with her.

Should have kept my mouth shut…

When no one answered the door, the muscles of Garret's neck and arms instinctively tensed.

He knocked again.

Still nothing.

He positioned the delivery bag that was slung over his shoulder between himself and the road, just in case anyone was watching him, and when he was satisfied that the front of his body was properly shielded, he reached down and touched the door handle.

But he hesitated before turning it.

What are you doing, Garrett?

Of course the door would be locked. Why bother to test it? And what did he plan to do after that? Break in?

He shook his head at the absurdity of it all.

To humor himself, he tried the door handle anyway. He'd come all this way, after all, and…

Interesting. It was unlocked.

That either meant amateurs, or…

They wanted him to enter.

He reached into the half-open meal delivery bag and wrapped his hand around the pistol grip, but otherwise left the weapon in the bag. With his other hand he turned the handle and opened the door.

He moved quickly when there was no resistance on the other side, slipping in and shutting the door behind him.

He removed the Glock and lowered the delivery bag to the floor. He assumed a defensive stance as he proceeded inside. His eyes were adjusting to the dim interior light that was made even darker by the sunglasses he wore.

The place was absolutely, utterly ransacked. The contents of the hallway closet had been dumped to the floor. The removable cushions from the living room couches were also strewn about, their fabric covers unzipped, their foam paddings torn out. The frames of the couches themselves had been over-turned so that they squatted upside down on the carpet.

In all that carnage, his eyes caught on a USB charger, incongruously plugged into a wall. He instinctively lowered his head, burying his face in the raised collar of his polo shirt. He was familiar with devices like these, which were used to conceal tiny, motion-activated cameras that transmitted data over the phone network. He wouldn't be removing his sunglasses anytime soon.

He continued onward. In the kitchen, the fridge and cupboards were open, their contents dispersed across the hardwood and the counter tops. He didn't spot any chargers this time, but there was a USB stick tantalizingly left out in the open next to the kitchen sink—likely a honeypot containing the spymaster's trifecta of tracker, microphone and camera rolled into one.

Upstairs, the two bedrooms fared little better: clothes were laid out all across the floor. The closets and wardrobes were open, the mattresses laying against the walls, the bed frames perching empty on the floor. The contents of two suitcases in one room —presumably Isabel's—were also dumped out all over the carpet. USB chargers protruded innocently from outlets next to the bed frames, disguised as actual devices someone would use while browsing a phone or tablet in bed.

Despite searching every room, Garrett found no sign of either Isabel or her brother, but multiple indications of continued remote surveillance.

He wasn't sure what shocked him more: the fact she had been kidnapped, or that he had known.

ISABEL REGAINED CONSCIOUSNESS. Darkness... she was blindfolded, and had her hands bound in front of her. A seatbelt was strapped around her waist. A moment later she heard the subtle click-click of a blinker switch, and her body swayed to the motion of a turn—she was in a vehicle of some kind. Likely a SUV or a van, judging from the leg room. From the smoothness behind her head, and the motion reported by her inner ear, she thought she was positioned on a jump seat of some kind against one of the interior walls, and facing inward.

To her left, she could feel someone's leg pressing against her own. The owner's breathing was ragged, forced.

"James, is that you?" she asked.

"Keep quiet," a stern voice commanded from her right.

"Yes," James answered quietly. "It's me."

She heard a sickening thud, followed by a sudden inhale from James beside her.

"Quiet!" Another voice, further to the left.

James pressed his leg harder against hers. She returned the pressure with her own leg, feeling terrified.

While upset that she'd dragged her brother into this ordeal with her, she was also utterly grateful he was here. She had no idea what she would do without him. To have to face this all alone seemed an unbearable thought.

In the darkness, she listened to the constant hum of the tires, a high-pitched sound that indicated they were traveling at speed, likely upon a highway. The hum was occasionally punctuated by a repeated clatter and thud, probably from the tires traversing different uneven surfaces on the road.

She wasn't sure how much time passed on that highway. An hour. Ten minutes. It seemed like an eternity.

Finally she was drawn to the side as the vehicle slowed down and made a turn. The tire hum transformed, becoming crunchy, earthy. A staccato percussion of sharp, metallic pings joined in which she recognized as bits of gravel striking the underside of the vehicle. The faint odor of dirt and dust began to permeate the air.

Once again she had no idea how much time went by while traveling down that road, but then the vehicle made another turn and the pings of gravel gave way to the scraping and grating of tall, untamed grass against the undercarriage. The dirty odor cleared from the air.

Finally the vehicle ground to a halt. She slid to one side from the sheer abruptness of it, pressing into James.

She heard movement. The crinkling of gear, the scuffing of thick boots, and then a door slid open in front of her somewhere. A breeze caressed her face, and the air carried the scent of fresh rain mixed with undergrowth. She heard the flutter of leaves in the wind; a raven cawed somewhere in the distance, and crickets chirped nearby.

Her brother's leg pulled away from hers.

"Get up." A voice said.

She tried to stand but the seatbelt kept her in place. A hand also came down hard on her shoulder.

"Not you."

She stayed where she was. She couldn't see, but it sounded like James was being led toward the open door. "Where are you taking him?"

No answer.

She heard the rustle of foliage outside and realized James and some of the captors were now walking away from the vehicle.

She couldn't help a rising sense of panic. They were being separated. She was going to be alone with her jailers. And James... what were they going to do with him?

"It's not his fault," Isabel pleaded. "Let him go. Please. I'll do whatever you want."

Her pleas were met with silence.

The door in front of her was still open. She strained her ears, trying to hear what was going on outside. Darkness was supposed to heighten one's senses, but she heard only her own tense gasps for air, and the more controlled breathing of her remaining captors. She couldn't tell if James was still walking.

She continued to listen intently, hoping to hear something that would reveal what was happening outside. The sound of a door closing. An engine starting. Anything.

There.

In the darkness, she heard a faint, mechanical murmur, initially almost indistinguishable from the ambient sounds of the breeze and the crickets. It sounded distant. Maybe two hundred feet away.

The mechanical murmur quickly grew in volume, escalating first to a high-pitched whine, and then to an all-out roar—a primal scream of steel and power that reverberated throughout her body.

A helicopter.

This powerful machine that she couldn't see would soon rise up and take away her brother if she did nothing. Perhaps forever.

She tried to suppress the rising panic she felt, but couldn't.

I'm not leaving him.

She rotated her bound hands far to the right, and then, trying to be as inconspicuous as possible, she quietly slid her thumbs along the lower portion of the seatbelt until she found the buckle release. The angle was awkward, and she had to bend her wrists painfully to align the thumbs of her bound hands with the button. Then she took a deep breath and pressed it.

When the belt retracted, she instantly leaped to her feet and made a run for it. Still blindfolded, she hit her head on the low ceiling and then either tripped or someone tripped her, because she fell forward.

Her cheek hit something on the way down—presumably the door frame of the vehicle, and the blindfold was ripped from her face. Thankfully the blow was a glancing one, so she had enough presence of mind to raise her bound hands to cushion her fall.

Her lower body landed on the floor of the vehicle, while her upper body fell through the door frame and gravity dragged her fully outside. She tumbled into the damp grass, scraping her arms.

Free of the blindfold, her eyes were unaccustomed to the light at first, and she blinked several times. Her face, arms, and thigh throbbed. She ignored the pain and frantically struggled to get up, intending to race after James.

In the time it took to rise, her mind registered that she stood in a clearing. The helicopter resided near the tree line across from her. Her earlier guess of two hundred feet had been wrong: the helicopter was more like five hundred feet away. Some kind of Blackhawk variant, she thought. Definitely a warbird, judging from the weapon mounts.

The rear sliding door was still open and James sat inside, surrounded by four black-clad, helmet-wearing men. The ballistic visors on their helmets were closed so she couldn't see their faces. James was still wearing a blindfold. The craft hadn't yet taken to the air, though the rotors were spinning full speed, a blur of steel and fury. She could feel the wash from here.

She started to run toward her brother. Instantly someone tackled her from behind and merciless arms hauled her to the ground.

She only caught a momentary glimpse of her attacker's face as she struggled to rip away from him. He was wearing a helmet like the kind special operators used, his face hidden behind the mirror-like ballistic visor. She fought against him with her bound hands, but it was no use, he was too strong.

Recognizing that escape was futile, she turned all of her attention on the helicopter, and James. The warbird was only just starting to get off the ground.

"James!" she called.

She wasn't sure what she hoped to attain by yelling at him. Maybe she believed she'd somehow invoke a rise in her brother, and instill the courage to fight back or somehow break free of his binds. Maybe she just feared abandonment. Or perhaps she just wanted to let him know that she loved him.

Either way, her brother wasn't a superhero. He was simply a human being, much like herself. And though an incredibly smart and gifted one, he couldn't help her now.

She continued to struggle against her captor, but then another man joined him, further pinning her down.

She couldn't help the tears that fell then. She was powerless to stop any of this. Absolutely powerless.

Through it all, she refused to look away from the Blackhawk. If this was the last time she would see her brother again, she intended to witness every moment.

Through the tears, she watched as someone aboard the helicopter shoved an oxygen mask into her brother's face. The aircraft continued upward, rising now well above the tree line.

That was when disaster struck.

A rocket slammed into the helicopter from beyond the trees. The Blackhawk exploded in a searing fireball that devoured its steel frame and strew fragments of molten metal across the clearing. One of the men on top of her instantly went limp, but she hardly noticed.

Her eyes remained glued to the terrible sight, her mind not entirely registering what was happening as she watched the helicopter's charred husk descend. It almost seemed to move in slow motion until finally it smashed into the ground in a storm of blazing shards.

"Go go go!" someone shouted behind her.

Again, she barely heard. Her tears had stopped, replaced with disbelief and utter incredulity. That wreckage… that terrible wreckage harbored the remnants of her dear brother, one of humanity's greatest minds. His beautiful mind, and person, burning in flames.

No… no. This can't be happening.

The grief was overwhelming.

Her greatest fear had come to pass.

Now she had no one else.

She was alone in this world.

She had lost her big brother forever, and she had no idea what she was going to do without him.

Worst of all, it was entirely her fault.

3

Someone hoisted the limp man off her. As strong arms drew to her feet, her eyes dropped to the man who remained on the ground: a long shard of metal from the helicopter stood up starkly from his back. A blow like that would have killed him instantly.

Good, she thought.

Two other helmet-wearing men hurriedly hauled her languid body into the black SUV that had carried her here. They had their ballistic visors lowered, hiding their faces. She didn't protest or struggle when they sat her down on the long seat that abutted the far wall, nor when they quickly slid a fresh blindfold down over her eyes, enveloping her in darkness once more.

I hope they kill me soon, too.

Her body was drawn to the right as the vehicle accelerated rapidly through the tall grass. She was jolted up and down, at least until the man beside her buckled her seatbelt.

The scraping of foliage against the underside

transformed into the rapid pings of small stones against the undercarriage as they spun back onto the gravel road.

She was continuously jostled about—the vehicle must have been traveling at a crazy fast speed on that road—but she hardly noticed. Her thoughts dwelled on her brother. How, growing up, he had always harbored her and tried to protect her. And more recently, how he took her in when no one else would.

I can't do this alone.

Fresh tears fell, soaking her blindfold, and she sobbed. She expected her asshole captors to tell her to shut up, but they remained quiet for once. Maybe they were just as stunned as she was about what happened. Maybe they were finally feeling some guilt over what they had done.

Doubtful.

Can't do this...

Her cheeks felt hot with sudden shame. She was being incredibly selfish. Her brother had just died because of her, and yet she was more worried about being alone than the fact he was gone.

Then again, wasn't that one side of the same coin? Part and parcel of losing someone?

She shook her head, trying to clear her conflicting emotions.

She realized the vehicle was accelerating faster and faster, as if under intense pursuit... the gravel sound was gone, replaced by the hum of the highway. She could hear the deep, throaty growl of the engine rising in pitch, only to momentarily fall again as a higher gear clicked in. The process repeated several times so that she had to wonder just how fast the SUV was going.

She heard a screeching and at the same time was

pulled sideways—hard—against the seatbelt. Another shriek came from the tires and she was wrenched in the opposite direction.

The alternating rising and falling growl of engine acceleration began to replay all over again, and then she was pulled to the left along with another screech.

She heard a series of sharp, resounding impacts, reminding her of hail. The clanging came at irregular intervals, concentrated on the rear and sides of the vehicle.

The SUV had to be taking gunfire.

Instinctively she tried to crouch lower in her seat. Right then three chilling, high-pitched thunks emanated from the vehicle frame almost right next to her head, and she started. The sound was more muted than the other impacts, and she guessed it had struck a window. She didn't feel any wind leaking from the area, which meant the glass hadn't broken. Yet. As far as she knew, bulletproof glass could only take so many impacts before it failed. She wondered how long the window would hold…

More high-pitched thunks came from the window, and she flinched.

Someone didn't want her falling into the hands of her current captors. They'd killed James already, and now they were back to finish the job.

That was what she wanted though, wasn't it?

A deafening explosion muted her hearing and she became weightless. She felt like she was in an amusement park ride gone bad.

The vehicle slammed into the ground, and the seatbelt that held her in place dug painfully into her body. As all the blood rushed to her head, she realized she was upside-down.

She couldn't hear anything except for a high-pitched ringing in her ears.

Someone tore the blindfold off her face. She was staring into the visored helmet of one of her captors. His body was inverted relative to hers, and he was on his knees before her, resting on the roof of the upturned SUV.

He reached up and pressed the seatbelt buckle release. She dropped toward the padded headliner that covered the roof and shielded her head with her arms to break her fall. Despite the padding, it still hurt. Didn't help that her hands were bound and she could only move her arms within a narrow range of motion.

The black-clad man shoved her toward the SUV's sliding door, which was closed. The other visored operative crouched next to that door with an automatic rifle slung over one shoulder in a ready position.

She crawled along the padded roof toward the door, keenly aware of how silent the world around her had become. Nothing could pierce the ringing tinnitus in her ears, and she vaguely wondered if that explosion had made her permanently deaf. One of the bulletproof windows had been knocked out of its frame, but was still intact and lying on the headliner—she crawled over it.

When she reached the door, the two men exchanged hand signals. The man closest to Isabel noiselessly opened the sliding door. It jammed partway—apparently the vehicle's frame had deformed during the impact. But there was still more than enough room to exit the vehicle.

The other operative immediately began issuing covering fire. Isabel couldn't see exactly who he was shooting at. As for the gunfire itself, she could only vaguely hear it, like the pop of some distant fireworks going off.

The man closest to Isabel hauled her out of the SUV, and when she emerged, she clambered to her feet, mimicking her captor's crouch. He led her directly into the line of trees that bordered the highway, then shoved her behind the closest trunk, pushing her to the ground.

He took cover behind the same tree, then leaned around the edge to issue covering fire.

Staying low, Isabel peered past the edge, wanting to get a look at her assailants... at the people who killed James. She spotted the upturned SUV, and saw the other black-clad operative racing toward her position. He never made it.

He took a hit to the head and dropped like a ragdoll.

The front door of the upside-down SUV opened, and another occupant crawled out. The man's visor was open, and from the trail of blood he left, he was obviously injured.

A rocket slammed into the SUV from somewhere farther down the road, and she was forced to close her eyes as the vehicle and injured operative alike were engulfed in an immense fireball. She ducked behind the tree for cover.

Rough fingers wrapped underneath her armpit and forced her to her feet. Her captor led her deeper inside the forest, keeping his fingers wrapped firmly around the crook of her right arm.

The two of them threaded their way through the trees and the dense undergrowth. The branches of small shrubs constantly whipped at her face and neck, but she hardly noticed for the adrenalin pumping through her veins.

She heard a distant voice, but couldn't understand the words. She realized the operative was talking, but her hearing was still muted. That latest explosion hadn't helped matters.

The man stopped to open his visor, perhaps hoping she might be able to understand him better, and she looked into a young yet hardened face. She might have even called him handsome under other circumstances.

And then his chest erupted and droplets of blood smeared her right arm. He dropped to his knees.

He had been hit.

He said something to her, but she couldn't quite make out the words. He dragged himself behind a nearby tree and opened fire.

He looked at her and mouthed a word again. This time she recognized it.

Run!

She tore away, running frantically through the undergrowth between the trees. She heard sporadic shooting. It sounded louder: her hearing was finally returning.

A final gunshot ricocheted through the forest, and the shooting stopped.

They got him.

Her heart was nearly thumping out of her chest at this point, and she was gasping for breath, but continued running. She was nearing her limit. Branches ripped and tore at skin and clothing like angry phantoms eager to claw her into the dirt.

Lungs on fire, she finally reached her limit, but pushed past it. Fear and adrenaline were good motivators.

All of a sudden her foot caught on something and she tripped, crashing through the undergrowth. The sound of all that breaking foliage seemed a little too loud for her, and she worried she had given away her position.

But she was too utterly spent to get up. So she lay there, panting and gasping, her lungs and muscles burning from the exertion. As her breathing finally began to return to some semblance of normalcy, she started to notice the sting of all the cuts and nicks the undergrowth had given her. Her arms, hands, cheeks, chin... they all smarted. She even had some tender areas beneath her jeans where her legs had caught on some of the bigger branches during her frantic escape. And those were just the external injuries: her muscles ached, her head throbbed, and mental fog clouded her thoughts.

So she continued to merely lay there, catching her breath. At least her hearing had returned. It seemed almost normal now—she wasn't permanently deaf after all.

She considered just giving up. She was too tired. Every fiber of her being felt heavy, like she'd run a marathon and smashed into a brick wall at the end. The adrenaline rush that had propelled her forward was fading, and she felt utterly drained.

Yes I should just give up. Let them execute me.

No.

I won't let his death be for nothing.

She took a deep breath and tried to imagine positive energy filling her. Then, gathering her strength, she pulled her upper body upright.

See, that wasn't so bad.

She heard the soft snap of a breaking twig not far from her and she flattened herself once more.

Her heart beat loudly in her chest and she barely suppressed a rising sense of panic.

Swallowing hard, she got her fear under control. Staying low, she quietly, carefully pulled herself toward a nearby fallen log. It was only three feet away, but seemed a lot farther.

When she reached it, she gazed over the log toward the direction of the sound she'd heard. She still felt a bit light-headed from the adrenaline hangover as she scanned those trees, but blinked the sensation away.

That was when she realized the forest was completely quiet. No birdsong, nor even any insects. She would have almost thought her hearing hadn't returned, if not for the sound of her own soft breathing barely audible above her raging heart.

She had a strange, uncanny feeling then, as if someone was watching her. She continued to sweep her gaze between the surrounding trees, and when she saw nothing, she had a sudden, horrifying thought.

They're in the trees.

Slowly, carefully, she looked up.

She scanned the upper branches, searching for signs of her foes, but saw no one. She rotated her head and upper body, scanning all the boughs above her, but there was nothing. Just empty branches.

Her shoulders slumped in relief and she slid down to lean against the fallen log.

She heard rustling, this time coming at repeated intervals, and she stiffened. The sound of snapping twigs, and of undergrowth scraping against fatigues. Getting louder.

She carefully peered past the uppermost edge of the fallen log.

Motion drew her eyes to two men meticulously making their way through the undergrowth. They wore combat fatigues and helmets, and carried automatic rifles. She would have been hard-pressed to distinguish the pair from the previous group of men who had kidnapped her and James.

She realized the two men were following the same path she had taken. Tracking her. Likely wasn't difficult, given the path of broken branches and trampled twigs she had left in her wake.

They were headed straight for her.

It was too late to get up now. They'd see her as soon as she arose. And there was nowhere for her to crawl: it would take too long to get anywhere without making a sound. Plus the trail through the flattened undergrowth would be obvious.

She would have to rely on mercy.

Or luck.

She flattened herself against the base of the log, hoping to blend in unseen with her surroundings. There was only a small chance that it would actually work, but she had to try.

The footfalls through the undergrowth became louder and louder, until one of the trackers towered almost directly above her. His automatic rifle was pointed at her.

So much for mercy then.

Isabel froze and held her breath. She hoped death would be quick.

The soldier didn't move. He simply stood there. The visor of his combat helmet was open, exposing a weathered, bearded face.

He looked right at her, but those hard, ruthless eyes didn't focus on her; instead his gaze moved right past as if he couldn't see her.

How was that possible? Isabel's cover wasn't *that* good. She knew it wouldn't hold up to direct scrutiny, especially not from a trained special operative. Or ex-operative.

He turned and made a signal—likely toward the other operative, whom she couldn't see.

Okay. Here it comes.

She braced herself for the gunshots.

But incredibly, the soldier continued forward, vanishing from her view.

The second operative passed her a moment later. Like the first, his visor was open, revealing a bearded face. His stern gaze also passed over her, and he too didn't seem aware of her. He continued forward without even stopping.

As the pair of rustling footfalls slowly receded, she slumped her shoulders and allowed herself to breath, taking measured, quiet gasps.

Perhaps she had overestimated how much of a trail she had left in the undergrowth. The foliage wasn't particularly dense here, it only seemed so because of the mad dash she'd made. But still, that meant she would've been easily visible to the men while she lay there in plain view.

She didn't get it.

Well, either way, she was still in the game.

She waited, listening as the sound of her trackers continued to recede, until just like that the footfalls were gone entirely.

4

Isabel started counting in her head. She wanted to wait a full ten minutes before moving and she didn't want to have to rely on her already skewed time sense, which made every little moment seem like an eternity.

So she counted. Focusing on the current number, then the next number. Trying not to think too much about what had just happened.

12. 13. 14.

How had they not see her?

15. 16. 17.

And what about that strange sensation of being watched she'd felt the moment before the soldiers showed up?

18. 19. 20.

Come to think of it, she wasn't actually sure whether that particular feeling had actually faded.

Something is still watching me.

So much for focusing on the current number…

21. 22. 23.

I'm being watched!

She started to imagine a balloon of resonant, protective energy surrounding her, then shook her head and laughed sadly. She was somewhere in a forest, surrounded by men who wanted to kill her, not safe and sound in her bedroom at home.

Meditation techniques aren't going to help me now.

She managed to count all the way to three hundred despite the distractions, and decided that was long enough.

She peered past the log that was her hiding place and surveyed the forest around her. For good measure she also checked the trees above again. No one watching her...

Tentatively, she stood up. When no bullets riddled her body and no shouts pierced the air, she decided she was good to go and started back the way she'd come. The trail was relatively easy to follow: she could see the telltale signs of broken branches and broken undergrowth, along with the occasional footstep. Once again it seemed impossible that her trackers had missed her...

Having previously worked on a military base, she had a lot of friends who were military or ex-military, so she had some idea of the M.O. of those who now hunted her. She didn't believe her attackers would hang around the crash site very long, not when first responders were likely be headed to the wreckage at that very moment. Their best option would be to deploy a small group of men to either look for or wait for her while the main unit relocated. When the small group captured or killed her, they'd radio for pickup.

She'd only encountered the two mercenaries looking for her so far. There were likely others, and she suspected there might be snipers deployed somewhere closer to the road—it all depended on how badly they wanted her.

Maybe she was being overly paranoid, but she definitely didn't want to walk into some sniper trap, so she swerved, turning roughly twenty degrees away from the original path she'd trampled through the forest. She did her best not to disturb the foliage too much, not wanting to give her hunters a new route to follow.

When she felt she had gone far enough, she diverted another twenty degrees to the right—at least she hoped it was twenty degrees—and continued forward in a path that hopefully ran parallel to her original, though was well to the left of it.

She still didn't hear any birds, and insects were conspicuously absent. The flies and mosquitoes should have been out in full force this time of year, but there was nothing. She wasn't quite sure what to make of that. It was as if the whole forest was holding its breath for her.

It only made her all the more careful where she stepped, wanting her advance to be as silent and untraceable as possible.

She was uncertain of how much time had passed —*I should have counted the seconds!*—but she figured she should be near the road by now. Still, everything was absolutely quiet. No traffic noise. Maybe the highway was way out in the boonies?

She finally heard a distant, Doppler-shifting siren, telling her that first responders were arriving on the scene at last. One would think the siren would guide her toward the road, but for the life of her she couldn't figure out the direction of the wailing. One moment the siren seemed to come from in front of her, the next behind her, and the next to her right: the dense foliage and trees were reflecting and scattering the noise.

When the howl of coyotes—or wolves, she wasn't quite sure—came in answer, as such animals were sometimes wont to do when they heard a siren, she was also unable to discern what direction the baying came from thanks to the distorting acoustics of the forest.

It was at that point she started to panic.

She turned right, hoping to find her original trail. It was risky, because she could very well run into her hunters, but she felt she had no choice. This time she purposely started counting, more to calm her nerves than anything else.

By the time she reached three hundred and still hadn't encountered her original trail, she realized she was lost.

She paused then, listening. The air was silent once more. No sirens, no birds, no howls.

She took several deep breathes. Positive, energizing air in, negative, debilitating air out.

Her path was here, somewhere. It had to be. She must have missed it. She decided to try retracing her steps. But she found it difficult, because she had been so careful not to disturb the undergrowth this time. It didn't help that the ground there was covered in moss that sprung back into shape after being stepped on, leaving no footprints.

She turned right once more, deciding that the original trail must just be a little farther. She started counting, and when she reached three hundred, she still hadn't found the trail.

So that's it, then. I'm lost.

She glanced toward the sun, which she could see through the thick canopy overhead. In the northern hemisphere the sun traveled across the sky from east to west of course. That didn't help her though, because she had no actual idea where the sun was when she had first entered the forest. In her shell-shocked state, she had been more focused on trying to stay alive than on seeking out the sun's position.

She lowered her eyes and wearily sat against the thick gray trunk of a towering white ash tree and rested.

Her thoughts instantly drifted to James and the exploding helicopter.

James. One of the greatest minds she'd ever known. Her dear brother. Gone just like that.

And he had died for nothing, apparently, because it was obvious she wasn't getting out of here.

If only the first group of kidnappers hadn't confiscated her phone. Then again, it was doubtful she'd get a signal out here in these woods anyway.

It would be dark sooner or later. She wasn't sure she'd be able to survive a night in the forest. She recalled the howling she had heard when the sirens came, and she was convinced it was a pack of wolves, not coyotes.

Unease settled in the pit of her stomach.

Yes, it was wolves.

She closed her eyes and took another deep breath.

Help me.

She wasn't sure to whom she had directed the request. She wasn't particularly religious. It was more a habit from meditation, where asking for healing energy and so forth was par for the course.

She opened her eyes and smiled sadly.

No one was going to help her out here. She was lost. Alone in the woods. Far from civilization. Hunted by men who wanted her dead.

She stretched wearily, leaning her head back onto the furrowed trunk of the tree she sat against.

A flash of light came from above.

Puzzled, she looked up. She saw only the empty blue sky between the overhead branches. She blinked, squinting.

There: she spotted a tiny, glowing dot. It shone a grayish-white against the blue sky, reminding her of the moon on a sunny day, though ten times smaller. A... star?

As she gazed at it, the dot drifted, vanishing behind a branch.

Curious, she stood up, moving out from under the white ash tree, and searched the sky until she spotted the dot again.

It continued moving across the sky.

Isabel had the sudden urge to follow it. She wasn't sure where that impulse came from. Natural curiosity, perhaps. Or maybe it was because she had no other recourse and nothing to lose.

So she followed it, moving in the same direction as the dot. She couldn't tell how far away it was nor how big it might be... the object could have been in the earth's atmosphere for all she knew, or directly above the trees.

Assuming it existed at all—it was possible she was imagining it or hallucinating. She'd just endured a very traumatic turn of events, after all. Weary, lost, depressed, shell-shocked, suffering from adrenaline hangover: who could say what state of mind she was in?

I wouldn't be surprised if I'm losing it.

The overhead branches intermittently concealed the dot so that it moved in and out of view. Each time it passed from sight, she wondered if she would see it again, or whether the illusory object would finally reveal itself to be the figment of imagination she was beginning to believe it was.

But invariably, when she advanced past the latest bough that blocked the sky, the dot reappeared to guide her.

She was just beginning to think the object was real when she emerged from the shadow of one particularly large tree only to discover the dot had vanished.

She furrowed her brow and repositioned several times, keeping her gaze skyward, but she didn't spot it again.

Well, that was a nice little distraction her mind had provided from the reality of her situation. Now it was time to face the truth.

She wasn't getting out of here.

She exhaled deeply, closed her eyes, and bowed her head.

A deep, distant whine floated on the air.

Her eyes shot open. She strained her ears, listening. The whine grew in pitch and volume, and she felt a subtle tremor underfoot. The noise reached a crescendo and then receded as quickly as it came, Doppler-shifting down in pitch as it did so. The tremor subsided.

A semi had passed by. It was close.

The road was somewhere just ahead.

Feeling a rising elation, she continued forward, moving in the same direction she'd been traveling in pursuit of the elusive dot. In moments she could see a strip of asphalt between the trees ahead, and was able to make out at least two lanes of a divided highway.

She suppressed the urge to run and instead made her way forward slowly, moving from tree to tree, carefully scanning the trunks and treetops as she did so, wary of ambush. But she encountered no resistance.

When she reached the road, she confirmed that it was indeed a two-lane highway. There were no vehicles visible in either direction: nothing but tree-lined wilderness on either side. She must have wandered miles away from the crash site because there was no sign of the wreckage or the first responders she'd heard.

As she thought about the strange course of events that had led her to this spot, goosebumps prickled her skin and she blinked rapidly a few times before swallowing.

First the mercenaries not seeing me, then the guiding light.

She looked to the sky once more. The bright dot was long gone, but that didn't stop her from expressing gratitude.

"Thank you," she whispered.

5

Isabel had no money on her, no credit cards, no phone. She had only her clothes on her back.

She stayed close to the tree line so that she could dash inside if she spotted anything or anyone suspicious. She managed to flag down a passing semi, and the kind trucker offered to give her a lift back to the city.

It got dark way sooner than she expected, and when the trucker told her the time, she was surprised it was seven already.

Amazing how time passes when you're having fun, she thought bitterly.

She had no way of knowing how long had she been unconscious when the first group of men had kidnapped her. Too long, she concluded.

The semi dropped her off at one of the more popular thoroughfares in the city, and the trucker gave her enough money to buy a meal and bus fare.

She asked him to write down his number so she could someday pay him back, but he refused, and she was basically brought to tears by his generosity. She gave him a hug and thanked him for renewing her faith in humanity.

She bought a small meal from a nearby bar, and then hopped on a bus to head home. As she sat aboard by herself, she reflected on how it probably wasn't the best idea to return home. But she needed to get her bank cards, or some money at the very least. She couldn't rely on the kindness of strangers forever. A change of clothes would be good, too.

She decided she was going to post up somewhere near the house and merely observe, with no intention of entering until she was absolutely certain no one was watching it or lurking inside. That meant she'd probably have to keep watch until dawn, at least.

The only other option was to impose on a friend, but she'd already decided she wasn't going to risk dragging anyone else into this. Not after what happened to James.

So she remained aboard the bus, getting off at the designated stop and proceeding on foot.

She passed a few residents who were going for an evening walk, and she exchanged hellos with them, though the quiver in her voice betrayed her nerves.

She definitely had a bad feeling about this but despite her misgivings she continued. When she reached the final bend on the way to the house, she hesitated only a moment before stepping past and peering down the street.

Nestled along the residential road, this affluent neighborhood bore the unmistakable marks of gentrification. On both sides, rebuilt houses with grand facades competed with older, weathered homes for the skyline. Towering trees attempted to cast shadows over the well-maintained sidewalks that lined either side, but bright street lamps banished the darkness.

The homes on the left were worth about double those on the right, due solely to having backyards directly abutting a golf course.

The house she shared with James was on the left, but it was seven houses down from where she stood, and she couldn't quite see it from here.

She crossed to the other side of the road and, thanks to the solar-powered outdoor accent lighting, finally picked out the characteristic brick flowerpot that was part of the home's frontage. She couldn't see onto the actual driveway at this distance though, but she didn't spot any unusual vehicles parked in front beneath the street lamps. The neighboring homes harbored the typical high-end SUVs and sedans one would expect on a street next to a fairway.

She considered continuing forward and walking past on the opposite side of the street, but given the circumstances, decided a more subtle approach would be more appropriate. She knew of a far better spot to post up.

She crossed back over to the side of the road that was closer to the golf course, and retreated until she came to a house with an open, unfenced yard—one of the older houses that hadn't been torn down and rebuilt yet. She quietly made her way into the back-yard, terrified that some pit bull or other dog would attack, but she reached the chain link fence next to the fairway without issue.

With shaking hands she climbed that fence; when she reached the top rail, she wrapped her small fingers around the bar between the triangular-shaped protrusions and swung one leg over and then the other. She leaped down onto the grass of the fairway on the other side.

The golf course was empty at this late hour. It

was a lot darker here, since there were no lights, but she just used the dark outline of the fence beside her as her guidepost as she advanced. She wasn't all that familiar with the backyards of any of these houses, but she thought she'd know hers when she saw it. It might take her a moment to recognize it in the dark, though.

Most of the yards were partially shielded from view by the hedges, trees, and bushes the home-owners had planted on their properties. Some had even built their own fences inside the chain link, tall panels of closely-spaced wooden slats that protected their yards from the prying eyes of lowly golfers. Trees and shrubs also grew next to the fence on the fairway side as well: have to keep the greenery pretty for the clientele, after all.

She was passing by a particularly thick set of bushes next to the fence when, without warning, the darkness moved.

A callused hand clamped down over her mouth, stifling the scream that instantly rose to her lips. A powerful arm wrapped across her chest, pinning her own arms to her sides and swooping her into the thicket.

It was the exact same hold her original kidnap-pers had used, except this time without the sevoflu-rane rag.

She expected a needle to prick her neck any time now. She should have never returned here.

Back at square one. Stupid stupid stupid!

She struggled frantically and opened her mouth to bite down on whatever flesh she could. It was diffi-cult to even open her lips because her attacker was pressing his hand so mercilessly hard against her face, but she thought she gave him a good pinch, at least.

"It's me," someone hissed, the breath hot in her ear.

She froze. That voice…

Garrett? What the heck was he doing here?

The ex-Navy SEAL must have sensed her relaxing, because he slid his hand from her mouth. He spun her toward him so that she could see the shadowy outline of his face, and she had the impression he was holding a finger to his lips.

He turned her around and wrapped an arm around her again, pulling her close. His touch was strong yet comforting somehow now that she knew it was him.

He leaned forward, moving her with him, until they were both peering beyond the thicket he'd drawn her behind. He looked both ways, then nodded in the direction Isabel had been walking.

She stared, not seeing anything out of the ordinary at first. There were just some bushes lining the golf course side of the fence, along with a scattering of trees. One of the fairway fountains had activated in an ornamental lake nearby, spewing water in an upward stream against the starry sky, but other than that she saw nothing. Wait, that might have a been a sprinkler, not a fountain… she couldn't be sure in the dark.

She was just about to ask him what it was she was supposed to be looking at, when about a hundred feet ahead a shadowy silhouette appeared, emerging from the bushes.

She suppressed a gasp.

They were watching her home from the golf course.

The shadow appeared to bob back and forth for a moment, then vanished an instant later.

Garrett pulled her back into the thicket and released her. He spun her toward him once more, and then motioned with his hands. She could barely see them in the dark, but got the gist of the gesture, which was "be quiet and follow."

He retreated, keeping the bushes that grew on this side of the fence between himself and the fairway proper, slowly making his way through the under-growth in the direction Isabel had come.

He seemed hyper aware of the branches and undergrowth, avoiding twigs and so forth underfoot as if it was second nature. She did her best to copy him, though found it difficult in the dark. When she stepped on a particularly loud twig, Garrett stopped, waited a few moments, then swapped places with her so that she could take point.

They continued forward in that manner, with her in the lead and Garrett bringing up the rear. It was only when the house was well behind them that she dared to speak, albeit softly.

"Why are you here?" she asked over one shoulder. "You have to go."

"No," came the gruff answer.

"I can't drag you into this!" she declared.

"Into what?" he asked calmly.

She turned back to look at him, but couldn't see his face in the light. "How did you even know..."

He didn't reply.

They reached the yard that Isabel had used to enter the golf course, and Garrett helped her onto the chain link fence before swinging himself over.

They quietly sneaked across the backyard and past the house. She held her tongue while trespassing, not wanting to attract any more attention than neces-sary, though her mind was reeling. Had Garrett been a part of this somehow? Maybe he was among the men who had taken her and James?

Finally she couldn't take it, and when they neared the front sidewalk, she repeated: "How did you *know*?"

Again he didn't say a word.

She was definitely starting to think he was involved somehow, until he finally spoke.

"Had a hunch," Garrett said gruffly.

"A hunch?" she asked. "What kind of a hunch?"

"Doesn't matter," he said.

"What do you mean, it doesn't matter?" She pulled him toward him. They had reached the sidewalk, and she could see finally his face under the dim light of the closest street lamp. He looked at lot older than the last time she had seen him, with crow's feet starting around his eyes, and lines on his forehead. He also seemed more haunted, if that was possible. Maybe it was just the light.

"I need you to be honest with me," she said. "I… I don't know who I can trust anymore."

He seemed to study her for a moment in the dim light before returning his attention to the street. "I had a hunch something was wrong. I tried calling you. When you didn't answer, for some reason I thought I should check on you."

"You're an ex-SEAL," she stated. "You don't worry easily. Why would you check on me over some mere hunch? I could have been out at a movie theater with my phone set to airplane mode."

"If there's one thing I've learned in this life," he said. "It's always trust your gut. Always."

She shook her head. "I haven't seen you in years. Why now? Why would you be thinking about me after all this time? And how did you even know my new address?"

"Your old neighbor," he replied.

She noted that he answered the last question but not the first two. She wasn't quite sure what to make of that, but she decided not to press the issue.

Up until that moment he had been alternately looking up and down the street as if keeping watch. But now he stared directly into her eyes. "Where's your brother James?"

She dropped her gaze, stared at ground.

"It's his house, isn't it?" Garrett pressed.

Her voice was hoarse when she spoke: "This is what I've been trying to tell you. This is why I can't drag you into this. James is…"

Why was this so damn hard?

"James is…"

Why couldn't she say the words?

Her lower lip was doing this quivering thing, and when she blinked, tears fell.

"He's dead," she said.

The finality of those words struck her like a freight train and her legs buckled.

6

Garrett caught her and held her close. She was like a limp doll in his arms.

"It's going to be okay," he whispered in her ear.

In answer, she wept softly onto his shoulder.

He didn't really know what else to do to comfort Isabel, one of his oldest friends, so he just held her as she cried her heart out into his old T-shirt. He instantly regretted not staying in touch with her over the past few years, and felt partially responsible for what had happened.

Maybe if I had been there for her, this wouldn't have happened.

Well, he had his own problems. He couldn't be there for everyone.

He was there for now, and that's all that mattered.

Knowing it would be a bad idea to let his guard down, he kept his gaze on the street and sidewalk while he comforted her. He held onto her for at least a minute, and finally the sobbing stopped and he felt strength return to her body. He relaxed his hold, and when she remained on her feet he tentatively released her.

She seemed reluctant to pull away though, so he did it first, taking a step back. Then he looked directly into her dimly lit face. Her eyes were puffy from the tears, but otherwise he was struck again by how little she had aged—she was just as pretty as he had always remembered her.

Headlights from down the street drew his gaze, and he quickly pulled Isabel into the shadows of a nearby hedge until a big truck passed.

"We have to go," he told her when the vehicle had gone. "I'll get my jeep. Wait here."

"I'm coming—" she began.

"*Stay.*" He spoke the word in his command voice. It was a tone he had learned and practiced well during his tenure on the Teams. A tone that promised consequences for any disobedience. She was safer here at the moment, whether she realized it or not.

She opened her mouth as if to protest but then seemed to think better of it and retreated into the shadows.

Satisfied, he crossed the street so that he was on the opposite side of the road, and then made his way back toward where he'd parked. Garrett walked on the sidewalk this time, with his head bowed and cap pulled low. He was well aware that if a drone watched from above on the thermal band, he'd only look suspicious if he abandoned the lamp-illuminated sidewalks for the shadows of the front yards.

Yes, he had kept to the shadows while in the golf course, and a thermal drone might have seen him there, too, but he hoped the thick canopy of trees lining the course had successfully hidden him and

Isabel. The tree coverage wasn't as thick out here so he couldn't rely on that.

He passed Isabel's house, which was on the other side of the street: the driveway was empty and the place looked deceptively quiet. If he squinted he thought he could make out a dark figure keeping watch from one of the upper windows. Might have been his imagination.

He continued onward, and studied every vehicle he passed, regardless of whether it was parked on the road or in a driveway. He noticed nothing out of the ordinary. There were none of the larger vans one might expect to find during a surveillance op. There were a couple of SUVs, but they were empty as far as he could tell. He made his observations all very casually of course—to any watcher he would have seemed just like an ordinary passerby going for a walk.

Several houses later he arrived at the jeep. It was parked on the road in front of an older house. He got inside and started it, but left the headlights turned off. He needed to make sure no one was following him, and turning on the headlamps was a sure-fire way to lose his dark adaptation—he'd miss any other vehicles that might choose to pursue with their headlights off. He planned to turn the lights on when he hit the main road.

Again, it was possible, even likely, that there was an MQ-1 drone or equivalent up there reconnoitering the neighborhood, but there was nothing he could do about that at the moment. Driving with the headlights turned off wouldn't matter on the thermal band, and in fact might attract a drone's attention, but he needed to be sure if a vehicle followed. Besides, any drone operators would've probably already flagged his vehicle as suspicious, but they'd still need men on the ground to actually engage. He'd be ready if they pulled the trigger.

Garrett kept an eye on his rear view mirror as he drove down the street, but saw nothing yet. As he rounded the bend he pulled over to the side of the road in front of the house where he'd left Isabel. He unlocked the doors and waited.

When she didn't emerge from the shadows he began to worry. Had they gotten to her already?

He was just about to get out and look for her when she finally appeared.

She hesitantly peered into the passenger-side window.

He realized she probably couldn't tell if it was him or not in the dim lit. And the lack of headlights certainly wouldn't have helped.

He leaned forward and rolled down the window: "It's me."

She relaxed visibly and opened the door.

When she was inside he continued down the street; satisfied that no one was following, he turned on his headlamps—just in time for the main road—and let rip on the gas. He quickly dialed back on the speed, however, making sure he was going the limit.

"How did you end up in the golf course?" she asked suddenly. Her tone seemed ambiguous. He couldn't tell if she was suspicious of him, or just wanted more information.

"When I got to your house there was no one home," Garrett explained. "They had ransacked the place, obviously looking for something. Oh, and they left the front door unlocked. At first I thought that was a rookie mistake, but I quickly realized these guys were anything but. It was a honeypot. They'd left behind camera systems to record any intruders, disguised as USB chargers and memory sticks. Motion activated, piggybacking on the phone network to transmit data."

"So they know you were there?" she pressed.

"They know *someone* was there," he agreed. "Not necessarily me. I had my cap pulled low, my collar raised, sunglasses on."

"But your jeep, where did you park it when you visited me?"

"In front of your driveway, unfortunately," he admitted.

"Then they have your license plate."

"It's possible." He decided not to alarm her by mentioning an MQ-1 drone might be silently stalking them at that very moment. Instead, he added: "We'll be dumping the jeep shortly."

"Just like that?"

"Just like that," he agreed.

"A man of resources," she said.

He grunted.

"Or a thief," she continued.

"The latter," he admitted. No point in sugar-coating what he planned to do.

She paused. He was expecting her to grill him on the morality of taking other people's property or some such, but instead she said: "So you still didn't explain how you ended up on the golf course. Or why you're helping me."

He glanced in the rear view mirror. He didn't think anyone was following them yet. But if a drone truly had them under surveillance, any observers likely thought the situation was under control. "I'm helping you because I can. And because your friendship meant something to me."

"You're risking your life…"

"I realize that," he said. "But it's my life, and I can risk it however the hell I want."

In truth, he was simply glad to have something real to fight for again. Something *worth* fighting for. But he couldn't tell her that. She wouldn't understand.

"And the golf course?" she gently reminded him.

"I left your house soon after realizing you weren't there," he explained. "I figured they'd send out a cleanup team to ensure there were no loose ends."

He could feel her inquisitive gaze upon him. "Loose ends?"

"It was obvious they left in a hurry." Garrett turned onto a side street. His destination was only a few more miles. He kept one eye on the rear view mirror, but so far no one was following on the road. "The place was ransacked. Totally ransacked. Because of that, I thought there was a chance that whoever took you didn't find what they were looking for, and might return to search again, but this time they would clean up the mess they'd made. You know, collect the cameras, restore all the furniture the way it was. Pack your suitcases and make it look like the two of you had left town. Something along those lines.

"Anyway, I was right. I observed your house from a rooftop a few homes down, and I saw a reconnaissance van arrive." He left out the part about how the canopy of a tall oak shielded that rooftop, keeping him from the view of any watching drones. "Four men left the van, and only one returned when it drove off an hour later. That's when I knew there was a chance either you or James had escaped. They had deployed three men on the property, waiting for you to return. I kept an eye out, and saw one of them leap the fence and take up a position in the golf course.

When I spotted you approaching on the fairway, I made my way down as quickly and quietly as I could, hopping the fence and stopping you before you could get us both into trouble."

"How did you even *see* me in the dark?"

"Wasn't easy." Garrett didn't want to admit that he partially got lucky, because he just so happened to catch her shadow passing in front of the backyard light of a neighboring home. If he had been looking any other way, he wouldn't have seen it. He wasn't even sure if it was actually her at the time.

"You haven't even asked me why they're hunting me," Isabel said. "And yet you're still helping me. Unconditionally."

"I don't care why they want you," Garrett told her. "No. That's not entirely true. I do care. I mean, it doesn't matter. I'm going to help you no matter what. No matter the cost. This is what true friendship looks like."

She studied him, then rested a hand on his arm while he drove. She squeezed. "Thank you. I appreciate that. Though I feel I don't deserve it. I wouldn't do the same for you. I'd be terrified. Tell you to go to the police."

"You probably would," he agreed. "And that's fine. Because you don't know the things I know. You wouldn't be capable of helping me. And just so you know, the people we're dealing with, they operate above the police. Well above."

When her grip only tightened on his arm, he worried he had said too much and was scaring her.

Finally she released him. "I think they're after me because of a whistleblower complaint I filed."

Garrett furrowed his brows. "How can you be so sure?" The military industrial complex had undoubtedly offed whistleblowers before, of course, but he wasn't entirely sure they were specifically targeting Isabel, given the timing.

"Do you want to know the specifics of the complaint?" she asked.

"No," he said. "It's not relevant. If they wanted you dead, they would have killed you as soon as the complaint was filed. They wouldn't have fired you and let you pursue legal action against them for wrongful dismissal."

"How did you know I did that?" the astonishment in her voice was obvious.

"Your old neighbor. He told me more than just your new address. He said you had to sell the house because of legal fees."

"Oh. What did you do in the military again? I know you had tours in Afghanistan and Iraq…"

He smiled sadly. "What did I do? Too much."

She shook her head. "Well either way, you're wrong. It had to be me they wanted. James didn't do anything. He was just a researcher at a university."

"But how can you be so sure it wasn't him they were after, and you just got caught up as collateral damage? Think about it. They killed *him*, not you. You're going to have to explain to me exactly what happened. I know it will be hard, but you have to do it. I need to get a better idea of what's going on."

She was quiet for a moment, as if stealing herself. And then she blurted out everything that had happened, as if dealing out the facts as quickly as possible would be less painful. From the moment they were kidnapped, to waking up in an SUV, to watching James escape in a helicopter, to the resulting attack that ended in her brother's life, to her escape in the woods, and hitchhiking back to the city.

He had the distinct impression she was leaving something out about her escape in the woods, as it seemed too convenient that her attackers would simply "give up and stop looking for her," as she put it, not to mention the way she fidgeted when she said that, but he decided not to question her on it. At least not yet. She was under enough stress.

Garrett tapped his chin. "So one faction tries to kidnap you and your brother. The second faction tries to prevent the two of you from falling into the other's hands at all costs, including murder. What kind of research did your brother do again?"

"Just about everything physics related, really," she said. "From materials science to high energy physics to differential geometry. You name it, he did it."

Garrett nodded. "And did he make any break-throughs lately?"

She paused, and when she finally spoke she seemed stunned. "In the confusion, I completely forgot what he told me. I hadn't even considered it might be him... I totally thought it was *me* they wanted."

"What do you mean? Did he or did he not make a scientific breakthrough?"

"I don't know if I'd call it a breakthrough," she said. "But an experiment he ran earlier today was a success, apparently. He didn't want to discuss the specifics. Told me he had some more tests to run before he could make it public. But he did mention it would change 'everything,' whatever that means."

"An experiment earlier today..." Garrett frowned. "That's a little quick. Too quick. They must have been monitoring his communications for a while. And when he made the discovery, they moved in. Do you know exactly what it was he was working on?"

"No idea, to be honest," Isabel told him. "Something about a tridekeract. A thirteen-dimensional hypercube, of all things. I can't believe they'd kill him over math."

"You might be surprised what they would do, especially if competing factions are involved." Garrett saw the building he was looking for. "We're here."

"The mall?" she asked.

In answer, he drove past the mall and headed directly toward the underground parking garage situated next to it.

7

I sabel sat quietly while he drove down to the second underground level of the garage. She wondered what the plan was. Assuming Garrett even had a plan.

She still didn't know what to think of him suddenly stepping back into her life, but she was grateful that she didn't have to face this alone. He'd already saved her life by preventing her from getting too close to her home. She owed him for that.

I can't believe I thought I could spy on my own home without getting caught.

Garrett parked and then tossed her a spare baseball cap he fetched from the backseat.

"Put this on," he instructed. "Tuck all your hair inside."

"Could be a while," she said. "I'm not the best at tying my hair into a bun without pins."

She managed to tame her unruly locks, tying them into a relatively messy ponytail, but that was all she needed to tuck her hair inside the cap as requested.

"Wear these." He handed her his sunglasses.

"Now, after dark?"

"This is a mall," he explained. "There will be security cameras."

She shrugged, then slid on the sunglasses. He also fetched her a wind jacket from the backseat, and she put it on. He raised the collar for her so the Rain-Guard fabric partially shielded her face.

"Good to go," he commented.

He grabbed another cap from the backseat and pulled it low over his own head. He didn't wear another pair of sunglasses, however. She supposed he didn't have any more.

"Got anything else back there, maybe something I could drink?" she asked hopefully.

"No such luck. Let's go. Walk twenty feet in front of me at all times. Don't make it obvious we're together. Use mirrors or shop windows to keep track of me, or use strategic glances. Keep your head bowed, don't make eye contact with anybody. Don't stand out." He adjusted the collar of his polo shirt so that like hers it covered a good portion of his face, and then he got out.

Isabel emerged as well and looked at him: he kept glancing over his shoulder, as if he expected men to leap out at any moment and attack.

Garrett waited for her to take the lead and she climbed the stairs to the main floor. She entered the connecting pedway and emerged shortly into the mall proper. She glanced back, confirming he was shadowing her.

Most of the shops were closed at this hour, but the mall itself was still open. She used to hang out in this place a lot when she was younger. The majority of the doors got locked after midnight, and unlocked again sometime before six in the morning. If you were caught inside after the doors got locked, security would unceremoniously escort you to the closest exit. There was quite some time left to midnight, fortunately.

There were only a few people in the mall at this time, and Isabel, keeping her head bowed, didn't make eye contact with any of them. Floor-to-ceiling columns plastered in mirrors were common to these hallways, and whenever she passed one she always spotted Garrett behind her.

At one of those mirrors, when she spotted him she realized he'd fallen behind—he was stopped at an ATM.

Isabel paused next to the mirror and pretended to check a non-existent smartphone in one hand. She thought using an ATM probably wasn't the best idea at the moment, but then again they'd need money...

Garrett walked by a moment later. "I'll lead."

She waited until he was about twenty feet ahead, then followed.

He led her to a drugstore chain on the second floor, one of the anchor tenants in the mall that remained open relatively late on a Saturday night. She entered and waited near the front tills as Garrett vanished into one of the aisles. She passed the time by pretending to look at magazines. Every year the magazine section got smaller and smaller, she noted. Wouldn't be long until they got rid of it entirely.

After a few minutes he reemerged carrying a shopping basket. He walked by her on the way to the till, and then she watched him unload a prepaid Visa gift card, two cheap smartphones, a pair of prepaid SIM cards that included data plans, a pack of paper clips, a screwdriver, a wire stripper—amazing what drugstore chains carried in their Tools departments these days—a cheap pair of sunglasses, a couple of pairs of shirts, a six-pack of bottled water, some protein bars, and some blond hair dye.

Her first thought when she saw the hair dye was, *that can't be for me.* But Garrett's hair was blond already. She sighed.

It's for me.

After he left the store, she followed at the usual twenty feet distance. He donned the sunglasses and then sat down at one of benches next to the second floor railing. He pulled out his old phone to dial a number.

Isabel walked by and paused about ten feet past the bench. She rested her hands on the railing, gazing down at the first floor below.

Without looking at him, she said softly: "Do I want to know who you're calling?"

"The police," he replied.

She was confused. "Without changing the SIM card?"

He ignored her and spoke into the phone. "Hello, I'd like to report a stolen vehicle." He shared his name and address, described his jeep, and told the operator when he last saw the vehicle. "I parked it in my driveway today at noon and it was gone when I woke up… no, I haven't seen anything unusual lately in the neighborhood. I'm not sure who might have taken it… my wallet and all major credit cards were in the vehicle, as well as my bank card. Yes, I'll be calling the card companies and canceling as soon as I can." He then gave a contact number, and hung up.

"Don't they usually send an officer out to take the report in person?" Isabel asked.

"That's what the operator told me," he agreed.

"But you won't be home anytime soon…"

"Nope."

She glanced at him and saw him switch off his phone. He produced the pack of paper clips and used one of them to eject the old SIM card. He didn't put in the new one.

He caught her looking at him.

"I'll set up the new phone tomorrow at an Internet cafe," he explained.

She returned her gaze to the first floor below. "Why take out the SIM card of your old phone then?"

"Just a precaution."

"Okay…" she said. "It's not like you need to teach me tradecraft or anything. It won't help."

She thought she felt his eyes on her, but she didn't look at him.

"I'm just some girl who's in way over her head," she clarified.

"You're going to need to learn some tricks if you want to survive," Garrett told her.

Those words worried her. It felt almost like he was trying to prepare her in the event something happened to him. She was starting to get that frightening feeling all over again of being alone in this situation and not knowing what to do.

"Promise me you're always going to be here for me," she told him without looking at him. When he didn't answer, she insisted: "Promise. Garrett. That you won't vanish from my life again." She added, as an afterthought: "Even when all of this is over."

But he didn't answer.

Guess we're done talking for tonight. That was a silly demand of mine to make anyway. Of course I can't demand that of him. He doesn't owe me anything. Not a thing.

He pocketed the phone, grabbed the shopping bag, and took the lead once more. She let herself fall behind thirty feet this time as he proceeded to guide her toward the mall's far exit, well away from where they had entered.

He left the mall via a surface exit and continued across the parking lot until he reached the street. It was a warm night, and she was getting hot in the Rain-Guard jacket, but she kept it on because of the high collar that partially shielded her face. She maintained her thirty foot distance from Garrett.

There were only a few other passersby on the sidewalk, and none of them exchanged a word with her or Garrett, who always kept their heads down and didn't make eye contact.

They continued along the sidewalk like that, following the road for a good ten minutes until reaching an apartment building. Garrett diverted toward the building and she followed. He made for the aboveground parking garage that was next to it. There were three levels.

Garrett entered the garage and waited for her several feet inside. When she joined him beneath the shelter of that garage, he started walking next to her.

"Guess that means we no longer have to trail each other," Isabel said.

"Good guess," he replied. "There are no cameras in here. And drones won't be able to get a bead on us."

"So this is where we're getting our next vehicle, huh?"

"Another good guess," Garrett told her.

The garage was well lit, and as she walked among the rows of vehicles with Garrett, she noticed a running pickup truck parked behind a Toyota Prius.

A pair of legs clad in dirty jeans and worn shoes protruded from the undercarriage of the Prius. She heard a whirring sound coming from underneath, like a battery-powered saw or something.

"Odd time to change the oil," she commented.

"Stay here." He handed her the shopping bag. "Don't let him see you."

Isabel took cover behind one of the concrete pillars in the parking garage and peered past the edge just as Garrett reached the the pair of legs.

"Piece of shit." Garrett dragged the man out by the ankles and hauled him to his feet. The man attempted to strike Garrett with the electric saw. She might have gasped any other day, but she'd seen so much violence today that the attack hardly registered.

In any case, the former SEAL easily caught the man's hand and batted the weapon away. The electric saw clattered harmlessly onto the concrete floor.

"Stealing catalytic converters, are you?" Garrett roared. "Get out of here." He shoved the man hard against the rear of the pickup.

The guy hit the steel frame of the truck and stumbled to one knee. Again, she felt nothing for the man. No empathy whatsoever. And it wasn't just because he was a thief.

Holding his shoulder as if injured, the man quickly clambered to his feet and hurried to the driver side of the pickup. He gave Garrett one last frightened look, and then entered the truck, slamming on the accelerator before even closing the door. The vehicle fled the garage in a cacophony of squealing tires.

Isabel emerged, rejoining Garrett. "Why didn't we just take *his* vehicle?"

"Because he'd report it right away. Well, assuming

it's not stolen itself." Garrett took back the shopping bag and advanced, studying the parked vehicles on either side. "Ideally, we'd want a car from airport longterm storage, but security can be tight in those places. And we're a little far from an airport at the moment. So we have to settle for the second best thing."

He paused next to one particular vehicle. It was an old, dirty, Honda Civic. Someone had scrawled "shitbox uncertified" into the grime of the angled rear window.

Garrett walked to the driver-side door and examined the lock in the dim light.

"This one." He produced the box of paper clips from the shopping bag.

"Don't tell me you're going to make a lock pick out of paperclips," she said.

"How'd you guess?" He reached into the bag again, this time grabbing the screwdriver.

She crossed her arms. "Is this something they teach all Navy SEALs?"

"You forgot that I used to steal cars in my teens?"

She paused. "I only remember you stealing one car."

He grinned widely. "Ah yes. The time I got caught."

She shook her head. "The more you know someone, the more you realize you don't know them."

He gave her a wink and returned the paper clips to the bag—apparently he was only being sarcastic about opening it with those—then ran his fingers along the thin elliptical gap that encompassed the door handle. He jammed the tip of the screwdriver into the gap right below the lock, and pried upward, jiggling the screwdriver a few times. She heard a soft snap.

Garrett tried the handle and the door opened.

He grabbed the wire strippers from the shopping bag next and, still holding the screwdriver, proceeded to sit in the driver's seat.

She couldn't see what he was doing, but in a few moments he had the compact sedan running. He opened the passenger-side door and beckoned her inside.

She went around and squeezed into the passenger seat.

"We might have to steal a car every day to be on the safe side," he said. "Can you handle that?"

"Yeah." She wasn't sure what else to say. She was thinking of James, and starting to descend into despondency again.

Suddenly Garrett's hand wrapped around hers and squeezed tight. She didn't think he had noticed the tremble in her voice. "Hey. Everything is going to be all right. I'm not going to let anything happen to you."

She decided to re-ask the earlier question he hadn't answered. "You're going to stay in my life when this is all over?"

When he didn't answer, she looked him in the eyes.

"I'll do my best," he told her, forcing a smile.

"It's all right, you don't have to. You don't owe me anything." She lowered her gaze. "You don't really think we're going to get through this, do you?"

"I know you will," was all he'd say.

"What about you?"

But he'd gone silent again. That was... worrisome.

As he drove the vehicle from the apartment garage, he told her: "Gas is pretty low, we're going to have to make a pit stop before the motel."

"A motel," she said. "Good. I need a rest after today. Longest day of my life."

"You might want to take a nap. I plan to take us well outside town before getting a room."

She was about to do just that, but thought of something. "There won't be any police roadblocks?"

"Doubtful," he said. "They won't shut down an entire city to stop you. That's too blatant a display of power. These guys operate in the shadows. Less accountability that way. They're modus operandi is: use a drone to track the target, then send in a quick reaction team to capture or terminate in the night."

She considered that for a moment. "Is that what I can expect to wake up to? A quick reaction team?"

"Not if I can help it," he told her.

She thought of something. "How much money did you get from the ATM?"

"I was able to get the daily maximum," he said. "A good sign. They haven't frozen my account. Yet."

"What's the daily maximum?"

"Five hundred," he grunted.

Wasn't much.

Isabel fetched a water bottle from the shopping bag and took a sip. Then she decided to take his advice and lay back on the headrest.

She had trouble falling asleep at first. Napping in a car wasn't easy at the best of times. Even so, she must have slept a little bit, because the next thing she knew the vehicle was rolling into a motel, and in a few more minutes she was lying in a warm bed.

Thankfully Garrett had purchased a room with two single beds, so she wouldn't have to worry about him moving around and waking her up during the night.

Her last thoughts before sleep came involved James. His easy smile. His genius mind. His caring nature.

I won't forget you.

8

G arrett left a note on the motel table for Isabel in case she woke up before he returned, and then made his way to the coffee shop on the premises. The Glock was neatly tucked into his rear waistband and hidden beneath his shirt.

He'd only slept intermittently last night, having kept watch on the parking lot from a chair he'd moved close to the window, so the first thing he ordered at the coffee shop was a triple espresso shot, paid in cash.

After downing that, he drove to a hotel a few miles away and asked to use their computer. Again he paid cash and they gave him a slip of paper with the password.

A member of the front desk staff showed him to the tiny room where two computers were housed. He thanked her and, being careful not to disturb his Glock, sat down at one of the machines.

He started up a TOR browser session, registered a new email at protonmail, and activated the Visa gift card as well as the SIM cards he'd picked up last night—he provided a fake name and address along with his newly registered protonmail account for both.

With the Visa, he also purchased and activated two eSIMs from an online reseller, using the same fake information.

He grabbed the new burner phones and installed a SIM card in each of them. He turned on the phones, and when they connected to the telephone network, he switched over each device to the new eSIMs.

He installed and launched Signal messenger on both phones. He turned on his old phone—which started in airplane mode—and copied the numbers of two particular contacts into the new devices. He turned off his old phone again, and picked one of the new phones to send each contact a quick text via Signal. He waited until receipt was confirmed, then he placed the new phones into airplane mode.

He hopped back into the stolen vehicle and drove back to the motel. When he returned to the unit, Isabel's unmade bed was empty.

He immediately drew the Glock.

I shouldn't have left her.

He glanced at the bathroom door—it was shut, and he could see light shining underneath the bottom gap.

He knocked on the door. "Everything all right?"

"I'll be out in half an hour," she replied.

His tense shoulders relaxed.

He sat next to the window and set down the pistol on the table in front of him; the wooden surface displayed the marks of years of spilled coffee and cigarette burns. The curtains were shut of course, but he was able to observe the parking lot through the gap between the edge of the fabric and the window: everything was normal out there.

He connected one of the new phones to the motel Wi-Fi, then launched Signal. One of his messages had a read receipt.

A response came a moment later. *I'll see what I can do.*

Garrett texted back: *Thank you. P.S. It's urgent.*

He left the phone connected to the Wi-Fi network, hoping for a reply soon.

He kept his gaze on the parking lot, doing his best not to become antsy. During a raging conflict, holed up in a hide, while scanning the battlefield through the scope of a sniper rifle, he could be the most patient of men as he waited for targets to present themselves. Incoming fire could be ricocheting around him, insurgents could be taunting from across the street, but always he remained calm and patient.

But in those moments before shots were actually fired and battle commenced? Those times were always the most trying. That was when the fear, the uncertainty, the regret—basically every negative emotion known to man—could take hold.

Give me a battle already.

He smiled grimly, wondering if he needed another triple espresso shot already. Then again, it would probably only make him even more antsy.

Isabel finally emerged with a towel wrapped around her head and another around her body. Her gaze momentarily dropped to the Glock sitting on the table, but she quickly averted her eyes to his face.

"I was worried you'd abandoned me," she said,

"You were sleeping like a baby," he said. "I didn't want to wake you."

She shrugged. "I saw the note soon enough." She

grabbed the jeans from next to her bed, and fetched one of the new T-shirts he had picked up at the drugstore yesterday.

She went back into the bathroom, shut the door, and came out in another five minutes. She was wearing the over-sized black shirt, which worked well with her jeans. And her hair was now dyed a bright, platinum blond, and cut short to frame her face; a few tousled bangs danced over her eyes.

He wondered for a moment if it was a mistake to dye her hair blond. He hadn't realized last night that the color would be so… bright. The point was to look different than she normally does, but also not stand out: hair like that definitely stood out, at least to him.

"You're going to have to keep wearing the cap," he instructed her.

She nodded. "Should be easier to put on with this haircut." She sat down on the bed across from him. "I just wanted to say thank you, once again, for helping me out. I don't know what would have happened if you hadn't found me when you did yesterday."

He pursed his lips. "That's what friends are for."

She smiled, but sadness suddenly filled her eyes, and she glanced down. "I wasn't much of a friend to you, was I? I should have kept in touch."

"It was my responsibility just as much as yours," he said. "Life, responsibilities, they get in the way sometimes."

She bit her lower lip. "You know, I was thinking about what you said yesterday. About how it wasn't me they were after. Like I told you, I completely forgot about what James had mentioned regarding his mysterious experiment… I was too shell-shocked after everything. But it does make sense. I still can't believe they'd kill him over math, though."

"Maybe he discovered a new type of physics," Garrett conjectured, thinking of the "hybercube" she mentioned.

"But again, why murder him for that? Wouldn't a discovery like that be helping humanity?"

He studied her as she sat there hunched on the bed, looking like she carried the weight of the world on her shoulders. He wasn't sure how to break this to her. She could be so naive, sometimes. "You're right, it would. Unless the men after you have already made the discovery themselves, and want to hoard the knowledge, or keep it from falling into the hands of adversaries. Clandestine wetwork operations have never been pretty, but they're always an option intelligence agencies and defense contractors keep in their back pockets, ready to use if it suits their purposes."

"Wetwork. That's an euphemism for murder, isn't it? How can any agency or contractor justify killing someone? Especially for this... what a terrible thought." She seemed to slump even further. "That some people would keep the rest of us down for their own stature and power." She shook her head sadly. "He told me his research could change the world. And now that will never happen. It's lost. All lost. Along with him."

Garrett studied her. "There's a small chance his research might not be lost."

She sat up straight. "What do you mean?"

"I collected a memory stick yesterday," Garrett replied carefully. "I suspect it contains a backup of his research. I don't know the password, unfortunately, so haven't been able to confirm anything either way. That's why I didn't tell you. But I realize, you deserve to know that there might still be a chance the research isn't lost. Though a small one."

"Where did you get this memory stick?" she seemed flabbergasted. Rightly so.

"I mentioned when I got to your house, the place was ransacked," he replied. "But I left something out. Something… odd. You see, literally a few seconds after I stepped inside..." He hesitated.

Isabel crossed her arms. "Tell me. I need to know everything."

"I received a text from an unknown number." He showed her the text:

Unknown Sender: UNDERNEATH THE MANTEL.

He continued. "So I went to the fireplace and checked for any loose bricks. Sure enough, there was one underneath the mantel. I pulled it out and found this bad boy."

Isabel blinked, confused. "Who would even know you were there? I thought you went to the house on a hunch."

"I did," he said. "I'm just as confused about it as you are. At first I thought it might have been you or James who sent the message. That there were some security cameras on the premises that I'd missed and you'd texted me from another phone when you saw me. But then after you told me what happened to you, I quickly ruled out that option."

She shook her head. "This doesn't make sense." Her face was full of suspicion.

Garrett nodded slowly. "Either we have some allies in high places, with technology that can track anyone's cell phones down to the GPS level—they knew I was there, and they knew where James was keeping his research. Or, the more likely scenario: the device is a plant. That's why I say there's only really a small chance the research isn't lost."

She tapped her lower lip doubtfully. "If whoever sent that message knew the memory stick was there, why wouldn't they just get it themselves? The device definitely has to be a plant. Filled with disinformation. Or a tracking device. Put there by the people who took me."

"Which is why I hid it in a secure location before returning to the house to wait for you," he agreed. "It's also possible that whoever is helping us couldn't get it themselves: maybe they'd compromise their position if they did so. Either way, we need to get it looked at as soon as possible. Just in case it has the research your kidnappers are looking for. Or something equally important."

"Like what?"

"I don't know," he admitted. "But right now we have no bargaining chips for your life. If we can get that stick cracked, and it has anything at all valuable on it, that might give us the upper hand against those who are hunting you. So here's the plan: I'm going to return to where I stashed the memory stick. And if nothing has been touched or disturbed at the site, and no one is waiting to ambush me, I'm going to deliver it to a certain analyst friend of mine to see what he can do."

"Did you try guessing the password yourself?" she asked.

"No," he said. "It's a LockKey S1000. I looked it up... this particular model allows ten guesses. After ten, it can't be unlocked, and you only have two options, destroy or reformat. When I plugged it in at an Internet Cafe, it informed me I had one guess left."

She considered everything he had said for a moment. "Last night you mentioned someone might have been monitoring my brother's communications. Why? How?"

"First of all, I need to explain something," Garrett told her. "Most emails are encrypted during transmission, but they're stored on the mail servers in clear text."

"That sounds... bad," Isabel said. "Then again, there's so much email being sent these days, it seems like it would be fairly hard to find anything."

Garrett smiled patiently. "Have you heard of QUASAR? A piece of software run by certain NSA actors that scans every email sent and received over the Internet. How do they do this? They've used zero day exploits to install software on mail servers and mail clients throughout the world. This allows them to index the messages in clear text before they are encrypted and sent out, or after receipt, when they're unencrypted.

"Not every server or client is vulnerable of course, but many of the university servers are. As for finding data... a little bird told me they've recently updated QUASAR to use AI to sort and tag messages based on keywords and patterns. I suspect James sent out an email at some point that caught the eye of that program or its derivatives. Either that, or maybe the program simply monitors high-profile university researchers for even the hint of a new discovery, and alerts the operators so they can deep dive."

"So you think one faction of the NSA kidnapped James and another faction murdered him because of something he said over email?" she asked.

He was a little surprised at how easily she was able to ask that question without tearing up or even a hint of emotion. It had only been a day...

Isabel is a lot tougher than I thought.

He supposed going through a court case against one's employer could do that.

"As I said, they would have done a deep dive," Garrett explained. "Likely hacking into his work computer, initiating surveillance on his house and workplace, before actually pulling the trigger. As for the actual kidnapping and killing part, the defense and intelligence communities don't like to do that sort of thing directly. They tend to hire private companies to do their dirty work, contractors falling under the auspices of special access programs or black projects. Let's them avoid FOIA—Freedom of Information Act—requests. But it's not clear the government is involved here… some of the bigger defense contractors are governments in and of themselves, with access to software even more powerful than QUASAR—since they are the ones who developed it. You used to work at a defense company. You know what I'm talking about."

Isabel seemed disturbed. "I only heard rumors about stuff like that. I was never directly involved."

"I meant that you know they can be governments in and of themselves. Shadow governments."

She nodded slowly. "If the government—the real government—isn't involved, I'm not sure whether that's good or bad."

"It's bad."

His phone beeped. He had a new Signal message.

He read it over and then glanced at Isabel. "Okay. Here's the deal. I sent out two messages this morning. The first to my analyst friend, telling him to expect a visit from me later today. The second to a gal who works at a cyber-penetration firm. I asked her to retrieve any emails your brother sent and received over the past month from his university account."

"Can she do that legally?" Isabel asked.

"You don't want to know," Garrett replied. "Anyway, she just got back to me. She was able to get access to the mail server, but apparently James hadn't sent or received anything for over a week. Before that he was emailing daily. Which tells me our shadow government friends deleted all his correspondence from the past week. His work computers would contain a local cached copy of any emails he sent, but I'm guessing whoever kidnapped you would have broken into his office at the same time and taken all his computers and any other research equipment."

Isabel appeared lost in thought. Then: "You said his work computer would have had a local cached copy of any sent emails? That means any colleagues he might have contacted could also potentially have cached copies on their machines."

"Depending on the email software and version they're running, yes. Mozilla Firefox is good at taking copies off servers. Do any of the names on this list ring a bell?" He held up his phone and showed her a list of names ending in .edu addresses. "These are the people your brother has emailed the most over the last month, according to my cyber friend, sorted by most contacted to least."

She pointed at the top two. "These are his colleagues from UC. They work in his department, and he had them over for dinner at least once a month."

"All right. Change of plans. We're going to get in touch with these two colleagues of your brother's first. They could be in danger. And their work computers might contain important pieces of evidence. After we've secured them, I'll pick up the memory stick and take it to my analyst friend."

"This analyst friend of yours, can we trust him?" she inquired.

"We were in Afghanistan together at the start of the war," Garrett explained. "He was a CIA case officer and I was assigned to work with him. It was an interesting pairing to say the least, a spook and a frogman. He was the one who recruited and briefed assets for intel, while I was the guy who got him to those assets.

"I'm going to be honest. We hated each other initially. But by the end, we became really close. How could we not after all the shit we went through together? So yes, I trust him. To a degree, anyway. Everyone knows you never really leave the CIA, even after you retire. Loyalties are entrenched deep. I do plan to feed him a fake cover story. Something like, the memory stick contains the notes from a sci-fi novel a client is working on."

Isabel's eyes dropped to his phone, which sat on the table next to his Glock. Or maybe it was the Glock she was looking at. "You've been communicating with these two friends of yours using your phone? Isn't that dangerous?"

Garrett pursed his lips. "Can be. But my two contacts and I are using Signal to keep in touch. And this is the new burner phone…"

"What's Signal?"

"A secure messaging app. Big on privacy. Data is kept encrypted at all times. No clear text. If subpoenaed, Signal can only provide two pieces of information for an account: the date it was created, and the date it last connected to the Signal service. That's it. And sure, there's malware out there that captures any characters entered via the built-in on-screen keyboard, but remember, I changed my SIM card. I also switched to a burner eSIM shortly after turning it on, and have fresh installs of the operating system and Signal. So we shouldn't have a problem."

He spoke with a confidence he didn't entirely believe himself. The men they were up against had incredible resources backing them. What did he have? Less than five hundred dollars in his pocket, a stolen vehicle, and a couple of burner phones. It was possible he missed something. Likely, even. And all it would take was one mistake for everything to come crashing down.

Whatever the case, he had already resolved that if it came to it, he'd take a bullet for Isabel. If he was going to die, dying for her seemed like a noble way to go. More noble than going out by his own hand, anyway.

"What would I do without you?" Isabel asked, smiling.

I guess we'll see, Garrett thought. *You might learn sooner than you think, unfortunately.*

9

B lackwell gazed at the satellite footage on his desk and watched as five small craft left orbit. A moment later, a fresh batch returned from outer space. The spy satellites confirmed that these craft always headed out to certain asteroids and moons.

16 Psyche was a common destination, as was Ceres—considered more of a dwarf planet by some than an asteroid, there were signs it harbored frozen salt water. Apparently cryovolcanism had caused the melted ice to seep to the surface where it sublimed into salt deposits. On Earth, the brine beneath salt flats contained large amounts of lithium, the metal essential for electric batteries. Whether or not these craft mined Ceres for lithium, Blackwell didn't know.

There was a lot he didn't know about these things. But one thing he did know, the trips to 16 Psyche and Ceres had been increasing. As had the sightings on Earth.

The Entities were planning something big.

He was determined to find out just what that something was, and to stop it.

And then there was the Lockwood matter. What a fiasco that was turning out to be. Blackwell had been furious when he'd learned James Lockwood had been terminated. The status of James' sister was unclear... Lieutenant Mitchell was convinced she had been killed in the forest along with the others, but Blackwell wasn't so sure as her body hadn't been recovered. That night an MQ-1 tracked an incongruous vehicle leaving the neighborhood of the Lockwood home and followed it to a local mall. Blackwell had sent in a quick reaction force but the team only recovered an abandoned vehicle.

A quick search of the plates showed it belonged to an ex-SEAL named Garrett Bennett. Not one of Blackwell's men. Military records indicated he had earned multiple medals and awards during his three tours of duty, which included a stint in Afghanistan and two in Iraq. One might think an exemplary military record and its awards could reveal a man's character, but Blackwell knew quite well how people changed after leaving the army. Often bitter, many suffered from PTSD, and had trouble reintegrating with society.

The two operatives sent to Garrett's townhouse had ransacked the place but found nothing. Blackwell had instructed them to remain there, lying in wait until further notice in case the ex-SEAL decided to return.

There were two options: either Garrett was working for the same men who had killed James, or he wasn't.

Blackwell had no idea, at the moment. And not knowing irritated him. That said, Garrett fit the typical profile of the men Jackson Kane liked to recruit...

As for who had terminated James, Blackwell was certain Jackson was definitely involved. The man had been a thorn in his side for the past two years ever since he had broken away to start a competing organization. Kane had taken a lot of men with him, along with the technologies they'd reverse engineered. Kane wasn't averse to funding his organization through illicit means such as human and drug trafficking, either, nor to killing anyone who got in his way.

Blackwell dismissed the satellite footage and launched a message request via his augmented reality display to his right hand man, Lieutenant Marcus Mitchell.

"Sir!" Mitchell said. A video stream from the lieutenant occupied the upper right of the display; he stood against the backdrop of a country lake—no doubt fly fishing, as the man was wont to do on Sunday afternoons.

The background quickly faded, becoming translucent so that only his face and upper body were visible —Mitchell had disabled background display.

"Tell me you have an update on the Lockwood target," Blackwell told him.

"Negative," Mitchell responded. "If she's alive, she still hasn't returned to her house. We followed and interrogated the driver of an Amazon delivery truck visiting the neighborhood, but he checked out so we let him go."

"What about Garrett Bennett?" Blackwell pressed.

"We have no news yet on his whereabouts," Mitchell replied.

Blackwell sighed.

"If she's alive, we'll find her," the lieutenant said confidently. "And the ex-SEAL, too."

Blackwell nodded. It was extremely hard to stay off the grid in this day and age. His group had facial recognition AIs running 24/7, scanning everything that ran through the nationwide video spigot... security cameras, ring cameras, cell phone cameras: if it was connected to the Internet, it would be processed at some point. That said, it didn't take much to fool the cameras. Something as simple as a Covid mask could outsmart the AI, or a shirt with a man's face on it.

"Have the remote viewers had any luck?" Blackwell asked.

"No," the lieutenant answered. "They're all drawing blanks."

"That's highly unusual, isn't it?"

"I suppose so," the lieutenant agreed carefully. "It's possible someone or something is protecting the targets."

"Or that remote viewing is bullshit," Blackwell said. "Come on, that's what you wanted to say, isn't it?"

Mitchell hesitated, then gave a diplomatic response. "We've had great success with it in the past. We've also had great failures."

"You've never really believed... the channelers, the remote viewers."

The lieutenant pursed his lips. "In all honesty, half the time I can't tell if they're just making stuff up. Even when we have them working in teams."

"Neither can I," Blackwell agreed. "But those times they've given us solid, actionable intel that turns out to be true, even when there was no other way they could have known that intel, outweigh the times they've failed us."

Because of the failures, Blackwell treated whatever the psychics gave him as a probability, as in, what was the probability that answer x,y,z was true, and he acted accordingly. Most of the time Blackwell relied on multiple sources of intel to get to the final answer.

His thoughts lingered on a certain sentence the lieutenant had said. *It's possible someone or something is protecting the targets.*

Someone or something. Blackwell believed the Entities could interfere at will with viewings, feeding misinformation and misdirection to further their own ends, or outright shielding a target from remote observation entirely.

It was something humans could do as well, and Blackwell had men working full-time to keep the facility shielded from prying, as best as they could. It was a mentally draining task, and men had to be cycled out every couple of hours. Mitchell wasn't convinced it actually worked, but Blackwell believed it made a difference.

Jackson Kane had men doing the same. Jackson had originally operated out of a mobile base, changing locations every few months. But Jackson had recently relocated to a more permanent base in Alaska, one that showed up like a beacon on the remote viewing side of things.

Because of that, Blackwell had suspected a trap, but he'd organized an attack to take out Jackson anyway. However, it turned out Jackson had made some new allies among the Entities, and the man repelled the attack with ease—firstly, equipment failures were widespread upon Blackwell's team, to the point of jets losing thrust and some even crashing into one another, as well as munitions depots self-detonating. Blackwell didn't know of any human psychics that could do that. Secondly, the orbs themselves also intervened, targeting personnel and equipment with energy weapons. Blackwell was forced to retreat with his tail between his legs.

So for now, Blackwell tolerated that base, but he planned to destroy it at some point. It wasn't like he could just drop a nuke on Alaska without the rest of the world knowing. Dealing with Jackson would have to be a subtle, surgical-precision thing, something that didn't involve a grand counteroffensive. It would likely have to be a two or three man operation. He was still working out the details.

Anyway, because of the remote viewing problem, Blackwell had resorted to spying on him the good old-fashioned way, with men embedded in Jackson's organization. Just as Jackson no doubt had men embedded in Blackwell's.

"Anything else, sir?" The lieutenant's voice brought Blackwell back to the present.

"Did you search the Lockwood residence again?" Blackwell asked.

"Yes," Mitchell replied. "But there don't seem to be any other backups of the research. The laptop we confiscated from Lockwood's home contains everything his work computer had on it."

"Well search again," Blackwell instructed. "And Bennett's place, too, for good measure."

"Yes, sir."

Searching their homes multiple times was most likely futile at this point, but at least it gave Blackwell the sense that he was doing something tangible. Even so, if Isabel Lockwood was alive and there was another backup copy of the research, there was a good chance she had it. Or knew where to find it.

And if that research fell into the wrong hands, Blackwell would only have more problems…

He took a sip from the water bottle he kept on his desk. He dismissed the call and removed his AR glasses entirely to rub his eyes.

Similar to the remote viewers, there was no news from the channelers as of yet. He'd instructed them to keep trying to contact the Entities, but these things took time.

Still…

I might have to try contacting them myself at this rate.

But that, he knew, was a very bad idea.

10

Isabel sat in the passenger seat while Garrett drove the stolen vehicle back to the big city. She had the phone in hand, and was gazing at the top two contacts in the list as returned by Garrett's cyber-penetration friend—the two UC professors James had been in contact with before his email trail went cold.

Isabel had met them both: they were good men. The first contact was Liam Malcolm. He had a wife, no children. He always was so happy-go-lucky and very easy to talk to.

The second contact was Dr. Noah Patel, also married but with two kids. He was the more reserved of the two, and Isabel often found herself talking more to his wife than him whenever he visited James.

Phone numbers and addresses were listed beside their names. She had wanted to call them from the burner phone, but Garrett hadn't let her.

"The whole point of burner phones is to avoid tracking," Garrett had scolded her. "If we start calling people who are potentially monitored, we lose that edge and have to toss the phones."

"But we need to warn them that their lives are in danger!" Isabel had exclaimed.

He'd given her a solemn look. "There isn't a way to warn them, not without endangering their lives, or our own. But I'll figure something out. I'll probably have to do it tomorrow when they're at the university. But before I do any of that, first I want to make sure they're still alive."

"Oh no… you think…?"

"I don't know what to think anymore."

She'd closed her eyes. "So where are we headed?"

"The airport."

"What's there?"

"You'll see."

According to the address in the contact list, Liam's house was en route to the airport, so she'd convinced Garrett to do a drive-by to at least determine the extent of potential surveillance. Garrett had seemed convinced that there would be no obvious on-the-ground monitoring, and instead, the houses would be solely surveyed by drones, but he'd relented.

"Only because it's on the way to the airport…"

She gazed longingly at the countryside outside the window. Out there, farmland stretched as far as the eye could see. Some farms produced crops such as wheat and corn, others raised livestock like cows and horses.

She could see her translucent reflection in the window, overlapping the landscape, and she was struck by how much things had changed in just a day. That's all it took to turn one's life completely upside down. Just one day.

As she gazed at herself, she didn't even recognize

the person peering back. Her eyes had become haunted. Her long black hair had been replaced by a blond, pixie haircut. She hated it.

"How are you holding up?" Garrett asked.

"Fine," she replied.

"You sure?"

She didn't answer. She was going to give *him* the silent treatment for once.

Well, her resolve lasted about thirty seconds. "And I thought having no money and being jobless was bad. But being hunted and on the run? It brings desperation to a whole new level. Not to mention losing someone you grew up with. Someone you thought would always be there. A brother ripped away from you for no reason." She closed her eyes. "Sorry."

"Don't be. What happened to you isn't easy."

"I just wish none of this had happened. James… meeting you…" She looked at him. "I don't mean to sound ungrateful. I do appreciate everything you've done, and are doing for me."

He glanced at her. "I don't mind. I have nothing better to do. And I'm not even kidding."

"What about your job?" she pressed.

"I quit," he said. "Got sick of the mercenary life. I like combat. Love it, even. It's the politics, and the morally ambiguous stuff I'm not big on."

"Like what?"

"I'll tell you about the job that made me quit. They wanted me to kidnap a child to get a certain Third World politician to cooperate."

"This was for the CIA?"

"Sort of. Officially I worked for a private contractor. But they were employed by the CIA, DIA, or some such. They don't tell us grunts."

"So you went through with it and quit after?"

"Nope," he said. "Quit as soon as I read the brief."

"And how long ago was this?"

"Six months, give or take."

"And what have you been doing since?"

He chuckled softly. "A whole lot of nothing. Tried to work at Walmart. Quit the same day."

She studied him. He was in pain, she could tell that much. "Ever find out what happened to this Third World politician?"

"Nope. But it's doubtful it would have hit the news either way. Ops like this, they are kept very secretive, with deals worked out under the table. No one ever talks to the media, and if they do, it's only to spread misinformation."

"It must have been hard to reintegrate with society when you left the military," she said. "I'm sorry again that I wasn't more of a friend to you."

"As I told you before, it was just as much my fault for losing touch as yours."

They continued the drive in silence and soon reached the city. Garrett donned his sunglasses and pulled on his cap; Isabel followed his lead.

Garrett stopped at a mom-and-pop coffee shop to ask for more specific directions to Liam's neighborhood: Garrett insisted on not using the burner phone's built-in GPS or search features, because "address data could be tracked."

She wasn't sure if he was being paranoid or pragmatic.

She leaned toward the latter.

It took about ten minutes after entering the city to reach the neighborhood, but before they even arrived at the home she knew something was wrong.

There was an ambulance and several police vehicles parked out front, as well as a police van. Several police SUVs had made a roadblock to cordon off the street.

After first Isabel panicked, wondering if Garrett was driving into a trap, but then she realized an officer was standing in front of the roadblock and turning vehicles around without stopping them. Garrett seemed to notice the same thing, because his white-knuckle grip on the steering wheel loosened slightly.

"He's not wearing a body cam, I don't think," Garrett said in regards to the officer. "Even so, keep your head down. We don't want to get caught on a ring camera or cellphone."

Indeed, she saw neighbors and other bystanders on the pavement, recording everything with their smartphones.

When Garrett reached the front of the line the officer signaled for him to turn around, and Garrett started to do precisely that.

Isabel meanwhile was gazing at the driveway leading up to the house. When she spotted two first responders pushing a gurney covered by a sheet, her breath caught in her throat. She could see the outline of a body beneath that sheet.

Liam… no. She imagined his face beneath that sheet, covered in blood.

Not you as well.

Garrett had seen it, too, but he said nothing as he turned the vehicle around.

"Oh my God," Isabel blurted when the house was behind them. "They killed him. They killed him. Just for being a *colleague* of James!"

"Give me the second address," Garrett

commanded emotionlessly. Of course it was easy for him, he didn't know Liam and…

"What about his wife?" Isabel said. "They killed her too, didn't they? We have to go back and ask the officer!"

"Give me the second address," Garrett intoned firmly.

With shaking fingers she opened the phone and read out the address of the next colleague on the list.

"Okay, I know where that is," he said.

Isabel dreaded what they would find there.

"What's the point of going?" Isabel said. "They've probably killed him and his family, too."

The mere idea tore at her heartstrings. Dr. Noah Patel slain in cold blood, along with his wife and two kids… the thought of those beautiful little ones being harmed in any way, shape or form was heart-wrenching.

"We're not actually going, and don't be so sure they're dead," Garrett told her. "If they wanted to flush us out, the first people they'd watch would be the folks your brother was in touch with the most."

"Then why did they kill Liam and his wife?" Isabel asked.

"Remember, we're dealing with two factions here," Garrett explained. "One faction—the faction that kidnapped you—would have wanted him alive. The other, not so much."

She thought for a moment. "So what you're saying is, the faction that wants me will do everything possible to keep Noah Patel and his family alive?"

"Most likely," Garrett agreed.

"And if they fail? Like they did with Liam?"

"Then they fail," he said simply.

She threw up her hands in frustration. "I hate

this. Mercenaries. Defense contractors. They're the lowest of the low. Scumbags among scumbags."

"I won't disagree…"

"You said we're not going, then why did you ask me for the address?" She was barely holding back tears. "At the very least we should call Noah and warn him and his family to get out."

"If we do that, and it becomes obvious we're not going to visit them, their use as bait drops considerably. The faction that wants him alive might pull their men back if there's no longer any value in protecting him and his family. As to why I asked for the address, mostly to distract you. I still plan to pay the professor a visit tomorrow, however, when he goes back to class."

"Won't our hunters be watching?"

"They will," Garrett agreed. "I'll have to be subtle about it."

"I'm coming with you," she insisted.

"No, you're not."

"We'll see. Where are we going now? The airport still?"

"The airport," Garrett agreed.

"What's at the airport?"

"Payphones."

"Oh." That wasn't a bad idea. If anyone traced the call, the first conclusion they would come to was that the caller was about to hop onto a plane.

Confusion and misdirection.

She might just learn this game after all.

She closed her eyes and did her best to forget about Liam. It wasn't easy. She just wished there had been a way to warn him in time. She dearly hoped they weren't too late with Noah.

They reached the airport. Garrett took the smartphone, then, despite her protests, he left her in the vehicle while he went inside the terminal. He wore his sunglasses and kept his cap pulled low.

He returned after fifteen long minutes.

"Tell me he's all right," she told him.

Garrett played a recording he had made with the smartphone.

She heard some soft dialing, followed by a ringing. There was a click and then a voice spoke. "Patel residence."

The voice sounded tinny: she could tell Garrett had recorded it by pressing the device against the payphone handset.

Another click came. That would be Garrett immediately hanging up.

He gave her a questioning glance.

"It's him," Isabel said. "I recognize his voice."

"Then we have proof of life." Garrett started the car.

"So tomorrow we try to catch him on campus without being surveilled," she said.

"*I* try to catch him, yes."

She decided not to correct him, for now. "So what's the plan for today?"

"It's time I paid a visit to my analyst friend. But first I have to retrieve the memory stick." He glanced at her. "I'm dropping you off at a motel beforehand: if there's a tracker in that memory stick, you're done."

Her shoulders tensed all over again. "But what about you?"

"I can take care of myself."

She knew he was right. She just hated the thought of being alone, especially now. After a few minutes she said: "At least tell me where you're going. As in, a location."

In reply he pulled into the parking lot of an old, beaten up motel and drove her to the front office. He dropped a wad of cash into her lap. "If I'm not back in two hours, ditch the motel and find somewhere else to stay. Assume the worst."

"That's a bit dramatic isn't it?" She grabbed the cash. "You'll be fine. Besides, it's not like I have anywhere else to go."

"You'll have to find somewhere, another motel, anywhere. Because if I'm captured, they have ways to make people talk. Even men like me."

"Then don't get captured," she said emphatically.

When he didn't answer, she reached out, squeezing his shoulder. He looked at her, and she saw a tenderness and care she hadn't seen before in his eyes. However it was quickly lost, replaced by determination.

"*Go*. I'll be back soon." He shoved one of the burner phones into her hands. "Don't text me unless it's an emergency. And if you do, use Signal. Connect to the motel's Wi-Fi. When you're done, immediately turn off the phone and remove the battery."

She nodded slowly and got out to watch the vehicle depart.

And so he's gone. My last protector.

She walked into the office and glanced at the digital alarm clock hanging on the wall behind the counter. She noted the time.

Two hours. She was supposed to give Garrett two hours.

If it came to it, she didn't think she'd have the strength to leave without him.

GARRETT STOPPED the vehicle two blocks away from the park where he'd stowed the memory stick. Said park was a swath of green land set atop a hill that overlooked much of the city. Some of the best views in town could be had there.

He got out and took to the sidewalk, noting the vehicles parked on the street, as well as in the driveways of the houses that resided on the opposite side. None of them stood out, nor were they occupied.

When he reached the park he made a beeline for a certain bench near the outskirts, which, in his opinion, afforded the best view of the city. Upon arrival, he sat down on the right-hand side of the bench. The view was breathtaking. In his youth he'd spent countless hours sitting in that same spot, pondering life.

But that wasn't why he was there today.

He waited several minutes. No one approached or accosted him.

He waited until a lingering dog walker left the park, and then he reached underneath the seat and retrieved the memory stick from where he'd lodged it between the small ledge formed by the corner brace and the front leg.

He glanced at the device, confirming it was the same USB stick he'd originally placed, and then got up and made his way back to the stolen vehicle.

Along the way, he kept expecting to take a bullet to the chest at any moment. Either that, or for special operators or mercenaries to swarm his position.

The walk back to his car proved quite long… not to mention tense.

But nothing happened and he reached the vehicle unscathed.

He started the sedan and pulled out onto the main road, heading for the mansion of his analyst friend, Archer Blake.

A quick glance in the rear view mirror confirmed that no one was following him.

He just had to hope that were no unseen drones in the sky watching him…

11

E van sat in a chair of some kind in the darkness. It was a hardback chair, with an unpadded bottom. Meant to make him feel as uncomfortable as possible. Whenever he tried to stand up, unseen hands pushed him back down again.

Hands was not precisely the correct word. More like a force, because he had felt the pressure across his entire body, squeezing with equal duration and pressure. Even his lungs and throat had constricted until he had stopped.

So he just sat there in the dark, waiting, wondering. Sometimes the shadows seemed to swirl and move around him, almost coalescing into shapes. Sometimes he saw glowing orbs in the darkness, orbiting, teasing.

And then, just like that, he awoke in the hotel room he had taken before that ill-fated flight. Confused, he rubbed his eyes and got up. The narrow bed with its frayed floral bedspread occupied one corner of the room. A battered leather suitcase, partially open, rested at the foot of the bed, revealing a jumble of clothing, wires, and electronic devices. Another suitcase, this one metallic, lingered next to it.

A wooden table resided near the window, next to a pair of threadbare armchairs that had seen better days. On the table, a laptop with multiple screens displayed a maze of encrypted codes, maps, and Boeing 777 blueprints.

The room was eerily silent, save for the faint hum of the laptop's cooling fan. A half-empty glass of water and a crumpled room service menu sat beside the computer, and the faint, lingering scent of exotic spices from a takeout container permeated the air.

"It can't be," he said.

His phone pinged on the table. He looked down and read the message.

Etihad Airways 473.

It seemed he was reliving the day before the flight. But how was that possible?

It wasn't. Somehow, his memories were being accessed.

Replayed.

I just won't get on the flight. I won't go along with any of this.

But what if it was real?

What if everything that had happened had been a nightmare, and the flight hadn't actually taken off yet? He pinched himself just in case this was a dream in and of itself. Well, *that* certainly hurt.

He went to the metallic suitcase where the bioengineered virus was stowed. He picked up the container and gingerly put it down on the table, then opened it and confirmed all the canisters and vials were intact, and that the deployment mechanism was intact and in working order.

He smiled sadly. The disaster was a nightmare after all, then. He hadn't yet completed the mission.

And yet…

Etihad Airways 473.

Why did the flight number seem wrong? In his nightmare, the plane had been *Lufthansa 778.*

That's because it was a nightmare, he reminded himself.

He closed the suitcase and set about packing his things. He had a plane to board.

ZYR'THALIAN STUDIED the biological container that called itself Evan. Time was nonlinear here, and the Evan was experiencing time in the same fashion Zyr'thalian experienced it.

Nonlinear time had many branches in the forward and backward directions, but only one of those branches was active at any given moment in the Evan's world. It was something the biological containers called the Present. But there were too many branches to follow at any given moment, an infinite amount of wave functions, which was why latching onto a biological container—tagging it—was the only way to properly track any of them. Otherwise Zyr'thalian would be peering into pasts that never existed or futures that would never come to be.

The branches were probabilistic in nature, but sometimes, just sometimes, those probabilities aligned so that they funneled into four or five distinct possibilities rather than the usual infinite. These inflection points were called branch alignments, or convergences, and they readily stood out from the ordinary branches. Whichever one of the alignments came to pass depended on the choices of the containers involved, which was usually a precious small few. It always both amused and amazed Zyr'thalian that so few biological containers could influence the lives of billions based on their actions, but such was the way of things.

Zyr'thalian and his cohorts had interfered with the Evan to prevent a particularly bad alignment, one whose outcomes had been extremely unfavorable. But that interference had only caused yet another adverse convergence to bubble up, this one even worse than the last. In fact, it almost seemed as if the Evan's sole purpose in this matter was to serve as a mere distraction, meant to shield the worse convergence from the view of Zyr'thalian and cohorts. In that, the Evan had nearly succeeded.

The Evan's memories itself were full of obfuscation and misdirection, making it impossible to expunge the needed information. That one was well-trained at mind guarding. The Evan would have to be returned to its realm of existence to experience time linearly once more. Its container had been properly tagged, and Zyr'thalian and cohorts would be able to watch the being.

Yes, they would observe this Evan, see which faction aided and abetted the container. There were a few possibilities, but Zyr'thalian needed to be sure.

Meanwhile, the containers that called themselves Isabel Lockwood and Garrett Bennett would be further investigated. The branches leading to the convergences were yet uncertain, but nonlinear time suggested those two had a part to play in the coming alignment...

12

G arrett went to an Internet cafe and asked for a Linux machine. After he paid the fee in cash, the proprietor gave him a bootable memory stick and told him to pick any computer.

Garrett went to the far side of the cafe and sat down at a computer that offered him a good view of the entrance and all the other patrons. He connected the memory stick and booted into Linux.

Once the machine finished booting, he attached the encrypted memory stick he'd gotten from the Lockwood residence, along with a new, fresh memory stick. He initiated the dd command, affectionately known as "disk destroyer" by those who recognized the true power of the tool, or "disk duplicator" by the more naive.

He created a special shell script with the help of an online AI tool and ran it on the bootable memory stick first to confirm everything would work as planned—AIs had a tendency to hallucinate, and he knew quite well he could unintentionally destroy the USB if he wasn't careful.

When all went as expected, he edited the script and used it to make a bit-by-bit copy of the encrypted stick. Just a little precaution in case something happened to the device while in Archer's possession.

Of course, just because he'd created a bit-by-bit copy didn't mean he'd be able to unlock the data. Even if he had the password, without knowing what algorithm was employed by the microprocessor inside the LockKey, he wouldn't be able to decrypt the data. He just had to hope that if something happened to the original device that there would be some way to reverse engineer the hardware algorithm LockKey used.

When the copy was done, Garrett did a quick online search for a non-disclosure agreement form and printed it out.

Keeping an eye on the the time, Garrett drove back to the park and stowed the copy beneath the same bench.

Then he took the original with him and began the drive to the house of the analyst.

Along the way he made a quick stop at a camping store to pick up a pair of thermo tarps. He'd need at least one for later today, but first he had to get his meeting with Archer out of the way.

The neighborhood Archer lived in exuded an aura of wealth and power, starting with the impeccably maintained hedges and tall, wrought-iron gate that marked the entrance to the community.

Garrett drove onto the winding, tree-lined drive. Though it was midday, the road was shrouded in shadows thanks to the canopy of those tall boughs. He caught the subtle gleam of security cameras placed beneath each and every street post, domes watching and cataloging every visitor. Those cameras made him uneasy. He reflexively pulled his cap low over his sunglasses.

The houses themselves, when not hidden by the trees, were concealed behind tall, imposing hedges. He did catch glimpses of a few of them, their exteriors a mix of cutting-edge design and subtle grandeur, with sleek lines and minimalistic facades. Some had no hedges at all, revealing sprawling, impeccably manicured front yards.

Archer's house stood at the end of the road, fenced behind an imposing stone wall. Garrett drove to the main gate and opened the window to activate the intercom but when the gate started to open of its own accord, Garrett drove inside.

Unlike the other houses, this one was a veritable mansion, adorned with ornate columns and grand double doors. Everywhere Garrett looked, he spotted security cameras—next to the gazebo, in front of the manicured garden, on top of the wall. The house itself had roaming cameras that tilted to follow the approach of his sedan.

Typical.

Garrett lifted his collar and got out, not feeling at all comfortable with so many cameras pointed at him.

Going to have to change cars…

He kept his head bowed as he made his way to the main entrance.

Archer met him at the front door.

"Froggie!" Archer said, extending his arms in anticipation of receiving a big hug.

Garrett nodded in acknowledgment. "Spook."

An awkward moment passed with Archer still holding out his arms while Garrett simply stood there making no move to hug the man.

Finally Archer smiled, then beckoned Garrett

inside. "Haven't changed a bit." He led Garrett through the foyer and expansive living room. "Would you like a drink?"

"That's all right," Garrett said. "I don't plan to take up too much of your time."

Archer shrugged, grabbed a water bottle for himself from a plastic-wrapped container of twenty-four, then led Garrett to his workroom. It featured an impressive array of cutting-edge hardware. Multiple high-resolution monitors, some curved, dominated the U-shaped desk, which had an open design. That desk harbored server racks underneath, stacked one atop the other and humming with computational power.

The walls were adorned with tech memorabilia—autographed CD-ROMs, NFT art pieces in luminous frames, a framed T-shirt emblazoned with the words "Spooky Action At A Distance" above an image of a remote control and a black, spherical bomb.

A single ergonomic chair was positioned at the center of it all. And beside it, a visitor's stool.

Archer beckoned at the latter. "Have a seat."

Garrett didn't move. "Think I'll stand. As I said, I won't be here long."

"Too bad, I was hoping we could catch up," Archer told him. "Those years of trekking through the mud in Afghanistan taught me a few things, such as you never know when you're going to see someone for the last time."

Garrett nodded slowly. He couldn't help the sudden emotion those words instilled in him as he thought of all the buddy's he lost both before and after his tours.

"Remember Kasik?" Archer asked suddenly.

That was the affectionate nickname they'd given

their first translator in Afghanistan. His real name was Ali Safi, but they called him Kasik after the dead carcass used in the traditional Afghan game of Buzkashi, where horse-mounted players competed to grab the kasik—a headless goat carcass—and carry it across a goal.

"I remember," Garrett said.

Archer's eyes became distant. "I think of him from time to time. I can still see his face. The betrayal in his eyes, when we left him there like that."

They were on a covert mission deep in enemy territory, gathering vital intelligence on a high-ranking insurgent leader known for orchestrating deadly attacks on coalition forces. In one particular village, they'd been ambushed by Taliban, cut off by a barrage of enemy fire, and unable to regroup. They were forced to depart, leaving Kasik to an uncertain fate. The translator was likely captured and tortured to death.

Archer looked at him. "I can understand why you stay away. Whenever I see you, I always bring up the more... unpleasant... side of our time in the suck."

When Garrett didn't answer, Archer nodded slowly, then took a seat at the ergonomic chair. "All business today. Got it. Nice wheels by the way." He tapped at one particular monitor, which showed the video feed from a camera pointed at Garrett's beaten up Honda Civic.

"I've been moving on up," Garrett quipped.

"What's that say on the back... shitbox uncertified?" He grinned widely. "You should get into the analytics business. Way less dangerous than your line of work and pays a helluva lot more."

"You're assuming I'm working at the moment..." Garrett said.

"That might be an incorrect assumption," Archer agreed. "So what do you have for me today? In your Signal you mentioned something about a memory stick in need of tender loving care?"

Garrett produced the memory stick. "A novelist client of mine put together some fictional notes for a technothriller he's working on. He put those notes on this memory stick, password protected it, and set the work aside. When he got back to it a week later, he forgot the password."

Archer took the memory stick. "Ooo one of these babies. A LockKey S1000. And I thought the S200 was bad. How many password guesses did you use up?"

"There was only one remaining when I booted it up," Garrett informed him.

Archer smiled. "Get that wrong, the 'flash-trash' self-destruct sequence engages! Gotta love it."

"Not really."

Archer shrugged. "Well, should be simple enough."

"You'll have to sign this NDA promising not to reveal the contents." Garrett handed him the NDA he had printed out at the cafe.

Archer raised an eyebrow.

"It's what the client wants," Garrett explained. "You know sci-fi novelists. They're a tad on the eccentric side. Always worried about people stealing their work and ideas."

Archer pursed his lips, then produced a ballpoint pen and signed the document.

Garrett didn't really expect Archer to obey the terms of the NDA, but he wanted to get a signature anyway to better sell the eccentric client story.

"Let's have a look." Archer plugged the stick into

a rack-mounted server underneath his desk. When a password pop-up appeared on one of the curved screens, he tabbed to another window and began typing.

Archer frowned. "All right, this is going to take some time. I'll work on it later after I'm done with my paying clients. Hopefully I'll have something for you tomorrow by noon."

"You can't crack it any faster?" Garrett pressed.

"Hey, come on, it's a Sunday." Archer pulled up the specs of the device from the manufacturer's website. "Okay, so, the password is hashed with a salted SHA-256 before being transmitted to the drive over a unique USB channel. After the password is validated in hardware the AES encryption key unlocks. There's also the password try-counter to worry about, also implemented in hardware to prevent memory rewind attacks. That's the first thing we'll have to disable, of course, so that we can retry as many times as we want." He turned around in his chair to look at Garrett. "I'm going to have to consult with an external team."

"So the great Archer has finally met his match?"

Archer rolled his shoulders. "Want the data or not? Look, I have some friends who have cracked a ton of S200s. To do it, they basically purchased a ton of them and dismantled them with the help of a CT scanner and laser cutting tool. Once they got to the microcontroller at the heart of the chip, they bathed it in nitric acid to decap it—which means they removed the layers of epoxy that supposedly made the chip 'tamper proof.' Then they basically filed it down a fraction of a micron at a time, taking photos of each layer with a scanning electron microscope, until they got a full 3D model of the microcontroller.

"Then they took another decapped microcontroller but this time instead of filing it down, they hooked up gauge wires to log all communications going in and out. That in combination with their 3D map allowed them to slowly reverse engineer the cryptographic and try-counter algorithms, given them a way to look for potential zero-day exploits. And they found some. A lot, actually. The design of these things is downright sloppy sometimes.

"Anyway they've also been working on the S1000 recently, so I'll need to pick their brain. Unless you want me to spend months on this, filing down and mapping microchips before getting back to you."

"No that's fine, do whatever you need to do," Garrett told him.

Archer smiled patiently. "Thought so. Oh, and, I also have access to a quantum computer, so that'll help. I'll have to get the processed queued in the cloud and pay out of my pocket to skip to the front of the line, though. Ain't cheap."

"How secure is this cloud processing?" Garrett asked.

Archer smiled patiently. "No one else will be able to access the data, if that's your worry."

Garrett wondered again just how much he could trust him. Well, he had no other choice really, not if he wanted to find out what James was researching.

Assuming the device wasn't a plant.

"If there was some sort of tracker on the memory stick, would you be able to tell?" Garrett hoped the question didn't tip his hand.

Archer gave him a suspicious look. "I thought you said it was for a sci-fi author?"

Garrett tried to act as nonchalant as possible. "I did say he was eccentric, didn't I?"

Archer stared at him a moment longer, then typed a few commands on his computer. He stood up, retrieved what looked like a portable radiofrequency scanner from a drawer, and held it close to the connected memory stick. "I'm not seeing anything that would indicate external communications, though admittedly there's quite a bit of interference this close to the computer." He unplugged the stick and kept the scanner near it. "Still nothing. I think it's safe to say it doesn't have a tracker."

"Thank you for doing this," Garrett told his friend. "How much do I owe you again?"

"How much is the client paying you?" Archer asked.

"Two hundred dollars," Garrett replied.

Archer laughed. "Unbelievable. You know I'll probably be out at least fifteen grand by the time I give you this tomorrow, right? Between the consulting fees for the external team and the computing time…"

"I'll find a way to pay you back," Garrett said stiffly.

Archer frowned. "It's worth that much to you?" That suspicious look momentarily flickered in his eye again. "This must be a fairly important client. Sci-fi novelist, you say? She must be super hot." Archer winked. Before Garrett could dispel that notion, the man raised a hand. "It's fine. It's fine. I got this. But afterward we're square. No more favors. Understood?"

Garrett nodded. "Completely."

"Anything else you wanted?"

"I don't suppose I could borrow that radiofrequency scanner of yours?" Garrett asked hopefully.

With a shrug, Archer handed him the portable scanner. "It's yours."

"Thank you once again, Archer," Garrett told his friend sincerely. "I really appreciate this."

Archer grinned. "Are you sure I can't offer you a drink along with my illustrious company?"

"I thought you had more work to do on this Sunday afternoon?" Garrett pressed. "Paying clients and all."

Archer smiled. "True. All right then. Until tomorrow."

"Until tomorrow."

13

Isabel sat near the hotel window. The curtains were closed, but she'd left them slightly open to observe any vehicles coming and going. She had repositioned the digital alarm clock, moving it from the nightstand to the table next to the window, allowing her to keep tabs on the time as well.

Garrett had instructed her to leave if he didn't return in two hours. Well, the clock was closing in on the two hour mark and she was getting worried. If Garrett didn't return, she had no idea what she would do. She'd have to live on the streets. Always looking over her shoulder. Never sure when someone would put a bullet in her head.

He'll make it back. He will!

She gazed at the clock. Five minutes left.

He's abandoned me.

Her eyes dropped to the burner phone. She could text Garrett, ask him what was wrong. But he'd told her not to contact him unless it was an absolute emergency. But wasn't his delay an emergency in and of itself?

She decided when the two-hour mark came and went, she'd take cover somewhere beyond the motel parking lot, it didn't matter where, as long as the spot was relatively hidden and afforded a good view of the suite. That way, she could keep an eye out for his return without putting herself in danger. She'd text him then, when she was safe.

She wondered how long she could afford to wait for an answer. An hour maybe? Depended on how secure her cover was.

No. He's going to make it.

She kept wavering back and forth like that, cycling through different scenarios in her head, and then, when there was only thirty seconds left, a vehicle pulled up outside. It was an older model Chevrolet Cavalier. A bit rundown.

She couldn't make out the driver and suppressed a momentary panic.

Did I overstay?

She tensed as the door opened. A well-built man in a polo shirt emerged. He wore a cap and sunglasses, and when he raised his head and looked her way she realized it was Garrett.

She slumped in sheer, utter relief.

His shirt was a dark brown this time, instead of blue, and he'd swapped out his cap as well so that it was black, not gray. His sunglasses were of the wrap-around variety, not dark like before, but mirrored now. In one hand he carried two bags: the brown one obviously contained fast food, judging from the grease stain at the bottom.

She opened the door before he could knock. His free hand was behind his back, no doubt ready to withdraw his Glock in case someone other than her stood in the door.

"Cutting it close…" she commented.

He came inside. "Any issues since I left?"

"Nope." She shut the door and then motioned at his changed clothes. "You've been busy."

He grunted in reply and dropped the two bags on the table: that characteristic aroma of food cooked in sizzling fat hit her nostrils and she couldn't help but swallow hungrily.

"Feel free to help yourself." He headed toward the bathroom.

She resisted the urge to open the bags. "How'd it go with your friend?"

"He has the memory stick," Garrett replied over his shoulder. "He'll have news for us tomorrow."

"Everything is tomorrow," Isabel said.

"It'll be a busy day," he agreed. "There's still something I have to do today, though."

"What?"

In reply, he entered the bathroom and shut the door.

What was he up to now?

She sat down at the table and opened the paper bag. Inside were three burgers, two fries, two chicken nugget containers, and two waters. She grabbed one of the burgers, unwrapped it and dug in.

While she ate she peered into the other bag. The receipt indicated a cash purchase from a camping store. She fetched the two large packages inside. Each one was labeled "thermo tarp." With a shrug, she put them back and concentrated on her burger.

She heard the toilet flush and several moments later the door opened. She'd finished the burger and half a bag of fries by then.

"Someone's hungry." Garrett sat down next to

her. He studied her uncertainly a moment, and then added: "I'm going to visit your house again."

"What?" She swallowed a mouthful of fries. "Won't they still be watching the place? What about the men stationed inside? You really think they've been pulled off the property already?"

"I'm counting on all of them still being there," Garrett replied. "It's time I had a little talk with these individuals. We need to know who they're working for and why they want this research so badly."

She nibbled her lower lip nervously. "Isn't that kind of dangerous?"

"I'm a dangerous guy." He grabbed the Glock from his waistband and his experienced hands swiftly released the magazine. With a practiced glance he verified the loaded rounds before checking the empty chamber. Apparently satisfied that the firearm was up to his specifications, he slid the magazine back into place with a click and tucked the weapon into his waistband.

"You didn't need the theatrics," Isabel told him. "You had me at *dangerous*. When are we leaving?"

"*I'm* leaving as soon as it's dark out," he told her, sitting at the table next to her. He opened the paper bag and grabbed one of the remaining burgers.

"I want to come with you," she stated flatly.

"Do you?" He finished his burger—already!—and grabbed the second one.

"And you say *I'm* hungry…" She crossed her arms. "I won't stay here by myself again. You don't know what it's like, alone here, waiting…"

"Sorry," he said. "It's too dangerous."

"I'm supposed to sit here, worrying, while you go out there and risk your life interrogating the men who tried to kill me?"

"Yep," he said casually. "And we don't know for sure that they are the men trying to kill you. We don't know what faction they're from. That's what I'm going to find out. Though I suspect I might encounter both factions while I'm out there."

"Both?"

He took a big bite. "That's my hunch. One faction will be watching the other. But we'll see."

He finished the burger and started on the fries, veritably wolfing them down.

Isabel sighed, then offered what remained of her own fries to him.

"You don't want them?" he asked.

She flashed a weak smile. "You're going to need them more then me."

"Do you still have the burner phone?"

"Of course. It's not like I'm going to throw out my only means of communicating with you."

"Same rules apply. Don't text me unless it's an emergency. And if you do, use Signal. Connect to the motel's Wi-Fi—"

"And turn off the phone and remove the battery when I'm done," she interrupted. "I know I know."

"If I'm not back by eight thirty, leave," he continued. "And if you have to make an emergency exit from the motel before then, follow the tree line west. Keep going until the forest transitions to a field, and then return to the road and wait for me in the ditch."

"In the ditch?"

"That's right, that's your muster point," he said. "You'll want to be lying down at that point. You've seen the thermo tarps?" He motioned toward the bag from the camping store.

"I have," she replied.

"You'll want a tarp covering your body at all times when you're out there."

"Why, so I'm not cold?"

He frowned. "It will hide you from the thermal detectors of any drones that might be watching."

She cocked her head, unsure what to say.

He studied her for a moment. "Just to make sure everything is clear: if you have to leave the motel for any reason, take everything with you. The phone. The tarp. Everything. And if I'm not back by eight thirty, get the hell out, and don't bother waiting at the muster point because I won't be coming."

"Do I use the tarp in that case?"

"Yes," he told her. "Spend the night in the woods, if you can. And then in the morning make your way to the road and hitchhike out of here."

"Should I text you with Signal if I go to the muster point? To let you know I'm there?" She realized she was just stalling at this point, because she didn't want him to go. Didn't want to be left alone again.

"If you can." Garrett stood up.

She watched him head toward the door. "You'll be back by eight thirty."

He refused to meet her eyes. "That's the plan."

GARRETT PROCEEDED through the dark of the golf course, making his way toward the house Isabel had shared with James. He had one of the thermal tarps with him, wrapped around his head and shoulders and draped across his body, just in case an unseen and unheard drone was surveying the house on the thermal band from far above. He formed a hood

underneath his chin by gripping the edges of the tarp
with his thumb and forefinger.

Keeping to the shadows, he weaved between the
trees and bushes that had been planted next to the
course's property line to his right. A chain link fence
separated the fairway from the backyards of the
bordering houses; those backyards sometimes had
their own fences, not to mention their own foliage to
shield the yards from the eyes of the golfers.

He kept his head on a swivel, sweeping his gaze
from the fairway to the backyards and back again.

When he was still several houses distant, he
moved away from the property line, heading toward
the cover of trees deeper inside the golf course. This
part of the course apparently wasn't part of the main
fairway, per se, which would explain why it had more
scattered trees. Then again, maybe the owners just
liked to keep the golfers challenged.

He moved from shadow to shadow, making a
wide detour on the way toward the Lockwood residence. He kept glancing back toward the property
line with its chain link fence to gauge how far he
had moved, and when he was satisfied with the
distance, he started moving parallel to the fence
once more.

He finally reached the spot he was aiming for, a
tall tree he had scouted the night before, situated
almost directly in line with Isabel's house, but roughly
two hundred feet out into the fairway. It gave him a
perfect vantage point to survey the house.

Staying low, he took cover behind the tree, and
then peered past the edge of the trunk. He concentrated on the foliage located directly in front of the
chain link fence on the golf course side. A man had
been lurking thereabouts the night before. Garrett

wanted to get an idea of where that man's hiding place was tonight.

So he waited, continuing to scan the trees and bushes, and started counting the seconds in his head. When he reached nine hundred, he reset the count and started over.

In that manner, he waited in the shadows for thirty minutes, but still he had caught sight of no one, and heard nothing out there.

He pursed his lips. Had the man deployed somewhere else? Maybe inside the backyard itself or in the house? Last night he knew three mercs were in the house because he'd seen them enter from the vantage point of a neighbor's roof. But tonight he had no idea how many were present, nor where they were positioned.

He decided to risk getting closer. He lined himself up with the next nearest obstacle between himself and the fence—a small bush. Then he dropped, flattening his body against the wet grass, and began snaking forward.

When he reached the bush, which appeared as a dark outline in the night, he pushed his upper body upright, and then gazed past the foliage.

He heard a soft click behind and above him. It was the sound of someone flicking off the safety of an automatic rifle. He tensed, but knew whoever had done that didn't want him dead, at least not yet. Turning off the safety like that was tantamount to announcing "I want you to know I have a gun pointed at you." Because if they'd wanted to kill him without any warning, the proper way to disengage the safety was by slowly rotating the selector, riding it between the thumb and forefinger so that it made no sound at all.

"Get up," a voice hissed.

Garrett had a fairly good idea of where the man was standing, thanks to that command.

I can take him.

But could he? It was too dark. One mistake…

Garrett held up his hands, then clambered to his feet.

"Turn around," the voice commanded.

Before Garrett had even completed a half turn, a gunshot rang out.

\

14

Blackwell sat on the porch of his cottage. It overlooked a lake framed by lush, emerald forests. Songbirds chirped somewhere among the nearby trees, accompanied by the occasional buzz of insects. The air carried a faint hint of pine and sod.

Doing their best to blend into the backdrop, two of his men stood guard inconspicuously on either side of the cottage. Another five were distributed across the property. Subtle reminders that his work was always with him, no matter where he went.

Work was life. It had to be. There was simply too much to do... and too many problems to deal with.

He received a notification on his augmented reality glasses. Lieutenant Mitchell.

Blackwell accepted the request immediately and a video of his man appeared in the upper right.

"Got some news," Mitchell informed him. "We have an eighty-percent positive match on Isabel Lockwood, and another at a different location of Garrett Bennett."

"Where was she recorded?"

"Her face was caught on a mall drugstore camera, not far from an unidentified man of athletic build, presumed to be Garrett Bennett. He was at the till, while she was perusing gift cards in another aisle. When he left, she followed twenty feet behind. This drugstore was located in the same mall where we found Bennett's abandoned vehicle."

"So she *is* with him…" Blackwell said, tapping his chin. "Why only an eighty-percent match?"

"She was wearing sunglasses and a baseball cap," Mitchell explained.

Blackwell steepled his fingers. "Do we know what she bought?"

"We were able to identify some of the purchases made by the man with the athletic build: wire strippers, blond hair dye, and what appear to off-the-shelf gift cards, and either a box of staples or paper clips."

Garrett considered that. "So she's likely blond now. Tell me about the second location."

"Garrett Bennett's face was caught on a dome camera installed in the overhead canopy of a gas station. We only have a sixty percent certainty on the match. Again because his face was partially occluded —he was wearing a baseball cap pulled low, with his collar raised and his head bowed."

"Sixty percent is good enough for me. What are the whereabouts?"

"About eighty kilometers to the west of the city," the lieutenant replied. "Rapid reaction forces are on the way to all the hotels and motels in the vicinity, looking for a man or woman of the respective descriptions. The forces have also been warned that the targets may have modified their appearances, with the woman expected to be a blond now. Perhaps with a haircut."

"Excellent news," Blackwell said. "Anything from the channelers?"

"Negative," Mitchell replied.

"Keep me apprised."

"Will do," the lieutenant said before the video winked out.

Blackwell sighed. Well, if they could get to Isabel Lockwood, at least one of his problems might work itself out. As for the other problem…

He gazed at the lake and watched a dragonfly swoop into view. It flitted back and forth for a moment and then caught a mosquito right out of the air in front of him.

Blackwell smiled wanly.

He could relate to both insects.

Sometimes he felt like the dragonfly. Other times the mosquito.

Today, he felt like both.

MOMENTS after the gunshot rang out, the shadow beside Garrett collapsed like a puppet whose strings had been unceremoniously cut; the merc who had captured him hit the ground with a sickening thud.

Footfalls in the grass drew his attention to the right, where another shadow emerged. Garrett could see the obvious outline of a pistol pointed at him.

"Do you have a weapon?" the shadow asked.

"No," Garrett lied.

"Walk forward." His new captor ordered. "Quickly."

Garrett advanced as instructed. The merc came

up behind him, leaving a good distance between himself and Garrett.

Garrett suddenly heard the chain link fence next to the house rattle, no doubt as the other mercenaries came clambering into the golf course to search for their fallen companion.

"Down," his captor ordered urgently when Garrett reached what looked like a small maintenance shed.

Garrett ducked behind the shed. The man positioned himself a good seven feet from Garrett, near the edge of the shed.

Neither of them made a sound. In the deep darkness, Garrett couldn't tell whether the man beside him was peering past the shed or pointing the weapon directly at Garrett's face. Either could be the case.

He decided to take a risk and assume the former scenario was true, and that his captor wasn't looking at him at the moment.

Slowly, carefully, he reached behind him, underneath the thermo tarp that draped his body, and lifted his shirt so that he could access the Glock secured in his rear waistband. He wrapped his fingers around the grip.

"Freeze," the man whispered.

Damn.

His captor must have been wearing night vision goggles. The one problem with the tarp in its current configuration was that it hid Garrett's thermals only from airborne cameras, not men on the ground.

"Toss the weapon behind you," the man hissed.

Garrett resignedly threw the weapon away. A lucky toss—he hit a tree, and it made an obvious thud in the night. The sound wasn't much louder than the whispering of his captor, but it might have been enough to give away their position.

He could only hope…

He listened, but heard nothing out there. If anyone was coming, they were being very quiet about it. Any approaching men would show up on night vision goggles, of course, and his captor was likely tracking them even now, waiting for the best moment to strike.

And then it happened. The man began opening fire past the edge of the shed. The muzzle flashes dimly illuminated his face, and Garrett saw the night vision goggles mounted to his caiman-style ballistic helmet, the same lightweight headgear favored by special operators. Or ex-special operators.

These types of goggles would be designed to account for the bloom of the muzzle flashes, adapting to the intensity so that the man could maintain situational awareness. He'd be well aware if Garrett attempted to dive for the abandoned weapon.

But Garrett didn't have to dive.

Because the man had mistakenly assumed Garrett had given up his only weapon.

While the man fired, Garrett reached toward his ankle, lifted the pant leg, and grabbed the backup Glock he kept holstered there.

As the shadow of the man seemed to spin toward him, Garrett unloaded the weapon.

He heard a gurgling sound followed by a thud as his captor collapsed.

Garrett kept his weapon aimed at the edge of the shed, waiting and listening for the others.

He heard nothing.

Don't tell me they're all dead?

He quickly knelt over the fallen man, who was no

longer breathing, and felt around until he found his face. The goggles would be swivel-mounted to the caiman helmet the man was wearing, so Garrett removed the entire helmet and secured it to his own head. Then he swiveled the goggles into place.

Instantly the world transformed. An eerie green hue washed over the golf course, revealing the shed and trees located on this side of the course in stark detail, along with the body lying at his feet.

Garrett aimed his Glock past the edge of the shed and surveyed the landscape. Strewn between the trees, he saw two other bodies sprawled on the ground. He spotted a third next to a trunk—that would be the first man who'd discovered Garrett.

Yep. All dead.

They all wore night vision goggles and carried assault rifles.

Garrett considered swapping out his Glock for one of those, but decided it would be too bulky and unnecessary for his needs.

So instead he retreated to where he'd thrown his main Glock and recovered it. He put his spare weapon back into the ankle holster, and shoved the other into his rear waistband.

Then he knelt next to the dead man beside the shed and searched him. He found a smartphone, set it to airplane mode and turned the device off. He planned to remove the battery later when he had the tools.

The man had two thick pouches attached to his MOLLE chest rig. Garrett opened them, confirmed that they contained grenades, then unclipped both pouches from the rig.

Don't mind if I do.

With each pouch, he threaded one of the clips

through a belt loop on his waistband, putting the first on the left side of his body, and the second on his right, so that the grenades were readily accessible if needed. He discarded the remaining clips.

Keeping the thermo tarp in place around his body, he advanced to the other bodies, moving slowly, carefully, keeping his eyes on the chain link fence ahead just in case any more operatives decided to make an appearance. It was also possible—probable even—that a sniper was observing from somewhere inside the house or on the rooftop. Just because he didn't spot anyone didn't mean no one was present.

As he reached each body, he stripped the phones and also turned them off. They had grenade pouches, too, but Garrett only had so many belt loops and decided that two was probably more than enough. No need to be greedy.

He considered approaching the house to look for a potential sniper, but decided it was too risky. He had everything he needed now anyway, courtesy of those phones. They weren't quite what he was looking for, but would suffice. Not to mention he now had two grenades—couldn't go wrong there.

With the thermo tarp in place, he began the trek back the way he'd come.

GARRETT KEPT an eye on his watch as he drove back to the motel. He had just enough time to make a stop at the mall to pick up the tools he needed to remove the smartphone batteries. Some devices still relayed tracking information even while turned off, and Garrett wasn't about to have his positioned monitored by the bad guys. If he wasn't careful, he'd lead them right to Isabel.

He reached the mall. Thankfully the drugstore was still open, and he purchased the mini screwdriver he needed—the screwdriver he used to jack cars was too big—then he returned to his parking stall in the underground garage and set to work on the phones.

These particular phones proved to be extra devious. In addition to the main batteries, they also had backups snuggled beneath the main circuit boards.

He had no choice but to assume he'd been tracked up until the moment he'd removed all the batteries. So he abandoned his latest vehicle and made his way out of the mall by means of a different entrance. He moved quickly, as time was short.

He found a new car to jack shortly and then headed back to the motel. He was cutting it close, but with some carefully planned speeding, he'd return a good ten minutes before eight thirty.

15

I sabel sat cross-legged on the floor with two pillows jammed underneath her for support. She had also lain a towel over the motel carpet—who knew when it had last been cleaned, after all?

She was trying to visualize a place that made her happy and filled her with peace. She chose the white sands of Virginia Beach, and each time she imagined the waves lapping against shore, she became more relaxed.

She visualized light flowing from her head, swirling around her body, and reentering through her feet, as if forming a balloon of protective energy around her. She imagined white light from the world flowing into that balloon, recharging her and her body.

Then her mind drifted to James, breaking her concentration. James was dead. She still couldn't really believe it. It had been a little more than a day since she'd witnessed his death. Just a day. It was still so very raw and real to her.

She tried to put him into the box in her mind

reserved for distractions, but couldn't. A part of her was repulsed that she'd even try. As if she could just sweep his death under a mental rug like it was nothing so that she could relax and feel good about herself.

No, she would relive that moment again and again for the rest of her life whether she wanted to or not. That image of the helicopter exploding with James inside was permanently seared into her very being. As was the guilt that she had survived.

Survivor's guilt is very real. Is this what Garrett had to go through during his tours? What a terrible thought… reliving that feeling again and again as your closest friends died off one by one. Your brothers.

Garrett. He was the reason she'd begun meditating in the first place: to distract herself from where he'd gone. She was taut with worry, and couldn't shake the thought that he was going to be captured or killed. What was she going to do if he didn't return when he said he would?

If I'm not back by eight thirty, leave.

She involuntary opened her eyes. It took a moment for the blur to leave her vision and for her eyes to focus on the digital clock she'd set on the floor in front of her.

8:00.

She shook her head. Meditation was useless.

Too many distractions.

She rubbed her eyes. There was no point meditating now anyway, not with only half an hour to go.

She was wearing most of her current worldly belongings—her T-shirt and jeans, with the Rain-Guard jacket draped across the chair beside her. She had the wad of money Garrett had given her tucked into one pocket.

She sighed, got up, put on her cap, and slipped her sunglasses into the T-shirt pocket. She'd placed her sneakers next to the towel on the carpet, and she slid into them.

Restless, she sat by the window, peered through the gap in the curtains, and waited. She would be ready to leave as soon as he got here—in case he needed to leave in a hurry.

And he *would* get here.

She fingered the empty chocolate bar wrapper and bag of chips on the table. Not only had she eaten the fast food earlier, but she'd also finished the protein bars from the drugstore. She couldn't stop herself from picking up more snacks from the vending machine near the motel office: emotional eating at its finest.

The bag from the camping store also sat on the table, and she idly retrieved the thermo tarp from inside. It was still in its packaging. She smiled sadly, turning it over in her hands before putting it back.

Can't believe the way I'm living, now.

She started thinking about James again, and Garrett.

A flash came from outside as if someone had taken a photo. Alarmed, she leaned forward and gazed past the gap between the closed curtains, but the parking lot seemed quiet. There were no new vehicles since the last time she'd looked out.

For some reason, she glanced up. Overhead, squatting among the stars, she spotted a familiar glowing dot in the sky, scintillating as it moved.

"Not you again," she whispered.

She felt the irresistible urge to follow it.

She grabbed her key card and opened the door. Hesitating, she scanned the parking lot one last time.

Seemed safe. She was about to go out when she remembered Garrett's words.

If you leave the motel for any reason, take everything with you. The phone. The tarp. Everything.

She hesitated once again, because she didn't plan to go very far, but a part of her felt like she had to obey Garrett's words to the letter if she wanted to survive. Even if those words didn't really apply in the current situation.

I'll be right back...

With a sigh, she reentered and grabbed the bag from the camping store like a dutiful little servant. She also put on her Rain-Guard jacket.

Don't know why I'm bothering... the light will probably be gone by now anyway.

When she returned to the door frame, the glowing dot was still waiting there far above, beckoning.

She shut the door behind her and, gazing skyward, walked into the expansive lot, walking by the rows of parking spaces. She continued to advance, quickly distancing herself from the motel units and the light pollution they generated.

She could see the glowing dot quite clearly. It was moving westward.

She followed, and soon left the parking lot behind for bare grass. She entered the forest adjacent to the motel and momentarily lost sight of the dot until she moved past the branches of the pine that concealed it.

She continued to follow it, but then, just like that, the dot winked out right there in the middle of the sky.

Puzzled, she repositioned several times, searching the sky for it, but the dot seemed thoroughly gone.

She didn't quite know what to make of it all. Had she imagined the light? Was it simply some satellite passing low enough to reflect the sun, a satellite that had rotated so she could no longer see the reflection? Or perhaps it was a meteorite that had burned up in the atmosphere.

With a shrug she made her way back. Garrett would be returning any time now.

She was worried for a moment that her little side trip had caused her to miss him, but when she reached the tree line and peered back into the parking lot, she saw no new vehicles parked directly in front of her motel unit.

But Garrett wouldn't necessarily park out front... she scanned the parking lot, searching for any newly arrived vehicles, but she wasn't entirely sure if any of the cars she saw hadn't already been there.

She concluded that he hadn't yet arrived.

But just as she took a step past the tree line, a piano-black SUV quietly pulled into the parking lot.

She froze. It was a carbon copy of the vehicle she had been kidnapped in, down to the make, model and color.

Hands suddenly shaking, she retreated into the shadows of the pine forest, not taking her eyes off the vehicle.

It parked next to the front office, and two men dressed in black emerged. They headed straight inside.

A moment later the pair returned. One of them carried a key card. They reentered and drove the vehicle circumspectly around the expansive parking lot, choosing a stall several suites down from her own. The side sliding door opened, and six men dressed in black camos emerged. They wore tactical helmets and carried assault rifles.

Her heart was practically beating out of her chest right now. All of her instincts told her to run, but she could only stand there, petrified, watching from the shadows as the men approached her suite.

They hugged the lot-facing wall of the motel, moving slowly, carefully. If she had been watching from the window of her room, she wouldn't have seen their approach at all.

When they reached her unit, one of the men made a hand signal, and three of them took up a position on either side of the door, their weapons at the ready. The man closest to the handle used the key card the manager had given him and then opened the door.

The men rushed inside, alternating their entry from the left and right sides.

Isabel pressed her lips together tightly as she watched this.

If I was still inside that room…

The glowing dot had saved her yet again.

Maybe I'm just lucky.

No. Once was lucky. But twice?

Maybe James is helping me.

She smiled sadly. No. It wasn't James. It couldn't be.

Has to be another coincidence.

One of these days her luck would run out.

The men emerged. They seemed somewhat less tense, as their weapons were pointed at the ground now.

One of the men scanned the parking lot, and his gaze reached the tree line… he looked directly at

Isabel, and she flinched, instinctively retreating deeper into the shadows.

His gaze moved on, and in moments the six men retreated at a jog back to the SUV and piled inside.

If these men were here, that meant they'd captured Garrett, and now she was completely alone. But he'd said to wait until eight thirty. It wasn't eight thirty, not yet. It had been eight last she checked, and certainly not more than ten minutes had passed since then.

Also, the men had stopped at the motel office first. If Garrett had been in their custody, they would have had his copy of the key card, and so would have headed directly to her unit.

We must have been caught on camera somewhere in the area.

They were probably searching all motels in the area for any recent check-ins matching her description or Garrett's.

She watched the SUV drive onto the service road, but instead of merging onto the highway it pulled onto the shoulder of the road and came to a halt. The vehicle's headlamps promptly turned off: obviously the men were waiting in case she or Garrett returned to the motel.

Feeling suddenly exposed, she retreated deeper into the trees, but not so deep that she couldn't still see the highway. She grabbed the thermo tarp from the camping store bag. She removed it from its packaging and unfolded the bulky thing. One side was coated with a reflective layer, the other was polyester. She wasn't sure which side should face her. She had a 50/50 chance of getting it right.

It made sense that the reflective side should face her body, since the whole point of a thermo tarp was to keep the contents warm by reflecting any heat. So she positioned the shiny side toward her and wrapped the tarp over her head and shoulders so that her upper body was covered, hoping that would be enough to block out any thermal signature a drone might pick up. She resolved to stay close to the trunks of the surrounding pines, just in case.

She grabbed onto the tarp with her index finger and thumb, forming a hood beneath her chin. Then she pulled out the burner phone Garrett had given her and inserted the battery with one hand, turning it on. She kept her back to the parking lot, shielding the phone with her body so its dim light wouldn't give away her position.

She left the phone in airplane mode, but activated the Wi-Fi. In moments, she had connected to the motel Wi-Fi. The signal strength was weak, and she was a bit surprised that it still worked out here at all actually, but she was thankful nonetheless. She'd entered the Wi-Fi password earlier, and didn't have to type it again.

She hesitated before launching Signal. Was it possible the men in the SUV had a way to intercept her Wi-Fi access? Well, there was nothing for it… she had to warn Garrett. He might arrive at any moment.

She launched Signal. There was only one number in the contact list, labeled: MAIN BURNER. She sent that number an encrypted text:

Motel compromised. Meet at muster point.

She deactivated the Wi-Fi, then turned off the phone and removed the battery, pocketing both.

She scanned the highway one last time, but had lost sight of the SUV. Just because she couldn't see it didn't mean it wasn't out there.

Worried that the men might have intercepted her

Wi-Fi transmission, she proceeded into the trees. When she was satisfied that she'd gone deep enough, she walked parallel to the motel parking lot until she reached the service road.

What was it he'd said? Think.

Follow the tree line west. Keep going until the forest becomes a field, and then head to the road. Wait for me in the ditch.

West had to mean moving away from the motel. Because if she went the other way she'd be out in the open, and there were no fields there, just a parking lot.

So, staying well inside the forest, she followed the road, moving away from the SUV and the motel, and sticking to the shadows of the trees. Hopefully she was headed toward the muster point she and Garrett had agreed upon.

She kept walking within the cover of the trees as the service road met with the highway. She was relieved when the trees finally ended in a field.

I'm going the right way.

She dropped, and repositioned the thermo tarp so that it covered her entire body from head to toe. As she crawled toward the ditch next to the highway, she kept pausing to readjust the thermo tarp, wanting it to remain in place at all times.

When she reached the lowest point of the ditch, she halted and waited.

That should be good enough.

She heard the vehicles roaring past, but could only see their blurry tops rushing by from where she lurked at the bottom of the ditch.

She wasn't sure how long she waited, but it seemed like an eternity. An hour. Two?

Surely it was long past eight-thirty by now. She

wondered what she was supposed to do if Garrett didn't show up. Should she leave?

No. He's going to come.

Finally she heard crunching in the grass beside her, and realized someone was approaching. Or something.

"Garrett?" she asked tensely.

The shadow stopped.

"It's me," Garrett said.

She slumped in relief. "Garrett."

When he came close, she realized he was covered in a thermo tarp similar to her own. Beneath it he wore an army helmet of some kind, with what looked like night vision goggles strapped onto his head.

"You've got some new toys," she commented.

"Tell me what happened."

When she explained, he nodded sagely.

"They probably caught us on a camera somewhere. We'll have to be more careful going forward." He glanced at the sky. "We have to assume a drone is providing aerial reconnaissance at this very moment. They would have seen me stop a few miles back."

"A few miles?" She was stunned. "No wonder it took you so long to get here."

"Indeed. When I got your message I pulled over right away."

She considered his words. "So we're not going back to the car, I assume?"

"Nope. Anything suspicious will be tagged and watched. Including a car that happens to stall a few miles away from a reconnaissance target."

They retreated toward the forest, and when they reached the cover of the trees they resumed an upright posture. They kept their thermo tarps in place around their heads and bodies.

"Should we be worried about these tarps getting too hot?" she asked. "As in, they might heat up from all our body heat and give away our positions?"

"We should definitely worry," he agreed. "But unfortunately there's nothing we can do about that. Keep it ventilated as best you can."

"I will. Where to now?"

Garrett thought for a moment. "There should be a farm nearby if I remember correctly."

Staying in the forest, they headed southeast, judging from their position relative to the motel, which they circumnavigated before joining up with the service road on the other side.

When the trees gave way to another field, she and Garrett switched to crawling. It seemed like they wriggled across that prickly field for an eternity—the wheat stubble poked up from the harvested land, relentlessly scratching at skin and catching at clothes. She got nicks and cuts all over her exposed hands and neck. She was thankful she was wearing a long-sleeved jacket and jeans.

Finally they reached a dirt road and the going became easier.

It must have been close to midnight by the time Garret and Isabel crawled toward an older vehicle. It was parked next to a farmhouse that had its lights off at the moment.

Isabel was familiar with farms, or at least she'd visited a few, and she kept expecting an angry dog to come running up to her, but thankfully the owners either didn't have a dog or they let the animal sleep indoors. There weren't any cattle for the dog to protect from coyotes and the like, so that probably helped.

Garret bypassed the car's lock using his screwdriver technique, but he only opened the door a crack, just enough to roll down the window. Then he shut the door again.

He turned toward her and said, quietly: "When I open the passenger door window, I want you to enter like this." Holding the tarp over his body, he carefully clambered into the open window and pulled himself into the vehicle.

Great. That looks really easy. And not painful at all.

She waited until he opened her window, then took a deep breath. Keeping one hand on the tarp to make sure it didn't fall off, she pulled herself through the window. Her hips caught on the frame and she flinched at the pain in her midsection.

Garrett's strong hands wrapped around her biceps and gently pulled her inside the rest of the way. When she was settled, she realized her face was extremely close to his, as was her body. She suddenly wanted him to wrap his powerful arms around her and never let go.

But then he released her and pulled back.

She was dazed for a moment, but quickly recovered. She scolded herself.

Nice. Keep acting like you're in high school.

She pulled the thermo tarp out from behind her and folded it up. Then she sat back in the passenger seat. Her hands and neck throbbed from the cuts she had, but she would survive.

When Garrett hotwired the car, the lights inside the farmhouse came on.

He immediately turned around and drove onto the dirt road.

When they reached the highway, Isabel, tired and exhausted, couldn't stay awake any longer. She closed her eyes and fell fast asleep.

16

I sabel awoke in a new motel. She was lying in bed, and there was another unmade bed to her right.

The nicks and cuts on her hands from the crawl through the wheat field had been bandaged. She touched her neck and discovered more adhesive bandages.

Nice of him.

She saw Garrett at the motel table, which as usual he had moved next to the window. He kept his eyes glued to the small opening in the curtain. In front of him was an empty bowl of cereal.

Isabel glanced at the digital clock. *4:45 AM.*

"Don't you ever sleep?" She rubbed her eyes but otherwise stayed in the bed.

"If you want breakfast this is the only chance you'll have for a while," Garrett told her.

With a sigh, she got up. She was wearing her T-shirt and jeans, and her jacket rested on the night-stand beside her.

She made a quick, groggy trip to the washroom

and when she was finished her business she joined him at the table.

He had prepared a bowl of cereal for her, replete with milk.

"Early bird gets the worm, huh?" She took a bite. Oats, honey and milk never tasted so bland. Didn't help that she wasn't all that hungry, groggy as she was, but she forced herself, knowing she was going to need the energy.

When half the bowl was done, she was feeling more talkative. "So what happened at my brother's house last night?"

"I was almost captured," Garrett revealed. "One guy took me captive, then another guy shot him—a mole, I suspect. Then two others from the house rushed the mole and he mowed them down. While he was doing that, I shot him with the Glock stowed in my ankle holster."

She was lifting a spoonful of milk and cereal to her mouth but paused. "You have an ankle holster?"

"I do," he said.

She glanced down at the hem of his pant leg: she noticed nothing out of the ordinary, but the jeans were just the right looseness that a concealed weapon could definitely be present.

She took the bite. "Interesting. I thought you only kept a pistol at your waist."

"So did he."

She considered for a moment everything he'd said. Her groggy mind was only just starting to function properly. "So wait. They were all shot? So you couldn't ask them any questions."

"Unfortunately not, but I retrieved their phones."

"Anything useful in their contact lists or call histories?"

"Didn't check yet." He met her eyes. "We'll have to wait until I acquire some new equipment. Their phones had two batteries each, one main, one backup. Which tells me they very likely harbor tracking devices that operate at all times, even when the phones are physically turned off: as soon as batteries are placed inside they start transmitting. And there aren't SD cards I can remove, so we'll have to turn them on to get access to the internal memories."

She took another bite. "How much is this 'new equipment' going to cost? Do we have enough?" She wasn't entirely sure how much of the original five hundred dollars remained. Likely Garrett's bank account was frozen by now, but they could always try to withdraw again. Probably a bad idea though...

"We have enough," he said in typical, stubborn Garrett fashion.

"Can I give you a hug?" she said suddenly.

He gave her a curious look.

"I wouldn't have made it this far without you," Isabel blurted.

"Neither would I," Garrett replied softly.

"What do you mean?" she asked.

But instead of answering he got up, leaving her to finish her bowl of cereal alone. He lay down on the second bed. "I'm taking a quick nap. Wake me no later than five thirty. Keep an eye on the parking lot."

So much for the hug. She wasn't entirely sure why she'd asked him. She was feeling thankful, she supposed, and glad that he was all right after yesterday's ordeal. Either way, grogginess was obviously affecting her judgment.

"Okay, but I want to take a shower after I'm done eating," she said. A cold shower would do wonders to wake her.

"I need you to watch the parking lot." He was starting to sound tired now himself.

"Then I'll take a shower after you get up," she insisted.

"No time."

She frowned. "What do you mean, no time? You said wake you at five thirty. That's still early."

"No time," he repeated.

Isabel thought for a moment. "It's Monday… this morning we're going to pay a visit to Professor Noah Patel on his way to work."

"That's the plan," Garrett agreed.

She realized something. "You don't know when he goes to work, do you? That's why you keep saying 'no time.'"

"That would be why," he agreed. "I have however narrowed down the potential parking garages he'll use, based on their proximity to the physics building. There are two. If we get lucky, we'll pick the right one and take him this morning. If not, we'll get him at the end of the day at the second garage."

"Take him…" She wasn't sure she liked the sound of that. "Wait, are we kidnapping him?"

"Yep."

She sat there stunned for several seconds. "Is that the best idea?"

Garrett was sounding sleepier by the moment. "It's the only way to keep him and his family safe. Not to mention us. If we do it right, no one will ever know we took him."

She considered that for a moment. Garrett was probably right. Still, that didn't mean she had to like it.

Something struck her. "I noticed you've been

using the word 'we.' So you're letting me come with you this time."

"I've decided I have to," Garrett told her. "He knows you. If you don't come along I'll have to hurt him. And I think we want to avoid that."

"We do. He's a sweet man."

"Completely the opposite of me," Garret quipped from the bed.

"Basically." With that, she let him take his nap.

NOAH PATEL WAITED at the crosswalk as the bleary-eyed students shuffled in front of his car. The bus had just dropped them all off and there was nothing he could do but wait. He should have passed the vehicle earlier when he'd had the chance, but that was what happened when you didn't seize an opportunity when it presented itself.

What a life a professor had. Get up each morning, have breakfast, go through an hour of traffic to get to work, stand up in front of a lectern all day reading notes off prepared slides, go home, have dinner, sit down and watch Netflix or Youtube or maybe read a few research papers if you had any energy left, and then go to bed.

Repeat.

A lifetime of missed opportunities had led him to this moment. There were so many other paths he could have taken, yet he had insisted on following this one through to the end.

I don't envy you, Noah.

One would think having a wife and children would offer some respite from all the wearying monotony, but any time he engaged with family it only tired him further. He did his best to play the role of engaged dad and eager professor, but often wondered if the world would see through his charade.

Finally the long line of students came to an end and the traffic started to advance. It was a relief to be finally moving again, and in a few more blocks he reached the parking garage.

There seemed to be some kind of construction going on today, with a cement truck in the other lane and a flagman holding a paddle to direct traffic. The paddle currently read STOP.

Noah obeyed.

More waiting.

The cement truck ponderously moved across the line of traffic, inching across the street until the road was clear. Finally the flagman turned the paddle to SLOW. With a resigned sighed, Noah drove past the man and turned into the parking garage.

He headed toward his reserved stall on the fourth floor. There was an SUV behind him, not quite tailgating, but still close… he didn't like having vehicles following him in parking garage, they always made him feel rushed. For example if the vehicle followed him all the way to his reserved stall and there were cars parked on either side of the spot, then he'd have to take time to properly park while the driver behind him waited. He couldn't relax while parking like that—it made him nervous, like he was inconveniencing the waiting driver or something.

So he stepped on the gas to put some distance between his vehicle and the SUV. His tires squealed slightly when he made the tight turn to the next level and he was forced to back off on the gas a little.

He reached the fourth floor. As luck would have

it, the row of parking spaces were all empty this morning so he was able to park with ease.

A good start to the day.

The vehicle that had been following took the stall two spaces to his left. That one belonged to Professor Müller. But either someone was parking in the wrong spot, or the professor had recently upgraded to a Land Rover.

Noah retrieved the laptop bag from the seat beside him. He waved at the other vehicle as he got out, but couldn't really discern the occupants and otherwise didn't pay them much heed.

He slid the strap of the laptop bag over one shoulder and made his way toward the stairwell entrance. He was vaguely aware as another vehicle turned onto this level of the garage behind him.

He opened the stairwell door outward and stepped onto the concrete landing inside.

A man wearing a baseball cap was walking down the flight from above. He had his head bowed and hid his hands in his jacket pockets.

Noah got a bad vibe from that one; he started when the door slammed shut behind him and he hurried toward the stairs of the next flight leading down.

Should have taken the elevator today.

Before he even reached the top step the man shoved him roughly from behind. Noah smashed into the concrete wall of the stairwell, and hard arms pinned him against the abrasive surface. He felt the warm breath of his attacker in his ear.

"You're being followed," his assailant hissed. "We're trying to save your life."

Noah was confused. "How does pinning me against a wall save my life?"

He heard loud pops coming from the direction of the garage behind him. He was reminded of a vehicle backfiring.

Someone opened the door a crack.

"They're coming!" a female voice said. The door closed again with a loud thud.

"Go!" his assailant commanded.

The rough hands tore him off the wall and hauled him toward the flight of stairs leading upward. Noah was shoved forward and he half ran, half stumbled after the woman in front of him.

When she looked back, he thought he recognized her.

"Isabel?" Noah asked.

GARRETT SLID a hand underneath the man's shoulder and physically hauled him up the stairs after Isabel.

"Move!" Garrett hissed.

They reached the landing between floors and made a 180 to continue up the next flight.

Garrett was halfway to the next floor when he heard the door of the previous level slam open, followed by boots scuffing against concrete...

Garrett looked back and caught a glimpse of a black-clad man walking backwards up the stairs with a pistol pointed his way.

"Down!" Garrett threw himself into the professor and at the same time drew his Glock. He opened fire at the pursuer and the attacker quickly ducked out of sight.

Garrett's back hit the concrete stairs, but the

impact was partially padded by the professor, who grunted painfully underneath him.

"Go!" Garrett shouted at Isabel. He shifted so that the professor could get out from under him, and meanwhile provided covering fire with his Glock.

When no one reemerged, with his free hand he fumbled with the buckle of the grenade pouch he'd attached to the right side of his waist.

Before he could open it the attacker appeared again, bringing the pistol to bear.

Garrett aimed and opened fire again. The man took cover.

Staying low, Garrett quickly unbuckled the pouch at his waist, fetched the grenade, squeezed the safety handle, and pulled the pin. He leaned toward the railing beside him and nudged the grenade over the bottom edge without looking. It fell to the landing below.

He heard a muted shout and hurriedly clambered to his feet. In two quick steps he reached the upper landing.

Isabel was holding the door open for him so he leaped toward it. Behind him, one of the men opened fire at him from the landing halfway between floors.

As he passed through the door and onto the next level of the parking garage, the explosion ripped through the stairwell. It was deafening. Plumes of smoke tumbled from the stairwell door, which Garrett quickly shut.

Garrett glanced at the professor and confirmed that the man still carried his laptop.

"Let's move." Garrett scooped up the laptop and passed it to Isabel.

When the professor merely stood there, Garrett

grabbed him by the underarm with his free hand and yanked him along. Isabel followed along beside him.

After a few steps the professor seemed to recover from the shock of what had just happened, and he struggled to break free. "I can walk on my own!"

"Then keep up," Garrett said gruffly as he released the man. Garrett kept looking over his shoulder at the stairwell door; he also scanned the parking garage, watching for more ambushers.

"What's going on?" The professor's gaze nervously dropped to the Glock Garrett held.

In answer, Garrett stopped beside the beaten-up Volvo station wagon he'd stolen from the farm the night before. "Get in."

Isabel opened the rear passenger door for him. When he didn't enter, for a moment Garrett thought the guy was going to try to make a run for it.

But Isabel gave him a reassuring nod and finally the professor entered.

When everyone was inside the station wagon, Garrett buckled his seat belt and started the engine.

He rapidly pulled out of the stall and steered the vehicle down the ramp toward the next floor. The Glock sat waiting in his lap. He grabbed the weapon and slowed down as he passed a black sedan that was illegally parked in the middle of the ramp, not far from the professor's car. The sedan had its doors open, but otherwise appeared empty.

Further on, the SUV parked beside the professor's vehicle was riddled with bullets. The doors were open on either side, and three black-clad men lay bleeding out on the cement.

The professor's breath caught when he saw the bodies. "We have to call the police!"

"Thanks for the reminder." Garrett glanced in his

rear view mirror at the man. "Give Isabel your phone."

"What?" the professor said. "No."

"Please, just listen to him," Isabel offered a hand to the professor.

Garrett continued past the SUV and glanced at the stairwell. The door bulged outward, apparently having successfully contained the explosion—incredibly it hadn't been blown off its hinges. Tough doors. There was no sign of the those who had been inside the stairwell when the grenade exploded.

He returned the Glock to his lap and accelerated down the ever-descending ramp of the parking garage, moving at a speed that caused the tires to squeal as he rounded each bend.

"Noah, please… your phone," Isabel pressed.

The professor finally gave his cellphone to Isabel.

"Good boy," Garrett commented.

He held a hand toward Isabel and she pressed the phone into his palm.

Garrett promptly opened his window and tossed the device outside.

"Hey!" the professor exclaimed. "You know how much that cost me?"

"Not as much as your life is worth, I'm sure," Garrett commented.

That shut him up.

With the tires squealing as always, Garrett continued down the remaining floors until he rounded the final bend that led to the ground level, only to drive almost head on into a Mercedes.

He slammed on the brakes, as did the other driver.

A man in spectacles rolled down the window and shouted. "What's your problem asshole? Slow down!"

Garrett felt a soft touch on his wrist. He looked down and realized Isabel was resting her hand on his, next to the Glock, which he hadn't even realized he'd picked up.

He set down the weapon and put the vehicle in reverse, backing up to give the Mercedes room. He made a flamboyant "go-right-ahead" gesture, and returned the other driver's glower as he passed.

When Garrett reached the exit, he slowly pulled onto the sidewalk, scanning the road on either side. Seemed safe.

A student started to walk in front of the station wagon but Garrett accelerated anyway and the irked kid gave him the finger.

Garrett pulled onto the road and ran a red light. The traffic on this side was relatively minor compared to the opposing lane, which was jammed-packed with the vehicles of university students headed to campus.

"Are you going to tell me what's going on, now?" the professor asked.

17

I sabel looked over her shoulder at Noah. "It's good to see you." Her vision became suddenly blurry. She tried to smile, she really did, but she couldn't help the tears that suddenly fell as she gazed at one of her brother's closest friends.

She quickly looked away.

"Isabel…" Noah said. "What's wrong? Has this man kidnapped you?"

She sobbed. "No. He's helping me. Helping us. Because you see… James is… James…"

"He's gone," Garrett finished gruffly.

"What?" Noah sounded stunned. "How?"

Wiping away the tears, she strengthened her resolve. She had to be strong. Somehow.

Taking a deep breath, she explained the ordeal as best she could, from the kidnapping at the house to watching James die in the helicopter explosion, and how she had been on the run with Garrett every since. She left out the parts involving the glowing dots in the sky of course.

"We think they're after us because of a recent

discovery James made," Isabel explained. "One faction of the military industrial complex wants the research behind that discovery very badly, while a competing group—or *groups*—wants to make sure it doesn't fall into the hands of the first faction. At all costs."

Noah rubbed his eyes. "So those men shot dead on the cement of the parking garage—"

"Part of the faction that was following and spying on you," Isabel finished. "Probably the same group that kidnapped me."

"And the others who were shooting at us in the stairwell belong to the other faction?"

"That's what we believe," Isabel told him.

"But why am *I* involved?" Noah asked. "What does any of this have to do with me? I've done nothing."

"Associates of James Lockwood are in high demand this week," Garrett commented coldly.

"What?" Noah blinked in confusion. He glanced at Isabel. "What does he even mean?"

"Liam is dead." Blinking rapidly, Isabel pressed her lips together. "Liam Malcolm."

"Impossible." Noah frowned. "I was just talking to him yesterday morning."

"We were at his house yesterday afternoon," she countered. "The street was cordoned off by police. And they were wheeling… bodies out… in bags."

His face grew very pale. "What about my family?"

"They'll be safe, for now," Garrett said. "If they wanted you and your family dead, they would have finished the job yesterday, like they did with Liam."

"But you don't know that for sure," Noah argued. "You can't. You're not them. Only *they* know what their intentions really are."

"Believe me, I have some insight into their intentions, given my background…" Garrett assured him. "I suspect your house is being observed 24/7 by one of the factions. Just as you are. Or were."

"What do you mean, *given your background?*" the professor asked.

"The Teams," Garrett answered simply.

"He used to be a Navy SEAL," Isabel explained.

"Navy SEAL?" Noah repeated. "But that's a… commendable… profession." He seemed to be picking his words carefully to avoid insulting Garrett. "These men are anything but commendable."

"Yes, but they come from similar backgrounds," Garrett assured him. "Mercenaries. Guns for hire. Private security contractors. Whatever you want to call them, I know how men like that think, along with those who give the orders. Ex-military. All of them."

"But now that you've kidnapped me, won't they simply hold my family hostage to get me to turn myself in?" Noah pressed.

"They're safe," Garrett said. "And will remain so for the foreseeable future. They'll be watched and guarded even more vigilantly now by the faction that wanted you alive. But the instant you contact your family, or those watching them, all that goes out the window. That's when they'll barge inside and take your family hostage and use whatever leverage they can over you. And us."

"You have to trust him," Isabel consoled Noah. "Garrett knows how these men operate. They won't harm your family as long as you're still alive."

"Ultimately, Isabel is the one they want," Garrett clarified. "As long as *Isabel* is alive, your family is safe. So remember that in case you decide to try anything. You have to protect her at all costs, is that clear?"

"Yeah, sure." Noah was staring out the window, clearly worried about his family.

Isabel wished there was something more they could do, but Garrett was right: if Noah dared get in touch with his family, he'd only be putting his wife and children at risk. And if Garrett and Isabel ever contacted either of the factions that hunted them, they'd have to deny any knowledge of Noah. That was the best chance his family had.

"We're going to have to watch him," Garrett told Isabel. He spoke as if the professor wasn't there, listening. "He's going to try calling his wife at the first available opportunity."

Isabel glanced at Noah, who wouldn't meet her eyes. Garrett was probably right.

"Did James email you this week?" Isabel decided she might as well try to coax some information out of him, considering that was the main reason they'd kidnapped him. The fact that they'd unwittingly saved his life by interceding at just the moment the second faction chose to attack was incidental, if a little disturbing. It made her wonder if Garrett was truly correct in his supposition that Noah's family was safe. Still, their hunters had nothing to gain by destroying the only piece of bait they had against the professor, and potentially Isabel.

Noah seemed distracted and didn't answer her question.

"Noah," Isabel pressed.

"What?" Noah glanced at her.

"There were no emails from James this week?"

Noah frowned. "Well sure. Is that why they're after me? Because of some emails James sent?"

"If he mentioned his discovery in those emails, then yes," Isabel said. "Did he?"

"I… don't know. I…"

"Think," Isabel encouraged him. "It's really important."

Noah remained quiet for a moment. "Well if I recall, there was something about one of his pet projects… on branes I believe. He's got this theory where he postulates ten extra dimensions above our own. But he didn't mention a discovery of any kind. And I also saw him in the campus halls during the week, but we didn't talk about any breakthroughs he might have had or anything of the sort. Just the usual departmental gossip."

"Do you usually check your email on your laptop?" Garrett chimed in.

Noah gave him a dubious look. "Yes, why?"

Garrett kept his eyes on the road. "When was the last time you checked?"

Noah thought for a moment. "Early Friday."

"You normally leave your laptop turned on and connected to the Internet?" Garrett pressed.

Noah stiffened. "Where is this going?"

"Just answer the question," Garrett told him softly.

Noah chuckled and muttered something under breath. Sounded like "military grunts."

"Noah…" Isabel tried. "Do you normally leave it turned on and connected to the Internet or not?"

Noah looked at her, then exhaled in capitulation. "I usually put it into sleep mode when I'm not using it. And yes, I have a docking station at work and home, so it'll connect to Wi-Fi as soon as I attach it to the docking station, before it goes back to sleep again."

Isabel glanced at Garrett. "You think he might have some unread, cached messages the laptop managed to catch before they deleted them off the university server?"

"It's worth checking." Garrett's gaze momentarily dropped to the laptop bag tucked away on the floor next to her feet. He addressed Noah: "You don't have a SIM card in your laptop, do you?"

"I don't," Noah said.

"Can I check the emails now?" Isabel asked.

Garrett looked at her sidelong. "Go ahead, but disable the Wi-Fi first."

She grabbed the bag and produced the laptop. When she pressed the power button it turned on almost instantly—definitely was in sleep mode. She found the option to disable the built-in Wi-Fi.

"What email client do you use?" she asked the professor.

"Thunderbird," Noah responded.

"Perfect." She loaded up Mozilla Thunderbird and scrolled through the inbox. Thunderbird cached data offline by storing a copy of all emails, attachments, and other settings from the mail server on the local device. This allowed the user to access his or her email even when not connected to the Internet.

She stopped when she reached the most recent email from James, dated Thursday of last week. She switched to Threaded view, so she could start at the top of the message chain, and began reading aloud.

"First message from James reads, 'I've made the discovery of a lifetime.' Noah's reply: 'Do tell.' James: 'Brane theory is wrong.' Noah: 'How so?' That's it. I should note that Liam Malcolm was also carbon-copied on the emails, but didn't contribute to the thread, at least not this cached portion of it." She turned toward Noah. "I thought you said James didn't tell you about any breakthroughs?"

"Actually I specifically told you 'I don't know,'" Noah replied. "I guess I forgot. We talk ironically like that in emails all the time. I probably assumed he was being sarcastic."

"Do you remember if there was anything else?" Isabel pressed. "You didn't delete any emails, did you?"

"No," Noah told her. "Whatever you see in my inbox is everything I received from your brother."

"Check the previous emails," Garrett told her as he drove.

Isabel scrolled through the remaining messages from James. "Just campus politics and gossip. Some mentions about coming conferences. A retirement lunch. But nothing else about brane theory or a discovery."

"Earlier you mentioned something about the emails being deleted off the university server?" Noah pressed. "What's that all about?"

Isabel glanced at Garrett. "Should we tell him?"

Garrett nodded. "Likely James expanded on his discovery, at least in some small way, but you never saw it. The military industrial complex got to the messages first and wiped them off your servers."

"Why would they do that? And how?" Noah seemed genuinely puzzled.

"They have their ways." Garrett nodded at the laptop. "Toss it."

Isabel closed the laptop and opened the window. The wind tousled her hair as the landscape rushed past. She lifted the laptop toward the opening…

"What! No!" The professor was grabbing her shoulder.

She threw the laptop toward the sidewalk and shut the window. She gave Noah a pitying look.

"Sorry. They could have planted a tracker at some point. You've seen what they do when they hunt you down. We can't let that happen again."

Noah merely shook his head, seeming despondent.

Ten minutes later Garrett took them into another multilevel parking garage, this one next to a popular office building, and on the third floor they switched cars again. Garrett's carjacking skills were impeccable as always, and perhaps improving—it only took him a minute and a half to break-in and hot-wire the latest vehicle.

Before allowing Noah inside the new car, Garrett searched the professor for any other electronics. He proved clean.

"Why did we switch cars?" Noah asked when they were on their way.

"As I told you, Garrett knows how these men operate." Isabel was adjusting the seat of the new sedan. It was hard to get comfortable. "Covertly switching vehicles is the only way to outwit their reconnaissance drones."

"I still don't know what you want with me," Noah said. "You looked through my email. Can you let me go now?"

"I'm not sure I made it clear," Garrett told him. "You're stuck with us for the foreseeable future. It's the only way you'll truly be safe. You saw what the competing faction will do to you. They're not afraid to kill the men that have been ordered to watch you. If you return home to your family, you'll only put them all at risk. Is that what you want?"

He closed his eyes. "No." He glanced at Isabel. "Why do they want her? You said it yourself, it's

James Lockwood's discovery they want, and he's out of the picture."

Isabel exchanged a glance with Garrett. He gently shook his head. They'd discussed this earlier… they weren't entirely sure how much they could trust Noah. If he somehow managed to get away from them and contact his family to arrange a surrender, he might betray any information Isabel and Garrett shared with him.

"You already *have* his research, don't you?" Noah realized. "Or a backup copy. That's why they want you."

"They think we have it," Isabel lied. "But we don't. And that's why we wanted to talk to you." Well, it wasn't entirely a lie. They didn't know for sure what was on the memory stick Garrett had obtained from the house. It might have been James' research, or disinformation.

"Like I explained, James told me nothing," Noah said. "I have no clue what his discovery is. You should have left me out of this."

"I'm not getting through to you, am I?" Garrett told him. "If we didn't intervene today, you'd be *dead*."

"What did he discover anyway?" Noah mused as if only half listening. "*Brane theory is wrong.* What does that even mean? And why would anyone be interested in this enough to kill for it?"

"I don't know," Isabel said. "None of us do."

"Obviously it has something to do with brane theory." Noah paused. "Could he have discovered free energy?"

"It's possible," Isabel said. "That would certainly be something people would kill for. Whoever controls free energy controls the world."

"How so?" Garrett asked.

"You could destroy the entire planet with the energy that could be tapped from the contents of an empty cup," Isabel replied. "Would you want that to be in the hands of the average person?"

"No," Garrett said. "I suppose not. But what do you mean, the contents of an empty cup? By definition, the contents of an empty cup is… emptiness."

"I'm by no means an expert, but my understanding is that free energy is a hypothetical, limitless energy source that can be harvested from the vacuum of empty space, known as vacuum energy." She glanced at Noah. "Am I right?"

The professor nodded. "It's rooted in quantum field theory, which suggests even in seemingly empty space, there are fluctuations in energy levels due to virtual particles constantly popping in and out of existence. The 'quantum foam,' as it were. While these fluctuations are usually too minuscule to harness for practical energy generation, there are some who theorize that it's possible to extract an immense amount of energy from these vacuum fluctuations— all that popping in and out of virtual particles requires energy and that has to come from somewhere, after all. Richard Feynman once said: 'one teacup of empty space contains enough energy to boil all the world's oceans.' I think that's what Isabel was referring to."

"Ah, yes, you got me." Isabel sat back. "So not enough to destroy the world outright, but just boil away all our oceans. Same difference. The question is, how would that relate to 'brane' theory?"

"I'm not sure," Noah said. "Quantum foam could be particles moving across different branes, though how we could extract energy from that movement I have no idea."

"Maybe it's related to dark matter or dark energy?" she asked.

"Hmm," Noah seemed lost in thought. "Dark energy could be the result of gravitational tension between our brane and others in higher-dimensional spaces. And dark matter could simply be particles existing in the extra dimensions of other branes, influencing the dynamics of our own braneworld. Still not sure how that would relate to extracting energy."

"What's dark energy?" Garrett asked.

"It's what physicists theorize is responsible for the accelerated expansion of the universe," Isabel told him. "We've been able to measure its effect, but we don't know what's causing it."

"And dark matter?" Garrett pressed.

"It's matter that's responsible for eighty-five percent of the gravity in the universe," she explained. "And we have no idea what it is, or where it is even, because it doesn't emit any light."

"All of this is well and good, but in the email James said brane theory was *wrong*," Garrett reminded her.

"He did… and what he actually meant by that, I have no idea."

"Neither do I," Noah chimed in.

She tapped one finger against her thigh in thought. "Brane theory. Would that have anything to do with a tridekeract?"

"Depends," Noah said. "So a braneworld is a theoretical concept that envisions our universe as a three-dimensional brane—a membrane or surface—embedded in a higher-dimensional space. If you

added on ten extra dimensions, you could mathematically represent everything as a tridekeract. A thirteen-
dimensional hypercube."

"Maybe tridekeracts are easier to work with mathematically, than branes," Garrett interjected.

Isabel gave him a curious glance.

"Okay I admit it, I don't have a clue what I'm
talking about," Garrett replied.

"You might be closer to the mark than you realize," Isabel muttered, trying to remember what her
brother had told her at the start of all this. It seemed
so long ago. What were his precise words? It was all
such a blur.

Wait. There.

"The tridekeract was the key. The math, it's irrefutable."

Garrett was definitely close to the mark.

"Where are we going by the way?" Noah asked,
drawing her back to the present moment.

"Just making a little diversion to a motel," Garrett
told him.

18

Garrett took Isabel and Noah to a new motel. Inside their new unit, he informed Isabel he'd be heading to Archer's mansion by himself. Garrett wasn't comfortable leaving the professor alone with Isabel, not unbound, so before leaving he secured the man to one of the chairs by tying a bed sheet around his wrists. At the very least it would prevent the professor from trying to overpower Isabel.

He hoped.

"What if I have to use the bathroom?" Noah asked.

"Hold it until I get back." Garrett leaned close and, in a menacing whisper, added: "If you hurt her, I'll be coming for you." He pulled back and looked Noah in the eye to make sure he completely understood.

As always, Garrett instructed Isabel to text him in case of an emergency, and informed her if he wasn't back in two hours she was to move to a new location. He mostly told her that as a formality, because he knew it might be difficult for her to move the professor alone, and had already promised himself he'd return on time no matter what.

When Garrett arrived at Archer's garish property with its ornate columns and grand double doors, as usual he felt unnerved by all the security cameras. Even though this was his friend's house, he still wore his sunglasses and kept his head bowed as he left the car and approached the main entrance. While he trusted that Archer kept his camera data feeds as secure as possible, it was always possible there was some zero-day backdoor that allowed eavesdropping by unwanted third parties.

There was also a chance his friend had betrayed him. Unlikely, true, but still a possibility. There were ways to get to anyone.

He was feeling more paranoid since the incident at the motel the day before, when Isabel had narrowly escaped capture. He resolved then and there to switch vehicles again as soon as he was done with Archer.

He swept his gaze across the grounds, from the gazebo to the garden topiary, from the wall to the rooftop, and then back again. He searched for signs of ambushers or snipers, but nothing seemed out of the ordinary.

He continued forward tensely, ready to grab the Glock hidden under the back of his shirt at a moment's notice. If a sniper was tracking him, he'd be dead before he realized it of course, but he couldn't help the instincts he had, ingrained from years of training and surviving in places where men would kill you for speaking the wrong language.

His analyst friend met him at the door.

"Well there you are, Froggie," Archer greeted him. "Back for more, are you?"

As usual he held out his arms as if expecting a hug. Garrett smiled, but didn't oblige him.

Archer lowered his arms. "All right. Come in big guy."

"Your Signal said you've cracked the memory stick?" Garrett asked.

"I have indeed." Archer beckoned him inside again. "I'll tell you all about it. Wasn't easy, I tell you."

"I'm sure you have a lot of work to do this Monday morning." Garrett remained where he was. Definitely feeling more paranoid.

"Actually, I don't." Archer studied his friend, then sighed. "All right. You want to go, I get that. Fine. I've brought your sci-fi writer's data back from the abyss." He produced the familiar LockKey S1000 USB stick and handed it to Garrett. "The password is *tridekeract.* It only took the quantum computer fifty-two trillion tries to get it."

"Fifty-two trillion?" Garret arched an eyebrow. "There was only supposed to be one try left."

Archer beamed with obvious self-satisfaction as he spoke. "Oh, that. I disabled the try-counter easily with the help of the consulting team I hooked up with, and the rest was done with a brute force attack courtesy of my quantum computer. I did have to send certain voltages through the power connection pins, but didn't damage the stick in any way, shape or form. All the data is intact. Some interesting concepts in there. If a little far-fetched."

Garrett frowned. "You read it?"

"Of course," Archer told him. "You know I like science fiction. Couldn't resist. Had to get my fix."

Garrett was a little disappointed, if not surprised. "You made a copy…?"

"Nope," Archer said. "Who do you take me for, some back-stabbing spook? Oh wait…" He paused expectantly, as if hoping for at least a laugh, but when Garrett didn't react in any way Archer sheepishly cleared his throat. "I kid I kid. No copies. I wouldn't want this sci-fi writer of yours to go after me when I launch my own book."

Garrett examined the memory stick he now held.

"I left everything on the device intact, including the password protection," Archer explained. "I did however reset the try counter to zero for you. So you have ten guesses in case you forget."

"Thank you," Garrett told his friend, and meant it.

Archer smiled. "We're even now."

"No, I owe you."

Archer waved a dismissive hand. "Forget it." He paused then, seeming to reconsider. "Actually, yes you do. Come in for a drink. Or snack. Catch up a bit. Then we'll call it even."

Garrett pocketed the memory stick. "Next time. If I didn't know you better, I'd almost think you were stalling."

Archer laughed. "Stalling? Naw. I'm just a lonely, unmarried, middle-aged man looking to catch up with an old friend and relive a youth spent sneaking among the Tally. Can't believe it's been twenty years since Afghanistan."

"Thanks again, Archer," Garrett said. "It's been good."

"It's been good," Archer agreed. He offered his hand and Garrett reluctantly accepted, squeezing firmly.

"Ah ha!" Archer nodded at their handshake. "The

famous Garrett grip. A vise that would crush a weaker man! Surprised I can withstand it, are you?"

Garrett smiled patiently. "I haven't even started applying my grip…"

Archer's face dropped. "Oh."

Garrett released him and gave a farewell gesture that was half salute and half wave, then made his way back across the grounds. He could feel Archer's eyes on him the whole time, and an unexpected sadness came over him. He could relate to what Archer wanted. Reminiscing about old times, the brothers they had lost, it was something he could have really used right about then.

I should have taken him up on his offer.

But he didn't have time. Isabel was waiting for him. Besides, he was eager to find out just what was on the memory stick that people would kill for.

He reached the stolen vehicle, got in, and drove off the property.

———

WHEN GARRETT RETURNED, he found Isabel and Noah watching TV.

"*Now* can you untie me?" the professor asked. "I really have to pee."

Garrett complied and escorted him to the washroom. While the man did his business, Garrett joined Isabel at the small table next to the window and placed a laptop in front of her.

Isabel gave him a confused look. "Where'd you get this?"

"Swiped it from some college student at a cafe while he was busy flirting with the hot barista."

Garrett plugged in the memory stick when the laptop was done booting. "Not my finest moment."

When the password prompt came up, he involuntarily held his breath.

"What's the password?" Isabel asked.

Now was the moment of truth. If this didn't work...

He typed the word "Tridekeract."

The USB opened up. He had full access to the unencrypted data.

Garrett exhaled in relief.

"Figures my brother would use that," Isabel commented softly.

Garrett loaded the only file on the device and was greeted by a scientific document full of diagrams and figures, not to mention big swathes of text.

As usual he'd taken the seat that afforded the best view of the parking lot outside through the gap in the curtain, but while Isabel perused the document, he did read bits and pieces over her shoulder... most of it beyond his understanding.

"Should we bring him in on this?" Garrett kept his voice low as he nodded at the bathroom.

"I think we have to," Isabel replied. "We're going to need his take on it, I think. Some of this stuff is way over my head."

"Have you talked to him much?" Garrett asked. "We still don't know how much we can trust him. He might try to sell this information to those who hunt us, or trade it for a guarantee of safety."

She scrolled through. "Without access to the prototype mentioned in this document, we don't know for sure whether it's real or misinformation. We can emphasize that, make sure that's clear to Noah."

"Let's show him only a part of the document, but

not everything," Garrett decided. "Can you pick a relatively safe section, something we could use to give him the gist without revealing the actual mechanics behind the discovery? We don't need to show him the schematics of the prototype, and so forth."

She pursed her lips, and continued to scroll through the document. "Here." She highlighted a section near the end and turned the laptop toward Garrett. "It's a continuation of the email chain we read earlier, started by James, with Noah Patel and Liam Malcolm as the recipients."

It was indeed a continuation of the email chain. Garrett skimmed through it quickly, and then nodded. "This will do."

On cue the professor emerged from the bathroom.

Garrett beckoned toward him. "Have a seat. There's something you should look at."

The professor arched an eyebrow and, his curiosity piqued, he borrowed a chair from the motel's small desk and carried it to the table. He sat down beside Isabel and began reading the laptop screen.

After a moment the professor said: "What is this? Where did you get it?"

"My brother's house," she revealed. "But it's possible it was planted as part of a disinformation campaign."

Garrett leaned in next to the professor and reread the messages he'd originally skimmed over, hoping he'd have a better understanding this time.

JAMES: *I've made the discovery of a lifetime.*
Noah: *Do tell.*

James: *Brane theory is wrong.*

Noah: *How so?*

James: *Our universe is not a four-dimensional hyper surface embedded within a higher-dimensional space, but rather, I believe our universe is a holographic hyper surface. And while the holographic principal currently theorizes that the information contained in our three-dimensional region of space can be fully encoded on a two-dimensional surface, there is more to it than that.*

It is my belief that the universe is comprised of not just one holographic hyper surface, but layers of these surfaces stacked one atop the other. "Holographic entanglement," if you will, with each stack containing information that can be represented and encoded in those below.

As you go down the layers, the information from the upper stacks is compactified and represented as tightly wound objects roughly the size of Planck lengths; each successive layer becomes more and more crowded with quantum information until you reach the final, bottommost layer—our reality. To us, the information from those upper stacks looks like 'quantum foam.'

I've found a way to insert a particle of matter into that foam and therefore up the stack. I can retrieve the particle at a time of my choosing and return it to our reality intact.

I've experimentally determined that there are thirteen stacks, one built atop the other, each of ever-increasing informational complexity, like an intricate, inverted pyramid. The mathematics of such a system proved exceedingly arduous until I simplified my equations by using a thirteen-dimensional hypercube.

Yes, I know, you laugh at the word simplify, which is little more than a generous euphemism in this case, because the math is still complex and riddled with conceptual hurdles, and I do admit my final solution is still scrawled across five pages. But consider the alternative: fifty pages of unsolvable equations without the hypercube versus five with the cube, along with an equation that actually solves. The magic of the tridekeract!

Those five pages weren't necessarily a walk in the park either. I've spent months on them, and the answer finally came to me a few days ago when I was away from the lab, during a walk on campus believe it or not. Is that not how all great discoveries are made? By relying on the gift of the subconscious mind as it processes the data we've fed it?

I know what you're thinking. I haven't proven Brane theory wrong, because branes can have multiple dimensions too. If you can show me how to do the math with branes, I'll concede the point. But remember: fifty pages of unsolvable equations versus five… holographic entanglement for the win!

"D<small>ID</small> J<small>AMES</small> always talk like this in his emails?" Garrett asked. "He sounds so… professorly."

"He often liked to use his 'paper' voice when discussing research in emails," Noah concurred. "His way of keeping things professional, I suppose."

Garrett nodded absently. He was already reading the remaining responses.

LIAM: *I don't think you can rule out branes as the true basis of quantum reality merely because of math. While hypercubes and holographic entanglement might provide a convenient solution mathematically, that doesn't necessarily mean the universe is actually composed of holographic stacks. Using a tridekeract as a simplification could apply equally well to a brane reality. I'd really have to look at your math, because as far as I'm concerned, actual reality is comprised of multiple branes: we live in a 3-brane, and you're simply storing your particle in a higher dimensional brane. Assuming your findings and measurements are correct. Also how did you come to the conclusion that there are thirteen stacks? Why not any other number?*

James: *My findings are correct. I'd be happy to show* *you my math on Monday. Along with the device I've hacked together to test my theory.*

Noah: *Gads! You have a device??*

James: *Only a prototype, but it works. A little clunky, I admit, but it does the job. It's surprisingly large, given how small the injected particle is, but that's something we've come to expect where the containment and measurement of particles is involved.*

I actually repurposed a Penning-Malmberg trap to contain the matter, and— well, I'll tell you more when you stop by my lab on Monday and I'll give you a demo. As I mentioned in my previous email, the particle can remain in a higher stack indefinitely, or at least until I summon it back into our three-dimensional realm. So far I've tested inserting a particle up the stack for two hours and then returning it to the chamber intact, replete with original charge and spin.

I'll be happy to show you my results.

THAT WAS the end of the email chain.

Garrett hadn't noticed Noah's reply during his first skim-through, and now he glanced at the professor suspiciously. "So… you claim you never saw any of these emails?"

"I swear I didn't," Noah protested, apparently picking up on Garrett's dangerous tone. "That's not me replying."

"If that's not you…" Isabel let her words trail off. She glanced at Garrett. "The military industrial complex?"

Garrett nodded. "Inserting themselves into the conversation… trying to tease out information before enacting their kidnap attempt. They've likely confiscated the prototype by now."

"But they still want his research…" Isabel said.

"The question is, why? They could probably reverse engineer the prototype easily."

"Remember: there's more than one faction chasing after it," Garrett said. "Those who have the device will want the research that goes along with it, if only to ensure the competing faction can't get it. And the competing faction wants it so they can create their own prototype, of course."

"Wait, I thought you don't have the research?" The professor's gaze momentarily dropped to the memory stick. "Is this the research? Can I have a copy?" Noah's eyes shone greedily as he tried to scroll up past the highlighted section.

Garrett's hand shot forward and wrapped around the man's wrist, stopping him in his tracks. "No. You cannot."

"Can I at least read it?" the professor pleaded.

In answer Garrett closed the laptop lid and slid the computer to his side. "We've shown you all you need to see."

The professor sighed, and looked down resignedly.

Garrett wasn't sure how much he could trust Noah, but that momentary flash of greed he'd seen in the man's eyes when he'd asked for a copy of the memory stick told Garrett all he needed to know in regards to the research.

The professor gazed at Isabel excitedly. "If this is true, James has discovered a way to store particles in other dimensions so that they take up no space in our own world… can you imagine where this is going? If we could miniaturize the tech and scale this beyond single particles to the point where we could store entire objects, or even multiple objects… what if you could pack a room-sized space into the confines of a thimble? Board an airplane with an entire walk-in closet tucked away in your back pocket? Store the entire contents of a cargo hauler into a device the size of your suitcase? It would revolutionize travel and trade, disrupting entire industries. It would be worth tens of trillions of dollars."

"And yet in the wrong hands it could destroy the world," Isabel countered. "One could secretly transport anything. Drugs. People. Even a nuclear bomb. I can see why some people would kill to obtain it."

"Or to suppress it," Garrett mused.

The professor continued as if he hadn't heard them. "If James is right, and holographic stacks are the basis for our physical reality, physics might have to be updated. What was that he said about using a tridekeract to simplify the calculations? A thirteen-dimensional hypercube. Fascinating."

"I still don't get it," Garrett said. "I can visualize stacks of information well enough, but have no idea what a thirteen-dimensional cube looks like."

"It could be a mathematical simplification," Noah told him. "Not necessarily a representation of reality. We don't know. Might be best to stick to stacks of information if that's easier for you to understand."

"James once told me a thirteen-dimensional hypercube contained more than three-hundred and fifty thousand tesseracts," Isabel volunteered.

Garrett stared at her blankly. "What's a tesseract?"

"May I?" Isabel gestured toward the laptop that resided safely beneath Garrett's protective arm.

He offered her the laptop and she opened it up, connecting to Wi-Fi. After visiting a website, she turned the display toward him.

He was looking at a picture of a translucent cube

drawn inside a cube, with the inner vertices connected to the outer.

"A cube within a cube," Isabel told him.

"So?" Garrett didn't understand the significance.

The professor chimed in. "That's the inference of a 4D hypercube. A tesseract."

"The inference?"

"The shadow," Noah explained. "Assume for a moment that the tesseract is a wireframe object with solid edges and vertices, but see-through faces, then the shadow of that tesseract projected onto a 3D plane appears to the human eye as a cube within a cube. We can't actually view a tesseract directly, at least not in its entirety, because our vision can't comprehend four spatial dimensions."

"I still don't get it," Garrett said. "If it entered our reality, we'd only see a shadow?"

"Not exactly," the professor replied. "If a solid 4D cube intersected our plane, we'd simply see a 3D cube emerging as if from nothing, slowly growing in size, and then shrinking again as it passed out of our plane. The closest analogy I have is an orange ascending through a sheet of paper.

"If you were a 2D creature living on that piece of paper, you'd see a dot eventually becoming a line and growing bigger and bigger as the orange ascended through the paper. The line would recede again as the orange continued past its widest point, until eventually it became a dot again, vanishing when it passed through the paper entirely.

"The 2D creature, if it had binocular vision like us, would be able to tell that the line was in fact a circle in the 2D plane thanks to its shading and the slight perspective incurred by its binocular eyesight. Just as we would interpret a 4D sphere passing through our space as a growing and shrinking 3D sphere."

"But I thought all of this was just so we could do the math, and it's not a representation of reality." Garrett sat back, stumped. "You just said that."

"No, I actually said it's not *necessarily* a representation of reality," Noah corrected. "The math might be an accurate reflection of what reality is, or it might not. I can't say. We may not be dealing with holographic hyper surface stacks after all, as her brother theorized, and instead we might be dealing with full-blown spatial dimensions. But again, I'd have to see the research."

Noah paused for a moment. Then he shook his head. "I have no idea how any of this is even remotely possible, to be honest. The energy requirements to transfer particles through the quantum foam and into higher dimensions should be immense, and far beyond current technological capabilities. Certainly beyond anything a university lab could provide. Unless James took a cue from illegal grow-ops and broke through the cement floor of the university to tap directly into the power grid or something."

"Or James came up with a new understanding of physics," Isabel hinted. "You said it yourself, physics might have to be updated."

Noah ignored her. "And he claims he's repurposed a Penning-Malmberg trap? That actually sounds ridiculous, now that I think about it. This has to be misinformation. Meant to throw you off track." He rounded on Garrett. "Your enemy has fed you disinformation, my friend."

Isabel was the one who answered. "You're forgetting that my brother only transferred a single particle… the energy requirements wouldn't be that great."

"Maybe so, maybe not. I'm going to have to err on the side of disinformation until I see all the data." The professor's eyes drifted to the laptop, focusing on the memory stick plugged into the side. For a moment Garrett thought he was going to try to grab the memory stick and make a run for it.

But then the professor slumped in resignation. "I'm at the mercy of some ex-army grunt who can't understand the importance of a proper review."

"Oh I can understand human greed all right." Garrett took the laptop and then disconnected and reconnected the USB stick. When the password prompt appeared, he entered random characters.

"What are you doing?" Noah asked in alarm.

"Incrementing the password counter."

Garrett entered five more invalid passwords.

"Wait, stop!" The professor glanced at Isabel urgently. "He's going to destroy your brother's research!"

"Garrett…" Isabel said warningly.

"Don't worry, I'm not going to destroy it," he assured her. "I'll leave one try, that way all it takes is a single invalid attempt to activate the 'flash trash' mode."

He entered three more incorrect passwords, and then, true to his word, he unplugged the memory stick and shoved it into his pocket.

"Now if anyone tries to enter the wrong password, it's gone," Garrett said.

Isabel didn't seemed convinced. "I'm sure the military industrial complex can crack the password, just like your friend."

"True. But it does mean we can wipe out the data in a pinch."

"Again, you're assuming it will become unrecoverable at that point," Isabel countered.

Garrett shrugged. "Either way, it could buy us some time." He shut off the laptop and closed it.

19

Time kept repeating for Evan.

He lost track of the number of flight numbers he'd boarded, the different oceans he'd flown over, the varying people who tried to hinder him at the airport.

Every flight ended the same: the Entities intervened before he could land and release his deadly cargo. They captured the plane and its passengers in all realities.

And each time, when the world reset and the darkness faded, he always found himself in a hotel room, so that when he finally woke up in his own bed he had to wonder if he was simply in yet another alternate reality.

This was definitely his home. He recognized the curtains and the furniture. The birds chirping softly outside, basking in the Florida sun.

Had the Verndari truly released Evan?

He checked the date on his phone. It was two full days after the flight—time had not reset again. That meant they had truly released him, and his memories were real, not nightmares: the Verndari had indeed taken the entire plane and prevented him from releasing the virus.

It was all so very strange, even startling. In the past, they had never interceded with humanity so blatantly as they had here. Why now? And why had they returned him to his life? What about everybody else who had been aboard that plane?

All he knew is he had to be very careful. They had released him for a very specific reason, and without a doubt they were watching him.

Assuming of course that all of this was not simply another of their illusions…

He heard movement in the kitchen and got up. When he went downstairs, to his great relief he saw his wife. His beautiful wife. She was cooking eggs for breakfast. Or lunch, he supposed, glancing at the clock.

When she finally saw him her eyes filled with a look of stunned surprise, and then relief. She rushed over to give him a hug.

"What are you doing here?" she said, sobbing. "I thought you were dead."

"What day is it?" he asked his wife, wanting to be absolutely certain. Maybe the date on his phone was wrong, and the Entities were playing tricks on him again.

"Monday," she said, sounding confused.

"The fifth?" he pressed.

"Yes." She pulled away from him and quickly wiped the tears from her cheeks. The confusion was obvious on her face. There was fear there, too. "What happened?"

Was she even real? How could he know for sure?

"Nothing," he lied. "I didn't get on the flight."

She nodded slowly. She didn't know about the mission. He hadn't told her. And the Guide wouldn't have, either.

"The Guide wants to talk," she said.

Ah yes. *The Guide*. It certainly would like to talk, wouldn't it?

He gave her a disapproving look. "You've been making contact?"

"Well, yes, I—"

He raised a silencing finger. "We have to be careful. They're listening even now."

"But the house is shielded…"

He sighed heavily. "You don't understand, time and space are no boundary for them and their adversaries. We have to be very careful. The Guide wants to talk, you say? Fine, we will do it at the cottage."

He knew the Verndari could not come there.

He ate the eggs his wife had made and packed some small sandwiches, planning to have a picnic while out there. Or at least, that's what it would look like to any watchers.

It took a couple of hours to drive out to the cottage. It was somewhat peaceful out there on the fringes of that lake. A lot of mosquitoes though.

Gotta love Florida.

He and his wife applied ample amounts of bug spray, then took their canoe and paddled out to the middle of the lake, which was more of a bog than anything else.

Then he set down the paddle and grabbed his wife's hands. He squeezed tightly, and she returned his grip reassuringly.

He closed his eyes and began inhaling and exhaling. His wife did the same. With each exhale, they produced a soft humming sound that vibrated the upper trachea. They were inducing the necessary trance-state to make contact.

When he pierced through the veil of reality, something seemed off this time. There was a strange…

NO.

He opened his eyes in fright, ending the trance. Who had said that?

His wife's eyes remained closed. He tried to break free of her grasp, but she wouldn't let go.

"Elnora!" he said. "Elnora, snap out of it!"

Her eyes shot open. The whites had become pure black, as had the iris, so it was like he stared into a black hole.

Terror filled him.

The Guide spoke directly through her. "Did you tell them anything?" Her voice was deep, like the guide. Misshapen.

"No! I told them nothing!"

"What did they do to you?" the Guide pressed, squeezing his fingers even tighter. He could feel bone breaking, snapping.

"They played through the event hundreds… thousands of times," Evan gasped through the unbearable pain. "It always unfolded the same way. Always… ended in the capture of the plane."

"And you told them nothing?" the Guide asked once more.

"Yes, nothing!"

The Entity that had assumed his wife's form smiled. "Good."

To his shock and horror, her hands darted to the right with inhuman strength and threw him into the lake. It felt as if his arms had nearly been torn from their sockets.

When he hit the water he gasped frantically. He couldn't remember it ever being this cold before…

"Elnor—" he tried, but a mouthful of frigid water interrupted him. He was struggling to stay afloat. His body felt heavier, somehow, like the depths of the lake itself were exerting a pull upon him, inexorably dragging him under. And the cold only further drained the fight from his muscles.

In seconds it was over.

Where Evan had been struggling to stay afloat only ripples remained, slowly spreading out across the pristine lake.

The canoe slowly paddled away.

20

G arrett had moved them to a new motel, just in case there had been a tracking device in the USB stick that activated when it was plugged in. He'd tested the unplugged memory stick with the portable radiofrequency scanner that Archer had lent him, confirming that the stick itself wasn't able to transmit location information while turned on.

When plugged into the laptop with Wi-Fi and Bluetooth turned off, the internal components of the portable computer produced a baseline of electro-magnetic activity that didn't change when the USB stick was plugged in. One would expect a spike in activity if there was a transmitter, but Garrett had decided to relocate anyway. As he always said, it was better to err on the side of caution.

Still, with all this motel swapping they were burning through the remaining cash at an alarming rate. Garrett was reduced to picking lodgings that were at the absolute bottom of the heap, the diviest of the dive motels. There was also an increased risk of getting captured by some unnoticed camera. Yes, there was definitely something to be said about hunkering down and staying in one place. Unfortunately, they wouldn't be able to do that for a while yet.

Garrett was sitting with Isabel next to the window of their new unit. The professor had excused himself to go to the washroom, giving them a moment of privacy. Garrett had checked out the washroom earlier… there was a small window near the top of one wall that could fold down slightly, but it was too small to fit a human being. Garrett had also patted down the professor once again, but found nothing: Noah wouldn't be able to cause any trouble in there.

"So what do you think?" Garrett asked. "Noah seems convinced this is misinformation. Is he right or wrong?"

"We haven't shown him the full document," Isabel replied. "I think Noah is wrong. My brother was definitely onto something, and he definitely succeeded in his experiment."

"But is it possible we're being misled in some way?" Garrett pressed.

"Of course anything is possible," she replied. "We won't know for sure until we have a word with the people who are after us. Even then, we'll have doubts about the veracity of everything, I'm sure. But somehow I doubt the military industrial complex would go through all this trouble of hunting us down if the research weren't real."

"I'm not saying your brother didn't make an important discovery," Garrett told her. "All I'm saying is, it might not be *this* discovery. We have two factions after us. One faction could have planted it as a red herring for the other faction. Then used me as the delivery mechanism: texting the location to *my* phone, because they saw me pull up in the driveway and enter the house."

She rubbed her forehead. "True. There are so many... strange... things going on. It's hard to tell what's real anymore. But I still think it's more than likely that this is the truth, and Noah's merely trying to convince us it's misinformation so we show him the full document."

Garrett peered into the depths of her eyes. "How well do you know him?"

"Noah? Not as well as my brother of course. He and his wife are good tablemates over supper, but otherwise, I don't really know much about him. I usually talked mostly with his wife whenever James had Noah over. For all we know he could be one of my brother's biggest rivals, and James only invited him over so often because he was trying to follow the 'keep your friends close, your enemies closer' proverb. Who knows? Maybe getting his hands on this research could turn around Noah's stagnant physics career."

Garrett cocked his head. "You said we won't know for sure until we have a word with the people who are after us?"

She studied him uncertainly. "I did."

His eyes drifted to the nightstand, where four cell-phones were stacked one atop the other, secured by an elastic. Eight batteries rested beside them. Those were the smartphones Garrett had purloined from the intruders on the Lockwood property.

When he returned his gaze to Isabel, he saw that she too was looking at the phones.

When her eyes met his once more, she nodded slowly. "Let's make the call."

"I'm going to have to pick up some equipment, first."

"Equipment?"

"I can't transfer the contact lists from the phones without turning them on," he explained. "And to do that, I need to put the batteries in. The instant those batteries go in, the phones will start emitting a tracking signal, revealing our location. Regardless of whether the actual phones are turned on or not. Airplane mode won't even matter."

"Ah," she said. "So you're going to build a Faraday cage."

"Basically."

She pursed her lips. "You know, we *could* just release the research to the world. Then they'll stop hunting us. Just email it to the editorial addresses of all the top newspapers at once: tips@nytimes.com, and so forth."

He gave her an incredulous look. "You said it yourself: in the wrong hands this could destroy the world. This tech, if ever developed by terrorists, would allow them to a) steal a nuclear bomb and b) smuggle it into the city of their choice. It would also be a boon to human traffickers. Drug traffickers. I'm sorry, humanity just isn't ready for technology like this."

"Then release *some* of it," Isabel countered. "No need for detailed specs."

"Then no one will believe it," he replied. "And that won't help us."

She sighed. "I hate it when you're right. You know, I've always been an optimist. Someone who believes that humanity is in general good. But there are too many who are misguided, operating on glitched mental models, mostly because of some level of human suffering. And somehow, those operating on these glitched models come to the conclusion that the only solution is even *more* human suffering.

"There are some who say technology is advancing at a rate far greater than the primitive human mind can keep up. But I would argue that we're capable of greatness. So many of us don't know the power we have. We can do great things when we put our minds to it. We're all spiritual beings capable of great love to one another. And I can't help but wonder, if we do release it, maybe things will just work themselves out. If this can somehow alleviate human suffering to a degree, then mental models might change across the world."

"Mental models," Garrett muttered. "I don't remember you ever being this naive. You'd think that being nearly murdered and hunted down by ex-military assassins would work that out of your system. Listen to me, Isabel: if we release this, nothing will just 'work itself out.' There's a reason why the general population doesn't have access to nuclear weapons, nor the blueprints and materials to make them. You're right about mental models, but you're wrong that these models will change anytime soon.

"Not everyone has the same moral compass as you. Even if the world were perfect and no one suffered, no one starved, there would still be greed and power lust. And there will always be, until we evolve. Spiritually, mentally, however you want to look at it. So no, we can't release this. When we're all loving each other and singing *kumbaya* together, maybe then we can let the common man have access to this tech."

She sighed. "Our ancestors were spiritual people.

Close to nature. What happened? How did we lose our way?"

"I wouldn't know."

She held up a hand and studied it. "The more we learn about how the world works, the material side that we can see and touch with our senses, the less connected we become to the immaterial side. The spiritual side."

The spiritual side.

Her words got to him, somehow. He thought of that moment on his patio, when he stared into the flames of his fire pit, with the Glock held to his head, ready to blow his brains out. And then somehow Isabel's face had come to him, and he'd heard those words.

She needs you.

Words that had set all this in motion.

He'd felt so… connected… to her in that moment.

He felt a soft hand on his arm and glanced at Isabel.

"What are you thinking?" she asked.

"Nothing important," he lied.

"What if we didn't reveal the research to the press?" she told him. "Just the story behind it? How they killed my brother and then hunted me down? It would cause a scandal that just might save us."

"Even if we wanted to get in touch with the press, we couldn't if we wanted to," Garrett explained patiently. "Not easily, anyway. Those tip lines you mentioned? Imagine the volume of mail those accounts receive on a daily basis. By the time anyone at the newspaper receives it, the email will have been long intercepted and likely deleted off the servers. Just like how they intercepted and deleted the emails James sent to his colleagues at the university."

Isabel didn't seem deterred. "Well, if we really wanted to, we could arrange an in-person meeting. Call them and book a time."

"Can't call," Garrett countered. "Again, the line could be monitored."

"Then stop by the building, camp outside, and ambush the reporters as they leave."

"That might work," Garrett agreed. "But even if they believed you, they'd have to take a ton of precautions to get the story done under the radar. They couldn't tell their editors. They'd have to prepare everything offline. It's just, not feasible."

"We could post what they're doing to us to online as well. Forums, social media, the usual outlets."

Garrett chuckled. "It's well known that intelligence agencies, not to mention defense contractors, have infiltrated the ranks of the big social media companies. They'll have any posts deleted within five minutes. And anyone who asks where the posts went will be met with manufactured vitriol."

"We have to try," Isabel pleaded. "Something. Anything. We can't just spend the rest of our lives on the run."

"We *will* try." Garrett beckoned toward the phones on the nightstand.

"You think calling them will make a difference?"

He didn't answer right away. "I don't know. It will be a first step, at least. To be honest, giving them the research might be our only real hope."

Isabel raised an eyebrow. "And how do we know they won't kill us once we do that?"

"Leave that part to me." His eyes dropped to the pistol on the table.

She followed his gaze and sighed. "It always comes down to guns and fighting, doesn't it?"

"Unfortunately, that's the only language our pursuers really understand."

The bathroom door suddenly opened and Noah walked out. The stench in the motel room became palpable.

"Sorry about that," Noah said sheepishly. "Blew up the place."

BLACKWELL SAT INSIDE HIS OFFICE, which was located two hundred feet below the air force base. It was a busy Monday morning, like all mornings.

He was examining a document containing an official write-up of the deaths of the agents assigned to watch the house of James Lockwood. All four had died on the scene the night before.

Blackwell again reviewed the MQ-1C thermal video that came with the write-up. One of the agents low-crawled across the grass of the golf course, then stood up not far from a bush and pointed his automatic rifle at an unseen target, or at least at a target that wasn't showing up on the drone's thermal feed.

Another agent had followed, ostensibly to provide cover fire or assistance, but then out of nowhere that second agent unloaded his combat rifle, killing the first agent.

Damn moles.

The remaining agent—one of Jackson's men, no doubt—beckoned with the automatic rifle, and Blackwell caught a glimpse of an arm behind the bush, but it vanished shortly. The unseen target had to have been using some kind of thermo-masking tarp. Likely an off-the-shelf variety. There were only a few on the market that would actually work—most of the tarps and blankets out there would quickly accumulate heat from the wearer, giving away the target's position after a few minutes.

The agent took cover behind what appeared to be a maintenance shed, and then opened fire at the other two men that were running in to provide backup. A moment later a muzzle flash erupted from beside the maintenance shed and the mole collapsed.

And that was it. No other thermal signatures were recorded.

When a cleanup team had arrived, they'd reported the phones of each man had gone missing. The phones themselves had continued to transmit their locations all the way to a local mall before the signal went black.

Only a very few people had the necessary evasion and combat skills to do what Blackwell just saw. And one of those people was Garrett Bennett. Trained by the US military, served for fifteen years, and then unleashed onto the real world to wreak havoc.

Blackwell shook his head. The military spent billions training men like this and then when their terms expired they simply let them go. Such a colossal waste. There should be some clause requiring men like Garrett Bennett to work for the military or an approved list of defense contractors for the rest of their lives. Blackwell himself tried to snatch up as many men of Garrett's ilk as possible, but he couldn't get them all of course.

We need more like him.

An audio alert went off and green text appeared in the center of his augmented reality display.

Incoming call from the Secretary of Defense.

With a sigh, he swiped at the air, dismissing the video feed, and answered the phone call.

A picture of the Secretary of Defense appeared in the center of Blackwell's vision. A partially transparent sound waveform floated just below that, and it changed in realtime to match the words coming over the connection.

"What the hell happened to that plane?" the Secretary asked.

A green indicator appeared beneath the sound waveform: *Vocal print authenticity confirmed.*

"All of our spy satellites have had their relevant data pulled," the Secretary continued. "USA-229 in particular was in the vicinity, and was recording the plane. But the data feed ends abruptly, moments before we lost the plane on radar. Where's that data? And what happened to the plane?"

"My apologies, Mr. Secretary," Blackwell said. "But there was a systematic failure of USA-229's camera system that caused us to lose the feed. We're working to determine the cause of the data blackout and will—"

"Systematic failure my ass," the Secretary growled. "You think that just because your company *built* the satellites that you own them? We paid you to develop this tech for us. Very well. To the tune of billions of dollars. You seem to think that we're merely renting the tech from you."

That's exactly what you're doing, Blackwell wanted to tell him. But the more diplomatic side of him took control just in time. "I'm sorry you feel that way. Look, I understand the pressure you're under. Whatever happened to Lufthansa 778 was a tragic accident. Debris has already started washing ashore, and—"

"USA-229 wasn't the only satellite with missing footage," the Secretary interrupted. "Are you trying to tell me they all suffered a very convenient systems failure, *at the same time?*"

"We've had to pull the data on some of the other satellites due to multiple classification issues. But I can assure you—"

"Multiple classification issues my ass," the Secretary growled. "I'm the Secretary of Defense! I have SCI clearance to *everything!*"

"You do, sir," Blackwell agreed. "But there are certain programs even you haven't been read into, and—"

"Don't try that waived bigoted crap on me. Read me in, goddamnit! Unless you no longer want your job."

Waived meant the Special Access Program was exempt from standard reporting requirements, while bigoted signified that only individuals on a specific list had full knowledge of the program. The latter word was a throwback to the BIGOT list of World War Two, in which only a handful of people knew the full details of the D-Day invasion of Normandy. The BIGOT list had worked extremely well: the specific timing and locations of the Normandy landings remained uncertain to the German forces up until the actual moment of the invasion.

Blackwell sighed. Not even the president was fully read in, not to this. Sure, he had been given a limited read in on some of the basics—enough to get by— but that was it. No, this was not something for the temporary government to deal with. Elected leaders and their appointments came and went, while Blackwell and the men who worked for him offered the only permanence the country ever knew. That

permanence allowed his group to transcend governments and policy, and to make the hard choices that
kept the country—and the world—safe.

His gaze involuntarily drifted to the tapestry of
the lone man with the glowing jewel holding the darkness at bay.

"I'm sorry sir, I can't," Blackwell finally said. "Nor
can I tell you anything more."

"I'll have your head for this," the Secretary spat.
"I'm going to send men down there to arrest you for
treason. I'm going to have your base searched from
top to bottom to see just what the hell you guys are
hiding down there. You think you can pull a fast one
on me, do you? We'll see how many more billion-
dollar contracts your company gets with the defense
department going forward. And your snug little headquarters beneath the air base? I'll revoke your EUL
and have you evicted by tomorrow morning."

EUL stood for Enhanced Use Lease. Basically a
lease used by the Secretary of Defense and the Secretaries of the Military Departments (including the
Secretary of the Air Force) pursuant to Title 10
United States Code, Section 2667, that allowed the
military to lease underutilized properties under their
control to the private sector for between five and
fifty-five years.

In Blackwell's case, the terms of his lease involved
the development of an extensive underground facility
beneath the base, which he would return to the military after thirty years when his private sector lease
expired. He built it to facilitate the transfer of crash
retrievals, so his company could jump to the top of
the queue among defense contractors competing for
access to the same materials. If you were the Air
Force, and you had the choice of shipping a recov-

ered non-human craft across the country to another facility or sending it across the street to a hangar on the same base where you'd already delivered the materials, logistics-wise you'd probably pick the latter. Of course, there were sometimes other reasons for choosing to send the material to an external location, but Blackwell's company won most of the contracts these days due to proximity alone.

"Did you hear me?" the Secretary repeated. "I'm going to revoke your damn EUL."

Blackwell smiled. He'd heard similar threats before, from people even higher up than the Secretary. In a few days time, when the Secretary realized that nobody would listen to him, he would learn just how powerless he really was, at least when it came to this.

Blackwell assumed his most jovial tone. "Is that everything, sir?"

In response the line went dead. Blackwell would have to make a call to the director of the CIA's Office of Global Access and get him to have a little talk with the Secretary. Hopefully the director could convince him to stand down before he further embarrassed himself.

A knock came at his door. "Come."

Lieutenant Mitchell entered. "Did you see the alert I sent you?"

"No," Blackwell said. "I was stuck on a rather unpleasant call with the Secretary of Defense."

"Professor Noah Patel has been kidnapped, and the two agents sent to watch over him have been terminated," Mitchell told him.

"Damn it!" Blackwell tore off his augmented reality goggles and tossed them onto his desk. "Was it Jackson?"

"Sort of."

"Explain," Blackwell stated flatly.

"We found two of Jackson's agents dead in the stairwell, not far from the bodies of our own agents," Mitchell revealed. "Killed by a frag grenade."

Blackwell tilted his head. "Oh really?"

"We identified the frag grenade. It's the same model as the grenades stolen from the agents we had watching the James Lockwood residence."

Blackwell threaded his fingers together. "This Garrett is good, I'll give him that. But he's not that good. He's going to make a mistake sooner or later. And when he does, we'll be ready."

"We will," Mitchell agreed.

21

Jackson Kane finished his trance session and emerged from the meditative state. He wearily rubbed his eyes.

Conversing with the Entities was always tiring. They kept wanting him to physically cross over to the other side for a "visit." It was all he could do to resist. They were dealers in temptation and had ways of manipulating thought and emotion that went way beyond any technology known to man. It was one thing to explore beyond reality with the mind and consciousness, another entirely to attempt such a thing with the body.

He was convinced that if he ever physically crossed over he'd never return. To what end the Entities wanted that, he did not know. The Nesut were similar to the Verndari in that regard—their intentions were never stated or even hinted at, their motivations entirely a mystery. They often feigned indifference to humanity, but Jackson knew they were interested. Very interested.

It was hard, sometimes, going through the day,

feeling like a pawn in a grander game. That's precisely what the Nesut believed he was of course, a simple pawn. But they would be in for a surprise.

They left humanity alone for the most part. As far as he could tell, this little plan of theirs would be the last major intervention for quite a while. And that plan was going well, truth be told. A little too well. A part of him had hoped they'd fail, but the other part of him was ecstatic. He wasn't sure if that was because the the Nesut were manipulating his emotions again, either.

One way or another, soon the world would be his. And if that meant the Earth's population would be reduced by a factor of ten, so be it. Such was a necessary step on the way to humanity's next evolution in consciousness.

He sat back in his office chair. It was an interesting feeling... having an office that was actually stationary, and one that afforded him privacy. Yes, it was located deep under a mountain, with rock walls that offered no windows. But that didn't matter: the wonders of augmented reality glasses meant he could make it seem like his office resided upon a white sand beach if he really wanted.

Still, it had been strange at first, sitting in an office that wasn't on the move, nor shared. He was accustomed to feeling the occasional bump or tug of motion, courtesy of the last few years spent inside a crowded semi-trailer, always on the go across Europe, South America, and various countries. When not aboard the trailer, he and his closest men had resided in a shipping container as it carried them between continents.

Yes, always on the move, to prevent capture or destruction at the hands of Blackwell. But they'd finally found somewhere that Blackwell could not reach, and allies who would stop at nothing to protect them from attack. Jackson was no longer on the run, and didn't care if Blackwell found him.

He received a voice call from Alastair Foreman, one of the moles he had embedded among Blackwell's men.

"We lost two of our agents to the renegades," Alastair told him.

That would be Isabel Lockwood and Garrett Bennett.

"I want that research," Jackson told him. Every single bit of technology that gave him an advantage over the Entities—*and* Blackwell—was a technology that Jackson wanted. No, *needed*. And there was no way he was going to allow Blackwell to obtain that tech.

"We believe they have kidnapped Noah Patel as well," Alastair continued.

"Have they?" Jackson mused. "Interesting. Thank you for the update. Keep me apprised."

Jackson hung up.

The Nesut had predicted the kidnapping.

So the games have truly begun, Jackson thought. *The next few days are going to be very interesting.*

ISABEL SAT next to the window, watching the parking lot from behind the curtain. In her peripheral vision, Noah perched on a chair in front of the TV, watching some mindless daytime talk show. He ate a bag of sour-cream-and-onion chips Isabel had purchased for him from the motel vending machine earlier.

Garrett, meanwhile, had gone to a sporting goods

store to grab some supplies and had left her in charge. She'd convinced Garrett not to bind Noah in his absence this time, but part of the deal required her to accept one of Garrett's Glocks.

The weapon sat on the table, ready in case she needed to deter Noah. Garrett didn't trust him, and truth be told, she wasn't sure how much she trusted him herself. She wouldn't be able to kill the professor of course, but if it came to it, she was prepared to shoot him in the leg or something.

"Want a chip?" Noah asked suddenly. He'd turned the TV volume way down.

"That's all right. Sour cream and onion. Can't stand the stuff. Plain all the way."

"My wife thinks I eat too many of these," Noah continued.

"Judging from the smell that came from the bathroom earlier," Isabel quipped. "She's probably right."

"Suppose so." He was quiet a moment. "How long have you known this Garrett?"

Isabel slid her gaze from the window. "Funny you should bring it up... he asked me the same thing about you."

"You've known me longer," Noah stated flatly.

She smiled politely. "Actually, I grew up with Garrett. We went to the same school."

"Oh." Noah sighed. "So you trust him more than me you're saying."

"Basically." She glanced at the TV, distracted by a flashy car commercial.

"How long are you going to keep me here?" Noah said, drawing her attention back to his face.

"You realize you're under our protection, right?" she explained. "I thought we made that clear earlier.

You know, after two people tried to kill you in a campus stairwell?"

"Can you at least let me call my family? Let them know I won't be returning tonight? It can be a one-way message. No replies."

She folded her arms across her chest. "No contact until we can arrange some sort of deal with our hunters. Remember, no one knows what happened to you. They'll leave your family alone only while that's still true."

"But if you're so sure they'll eavesdrop on my phone line, why not just call my number directly?" Noah pressed. "Then these men can interrupt the call, tapping in or whatever it is they do, and you can have your little negotiation right then and there. Why go through all this cloak-and-dagger BS?"

"I'd prefer to keep your family out of it," Isabel said quietly. "Let's say we get a number from those stolen phones, and we call it. Then no one has to know we have you. But if we call your family, they'll know. Do you see now?"

Noah stared at her. When he spoke, his words were cold. "I see completely. You don't want them using my family against you. And that's fine, I get it. You don't want the guilt. The burden. So how about this: if they bring up my family, simply say you don't have me and don't know where I am. And if they threaten to kill my family, say you don't care."

"That's actually what we plan to do already," Isabel revealed. "Assuming they even bring you up. But if we call your family, we can't do that, because it'll be obvious we have you. Don't you see it? We can't call your family."

Noah stared at her for several moments as if trying to think of a comeback, but then he looked away and turned up the volume on the TV, signifying the end of the conversation.

With a sigh, Isabel returned her attention to the window. Her gaze momentarily dropped to the Glock.

Garrett couldn't get here soon enough. At least she wouldn't be alone with Noah and his lingering questions.

The professor was right of course, even if she didn't want to admit it to his face. She didn't want her hunters to know she had the professor, if only to reduce the likelihood that they'd attempt to exploit the relationship by involving his family.

It was probably too late for that though. Garrett had used one of the two grenades he'd taken from the bodies outside her brother's house to take down the attackers in the stairwell. Was the grenade traceable? Probably. And if they didn't know that she and Garrett had Noah with them, they at least suspected.

Even so, she thought it best not to reveal that to him.

BLACKWELL THRUMMED his fingers on his desk. He had removed his augmented reality glasses to take a break for a moment. The constant bombardment of information those glasses inflicted was tiring not just to the eyes, but the mind.

How should I deal with this latest problem?

The Secretary had already made good on his promise of sending men down to search the base. Those men had been denied, of course, but unfortunately the Secretary, in his infinite wisdom, had also come in person. He was demanding a face-to-face meeting with him immediately.

Blackwell rubbed his eyes with his thumb and forefinger. He didn't have time for this. He really hated talking to politicians. But he supposed there was nothing for it.

A green light flashed on his augmented reality glasses, accompanied by a persistent, audible alert.

With a sigh, Blackwell retrieved the glasses and slid them on.

He was receiving an incoming call request from Lieutenant Mitchell.

Blackwell accepted. "What can I do for you, Lieutenant?"

"Got another lead," Mitchell responded. "QUASAR had a hit on two search terms this morning: LockKey and crack. The terms were detected inside a certain email thread on the servers of the UC Berkeley computer science department."

QUASAR was the name of the massive AI system that his team helped create for the NSA. It monitored the Internet 24/7, utilizing zero-day exploits to get its hooks in email servers and the like, grabbing clear text before it was encrypted. Some of those exploits were developed internally by his employees, while others were purchased from private companies. Not all providers were vulnerable, but academia targets were particularly easy to penetrate. Especially the computer science departments, which one would think would be the most secure.

"The gist is, a man named Archer Blake requested the help of a UC Berkeley team to crack a LockKey S1000," the lieutenant continued. "And get this: he's ex-CIA. Garrett Bennett's former case officer."

Blackwell's face lit up. "Interesting… and as we all know, no one ever really leaves the agency."

"True," Mitchell agreed. "But I plan to pay this Archer Blake a visit personally. Just in case."

"Not a bad idea," Blackwell told him. "How long will it take you to fly out there?"

"An hour and a half tops," the lieutenant replied.

"Keep me posted." With that, Blackwell disconnected the call.

He couldn't wipe the smile off his face.

Finally some good news.

If Garrett had asked this Archer to crack a LockKey S1000, likely the ex-SEAL had James Lockwood's research.

And best of all, the ex-CIA case officer might have even made a copy.

Either way, Archer would know how to contact Garrett, allowing Mitchell to set a trap.

Good news indeed.

That was the mistake, on Garrett's behalf, Blackwell was waiting for.

22

G arrett placed the ammo can onto the table. It was the tallest the sporting goods store had available. He closed the lid of the laptop and tried to slip it inside.

"Looks like a fit," Isabel commented.

Garrett nodded. He glanced toward the bed, where the professor sat sulkily watching the motel television on low volume. Isabel told him that Noah had complained about not being able to call his family and hadn't been very happy when she'd repeatedly denied him. Garrett was glad she hadn't folded, because allowing the professor to call would have only put them all in danger. He was actually quite proud of her, though he hid it well.

Garrett returned his attention to the task at hand. He removed the portable computer from the tall ammo can and set it aside. He lined the inside of the container with aluminum foil, sealing every seam with duct tape. When that was done, he instructed Isabel to keep watch on the parking lot, and then carried the laptop and ammo can to the bathroom.

The professor grunted in annoyance when Garrett walked in front of the television set and blocked his view, but otherwise the man remained silent.

In the bathroom, Garrett grounded the ammo can with a copper wire he connected to a pipe underneath the sink.

He booted up the laptop and connected the first smartphone to it via a USB cable. The phone had both batteries removed, but he'd installed software on the laptop to auto-copy the contents of the connected device the instant it turned on.

He closed the laptop lid and slid the portable computer into the ammo can, along with the connected smartphone. He positioned the latter so that the battery sockets were easily accessible, yet still shielded inside the can.

Once the device and laptop were placed, he took a deep breath, then reached in and hastily inserted the two batteries. He turned on the smartphone and quickly sealed the lid of the container and waited.

When he was satisfied that enough time had passed for the auto-copy to complete, he reopened the can and quickly reached inside to pull out both of the phone's batteries.

"Isn't there a chance the phone managed to transmit before you turned it off?" Isabel was standing in the bathroom door. "While the ammo can was open?"

"A small chance, but that's why we're leaving when I'm done," Garrett told her. "Now watch the parking lot like I told you."

She raised her hands defensively. "Sorry." She vanished from view.

He proceeded to place the other phones inside

one at a time and copied them the same way, removing the batteries when he was done.

When he finished with the fourth and final phone, he took everything with him and left the bathroom. He turned off the television when he walked in front of the professor.

"Let's go," he told the man.

Noah sighed, but got up.

In moments all three of them had loaded into the stolen vehicle and were on their way out of the parking lot.

Garrett handed Isabel the laptop. "Tell me what we got."

Isabel opened the lid and started to work the touchpad. "Okay. So I see four data files, labeled dump one dot t-x-t, dump two dot t-x-t, and so forth. Does that sound right?"

"It does," Garrett confirmed.

She clicked the touchpad a few times. "When I load them into the text editor, I get nothing. Well, I get different headers, like Contact List, Call History, Message History, and so forth, but otherwise all of the actual fields are empty. And when I load the files up in the hex editor, it's no different. There's… no data."

The professor snickered in the backseat.

Garrett glanced in his rear view mirror, giving the guy a warning look. When Noah saw his glower, the man quickly bit his tongue and looked away.

"Is it possible there was something wrong with the transfer program you used?" Isabel asked.

"A small chance, but unlikely." Garrett exhaled in defeat. "I was afraid of this… either the phones are designed to factory reset if they're tampered with, or the contractors memorized any phone numbers they needed."

He drove on in silence. It made perfect sense. If captured, they wouldn't want any incriminating numbers or call histories on their phones. It had been a mistake to assume he'd get anything out of the devices.

Finally, Isabel asked: "So what do we do now?"

That's a good question, Garrett thought.

LIEUTENANT MARCUS MITCHELL sat in the front passenger seat of the operations van. He was parked on the road a few houses down from the property of ex-CIA operative Archer Blake. It was quite the impressive neighborhood.

Marcus had researched him during the ride over in the Gulfstream G800: Archer got rich after leaving the CIA, selling his skills to the highest bidders. Some of the jobs were of questionable legality, to clients who were dubious at best—the Saudi prince who wanted to cover up the accidental death of a pretty influencer who died in the hot tub of his Dubai penthouse; the Mexican drug lord who hired Archer to come up with the optimal drug smuggling route off the Florida Keys. There were also indications he was still involved with the latter business, providing ongoing consulting services to the cartel.

Marcus could use those jobs against the man, if he needed to. Marcus wasn't one to judge, of course —he'd done some questionable jobs for questionable people himself. Including this job.

"That's a lot of cameras," the drone operator commented.

Marcus maximized the video feed from the drone on his augmented reality glasses so that the video consumed most of his vision. The near-silent device was using machine vision to catalog all the tiny cameras dotting the property.

He minimized the feed and turned toward the rear of the van to address the agent seated behind the drone operator. "Cut the power to the house, disable the land lines, and start up the jammer."

The latter would interfere with the solar-powered cameras sprinkled across the property, and would also prevent anyone from making calls. It would affect the neighboring houses as well, so if anyone decided to be a boyscout and call in the incident, they wouldn't be able to get a dial tone.

"Roger that." The agent messaged the other operators who were working upstream of the team.

Marcus heard a series of thuds on the roof of the van. That would be more drones launching—they contained the jamming devices that would blanket the neighborhood.

A moment later the agent turned back to Marcus: "It's done."

Marcus signaled the men to begin the approach. The rear doors opened, and he followed the black-clad men onto the winding, tree-lined drive. Songbirds chirped somewhere in the branches above.

Such a beautiful day to be working.

He smiled grimly and continued forward, scanning his surroundings as he did so.

The group reached the tall imposing stone wall that fenced in Archer's property, and then launched their grappling hooks.

In moments, Marcus and his men were over the fence and on the way to the mansion proper.

ARCHER WAS in the middle of a breaching hack against a South Korean company when his uninterruptable power supplies kicked in.

"Damn it," he muttered as the myriad of audible alarms from the UPS units filled the room with a cacophony of beeps. That was the third outage this month. "Knew I should've bought a house in a different neighborhood."

He quickly saved all his work and logged out. The different rack-mounted computers under his U-shaped desk would have already begun safe shutdown procedures. He turned off the multiple high-resolution monitors on his desk one by one, and as the computers began to shut down, he disabled the UPS devices, shutting off the alarms. His noisy work room quickly became unnervingly silent.

He sighed, staring at the NFT art pieces in their luminous frames. Some of those were worth a fortune. Or at least they had been in their heyday.

The things I waste my money on.

He retrieved his satellite phone from its mount on the far right side of the desk. He had the power company on quick dial. He pressed that button…

Odd. The phone didn't work.

Why am I paying for a satellite phone if I can't get a signal when I need it most?

He made a mental note to switch satphone providers, and then tried his ordinary smartphone next.

Also no signal.

What?

He grabbed the landline phone he kept on the opposite side of his desk. Maybe there was a big solar flare or something going on.

When he picked up the headset, he realized there was no dial tone.

Okay. This is getting weird.

He was starting to become a little afraid now.

Motion drew his gaze to the French doors that framed the entrance to his workroom.

A black-clad man wearing a balaclava stood at the open entrance, casually holding an AR15 with the muzzle pointed at the floor. Other men silently padded into view, joining the first individual. They all carried automatic rifles. None of those weapons were pointed at Archer.

For the moment.

He suddenly felt sick to his stomach. "I surrender?"

23

A prisoner in his own house, Archer sat on a bar stool at the sleek center island of the modern kitchen. He wore a facade of calm despite the underlying tension in the room. The stainless steel appliances gleamed under the soft overhead lights as he exchanged guarded glances with the balaclava-wearing men flanking him, the only sound the muted hum of contemporary appliances.

His gaze lingered on the rifles casually slung over those shoulders, and he vaguely wondered if he'd be able to snatch an AR15 before the others shot or subdued him.

Probably not.

He returned his attention to the closest man and waited. Still no one said a word. The quiet was becoming unnerving.

Maybe that was the point.

"What do you want?" Archer finally said. He was trying to sound annoyed, but a slight quiver on the last word betrayed his nerves.

Dammit. Out of practice at this crap.

"You used to work for the CIA," his captor stated.

"So?" Again Archer tried to sound nonchalant, but his mind was racing. The CIA? Was his past involvement with the agency finally going to get him killed?

"Do you still serve your country?" his captor asked.

Archer was nonplussed. "Of course I do."

"Except when it otherwise profits you."

Archer didn't answer immediately. "I don't know what you're talking about."

The interrogator sat back and folded his arms. "Helping smugglers plan and optimize their drug-running routes from Mexico to America hardly seems like a man serving his country."

Archer slouched.

So that's it.

He knew that particular gig would come back to haunt him. He started talking fast. A little too fast, perhaps, but he couldn't help himself. "Okay, look. They're just a client. I've never even met the cartel leader. I do everything remotely. I don't even know their real names. It's all code names and encrypted messages. I swear, I'm just a cog in their digital machinery. They send me coordinates, and I analyze the fastest and safest routes for the shipments. It's all business, man, no personal involvement. I can't afford to mess around with dangerous people like that. You've got to believe me!"

He fumbled nervously, glancing around the kitchen as if searching for an escape route, all pretenses of calm thrown out the window. "I've never been to any secret cartel meetings or anything. It's all virtual. They just trust me with their data because I've got the skills. I never thought it would lead to this. I mean, I just thought I was freelancing for some shady import-export business. They never told me it was drugs until it was too late, and by then, I was in too deep. I've been trying to find a way out, I swear!"

As beads of sweat formed on his forehead, he continued, "You've got to understand, I'm not the mastermind here. I'm just a guy trying to survive in a world that got way too complicated. They never told me what they were shipping, just the coordinates and a deadline. I'm begging you, if you let me go, I'll disappear, change my identity, anything. Just don't let them find me. I'm as much a victim as anyone else here!"

The leader glanced at his comrades. Some of them had cocked their heads, as if they found all of this very amusing.

"We don't care about the cartel," the man said simply.

Archer stiffened.

Shit. I caved like a little bitch. Definitely out of practice.

He reminded himself of who he had been. Who he *was*. In Afghanistan, he would have never let the Tally walk all over him.

I'm no one's bitch.

Archer straightened, and defiantly studied the calculating eyes behind that masked face. "What do you want then?"

"Garrett Bennett."

A chill passed down Archer's spine when he heard those words. He was being asked to betray the friend who had saved his life multiple times.

"I can't help you," Archer said.

"I thought you still served your country?"

"You don't know the hell we went through in the

suck. He's saved my life more times than I can remember."

But hadn't Garrett told him earlier that all debts were now repaid?

"Garrett Bennett is in possession of documents that don't belong to him," the man told him. "We need your help to find him."

Archer held his tongue.

The man sighed beneath his balaclava, then removed the mask, revealing his face. "Look, I'm going to level with you. My name is Lieutenant Marcus Mitchell. I work for the Department of Defense. Indirectly."

"You're a defense contractor," Archer stated.

"More of a security contractor working for a defense contractor, but close enough," Mitchell replied. "Now as I was saying, your friend Garrett is in possession of certain documents. It's likely he doesn't exactly know the full implications of these documents, but believe me when I tell you, if they fall into the wrong hands, the United States will become vulnerable to strategic surprise."

"Can't have that, can we?" Archer considered what this Mitchell was saying for a moment. "The USB stick. You're talking about the LockKey USB stick. Garrett told me it was for a client's sci-fi novel. Something about... inter-dimensional storage, I think."

When the contractor didn't answer, Archer blinked. "You mean that crap on the stick is real? Holy shit. It is."

"Did you make a backup?" Mitchell asked finally.

Archer studied him uncertainly. He could lie... but somehow he suspected this man would see right through it. "Yes, I made a backup."

"Can you tell us where it is?"

Arched smiled bitterly. "And after I do, that's when you kill me, right?"

Mitchell returned the smile with a patient grin. "You're not dying. At least not today."

"No, no, this isn't going to work." Archer folded his arms. "If I'm going to betray my friend, at least threaten to kill me first or something. Or my dog. Say you're going to kill my dog if I don't do as you ask. I need something for when Garrett comes over to whoop my ass."

"You don't have a dog..." Mitchell said.

"Not yet..." Archer agreed.

Mitchell glanced at one of the operatives seated at the desk behind him, and they both shrugged.

"If you don't give me the memory stick, I'll shoot your dog, and then you, in that order," the self-proclaimed lieutenant replied casually.

Archer stared at him, but didn't move. "I thought that would work," he lied. "I really did. But I'm sorry, I can't in good conscience give you the backup."

"So you have some backbone after all." The lieutenant sat back and folded his arms.

Archer gave him a defiant look. "Ratting out a cartel is a lot different than betraying my friend. A helluva lot different. What kind of a man do you think I am?"

I'm not so weak huh? You sonofabitch.

Mitchell apparently decided to try a different tact. "Don't do it for us, do it for you country. Remember who you were at the CIA."

Archer chuckled sadly. "The CIA. I thought I was making a difference. But I was just a grain of sand in the Afghan desert. In the end, I made no difference. None of us did over there. Didn't you see what happened after the withdrawal in 2021? The Tally are back in control. It's like nothing changed."

"You can make a difference for *real* now," Mitchell told him.

But Archer didn't answer. He thought about the document they wanted.

Inter-dimensional storage. It's real. Or the theory is. What the heck did you get me mixed up in, Garrett?

He wasn't sure how wise it would be to give such a document to these men. He had no idea who or what they represented. If inter-dimensional storage was real, and Garrett was keeping it from them, he probably had good reason. You didn't want something like that in the possession of the wrong people.

Mitchell exhaled wearily. "All right. So, on the one hand, you helped a Saudi prince cover up the accidental death of an influencer in his Dubai penthouse. We got, what, obstruction of justice, concealing a corpse, being an accessory after the fact?

"And on the other hand, you're helping a drug lord come up with the best routes to smuggle drugs from Mexico into the USA. So we tack on federal drug trafficking conspiracy, money laundering conspiracy, RICO violations, drug importation conspiracy, and likely a CCE charge. Your choices have left you in very deep federal waters. There's enough to lock you up for life. Would you like that?"

"What's a CCE charge?" Archer asked, feeling suddenly meek.

"Continuing Criminal Enterprise," the lieutenant replied.

Archer swallowed. "I'd like to talk to my attorney."

Mitchell smiled patiently. There was a dangerous glint to his eyes. "This is your last chance." When Archer didn't answer, the lieutenant pressed his lips together. "You know in movies when one character says 'we can do this the easy way or the hard way?' And when the other character doesn't answer, the first one says 'the hard way it is,' and proceeds to brutally interrogate the subject? I bet you never imagined the same thing would one day happen to you. Because… did you really believe I made my earlier threat only because you suggested it?"

Mitchell retrieved a Sig Sauer P320-M18 from his belt and pressed the barrel against Archer's temple. "I won't ask again. Where is the backup?"

"You won't shoot me," Archer stated, doing his best to act confident and calm though his heart was racing. "If you do, you'll never find the backup."

"I'm sure we will, once we ransack your work-room." Mitchell pressed the barrel harder against Archer's forehead. Painfully harder.

Damn. Should have stored the memory stick somewhere safer.

But he decided to attempt a lie. "The backup is stored off-site. You think I'm dumb enough to keep it in my workroom?"

Mitchell smiled coldly. "You already admitted that you thought the research on it was a work of fiction and therefore not worth paying attention to, so yes, I think you were dumb enough." Yep. The man could see right through it, of course. "The choice is yours. Tell us where to find it, or I squeeze the trigger and we find it on our own."

"Okay okay," Archer said. "It's yours. I'll take you to it."

A weak little bitch after all. What have I become? I'm obviously not the man I was in Afghanistan. Pathetic.

Mitchell holstered the pistol. "It's in your workroom?"

Archer sighed. "You got me."

Mitchell glanced at two other contractors. "Nac, Sergeant, with me. Mask off."

Nac removed his balaclava and gave Archer a mock salute before lifting a laptop bag off the counter and standing.

Sergeant meanwhile remained seated. "If it's all the same, I'd rather keep mine on."

"Whatever you want." Mitchell turned toward Archer and beckoned him forward.

Archer led his three captors through the elegant halls with their dark mahogany-paneled walls. At intervals, those walls opened up to chambers harboring floor-to-ceiling windows that allowed natural light to cascade over the polished marble floors, creating a bright and airy mood that was at odds with the tension in the air.

Archer's footsteps echoed loudly upon the marble floor, while those of his captors remained muted. The repetitive thud of his gait sounded to him like a ticking clock. A countdown to his doom.

When he originally told them he'd lead them to the memory stick, he thought he'd try to make a run for it, but now that he was on the move, he lost his nerve.

Why can't I find the courage?

He glanced at the men escorting him. They were Garrett's type. Hard. Deadly. If he tried to escape, he knew they'd either catch him right away or mow him down. Neither option was very appealing.

He reached the French doors of his workroom and led them inside. He promptly retrieved the memory stick he'd placed in the third drawer on the right side of his U-shaped desk and handed it to Mitchell.

Nac retrieved the laptop from his bag and Mitchell inserted the USB stick into the portable computer. Nac set the laptop down on the desk to more easily utilize the touch pad.

"Password?" Nac asked.

As per his policy, Archer had put a new password on the stick, which was *Nabopolassar626BC*: the name and birth year of the first king of the Neo-Babylonian Empire.

He'd entered nine incorrect passwords so that the next wrong entry would render the drive useless. It appeared that Nac hadn't noticed there was only one try left. If he had, he didn't mention it to the lieutenant.

"The password is *Albuquerque*," Archer replied, and spelled it.

Elation filled him. He'd finally found the man from Afghanistan buried deep inside him. The man Archer truly was. The case officer who would never betray the Navy SEAL who had risked life and limb for him multiple times.

He found it hard not to tear up in that moment.

I did it. I passed the test.

Nac entered the password. He glanced at the lieutenant. "That wasn't the password. Little shit lied: looks like we can't access the data."

Mitchell grinned ferally. "That's fine. Send it to HQ and schedule a password reset and breach."

"On it." Nac left the room, bringing the laptop and memory stick with him.

The lieutenant sat Archer down on the main ergonomic chair. "How do you communicate with Garrett?"

"Fuck you," Archer told him.

Mitchell casually turned around and grabbed the iPhone that was sitting out in plain view on the desk. He spoke into the radio built into his helmet, which evidently was set up to punch through whatever interference they were using to disable Archer's cellphone. "Charlie Bravo, deactivate the jamming devices, over."

Mitchell swiped up to unlock the iPhone and when presented with the lock screen he held the device toward Archer's face.

Archer immediately looked away so that Face ID authentication would fail.

"Hold him," Mitchell instructed Sergeant when the phone remained locked.

The other man positioned himself behind Archer; he wrapped his huge arms underneath Archer's armpits and pressed his palms flat against either side of Archer's head.

Mitchell once again held the iPhone to Archer's face.

Archer couldn't break free—Sergeant was pressing too hard—so instead he simply closed his eyes. Sometimes that was enough for Face ID to fail.

But not today, apparently.

Mitchell swiped through the unlocked phone and looked at the apps.

"Interesting. You're a Signal user." The lieutenant paused, tapping the screen to load an app. He turned the phone toward Archer again. It was indeed Signal, and the screen displayed an unlock prompt once more.

Archer closed his eyes defiantly, but as before the Face ID succeeded and the app unlocked.

He opened his eyes to a beaming Mitchell, who

was repeatedly swiping his finger up the screen to navigate the messages. "This will do. This will do nicely." Mitchell stepped back. "You can release him."

Sergeant let go of him and Archer slumped.

Sorry, Garrett. I tried.

T'VAAL WAS QUITE ENJOYING this new biological container. She couldn't help but pause to admire herself every time she passed in front of a reflective surface. The long blond hair. The sea-blue eyes. The thin body with its wide hips and voluptuous bosom.

T'Vaal reveled in the way the male containers looked her way as she walked through the shopping mall. Certainly an excellent container. What was its name? Elnora. Yes. Mate of the now inoperative biological container Evan.

T'Vaal had never intended to hold onto it for so long, but she was so thoroughly enjoying the body that she couldn't help herself. It had been too long since she had experienced this realm in a linear way. Besides, if her plans and those of her cohorts came to fruition, then this might be the last chance to enjoy such a container.

Even so, T'Vaal was vigilant, ever aware of her surroundings, both on this plane and above. There were many dangers in this realm, and she could lose the container in an instant. Look at how fragile the Evan container had been, after all.

She could still sense time nonlinearly while experiencing it the manner of her container, and as she left the mall and approached her car, she perceived danger.

Another being was observing... a competing faction with a biological container of its own? Or was the watcher one of the owners of the containers themselves, one of the "humans?"

While she physically moved between the different cars arranged in their grid-like patterns, T'Vaal searched her surroundings with her consciousness, scouring forward and backward in time as she did so.

There: T'Vaal saw a metallic, cylindrical object, with a tail of sharp, red bristles. Couldn't pinpoint the source. Nor could she discern the significance. There was a strange... fog... clouding her extrasensory vision. Some kind of interference. A limitation of her current container? She could sever the connection and unleash the full extent of her abilities, but then she'd lose access to the container she was so thoroughly enjoying. And as mentioned, this might be her last chance to savor such a thing...

T'Vaal found the car and entered. She accessed that part of the biological container's mind responsible for operating the machine and then directed the car onto the path of black concrete the containers called a road.

As she drove, her danger sense pulsed faster than ever. T'Vaal increased the forward motion of the vehicle. She scanned the exterior with her physical eyes, and at the same time reached out with her consciousness, searching, probing to the outermost extents of the local environment.

But there it was again: the incessant fog. She couldn't see past it. She had never experienced anything like this before.

Was it a competing faction? Had they found some way to interfere? Or perhaps the human themselves were somehow causing this?

Though T'Vaal was reluctant to do so, she was going to have to disconnect from her container. It would be a shame to lose it so soon, but she had no choice.

Right then T'Vaal felt a sharp, excruciating pain in her biological midsection, just above the seatbelt strap. She glanced down.

"No," she murmured.

A small cylinder with a tail of sharp, red bristles protruded from the waist of her container.

Too late she saw the small nozzle protruding from the bottom of the steering column where the dart had launched.

T'Vaal had been too focused on the external beyond the vehicle: the trap had been set inside her very car.

As her world became black, the car rolled into the ditch.

24

G arrett pulled into a new motel, a long way from the previous, and sent Isabel inside the main office to book a room. When she had the key card, he parked in front of their unit, then all three of them got out and entered the motel.

"Why is it all these roadside motels look the same?" Noah complained. "It's like we're stuck in a '70s time loop. The moment you step in you see those hideous floral curtains, walls covered in ugly floral wallpaper peeling all over the place, worn-out single beds, and that godforsaken foldable couch bed with more lumps than sour milk. Then there's the ancient TV with half the channels not working, and the bathroom is usually a moldy mess. It's like they copy-paste the same dreary design everywhere you go."

Garrett gave him a suspicious glance. The professor seemed a little too talkative, especially given his earlier, constant sulking. Then again, since his kidnapping, the one thing Noah had done consistently was complain.

"You get the couch bed," Garrett told him.

"Wonderful news," the professor replied. "Can't wait to wake up with an aching back and a body covered in bed bug sores."

Garrett went to the washroom straightaway and confirmed that the professor would not be able to make an unexpected getaway from the room—this particular bathroom didn't even have a window. He returned to the main living area; Isabel had taken up a position near one of the beds.

"Come on, it's not that bad," Isabel was consoling the professor. She lifted up the comforter to reveal the mattress sheets underneath. "See, no bed bugs."

"They burrow in deeper than that." Noah went to the bed and pulled back the sheets to expose the mattress underneath, which had seen better days. With a furrowed brow, he began inspecting the seams and corners. "They like to hang out in the seams and crevices of the mattress, where it's all dark and cozy. Can you turn on the table lamp?"

With a shrug, Isabel did so.

"Hmm, wish I had my smartphone, it's hard to see anything." He went to the headboard and peeled back the fabric, but evidently found nothing. "Well, they can be anywhere. Around the joints and screw holes of the bed frame. In and around nearby furniture like nightstands, dressers, chairs. Along baseboards, in cracks on the walls, beneath loose wallpaper. Underneath or within the folds of the carpet. Or even behind electrical outlets."

"For a physics professor, you certainly know a lot about bed bugs," Isabel commented.

He shrugged. "Travel is one of the upsides and downsides of academia. Research conferences, academic collaborations, and so forth. We don't travel so much anymore these days, given the advent of virtual collaborations and conferences. But I've been to my fair share of dives back in the day."

"Really?" Isabel arched an eyebrow. "Whenever James went to conferences, he always had luxury accommodations."

"Not everyone has the same tastes as your brother," the professor snapped. "Nor the freedom. I have a family, if you recall. One that you won't let me contact. The way it works at our particular university is, we receive a stipend for travel. Any accommodations above and beyond that stipend are paid for out of pocket. If the travel costs come in below the threshold the professor is allowed to keep the remainder. Your brother always used up his entire stipend, often paying out of pocket to further upgrade his hotel room, whereas I chose to save as much money as I could. For my family."

"Noble," Isabel commented

"Necessary," the professor countered.

Garrett was only half listening. He was trying to figure out what the next step should be. They couldn't live in motels forever. He supposed they could steal a large van and use that for a while, at least until they found an unoccupied cabin somewhere in the woods. He was fairly good at hunting, so food wouldn't be a problem, and if necessary could be supplemented with extras shoplifted from grocery stores. But he wasn't sure how well Isabel would adjust to such a life.

Plus there was the problem of Noah. They couldn't just let him go. Or could they? They'd made the professor well aware of the risks, and if he chose to go back to his family and endanger not just his life, but the life of his wife and kids, that was his choice, wasn't it?

His burner phone vibrated in his pocket, bringing him back to the present moment. He immediately went to the window and peered past the floral curtains. There were no new vehicles in the parking lot.

Puzzled, he pulled out the burner phone. The device was supposed to be turned off but apparently he'd left it on the last time he'd used it.

Already starting to make mistakes.

He had received a new Signal message.

It was from Archer: *I found something else on that memory stick you might be interested in.*

Puzzled, Garrett texted back: *I told you not to keep a backup. You also signed an NDA…*

"What's going on?" Isabel asked, joining him near the window.

"It's Archer." He kept his voice low, not wanting Noah to hear. "He says he found something else on the memory stick."

"What?" Isabel pressed.

Garrett was about to answer when his phone vibrated again. He read the message, and then tilted his phone toward Isabel so she could read it.

I couldn't resist. Sorry. But trust me, you'll want to see this. It changes everything.

Garrett texted a reply: *What did you find? There was only one file when I unlocked the device.*

He waited. Then: *I don't want to reveal anything over the phone. Meet me at my house in an hour.*

Garrett raised a dubious eyebrow. "He wants me to meet him at his house."

"Who wants you to?" Noah asked.

Garrett had spoken a bit too loudly, apparently. Didn't matter. There was no reason why the professor couldn't hear this next bit.

"You're not going, of course," Isabel said. "It's a trap."

"Definitely a trap," Garrett agreed. "Which is why I'm going alone. They flipped him somehow. Got dirt on him, I suppose."

Isabel grabbed his arm urgently. "But why go at all?"

Garrett glanced down at her hand; she seemed to realize only then that she was tightly gripping his forearm, and finally let him go.

"We need to find out who's behind this," Garrett told her. "It's the perfect opportunity. It's either do this or head back to your house. Or mine, for that matter. I also plan to send them a message."

The professor chimed in. "Oh yeah? What kind of message?"

Garrett's mouth fixed in a grim line. "Don't mess with us or our friends."

He grabbed the spare Glock from his ankle holster and set it down on the table in front of Isabel. He nodded at Noah. "Watch him."

GARRETT DROVE through the expensive neighborhood in his newly stolen Ford Lexus.

Ahead, a white van parked on the street stood out like a sore thumb. In a neighborhood whose vehicles typically included gleaming BMWs, Mercedes-Benzes, and Range Rovers, it was quite obviously a surveillance unit. The van was only two houses down from Archer's, and the upper floors of the mansion were readily visible from here.

At least the operators had gone through the trouble of plastering fake logos onto the exterior of the van to at least pretend it belonged to a real business: next to a picture of a plunger and a toilet were the words "Plato's Plumbing."

Garrett continued forward, reaching Archer's property a moment later. He turned into the seemingly empty driveway—the main gate was already open, as if inviting him inside.

He drove to the far side of the circular driveway, which had space enough for several cars. Garrett chose a spot on the far side of the bubbling fountain that served as the centerpiece and parked.

He stepped out of the vehicle into the full view of any hidden ambushers. He gripped the last grenade in his possession, his arm extended so that it was obvious what he held. His left hand was wrapped firmly around the safety handle, and with his right hand he dramatically pulled the pin.

"You can come out now," Garrett announced loudly.

He scanned the gazebo, the manicured garden, the upper windows, the rooftops.

No one appeared.

"All of you," Garrett shouted.

Still nothing.

"You think I'm afraid to die?" Garrett smiled wildly, then loosened his grip on the safety handle, opening it halfway so that inside the grenade the striker would be descending perilously close to the primer. When it touched, the delay element would activate, giving Garrett three to five seconds before detonation. He had no way to know when the delay element activated—these grenades were intentionally designed to be noiseless in order to avoid alerting potential targets. For all he knew, the delay element might have already activated, especially if the primer was particularly tall in this unit…

But five seconds passed without incident. So he had a little more room, then. And a little more time.

Someone must have given the order, because snipers suddenly stood up on the roof. Others arose from behind the gazebo, along with more hidden behind strategic spots in and around the garden. Some appeared in the upper windows of the mansion as well.

They were all dressed in black, their faces veiled behind sunglasses and balaclavas, their heads topped by helmets. They carried assault rifles—every single one was pointed at him.

Garrett pursed his lips, then squeezed the safety handle of his grenade all the way down once more in a gesture of conciliation.

"Who's in charge?" he asked.

A man on the ground stepped forward. "It's my unit."

Garrett studied the man. Behind that balaclava, two penetrating blue eyes returned his stare icily.

"Have your men lower their weapons," Garrett instructed.

The leader glanced at his comrades; he must have issued a quiet order over the radio because they all pointed their automatic rifles at the ground.

Garrett nodded at the leader. "Toss your weapon."

"Just me?"

Garrett smiled patiently. "Yep."

The man lowered his rifle to the ground.

"*All* of your weapons." Garrett nodded at the pistol grip that protruded from his cargo pocket.

The leader removed a Sig Sauer and set it on the grass next to the rifle.

Garrett thrummed his fingers on the explosive device he held. "Grenades, too."

One by one, the man removed the grenades from his vest pouches and placed them on the ground.

"Lose the satphone and the helmet," Garrett continued.

The man doffed his helmet, which contained the headset he used to communicate with his men. He set it, and his satphone, on the ground.

"Where's the backup memory stick?" Garrett asked.

"I don't know what you're talking about." The man put just enough confusion into his voice and expression that Garrett almost believed him.

Smiling, Garrett allowed the safety handle of the grenade to return to its former precarious position.

"It's on the way to headquarters," the leader admitted.

Probably the truth. Garrett squeezed the handle tight once more.

"Get in." Garrett beckoned toward the Ford Lexus. He glanced at the other contractors and added: "Don't follow. If you do, there won't be much left of your esteemed leader when you find him."

Garrett entered the driver's seat and promptly held the grenade—still in his left hand—close to the window so that everyone outside could see it.

He waited for the other man to sit down in the front passenger seat.

"You don't have to do this," his captive said after shutting the door.

"Oh yes I do," Garrett responded.

He turned on the car and exited the circular

driveway. He kept glancing at the rear-view mirror to keep an eye on the contractors. They all remained standing in place and otherwise made no attempt to pursue.

In moments the property was receding behind him. When he neared the surveillance van, he pulled over next to it, opened the window, grabbed the Glock from his waistband and fired at the closest tires. Judging from the way they remained partially inflated, they appeared to be some sort of "run flats," but that was fine—in their current state, they could likely only be driven at a maximum speed of around fifty miles an hour.

Garrett slid the Glock back into place at his waistband, situating it away from his captive, not at all worried the man would try to grab it. Any sort of scuffle between Garrett and himself would end badly for the both of them while Garrett held that live grenade.

He shut the window and floored it.

When the house was well behind and it appeared no one was following, he felt more at ease. Even so, he knew there were likely eyes in the sky watching at that very moment.

"What's your name?" Garrett asked.

The man didn't answer immediately. "Lieutenant Marcus Mitchell."

"Lieutenant, huh?" Garrett commented.

Defense contractors commonly allowed employees hired directly from the military to retain their former ranks as part of their job titles, especially when their roles closely aligned with their previous positions. It helped maintain a sense of hierarchy, discipline, and organizational structure that the now civilian employees could relate to, and helped with retention and discipline, among other things.

Usually they had multiple titles, one for use inside the organization and one for outside. For example, a retired U.S. Army officer who held the rank of Major might be referred to "Senior Project Manager" outside the organization, while Sergeants might be "Team Leaders," and so forth.

"You might as well take off your mask, Lieutenant Mitchell," Garrett told him.

Mitchell only hesitated a moment before removing his sunglasses and yanking off the balaclava, revealing a weathered face that bore the weight of years of service. He had the salt-and-pepper stubble and wrinkles of a man in his middle years, but the set of his broad shoulders beneath those black fatigues hinted at a strength and discipline more common to a man half his age.

"So you're either part of the group that kidnapped Isabel and her brother," Garrett told him. "Or the faction that killed him. So which is it?"

"We never intended for her brother to die," Mitchell claimed.

Garrett smiled coldly. "So part of the kidnapping group then, got it. Though it's up in the air whether I believe you or not. So... the backup is on the way to headquarters, you say? Where exactly is this HQ?"

"If you and Isabel surrender, I'll take you there," Mitchell promised. "You won't be harmed."

"I'd believe you if circumstances were different, really, I would." Garrett thrummed his fingers on the steering wheel. "But unfortunately, when I arrived at my friend Archer's mansion, I was greeted by a squadron of rifles pointed at my face. I didn't really appreciate that."

Mitchell raised a defensive hand. "We didn't know what to expect…"

Garrett guffawed. "Bet you certainly didn't expect me to threaten to blow myself up with a grenade." He teasingly relaxed and tightened his grip on the grenade's safety handle. "Where is Archer by the way? You haven't hurt him, have you?"

Not taking his eyes off that grenade, Mitchell shifted uncomfortably. "He's fine. Safe. In our custody."

Garrett gave him an uncertain glance. "Let me talk to him."

"You made me drop my phone, remember?" Mitchell told him.

Garrett retrieved his main burner phone and handed it to him. "Use Signal."

"My men don't have Signal installed. And if you're hoping to reach your friend's phone, it'll be locked away by now."

"Fine. Make an ordinary call." When Mitchell hesitated, Garrett added: "Go on."

The lieutenant entered a number and pressed the call button.

"Put it on speaker," Garrett instructed.

Mitchell obeyed.

"Hello?" a gruff voice asked.

"Can you put the prisoner on the line?" Mitchell asked.

A moment later Archer's familiar voice echoed through the car. "Hello?"

"Are you hurt?" Garrett asked.

"Garrett!" Archer replied. "No. Not yet. I'm so sorry. I did my best to stop them. But I couldn't."

Garrett extended a hand toward Mitchell. "The phone."

Mitchell gave him the device and Garrett promptly hang up.

The lieutenant arched an eyebrow. "That's it?"

"That's it," Garrett agreed.

"You know, I could threaten to have him killed if you don't cooperate with me."

"You could." Garrett grinned toothily. "But it won't work."

"Are you sure?"

"Positive." Garrett met the man's icy stare for a moment, then returned his attention to the traffic.

"I believe you." Mitchell sighed. "Let me bring you in. We can protect you from the men hunting you. Protect *her*."

"You're hunting us as well in case you forgot." He passed the phone back to Mitchell. "Enter the number of your boss into my contact list."

"My boss?"

"That's right," Garrett said. "And don't try to tell me you don't have the number memorized. I know how this game works."

Mitchell entered a number. He left the contact name as "Unknown."

"Now switch the phone to airplane mode, shut it off, and take out the battery," Garrett instructed.

The man complied. The burner phone's lid could be removed without a screwdriver, so Mitchell easily unplugged the battery.

"Now deposit the phone and its battery in the center console," Garrett instructed.

Mitchell opened the lid of the center console and placed the requested items inside the storage box.

"Whenever you're able, let your boss know he's going to get a call from me," Garrett told the lieutenant. "Tell him to install Signal. There's a few things he and I need to clarify."

"I'd be happy to clear up what I can right now," Mitchell told him.

Garrett flashed a patient smile. "I'd rather talk to the head of the snake than the body obeying it, if you don't mind. And remember: install Signal."

Mitchell shot him a defiant glance. "This will only end when you're in our custody, you know that don't you? We'll never stop."

Garrett knew the man was probably right. He decided he'd heard enough. "If you entered the correct number then this will end, believe me. Now open the glove compartment. There's duct tape inside. Use it to seal your mouth."

"But—"

"Do it," Garrett hissed.

With a resigned exhale, Mitchell opened the glove compartment and ripped off a piece of tape, securing it to his mouth.

Shortly thereafter, Garrett pulled into a tall parking garage downtown and parked on the fifth floor.

"Hold the grenade." Garrett gingerly transferred the grenade to the man's grasp, and as soon as Mitchell's fingers squeezed the trigger, Garrett immediately duct taped the man's wrists together. When that was done, Garrett taped Mitchell's arms to the steering wheel.

Garrett had expected the man to put up more of a fight by attacking him or otherwise trying to break free, but for some reason Mitchell restrained himself. It was almost like he was… relieved? Odd behavior for a hardened man of his background. Unless Garrett had completely misjudged his character.

Garrett retrieved the phone and battery from the center console and placed them in a bag he grabbed from underneath his seat. The only other items in the bag were a can of spray paint and a screwdriver.

As he left the vehicle he gave Mitchell a mock salute… the man still held the grenade, his wrists firmly duct-taped to the steering column.

Garrett's fingers were sore and stiff from having kept the grenade safety handle depressed all that time, so he massaged them as he walked away. Even the tendons in his wrist hurt. He'd definitely held onto that thing too long.

He reached the stairwell and took the pedestrian skyway toward an adjacent building. The skyway was about two stories up, and when Garrett was halfway across he glanced back, peering through the floor-to-ceiling windows toward the parking garage. As he watched, black SUVs pulled up in front of the entrance and exit, blocking all vehicle traffic to the building.

So he had been right about eyes in the sky.

Garrett suppressed the urge to run. He kept his head down, with his cap pulled low, and continued walking.

He entered the building and followed the signs to the next skyway, and continued in this manner through the downtown pedway system, moving between towers via skyways and tunnels until he reached a skyscraper ten blocks away that also had underground parking.

He went down to the parking garage and used the can of spray paint to cover up a couple of surveillance cameras.

Then he found an appropriate car, used the screwdriver to break in, then hot-wired it and drove to the exit. He did have to pay a small fee to activate the exit gate, but otherwise everything proceeded smoothly and without incident. The streets were clear outside, much to his relief.

At a red light, he gazed into the bag beside him, focusing on the phone and its battery.

He hoped that little trip was worth it. He considered just calling the number that Mitchell had given him right then, but decided against it.

Isabel needed to be involved. She was the one they wanted.

I just hope we can work out some kind of deal. And if not…

Well, he tried not to think about that.

25

T 'Vaal felt her link to the biological container known as Elnora strengthen once more, and she was finally able to open her physical eyes. A mistake… blinding rays hit the light receptors. No matter which direction she looked, the powerful white light was there. She wanted to shield herself with her biological hands, but her limbs were bound to her sides. She wanted to stand, but again, restraints dug into her flesh and prevented any such movement.

Growing angry, T'Vaal reached out with her consciousness, searching for those who trapped her. It should have been easy, because the body she was linked to acted as a beacon in this realm, allowing her to hone in on the precise time and place, but once again she struck an impenetrable layer of… fog. That was the only way to describe it. White, all-consuming fog.

T'Vaal attempted to move her consciousness forward and backward in time, but again was met by that fog, as if she was entirely constrained by the limitations of her biological container now, which should have been impossible.

Once again she realized that the only way to escape would be to abandon the container entirely. And yet, why had she been unaware of her existence when the dart had struck her? T'Vaal had lost all sense of awareness, like a human, and had only revived moments ago.

Something was very wrong.

She needed to break the connection to the container immediately. She reached toward it with her consciousness, and…

The link would not sever.

She tried again.

The dissolution failed to take.

How could this be?

She drew upon all her internal reserves and focused upon the lines of force linking her to the energy centers of the container, and concentrated all of her being on rending those connections.

And though she put everything into it, all of herself, the link merely flickered.

She was trapped.

"Good day to you, Elnora, and to your controlling entity," a pleasant male voice rang into the white light. "What would you like us to call you today?"

T'Vaal recoiled at the sound and couldn't help but hiss like some feral feline organism. Yes, she hissed, and snarled, reduced to the basest of biological instincts.

"I ask again, what would you like us to call you?"

She suddenly understood why the words had instilled in her such a primitive, savage response. That voice was… compelling her.

There was something wrong with her container's mind. Likely some kind of foreign matter circulated in its blood, influencing its neurochemical signaling to invoke feelings of trust and loyalty, along with compulsion. A state of mind directly mirrored in T'Vaal, because in that moment, unable to sever her link, she was completely human, and utterly susceptible to the constraints and limitations of her biological body.

She would not be able to resist.

She gave out one last defiant hiss, and then:

"Call me T'Vaal," she said via the container's oral aperture.

"Excellent," the voice said. "I'm sure you've realized by now that your consciousness is trapped here, and you're perceiving reality and time as we do. You're one of us now, and entirely at our mercy. You're going to tell us everything we want to know."

T'Vaal continued to fight against the compulsion to bow and scrape. It would be so easy to give in. So easy.

Must… not.

"Will I?" T'Vaal asked, her voice sounding more desperate to her auditory receptors than defiant. "We shall see."

"We certainly will."

ISABEL OPENED the door when Garrett returned, and he huddled with her at the table before quietly explaining what had happened to him when he visited his friend.

Noah turned down the television volume, and it was obvious he was trying to listen in, but Garrett doubted the professor would hear very much—he and Isabel were barely speaking above a whisper.

"So you have the number of their boss," Isabel said when he finished.

"I do."

"And you're sure Archer is safe?" Isabel shuddered every so slightly. "What if his voice was AI-generated?"

Garrett rubbed his chin. "It's possible, but I don't think they'd harm him, not when there's still a chance they could use him against me."

She pressed her lips together. "Will they?"

"If they do, it won't work," he assured her. "I'm not giving you up. No matter the cost."

"Are you sure?" she said. "I can't imagine what they might do to him if it comes to it."

"Then don't imagine it," Garrett snapped.

She blinked, taken aback. "You know, you can be heartless sometimes."

He inclined his head. "I have to be."

She studied him, then her gaze dropped to the bag he had deposited on the table. She could see the burner phone sitting inside. "So we're going to call this guy?"

"We are. But not here."

An hour later found them parked on the second floor garage outside the airport arrivals terminal. The lot was packed. Garrett had told her he'd chosen this particular location to make the call in case there was some zero-day exploit in Signal he didn't know about. While he was confident Signal was impregnable, it never hurt to play things on the safe side. The theory was, it would be more challenging to track them with so many other active devices around, what with the potential for signal interference and so forth.

Garrett also explained it was possible there were Stingrays set up somewhere in the area, either legally or illegally, portable devices that simulated cellphone towers, logging and retransmitting all data sent and received, essentially acting as man-in-the-middle attacks to eavesdrop on calls or messages. Stingrays were originally meant for use by law enforcement, but other bad actors had since co-opted the tech. In theory Stingrays were useless against Signal, since the app used end-to-end encryption for all data, including voice calls. Keeping in mind the aforementioned potential for zero-day exploits.

Of course, it was possible that Mitchell's boss hadn't even installed Signal as per Garrett's request. Isabel wasn't sure what they would do then. Maybe call the number anyway. Probably a bad idea, though.

Noah sat in the backseat, while Isabel was in the passenger side. Garrett remained behind the wheel.

"So you're going to let me listen in on this call of yours?" Noah asked.

"Today's your lucky day," Garrett agreed.

Isabel and Garrett had already decided that Noah could stay. The other option was for Garrett to take Noah on a walk while Isabel made the call, but they had concluded there was no point in hiding everything from the professor anymore. They were all in this together. They still had no intention of letting him read the entire research of course, but it probably didn't matter anymore if Noah knew that they actually had it. They owed him that much for depriving him of his family, even if it was for their own good. He deserved the truth.

Garrett looked at her. "Let's do this. Are you ready?"

She swallowed nervously and produced the phone.

On the drive here she'd turned on Garrett's burner—it had booted in airplane mode—and found the phone number "Lieutenant Mitchell" had entered. She'd manually transferred that number into the contact list of her burner phone, and when she'd pressed the last digit, she'd immediately turned off Garret's burner and removed the battery. She'd returned the original phone to Garrett, who had promptly tossed it out the window.

She turned on the remaining phone now and launched Signal. She navigated to the newly added contact, took a deep breath, and pressed the encrypted call button.

She tapped the loudspeaker icon to put the call on speaker phone.

"What if he doesn't have Signal?" she asked.

"He'll have it," Garrett promised.

The app emitted a ringing tone, and her heart rate picked up as the seconds passed, because she kept expecting the man who kidnapped her to answer at any moment. After ten seconds she finally realized he wasn't going to pick up, and couldn't help an exhale of relief.

It was so strange, she had been waiting since the start of all this to confront the man who had done this to her, and now that the time had come, she wasn't quite sure she could go through with it.

She glanced at Garrett. "He's not picking up."

"Hang up, and message the contact first," Garrett told her. "On some phones, Signal calls display a notification on the lock screen, not a ringtone, so it's possible the recipient missed it. Text to let them know you'll be calling in two minutes."

She did as he asked and entered four words: *Calling in two minutes.*

She pressed send and waited. Roughly a minute and a half later she received a return message:

Ready.

Her heart rate shot through the roof once more. She showed the phone to Garrett, then initiated the voice call again and activated speaker phone. The hand holding the phone shook visibly.

She met Garrett's eyes and could see the concern there. She quickly looked away.

Relax, she told herself. *I'm just calling some ex-army dude who works for a defense contractor. He can't harm me.*

Except she knew that wasn't true, not at all.

The ringing abruptly ended.

"Hello," a friendly male voice said.

"Hello." Isabel's heart felt like it was going to throb out of her chest. "I'm Isabel Lockwood." Her voice sounded shaky even to her own ears. She glanced at Garrett once again—the concern in his eyes had only deepened. She averted her gaze, wondering if she should've just let Garrett make the call.

But the whole point of having her on the line was to prove that she was alive. As the sister of the man whose research they wanted, she had more leverage than Garrett.

Still, she could hand the phone over to Garrett at any time. Let him take over. He'd know what to say and do.

He—

No.

She took a deep breath and gathered her resolve.

I can do this. This man can't harm me. I'm in control.

"Isabel Lockwood," the man was saying. "What a

delight to finally speak with you. I hope my men have not caused you too much inconvenience?"

"Oh no, not at all," she said sarcastically, her nerves quickly giving way to a rising anger. "They only just kidnapped me and my brother, and then let him get killed. No inconvenience at all."

"I'm very sorry about what happened," he said. "There are factions at work here that don't play very nicely. They took us by surprise. I lost a lot of good men myself. Again, my apologies. Things weren't supposed to play out as they did."

"And who am I speaking to, exactly?" she asked forcefully.

"I'm Jackson Kane," he replied.

26

I sabel frowned. "Jackson Kane?" The name meant nothing to her.

"I run the company that wants your brother's research," he told her. "I'm the Managing Director."

"I see," she said. "And what company is this?"

"I'd prefer to leave out the name for now. It's not important. Just think of us as a random entity involved in the defense contracting business."

"Uh huh." She couldn't help a feral smile. "A random entity. Well that makes sense your company prefers anonymity, I suppose, given you're in the kidnapping business. You say it wasn't supposed to play out this way? What did you expect would happen? You'd kidnap us and we'd all live and work together like one happy family?"

"Your brother would have been well compensated," Jackson said. "We would have paid him more than the university. Much more."

She clenched her jaw angrily. "He had a very

good salary already! And he would've turned down your offer. He was quite happy where he was."

She heard what could have either been a cough or a laugh over the line. The thought that Jackson might actually be laughing only further enraged her.

"Excuse me," Jackson said. "I have a bit of cough. In any case, I want to clarify something: if he refused to work for us, we would have ruined him. We would have made that very clear to him. So he would have accepted, I guarantee you. We couldn't allow him to release his discovery to the world."

"Ruined him? Is that supposed to be an euphemism for kill him?"

"Not kill him. I'm talking financially. We'd arrange a scandal… something big enough to get him summarily dismissed from the university, and prevent him from being hired or funded ever again. We're very good at that sort of thing." From his tone of voice, she had the distinct impression the man on the other end of the call was smiling.

She couldn't keep the growl out of her voice when she responded: "You're no better than the other faction."

"I'm sure you've realized by now, in the wrong hands, the tech your brother was developing would be very dangerous."

She did her best to feign an innocent voice. "Oh really? What tech are we talking about?"

"You take me for a fool?" Jackson spat. "Your ex-CIA contact revealed everything. I know you have his research."

She could feel Noah's eyes boring into her back. She felt kind of bad for lying to the professor about that, but she reminded herself that she was rectifying that particular misstep by letting him listen-in now.

She considered her next words carefully. "Let's say I do have it. So what? Apparently you already have a backup copy on its way to you anyway. You don't need me."

"Yes, but I want every last copy of that research. I can't allow you to release it to the world." What he said next shocked her. "You don't know this, but our scientists have already built similar devices. You see, we've had our own breakthroughs in physics and metamaterials manufacturing. We can store particles in higher dimensions already, and in the coming months we have plans to expand the storage capacity to include atoms, molecules, and nanoparticles, and eventually larger constructs like minerals and tissues. We only want the research to keep it out of the hands of everyone else."

She was stunned, and didn't know what to say for several moments. Her ire flared yet again. "What the hell? You're keeping breakthroughs in physics to yourself so you can be the only ones to profit from the technology? What is this, some kind of power play? Withholding new physics and technology from the rest of the world to enrich your pockets? You know that rises to the level of a crime against humanity, right?"

"Not if that physics and technology is too dangerous," Jackson countered in a patient, albeit patronizing, voice.

Isabel refused to be talked down to. "You could release the basic principals behind the physics. Just don't tell people how to build the devices. The same way we don't teach people how to build nuclear bombs, or at least, we make sure it's very hard to acquire all the parts."

Jackson's laugh was very audible this time. Definitely not a cough. "Hard is an understatement. The production, handling, and transport of enriched uranium and plutonium are subject to extreme security measures. Governments, nuclear regulatory agencies, and international organizations closely monitor and regulate the use of the materials.

"Building a nuclear weapon itself requires highly specialized knowledge and significant infrastructure. It's not something that can be done easily or secretly in a backyard, garage or university lab. Obtaining the necessary resources and equipment without attracting attention is *extremely* difficult.

"Also, there's a big distinction between basic nuclear physics principles and classified weapons design. Knowledge of the latter is closely guarded by governments and tightly controlled within the scientific and engineering communities. Access to this expertise is restricted, and those with the necessary knowledge are monitored by security agencies. For good reason.

"Conversely, the technology your brother has come up with is a lot easier to build than a nuke. Anyone working in a physics lab could do it, and they wouldn't need too much money, either. I don't even want to think about the Pandora's box we'd be opening if we released this tech, let alone the physics behind it. Society, as we currently know it, would be destroyed. Literally, not just figuratively. Let sleeping dogs lie."

She paused. Some valid points, and she was reminded of her argument with Garrett on the same subject earlier. Even so, it was obvious to her that she'd never change his mind on this. "And what does the US government have to say about all this... subterfuge?"

"The Department of Defense is all in," Jackson answered. "They're more interested in the weapons applications of the technology, of course, and we're happy to present that to them. But they agree that most of this stuff needs to remain secret, including the physics. If anyone got a hold of this, particularly nation state adversaries, things would get real messy, real quick. The DOD doesn't necessarily know the full extent of what we're capable of already, but it's better that way."

It was Isabel's turn to laugh, though hers was in disbelief. "So you're withholding information and technology from the very people funding your research."

"Like I said, sometimes it's better that they don't know the full extent of what we're capable of."

"So that way when you turn on them and take over the country, they won't know what hit them, huh?"

"More like, plausible deniability."

She waved a hand dismissively at the phone as if to bat him away. She took a moment to swallow down her anger before continuing. "Tell me about this other faction. About the men who killed my brother. Do they have this technology, too?"

"They do," he said. "They're led by a former general named Blackwell. I used to work for him two years ago. He's an idealist turned war profiteer—he won't let anyone get in the way of corporate profits. If you have something he wants, and you don't give it to him, he'll kill you to prevent it from falling into the hands of anyone else."

"Sounds a lot like you," Isabel sniped.

Jackson sounded taken aback. "We're completely different. He kowtows to the military industrial complex, offering stripped-down versions of the tech-nologies his company develops to the highest bidders. He has no plans beyond padding his wallet, no vision beyond which politicians he can bribe into his back pocket. Needless to say, I wasn't happy with how he was running his business, so I left the organization and founded my own. I have higher goals than simple money and power. Goals for humanity."

"Oh really, and what are your goals exactly?" Isabel pressed.

"They're quite simple, really. The preservation and protection of humanity and this world. I plan to gently guide us into a new age of technological achievement and enlightenment."

"Oh, so you want to be emperor of the world," she scoffed. "Nothing big. And who better to guide us into the Age of Aquarius than you, right?"

"I do hope to install a one-world government at some point, yes," he admitted.

She paused in disbelief, waiting for him to say more. Finally: "Care to expand upon that?"

"At the moment, no. But I'll be happy to during our in-person meeting. I've said enough for now."

Isabel couldn't help a sarcastic smile at that, though she knew he couldn't see it. "Funny, but I can't see an in-person meeting happening anytime soon. Something doesn't quite add up with your story. If you and this Blackwell already have the tech, why would either of you kill for it? Why go through all these lengths to hunt us down for the research? You say you want no one else to have it. That's fine, and that part is probably true. But there's something else you're not telling me. James has discovered some property or technique that has eluded your scientists, hasn't he?"

"Why don't you come in?" Jackson asked casually. "We can talk about it more, and also discuss your future at our organization. Last I heard, you had a hard time finding a job. We could put someone with your skills to good use. We pay extremely well."

"I'm sure you do." She pressed the mute button and turned to Garrett. "Heard enough?"

"More than," he replied.

She un-muted. "We'll be in touch." She ended the Signal call, and at Garrett's prompting she removed the battery and tossed the phone out the window.

"Well that was interesting," she said to no one in particular. "If a little disturbing."

"I get the sense he's definitely holding something back about the research," Garrett told her.

She nodded. "The question is, what?"

GARRETT LOITERED inside the washroom of a popular coffee chain not far from the airport. Noah was in one of the stalls—he'd begged to use the bathroom, claiming extreme diarrhea, something about how Isabel lying to him about the research had made him sick. Meanwhile she remained outside, sitting in the car, no doubt further contemplating the phone call.

Just as Garrett was. The purpose of that first call had been mostly to extend a feeler, and see what one of the factions pursuing them wanted. Now that they knew, they could plan their next move. Whether that meant a trade for the research, or going into hiding indefinitely, was something they would have to decide. Garrett still wanted to get in touch with the other faction at some point. He was curious what this "Blackwell" had to say.

Garrett paused. The bathroom was completely silent. He hadn't heard anything even remotely resembling the explosive, watery eruption one might expect from diarrhea. Either the professor had developed a sudden bout of constipation, or he was lying about the need to use the washroom.

"Yo, what are you doing in there?" Garrett asked.

No answer.

Garrett had just searched him, and was positive the professor had no communications devices on him...

He peered through the crack between the door and the edge of the stall. Noah was sitting on the toilet all right, but the lid was closed and his pants were on. He wasn't texting or anything like that... his hands were empty, resting flat on his knees. His eyes were closed, though his head was leaning forward, as if he struggled to stay awake.

Growing suddenly angry, Garrett kicked the door, hard. "Wasting our time, are you? All right, that's enough. Let's go." He peered through the crack once more. The professor hadn't moved: his eyes remained closed. "What the hell are you doing?"

He was starting to wonder if the professor had found drugs or something in the stall and had taken them, so when Noah still didn't answer, Garrett grabbed onto the top of the stall and hauled himself up and over.

He landed inside, in front of the professor, and physically shook him. "Hey!"

Noah blinked several times, then finally met his gaze. "Sorry. I don't know what happened. I... blacked out or something."

"Uh huh, and where's the diarrhea? How come I don't see it dripping down your leg?"

Noah gave him a weak smile. "Oh, wouldn't you know it? Seems like I've miraculously recovered."

Garrett patted him down again, but found nothing concealed on his person.

The main bathroom door creaked as someone else entered.

Suddenly apprehensive, Garrett peered through the crack into the bathroom common area: all he saw was a middle-aged gentleman washing his hands at one of the sinks.

Garrett roughly opened the stall and hauled the professor out with him.

The gentleman met his eyes, and when the man saw Noah behind him he flashed a knowing smile.

Garrett ignored him and proceeded directly to the exit.

When he reached the car, Noah suddenly threw up, vomiting all over the hood.

"What the hell did you eat?" Garrett asked.

"Noah!" Isabel had rolled down the window. "Are you all right?"

"I need to go the bathroom again," the professor said. "Swish some water in my mouth. Get the taste out, or I'm going to vomit again."

Garrett sighed impatiently. He scanned the parking lot and the road beyond. Everything seemed safe.

For now.

"Let him go," Isabel said. "It's my fault for lying to him."

"He's not sick because of you," Garrett growled.

He took the professor back to the washroom. He watched as Noah bent over the sink and sucked water into his mouth. The professor swished it around and then spat out the now murky liquid.

After three more times of this, Noah finally turned off the tap and stood straight. "I'm good. Could use some bottled water, though."

Garrett left the bathroom and lined up with the professor. He kept his eye on the vehicle outside, which he could readily see through the floor-to-ceiling windows. The queue moved slowly, and with each moment Garrett felt his impatience rising.

Finally he just skipped to the front of the line with the professor and picked out a water from the open shelving unit next to the till.

"I just want a water," he told the clerk, setting down the bottle.

He paid for it and then handed it to the professor.

When they walked out, Garrett swept his gaze over the parking lot once more. Everything was quiet.

They neared the car.

"I'm sorry for doing this," the professor announced.

"No problem," Garrett said. "It happens to everyone. We can't control when we're sick."

"Actually, I can," the professor mocked.

Garrett had only just touched the driver-side door handle but paused, feeling the hairs on the back of his neck stand on end. He shot the man an angry look over the roof of the vehicle. "What—"

"I was stalling," the professor admitted.

Garrett stared in disbelief. "Stalling?"

"To give them time." The professor nodded toward the entrance of the parking lot. Three SUVs swerved into the lot and surrounded Garrett and the vehicle.

Garrett immediately withdrew the Glock he had tucked in beneath his shirt.

Several black-clad men emerged from each vehicle. Their faces were covered in balaclavas, their eyes shielded by mirror-like sunglasses. They pointed assault rifles at him from all sides, and looked almost identical to the group of men he'd encountered at Archer's property.

Except there were a lot more of them.

"Drop it!" someone shouted.

Garrett slowly rotated in place, letting his Glock's aim pass over those who surrounded him. When his sights reached the professor, Garrett paused, and he cocked his head. The anger had been simmering inside him ever since the professor had admitted to stalling, and now that the man was firmly in his sights, that rage began to boil over.

"Drop it..." one of the surrounding gunmen ordered once again.

In answer, Garrett merely smiled, baring his teeth in a rictus. He aimed directly between Noah's eyes.

The professor had already raised his hands, but he raised them even higher, now. "I'm sorry! I had to do it. For my family!" He was sobbing.

Garrett's finger twitched on the trigger.

"Don't do it!" Isabel shouted from inside the car. "Stand down! Please!"

While he was willing to die for her, now was neither the time nor place. Still, it was tempting to end it right there, right then, by eliminating the man who had somehow turned them in. How Noah had done it didn't even matter in that moment. All that was important was that he *pay*.

Going out this way would be almost a relief. And it would be satisfying, too.

At least in the microsecond immediately after he pulled the trigger.

But that was the easy way out and he knew it.

He'd almost taken the easy way out before.

But now he had something to fight for. *Someone.*

He'd nearly forgotten about her these past few years. And she'd come back into his life so breathtakingly quickly. All because of a daydream.

But… was it even a mere daydream?

Either way, if he squeezed that trigger, Isabel would be left to deal with this conspiracy all alone.

That decided it for him.

He removed his finger from the trigger and held the weapon wide, raising his hands in surrender.

27

I sabel was inside a moving vehicle with her hands tied behind her back and a black hood over her head, a scenario that was all too familiar to her. She was positioned on a jump seat that backed against an interior wall. Garrett was beside her, and Noah was somewhere else in the SUV. She knew all this because before her latest captors had slid the hood over her head, they'd loaded her into the vehicle with her companions.

So I'm captured again. Heading toward who knows what?

Maybe it was for the best. She getting so very tired of running.

Which faction had her now? Was it Jackson's? Or did the men belong to the former general named Blackwell? The man who had apparently ordered the execution of her brother?

A sudden jolt to the side told her the vehicle was slowing down.

Already?

"Was this roadblock here on the way in?" someone asked.

"Negative," came the tense reply.

"Be ready for anything," another answered.

She heard the subtle metallic clinks and muted thuds of rifles being slung down from shoulders.

She suddenly started giggling like a madwoman.

"Shut up!" one of her captors said.

But she couldn't help it. "It's happening again. Again and again and again. I'm stuck in an endless loop. I— oof!"

Something hard struck her in the ribcage and she doubled over. Felt like a rifle butt.

"Isabel?" Garrett hissed.

She was in too much pain to answer. His leg was pressed against hers, and she felt it tense up.

"I'm fine," she finally managed, hoping to prevent him from doing anything rash. Her side still throbbed painfully, but she'd live.

A knock came at the front window and she heard muted talking.

All of a sudden all hell broke loose.

Her heart quickened as sharp reports emanated from the front driver-side area; each shot reverberated through the enclosed space, jolting her senses and heightening her rising sense of fear. She felt blind and helpless.

She hadn't actually believed it was going to happen again. Or had she? She didn't know anymore. Either way, life had decided to play one big, cruel practical joke on her.

She had been laughing moments before. Now, her hood was wet with tears.

Why me? Why why why?

Everything was repeating. Garrett was going to die, just like her brother.

While she lived.

Please not again. Please make it be me this time. Or both of us.

"Go!" It sounded like the sliding doors of the SUV flung open then, and the muffled thuds of men disembarking echoed throughout the confined space. Gunfire erupted shortly from the right side of the vehicle. Instinctively she ducked.

It's all going to repeat. Garret is going to die.

"Garrett, what do we do?" she asked frantically.

In answer he leaned his upper body against her and pressed his hooded face into hers as if probing, searching… and then without warning he bit into the cloth next to her chin. She pulled away in shock and in the process tore off the hood entirely.

Beside her, Garrett held the empty head covering between his teeth, having bitten through the fabric of his own hood to latch onto hers.

Repeated gunfire drew her gaze from Garrett toward the right side of the SUV, and she watched her captors return fire from behind the cover of the half open doors. One of them dropped right in front of her with a gunshot wound to the head.

No no no!

She returned her attention to the interior of the SUV and gasped.

NO!

At her feet, Noah lay collapsed on the floor next to the jump seat opposite her. Either a lucky gunshot had ricocheted from the interior of the SUV and struck him, or the attackers had specifically shot at him in that initial exchange at the front, as he would have been readily visible from the open driver-side window. That latter thought only heightened her sense of dread—Blackwell had definitely sent in men to eliminate her once and for all.

"Isabel! My hood!" Garret's voice drew her eyes back to him. He still had the hood over his head.

Her side still throbbed from where she'd taken the rifle butt earlier. She took a moment to push down the pain and the nearly overwhelming fear. Then, doing her best to mimic what he'd done, she leaned forward and latched onto the bottom rim of his hood with her teeth.

"Agh!" Garrett exclaimed.

She'd bitten too deep, chomping down on some of his skin beneath that hood.

She immediately released him. "Sorry!" Her eyes stung with tears.

I can't do this.

She trembled as more gunfire echoed behind her.

"Try again!" Garrett ordered.

She blinked away the wetness and tried to ignore the loud gunshots as she latched onto his hood once again with her teeth. She strove to be more careful this time and only bite fabric... judging from his silence, she'd succeeded.

She still had her hands bound behind her back of course, so all she could do was yank her chin upward and hope that would be enough to lift away the hood. Garrett helped her by sliding downward at the same time, and in moments the hood slid off completely. She let the fabric fall from her mouth.

She saw a big red bite mark at the bottom of his chin, but Garrett seemed hardly aware: he stood up immediately and hurled himself between her and the half-open doors of the SUV. She hadn't realized it, but their two remaining captors had stopped firing and had instead turned their rifles toward her.

Garrett was shielding her with his body.

She screamed, and it was heart wrenching. "No!"

The men opened fire.

Isabel collapsed to the floor of the SUV and sobbed. "No. No. No."

She couldn't bare to gaze at his dying body. Couldn't bare to even look up. She simply wept there at the floor of the SUV, her body in a pile.

"No… Garrett…"

It had happened again. Why? Why!

But then, incredibly, he was kneeling beside her. "Isabel."

"Garrett?" she asked hopefully. She saw no signs of injury. No blood, no nothing. Was she imagining it? Or looking at his ghost?

She studied him in confusion. "How? They fired…"

"No, they didn't get a chance." He nodded toward the opening. "Look."

Still puzzled, she leaned sideways to peer past him. The two men had dropped to the road, where they lay lifeless, their limbs arrayed in random positions. Beyond them, she saw other bodies: it looked like all their captors were now dead.

She wasn't sure if that was good or bad.

"If you can untie me, I can get to their weapons…" Garrett rotated so that his bound hands faced her.

She spun her upper body in kind, turning her hands toward him, and felt around for the bindings with her fingers. She found hard plastic bands of some kind wrapped around either wrist, connected to what felt like a central ratchet mechanism. Two tapered ends, each serrated on one side, protruded from that mechanism. She couldn't push the ends through the ratchet mechanism, and if she pulled on them she'd only tighten the binds.

"I think we're zip-cuffed," she told him.

She heard footsteps and glanced toward the open doors; two armed men stepped into view and she started in fright.

The newcomers were dressed all in black and wore balaclavas, and otherwise looked identical to her former captors, down to the mirrored sunglasses. They had their assault rifles pointed directly at her and Garrett.

She took a deep breath and closed her eyes.

So this is it. Please make it be quick.

"Weapons down!" someone shouted from outside.

She opened her eyes in shock. The two men lowered their weapons.

One of them entered. The second remained by the door, his gaze locked on Garrett. From the mercenary's posture, she knew he was ready to raise his weapon at a moment's notice should Garrett decide to do anything.

"Who are you?" Isabel blurted out. "What do you want? How did you find us?"

In answer, the first man picked up the black hoods from the floor. He slid one over Garrett's face, the other over hers.

Here we go again.

JACKSON KANE WAS ENTERTAINING delegates from the landlocked African Republic of Mali. His media team had prepared a presentation showcasing all the different ways his company could help Mali.

As the holographic multimedia presentation played across their augmented reality goggles, Jackson narrated in real-time. "We'll build you roads and railways, we'll erect hospitals, supply medicine… we'll construct tech hubs and provide extensive STEM training… you'll be the envy of your neighbors."

The translator echoed his words in Bambara, the native tongue of the delegates, via the speakers embedded in the goggles.

One of the men spoke in response. Jackson received the translated reply a moment later. "And in exchange all you want are the rights to twenty-five percent of our nation's gold mines?"

"I wouldn't put it quite that way," Jackson said. "More like a two-year lease. The rights revert back to you in two years."

He suddenly snapped backed to the present moment. That meeting had happened over two years ago. He'd arranged similar agreements with other African Republics, and had harvested enough gold to satisfy the needs of the project the Entities had read him into. He was at the culmination of his plans. Or rather, theirs.

In the trance state, he was able to elevate his consciousness to the plane where all life arose. To the Source, as it were. Time was experienced differently here.

He focused on what he wanted. The future. Specifically, tomorrow, when the convergence was meant to pass. He still couldn't get a clear reading on it. There were supposed to be only a few possible outcomes, but he hadn't been able to get a bead on a single one of them. He tried for a few more minutes, but finally in frustration he gave up and abandoned the Source.

He blinked, opening his eyes. He lay on the stone floor of his office. The binaural beats continued to play over the loudspeakers he had installed in the rock walls of the room.

A ringtone sounded from the shaved boulder that served as his desk. Serendipitous timing, as always.

He clambered to his feet and shut off the beats.

On the desk, a green light flashed on and off on his augmented reality goggles in time with the ringtone. Jackson retrieved the goggles and slid them on so that the device's heads-up-display overlaid his vision.

His turncoat Alastair Foreman was making an incoming voice call.

Jackson took a seat and accepted.

"They never made the rendezvous," Alastair told him. Floating at the center of the heads-up-display a semi-opaque sound wave represented Alastair's voice. A green check mark appeared beneath the waveform, next to the the the words: *Vocal print authenticity confirmed.*

Jackson suppressed the urge to curse. He could curse all he wanted when the call was done, but not in front of his men. Never in front of them. "Do we know what happened?"

"It was Blackwell," Alastair said simply.

28

Blindfolded and with her hands securely bound behind her back, Isabel heard the distinct chime of what sounded like an elevator arrival tone. Garrett was beside her—she could pick out his deep, almost relaxed breathing amongst the others around her. She wasn't sure how he could stay so calm given everything that was going on, but the fact that he was seemingly at ease certainly helped her keep it together.

She was escorted forward, and a moment later experienced that weird, floaty sensation in her stomach that she always got when an elevator started heading down. The subtle vibrations around her were another telltale sign.

As the descent continued unabated, she wondered just how deep they were going, and couldn't help a growing sense of dread. Her wrists throbbed painfully from the flexicuffs, the binds seeming to be growing tighter every moment, digging into her flesh. Meanwhile the pain in her ribcage from the rifle butt jolt had faded to a distant memory.

Finally the elevator came to a halt and she and Garrett were led forward. Judging from the way her footsteps resounded, she thought she was in a corridor of some kind. Her captors made her change directions after a few steps, evidently heading down another passageway. After a moment, they turned her again.

Each new corridor seemed to have its own particular acoustic character, from the hollow echoes of stark linoleum floors to the muffled whispers of confidential conversations. The sounds of distant footsteps, shuffling papers, and the occasional clatter of equipment reverberated through the narrow passages.

It was altogether unsettling. Her bare arms occasionally grazed the cold, indifferent walls, and she couldn't help the shiver that passed down her spine whenever she made contact like that.

Finally the echoes vanished, her footfalls becoming muted, and she realized she'd stepped into a carpeted room.

"Cut their binds," someone said from the front of the room. Someone sitting down, judging from the source of his voice. "And remove the hoods."

Isabel felt the binds momentarily tighten if that was possible, and then they broke away entirely. She flexed her stiff hands in relief. Her wrists continued to throb painfully.

The hood slid off her face. She was in an office of some kind… beside her stood Garrett, which was a consolation. Somehow, she felt safe with him present, even if she and him were flanked by four armed men.

The mercenaries kept their rifles lowered; they'd removed their balaclavas so that their faces were visible, but still wore helmets. Even so, she didn't recognize any of them. They also wore thick glasses whose lenses had strange, purple-blue patterns on them, hinting at personal heads-up-displays. She suspected those were the same goggles she'd mistaken for mirrored sunglasses earlier, which meant the lenses could be tinted on demand.

She swept her gaze past them, surveying the office, which exuded an air of authority and strategic precision. The space was surprisingly expansive, given its presumably underground location, with walls adorned by military memorabilia and awards. Shelves lined with replica aircraft flanked the room, with models ranging from the vintage biplanes of the early days of flight to the cutting-edge F-35s of the modern era. A tapestry on one wall depicted a lone man standing atop a rock pile, holding a glowing jewel that seemed to hold the darkness at bay around him. A grand oak desk stood at the back of the room, its polished surface reflecting the glow of the large LED world map hanging on the wall beside it.

Seated on a stately leather armchair behind the desk was a broad-shouldered man. His posture was somewhat slumped, as if he carried the burden of years of service and responsibility. Time had etched lines of experience and gravity into his face, giving it a weathered, thoughtful look.

His pristine and well-put-together business attire gave him an air of impeccable discipline. The glint in his eyes, though fatigued, was also intelligent, reflecting the cunning of a man who had climbed his way up the ranks with Machiavellian efficiency.

One of the mercenaries stepped forward and placed a small device in the center of the desk before returning to his place beside Isabel. She recognized the device as the original LockKey USB stick that contained all of her brother's research.

"So we finally meet," the man behind the desk solemnly intoned. "Isabel Lockwood and Garrett Bennett. I'm Derek Blackwell, managing director of this facility. Some call me The General."

Isabel stood defiantly in the center of the office, glaring at the man who sat so calmly and imposingly behind his large oak desk. She wasn't cowed by him. Not in the least. "You killed a good man. Noah did nothing to you. Nothing. He wasn't involved in this in any way."

"Noah Patel?" Blackwell inquired. "According to the report I received, he fired at my team."

Isabel took an angry step forward. "That's wrong. He was unarmed... he got shot when your men attacked!"

Blackwell glanced at one of his mercenaries, then returned his eyes to Isabel. "Your version of events is entirely possible. If true, I apologize, and I'll have the man involved punished."

"You apologize?" Isabel spat. "Just like that. You can't kill someone and then *apologize*. What about his family? Who's going to take care of them now?"

"I have men watching over them at this very moment," Blackwell said. "And I'll see to it that her bank account receives a sizable monthly stipend. That's the best I can offer."

"So that's your MO," she sputtered, barely able to control her rage. She was standing before the man who had killed her brother and his colleagues, and it was all she could do not to throw herself at him and start hitting. Not that it would do any good. "You think you can buy off everyone with your blood money. Do you plan to offer me cash, too, for what you did to my brother? How much is his life worth? One million? Ten?"

Blackwell frowned. "What happened to your brother was not my fault, I—"

"You had him killed!" She took another step forward.

Garrett held a warning hand in front of her, and when she met his gaze, he nodded toward the armed men, who had lifted their rifles ever so slightly and looked ready to intervene.

She gave Garrett her best attempt at a reassuring smile, then she closed her eyes and took a deep breath to calm herself. When she returned her gaze to the man behind the desk, she felt her anger roil again.

Blackwell sat back. "So that's what this is about. You're misinformed. It wasn't me. Jackson's team attacked our helicopter."

"Jackson said *you* did it," she told him firmly.

Blackwell sighed. "This is why I wanted to get to you first. You talked to him? What did he tell you?"

She crossed her arms. "It doesn't matter."

"It *does*." He smiled sadly. "Because if he lied about the wetworks operation involving your brother, he probably lied about everything else."

"Just as you're lying at this very moment!" Isabel snapped. "Look, even if it's true you didn't intend to kill him, you're the one who set all of this in motion in the first place by kidnapping us."

Blackwell pressed his lips together. "We had no choice. If we hadn't acted, Jackson would have gotten to you first."

Garrett interjected next. "How did you find us back there, after Jackson's lackeys took us from the coffee shop?"

Blackwell studied the ex-SEAL for a moment, as if trying to decide whether to answer or not. "We have moles in Jackson's organization, just as he has

moles in mine. When his men took you, we were noti-
fied of your position almost immediately and
dispatched a Gray Eagle."

Isabel blinked in confusion. "Gray Eagle?"

Garrett was the one who answered. "A medium-
altitude, long-endurance unmanned aircraft system.
A drone."

Blackwell grinned widely. "Correct! In any case, it
wasn't hard to extrapolate where you were headed—
there was a private airfield nearby we suspected Jackson's team might utilize. We had the quick reaction
force set up a roadblock, and here you are."

Isabel thought of something. "How did Jackson's
team find us in the first place?"

The question was meant more for Garrett, than
Blackwell, but the latter man answered.

"I'm not entirely certain about that," Blackwell
admitted. "I'd ask them, but unfortunately there were
no survivors." He gave the mercenaries beside Isabel
an annoyed look.

"The professor might have told them," Garrett
volunteered.

"Noah?" She regarded him uncertainly.
"What? How?"

Garrett met her gaze unflinchingly. "It's true.
Remember how he got sick, throwing up all over our
car? After I was walking him back from the washroom, he apologized to me, and implied he'd vomited
only to stall us."

She frowned. "You're saying he shoved his fingers
down his throat so that we could be captured?"

"He implied as much," Garrett agreed, his face
grim. "Funny thing is, I never saw him stick his
fingers down his throat before he threw up."

Isabel studied Blackwell closely: she thought she

saw a glimmer of insight in the director's eyes when Garrett had said that, but Blackwell hid it quickly.

He knows something.

"As to how the professor contacted them," Garrett continued. "I have no idea. I searched him twice, both before and after taking him to the bathroom. So unless this Jackson has some sort of new communications tech we don't know about, the most likely explanation is a zero day vulnerability in Signal. But again, I don't know how the professor could have known they were coming."

Isabel kept a watchful eye on Blackwell the whole time, but the man betrayed no further hints that he knew how Jackson had found them.

Instead, Blackwell said, very carefully: "Either possibility could be correct." He studied the LockKey USB stick that rested in the direct center of his oak desk, and then picked it up. "So much fuss over something so small."

"So you didn't plant that?" Isabel said. "It's real?"

"Very real," Blackwell agreed.

"Unless *Jackson* planted it," Garrett commented.

Blackwell pursed his lips. He twirled the USB stick between his index finger and thumb, rhythmically tapping the bottom against the oak desk with each swing. "Unlikely."

"We're not giving you the password, by the way," Isabel said. "Just wanted to put that out there."

Blackwell froze, met her eye, and set the USB stick aside. "We already have the research, courtesy of Garrett's ex-CIA friend. And we've unencrypted the contents, despite said friend's best efforts to hinder us. Rolling back a hardware password retry counter is relatively easy for a handpicked team of their caliber…"

Isabel exhaled in defeat. Garrett had told her he hadn't been able to recover the backup memory stick from Archer's house, and that the defense contractors had taken it to their HQ to decipher. She hadn't expected them to crack it so soon.

When he spoke, Garrett sounded genuinely puzzled. "Then what do you want with us if you have the research already?"

Blackwell glanced at the mercenaries. "Leave us."

"Sir?" one of them asked, confused.

"Go," Blackwell repeated.

The mercenary saluted, then he and the other three left, closing the door behind them.

"I'm impressed with your backgrounds," Blackwell said. "And I want to offer you both a position in my organization."

Isabel's jaw dropped. She stared at him, flabbergasted, and laughed aloud. She glanced at Garrett, and when he met her gaze, he started laughing too. They both doubled over like it was the most hilarious thing in the world. It helped that Blackwell had dismissed his men—she felt a lot more confident without armed men watching her every move. It was perhaps a false sense of security, because Blackwell himself was likely armed, but she enjoyed the moment while she could.

When she had gotten that laugh out, she straightened, and looked him in the eye: "I'm sorry. I can't work with my brother's killers."

Blackwell seemed disappointed. "I told you, I didn't have your brother killed. I had nothing—"

"Well you already admitted to killing Noah," she interrupted. "So that *does* make you a killer. Who else has died getting in your way? Sorry, can't work for you. And if you think I can help you expand and develop the device my brother outlined in his research, you're wrong. I'm a molecular biologist, not a physicist."

Blackwell smiled patiently. "We don't need help with that. You see, we already have a machine."

"So it's true!" Isabel exhaled in disbelief. "Like Jackson told us. You already have the technology. He wasn't lying after all."

"About that, he was not lying, no, because we do have a machine," Blackwell admitted. "Several proto-types, in fact. We've managed to miniaturize them as well. We're able to store matter roughly the size of this room in a device the size of a lunch box. But only for thirty seconds at a time. If we don't bring it back before then, the inter-dimensional bubble breaks and the contents are lost forever, floating between dimensions."

Isabel couldn't believe it. They had devices *already*. James had died for nothing. "If you already have a machine, why do you want the research? Oh wait, let me guess, to prevent others from having it. Just like Jackson's excuse."

"Partially… but not quite." Blackwell leaned forward. "If the results are reproducible, your broth-er's research will allow us to upgrade the time limit of our storage containers beyond the thirty second mark. We'll be able to store objects in higher dimensions perpetually."

29

I sabel stared at him... his previous words still registering. They already had devices. And those devices were the size of a lunch box, and could store the contents of... "Wait, you said you could fit this entire *room* into your devices? But Jackson told us there were only prototypes that could store single particles?"

"Ah, so some of his lies are coming out," Blackwell nodded knowingly. "We're so much further along than that. We can store entire objects in our prototypes. Multiple objects. Can be organic or inorganic, doesn't matter. Even human beings, if proper life support is provided."

"Unbelievable." Isabel crossed her arms in exasperation. "And you're keeping it from humanity. What else are you keeping? Free energy? Anti-gravity tech? Like I told your friend Jackson, I consider the withholding of technology a crime against humanity. And to what purpose? To keep your corporate profits super high? To ensure the old world order remains undisturbed? So we all keep paying our bills with our heads down, being good little obedient citizens in the rat race?"

Blackwell clasped his hands and steepled his index fingers. "There are reasons we haven't released any of this. Personally, I'm against any sort of release. Or even disclosure that we have this tech. I'd prefer we maintained full-spectrum dominance... as soon as our global adversaries get wind of this, the cat's out of the bag, and everyone will have it. I don't want to live in a world where nukes can be transported in just about anyone's pocket. Do you? Not to mention there are the lawsuits we'd have to face for being given an unfair corporate advantage by having access to materials other companies never get to see."

She was torn. On the one hand, she felt it was wrong to hold back this tech. On the other, she knew he was right, that some people would definitely abuse it, to the detriment of humanity.

She sighed. "Okay, fine. We'll debate that later. But tell me, you say you're limited to thirty seconds at a time with your current prototypes and understanding of the physics? Does Jackson's tech have similar limitations?"

"It does."

She glanced at Garrett. "So he hid that from us, too. Assuming this is true. Well I think I've heard enough." She returned her gaze to Blackwell. "You might as well let us go. We're never going to work for your organization."

Blackwell wore a wan smile. "I'm afraid I can't do that. You see, if I release you now, Jackson will hunt you down, and either kill you or force you to work for his own organization."

Garrett returned the man's smile, but his was

menacing, not wan. "So we're going to be prisoners, then."

"For your own protection, of course. I'd prefer that you worked for my organization, but if you choose not to, I understand. But you should know, the Entities have chosen you. They want you to work for me even more than I do."

Isabel exchanged a confused glance with Garrett. "The who?"

Blackwell studied her intently with those cunning, piercing eyes. "Have you ever heard the acronym NHI? It stands for Non-Human Intelligence."

Garrett laughed. "Aliens. You're going to bring aliens into this."

But Isabel felt her face suddenly go very pale.

Blackwell nodded at her. "You see her face, she knows. Did you ever bother to ask her what her whistleblower complaint was about?"

Garrett studied her uncertainly. Isabel looked at him, opened her mouth, but couldn't manage to say a word. She was in shock.

I was right. I can't believe it. I was right all along.

She returned her gaze to Blackwell. "So they *did* give me a tissue sample from a human-alien hybrid to study."

"We'll get to that," Blackwell told her. "And I wouldn't precisely call them alien. These Entities I'm referring to, they're a race of beings who've been on our world since the dawn of time. We have some working theories as to their origin. The first: they came here and colonized the planet millions of years ago.

"The second: they evolved here, long before us, likely during the Cretaceous Period. Either way, they had over one hundred and sixty five million years to develop hyper-consciousness. They're the original Earthlings. There are other, more esoteric theories, but one thing is for certain: we are not alone."

He looked at the LED map on the wall beside him and his eyes momentarily defocused. "I remember what it was like when I learned humanity wasn't at the top of the food chain. That there were inter-dimensional beings who existed on this planet with us, unseen and unheard unless they desired otherwise. Beings that could influence events at their whim, shape the course of human history.

"Beings who likely had a hand in the leap forward in human evolution 70,000 years ago. What are we to them? How would they hold us to account for what they had given us? I don't know... no one does. Oh, some of the Entities have revealed certain things to certain people, but much if not all of it is disinformation as far as I can tell. They keep their real intent to themselves, secret from humanity."

This was a lot to take in. It would upend everything. "Why are you telling us this?"

"Disinformation," Garrett commented.

It was Blackwell's turn to laugh. "Oh no, it's true, all of it. You're lucky, you know. We usually give new people a limited read in, revealing bits and pieces over many months, with the full read in coming at the end of a probationary period. You guys are getting the whole tamale up front. And the only reason I'm fully reading you in is because the Entities want it this way."

She stared at him. "They communicate with us? With you?"

He grinned knowingly. "They have ways, yes."

She immediately thought of all the strange and sometimes coincidental events leading up to the current moment. That feeling of being watched in the forest, the rogue mercenaries not seeing her when she cowered in plain sight—the Entities had masked her presence somehow. Then the glowing dot in the sky that had guided her out of the woods, and the urge to "follow" bubbling up in her head.

And what about the anonymous tip Garrett had received on his phone regarding her brother's research? And the light that had guided her out of the motel and saved her from capture?

The Entities had been communicating with her, *helping* her, the whole time.

She had to wonder, were all of these Entities on the same side, or were some from competing factions. Was that possible? That they would have factions too, like humanity? Blackwell had already said they often spread disinformation, which was another human trait. So why wouldn't they have factions, too? And if so, what if some of them were helping Jackson?

If they are real, probably best not to anthropomorphize them too much…

She thought of something else. "You said, 'how would they hold us to account for what they had given us?' And then before that, something about the lawsuits you'd have to face for having unfair access to materials no one else gets to see… what precisely have they given you? The technology or physics to create those storage devices you told me about?"

"Not directly," Blackwell admitted. "We've reversed engineered some of it from crashed UAPs—Unidentified Anomalous Phenomena. We believe the Entities sometimes crash craft purposely, usually at the same time among different superpowers, to set off technological arms races. At other times, the technology comes from craft they shoot down for us—

presumably craft piloted by NHIs from opposing factions, or actual extraterrestrials. We also sometimes engage in direct kinetic exchanges with them."

Isabel studied him a moment, trying to make sense of everything he was saying. "These... Entities... crash them *only* among the different superpowers?"

"Not at all: they do occur worldwide. Often the crash sites are radioactive, and even harbor pathogens, so the countries involved usually invite our military in to help with the cleanup. Other times, if it's a Five Eyes country or a neutral nation-state, the military simply goes into the country in question and takes the debris. Okay... I see the disbelief in your eyes. I'm going to break down the retrieval process for you in detail, to make sure there is absolutely no doubt in your mind that what I'm saying is true.

"So, the CIA runs a little side office called the Office of Global Access. Basically a facilitator to get JSOC's Special Mission Units in and out of countries where crashes occur. As long as its not China or Russia, the OGA will get the units in. Iran and North Korea can be a bit tricky, but sometimes the OGA can open doors there, too.

"They'll send in either Delta Force, DEVGRU, or the 24th STS... whichever JSOC unit is closest and has the necessary capability. The mission unit recovers the materials and hands them over to Special Operations wings who handle the transportation. These wings in turn give them to private defense corporations such as mine, and then the fun really begins. For the bigger crashes, or if there aren't any units nearby who have the needed capability, the OGA just tasks us directly and we send in our own extraction teams from barracks we operate around the world.

"A little side note… we developed the satellite-based sensor tech the CIA uses to detect the crashes, and we utilize it ourselves of course, so half the time we already have a retrieval team on the way before the OGA even contacts us. We'll back down if they have a closer JSOC unit in place, of course."

She shook her head. "Wait, go back a bit. The retrieval process… that's great. But you're going too fast… this is too much. Clarify something, please. First you say the Entities crash their ships on purpose, then they shoot down enemy craft, then they shoot down extraterrestrials, as in actual aliens. Then *we* shoot them down. So which is it? The last three I could probably believe, but the first? You say they possess hyper-consciousness, and are highly advanced inter-dimensional beings. And yet they send craft here from higher dimension and crash them on purpose? So basically giving us tech? Why?"

"Why did Prometheus steal fire from the gods and give it to humanity?" Blackwell posed. "We don't know for sure why the Entities would do this. But it does seem like they want us to develop the tech on our own, using human ingenuity to reverse engineer it rather than giving us the blueprints and physics outright. They want us to work for it, and compete for it… like I said, they sometimes gift craft to multiple superpowers to set off technological arms races."

"Prometheus…" Isabel mused. "The way you said that… you talk almost as if you believe Prometheus was actually real."

Blackwell smiled patiently. "Some believe he was an Entity."

Isabel smirked. "And you're one of those believers, right?" When he merely continued to smile, she tapped her lower lip with her index finger. "You've seen Star Trek? The Prime Directive in that show is basically a guiding principle for humans… it's meant to prevent interference in another world's natural development. Something like gifting technology would be expressly off limits."

Blackwell stood up to pace behind his desk. "The fictional constraints of a show developed by human beings can't offer us any insights into the goals and motivations of a mind that is utterly *alien* to us. Trust me when I tell you that our Entity friends have no such guiding principal. As I said, they evolved long before we did and co-inhabit this world with us, though at a higher level of existence. It would be the same as if we decided to drop a bunch of AK-47s in the territories of different African apes just to see which species could reverse engineer them first, let alone figure out how to use them."

"So we're just lower animals to them?"

He stopped pacing. "I didn't mean to insinuate that. I'm not trying to say they have no guiding principals at all… I'm sure they do. We just don't know what those principals are. I don't think they really consider us *lower* animals, in the basest sense of the word. There is even some evidence to suggest they created us, which would imply they have more than a passing interest in us. I mentioned that 70,000 years ago we made an evolutionary leap forward in intelligence. Some would say it's not quite natural to evolve such a leap so suddenly."

"I know some evolutionary biologists who would disagree with you…" Isabel countered.

"I'm sure you do," Blackwell agreed. "In any case,

they are here, and they have been 'gifting' us technology, whether by faking crashes as an excuse to give us tech, or by accident. Even so, it's not like we can understand most of what we recover. These ships we've captured have only revealed bits and pieces of information. And every ship is different—they're not made on an assembly line. Some of my channelers would argue they're constructed via consciousness itself, but I'd debate that.

"Despite these so-called 'gifts,' we can't figure out how eighty-percent of the stuff works. Sometimes we get lucky, like with the storage tech, other times not so much. To be honest, it's almost like these craft aren't entirely in our dimension, as in: parts of them exist in three-dimensional space, and other portions such as the controls and engines reside in four-dimensional space.

"For some of the more obtuse stuff, we've gotten hits from our channelers, who use consciousness to power parts of the devices on and off, but they're working in the dark. Let me give you an analogy: imagine a wired camera looking at a fish. The controls and video feed are located in a boat floating on the surface. The fish has no idea how the camera works, and can't even get access to the controls. The only way for the fish to reach it is to use certain esoteric parts of its mind it doesn't even know it has, by tuning its consciousness a specific way and reaching into the dark and fumbling around. This is the conundrum we face."

She exchanged a dubious glance with Garrett. "This is sounding more and more far-fetched all the time. He mentioned 'channelers' twice now?"

Blackwell sat down again. "Adepts, we get them from Kundalini retreats in India and Pakistan and

Malaysia, or grab gifted minors from local schools. People who can quickly be trained to harness their consciousnesses in ways we can use."

"Minors?" Isabel asked. "As in kids? Why?"

Blackwell opened his mouth to answer, but then shut it again as if to rethink his reply. Then: "Because they actually believe it's possible. In any case, we've moved away from using minors... too many problems. We use Kundalini adepts a lot these days, though they burn out quickly, unfortunately."

She shook her head. "This is all very confusing."

"It will get clearer as you become more familiar with everything," Blackwell promised. "For now, all you need to know is that different NHI groups have allied with different factions of humanity. These NHI groups have set up different permanent bases in our world. These stations are mostly automated, running courtesy of an advanced AI. We know of eight. Two are in the ocean. Two in the Andes. One in the Alaska Range. Two on the far side of the moon. One on 16 Psyche."

"16 Psyche?" she asked.

"The largest and most massive M-type asteroid. On 16 Psyche there's enough gold to make every person on earth a billionaire twice over, or to collapse the gold market and destabilize the entire global financial system. Basically seven hundred quintillion worth."

Garrett spoke up. "What use would inter-dimensional beings have for gold and money?"

Blackwell chuckled. "Oh, they don't use it as money. Gold is a key component in their metamaterials. Our NHI allies have embargoed the asteroid, but the biggest faction opposing them has found other ways to obtain gold. You see, the base beneath the

Alaska Range, it's operated by one of the opposing factions, and they are building something... dangerous... and Jackson Kane is assisting them. We want you two to help us stop them."

Isabel remained quiet for several moments. "This is a lot to take in. And despite your claims to the contrary, it still feels like Garrett and I are on the receiving end of some sort of disinformation campaign."

"I assure you, all of this is very real. Of course, if you ever went to the press, we'd disavow all of it and paint you as nutjobs."

Her lips twitched, forming a wry smile. "Wonderful news. Care to share a little more about this Jackson Kane? What does he want? And what is this so-called opposing faction building beneath the Alaska Range that's so dangerous?"

Blackwell cleared his throat. "I'll answer your question, but first, let's get back to your whistleblower complaint. You accused the defense contractor you worked for of tasking you with the analysis of certain exotic organic material. Earlier, you called it a 'tissue sample from a human-alien hybrid.' Can you describe the precise nature of this sample, and what it was you were tasked to do with it?"

30

I sabel looked at Garrett, and kept her eyes on his as she spoke. "About three years ago, I was tasked with sequencing the DNA of a tissue sample for a working genome. They fed me some BS cover story about how it was taken from someone with an inherited genetic defect, but that was an understatement. The resulting genome was... decidedly odd."

She turned her gaze on Blackwell. "You're familiar with the concept of junk DNA? Basically intergenic DNA sequences that don't code for any proteins. The remnants of ancestral genetic elements that were once functional but gradually accumulated mutations over evolutionary time to the point where we don't use them anymore. The tail-related genes, the gill-related genes, and so forth.

"Not all of it is 'junk' though, a good portion still have regulatory functions, or are used as histone anchors, buffers against radiation, alternative protein-coding pathways, and so forth. But my point is, these intergenic sequences are supposed to be all over the place.

"In the samples I was given… the intergenic sequences were repeated throughout, at regular intervals. No organism on Earth has such a neat and tidy layout of junk sequences. No evolutionary pressure could form that.

"Meanwhile, the intragenic—non-junk—sequences were even more disturbing. It looked like some genes were basically copied and pasted from human and animal genes. We're talking nucleotide by nucleotide. There were also many genes not even found in our biosphere that I had no idea what they did. *Alien* genes.

"There was also evidence that certain combinations of base pairs and palindromes functioned as unique identifiers for not only numerically identifying a given gene, but its chromosomal location, pointing at advanced engineering completely beyond what we're capable of. CRISPR gene-editing comes nowhere close. So basically whoever made the tissue sample could insert and remove genes in a far more targeted and methodical manner than we're capable of.

"I raised my concerns with my supervisor, explaining that the sample couldn't have been from someone with a 'genetic defect' and had to have been engineered. A day later, just like that I had my clearances on the project pulled and I was assigned to a completely different division. I sat on that information for two years. Two whole years. And when I finally came out, I accused the company of having access to samples of what could best be described as human-alien hybrids." She glanced at Garrett as she finished, and he nodded slowly.

Blackwell meanwhile remained quiet, as if unsure whether she intended to continue and didn't want to interrupt.

When she stayed silent, he spoke. "You're not far from the mark. But what would you do if I told you the tissue sample you were given was part of an effort to reverse engineer avatar tech?"

She stared him uncertainly. "Avatar tech?"

He chuckled sadly. "Yes. Sometimes the downed craft we recover are unmanned. Other times, we find pilots... non-human pilots. Their bodies have DNA sequences similar to what you've described. We believe the Entities occasionally build these bodies or avatars to experience our physical three-dimensional universe directly, when a full-blown human body isn't required."

"A full-blown human body?"

He threaded his fingers. "They also have avatars that are indistinguishable from human bodies. What better way to study humanity than to live among them, after all?"

"Like the animatronic baby robots researches embed within gorilla troops..." Isabel mused skeptically.

"Exactly!" Blackwell exclaimed. "So how does this relate to Jackson Kane, you might ask? He's gotten his hands on this avatar tech and modified it to allow human beings to pilot the bodies. As for the bodies themselves, he's managed to create full clones of human beings based on DNA extracted from hair samples. Which means he could easily replace the president with an avatar and no one would be the wiser.

"I should add that, while this was all still in development, Jackson was the one who secretly funded the counterclaim lawsuits against you. He's the one who sent you to the poorhouse. He couldn't have you releasing this tech to the public, regardless of whether you called it an alien-human hybrid or otherwise."

"Convenient of him," she commented, unconvinced. "He just so happened to do this so I'd be convinced to join your side, right?"

"He used compartmentalized proxies to get the samples sent to the company you worked for," he continued as if she hadn't spoken. "Making the reverse engineering work very difficult to track down. By the time we got wind of what he was doing, it was too late. He used my own tradecraft against me. I shouldn't be surprised, I suppose, given I trained him..."

Isabel flashed Blackwell a wide grin. "So you're throwing out all these revelations one by one… interdimensional storage tech, entities who have lived with us since the dawn of time, crash retrieval programs, avatar tech. It's almost like you're trying to see which one will stick, which one will convince us to join your side. And you're even trying to claim Jackson was behind the lawsuits against me. That's a nice touch. But to be honest, I don't believe any of this. And I'm not convinced you're being truthful about why you want us here. You say you won't let us leave if we refuse to join you? What happens to us then? We're prisoners, and that's it?"

"I'm sorry you don't believe me," Blackwell told her, seeming earnest. "As to what happens to you, nothing. I'll assign you a room on the base, where you'll live indefinitely, or at least until I've determined it's safe to release you. Because as I already said, if I let you go, Jackson will likely kidnap or kill you shortly thereafter."

"Uh huh." Isabel folded her arms. "Speaking of Jackson, you still haven't answered my original question… what is he building beneath Alaska that's so dangerous?"

Blackwell sighed. "The machine Jackson and the rogue Entities are building will either decimate Earth's population when it's turned on, or it will rip apart the fabric of space and time, collapsing the barriers between dimensions so that our universe as we know it no longer exists."

"Nice," she said. "I assume the ripping-apart-the-fabric-of-space-and-time part would be accidental?"

Blackwell frowned. "Not necessarily. There are some entities who dislike the fact we experience space and time as we do. Call them jealous. And they'll do anything to end what we have here. They've sown so much confusion into the time stream, it's hard to tell which outcome is planned. Either is bad, of course, but losing a tenth of the population is preferable to losing all of space and time."

Blackwell looked like he pressed a button underneath his desk; an instant later the door shot open and the four mercenaries piled inside. "Here, come for a walk. Let me show you a little of what we have going on here. Maybe it will help convince you I'm someone worth working for."

The four men escorted Isabel and Garrett outside, while Blackwell followed behind them.

They were escorted through the brightly lit corridors of the underground facility, her footsteps echoing in the quiet, sterile environment. The white walls, cold and uninviting, bore no discernible marks or signs, revealing nothing of whatever clandestine work was carried out within. Nondescript closed doors lined the passageways, their secrets hidden from view. From some of them, she could hear strange hums, as if they contained advanced technology. From others, she heard hushed, incompressible conversations.

Finally Blackwell paused next to one door, opened it, and beckoned her and Garrett inside. The four mercenaries went with them.

In the large room inside, intricate analysis equipment had been placed in front of a large, smooth metallic egg, approximately ten feet by six feet in size. Electrodes and other measuring devices were attached to the egg, while three scientists in white lab coats momentarily looked up from their screens when Blackwell entered. They didn't seem to care that Isabel and Garrett accompanied him.

"I'm supposed to be impressed?" Isabel asked. "You have electrodes attached to the sculpture of an egg. Let's see it float or something."

Blackwell wore a wide grin. "We haven't cracked the shell of this one just yet."

"Very punny," she said with an eye roll.

"Sometimes," Blackwell continued. "When a person with a strong emanation touches it, it will start to vibrate. Would you like to try?"

"A strong emanation?" she asked.

He nodded.

She shrugged. "Whatever that means." She walked up to the large egg and stared at it.

Why not?

She rested a hand on the surface. It felt cold to the touch. She held it there for ten seconds, but felt no vibrations from the device.

"I don't think it's working." She glanced at Blackwell, and noticed the three scientists were very careful not to meet her eye. In fact, they seemed to bury themselves in their screens even further when they sensed she was looking at them.

She withdrew her hand and returned to the entrance. "Fascinating. Can we go?"

Blackwell nodded and led her outside.

They passed another door, this one with a wide window situated next to it. She peered through the glass into the darkened room. Two individuals in lab coats sat next to what looked like a high-powered laser. Beside it, a plate had been placed on a table, and she could see the red dot of the laser striking it. On the opposite side, a pattern of alternating light and dark red bands was cast on a distant screen.

A dark-skinned man sat next to the table, beside the plate, and his eyes were closed as if he was concentrating. He wasn't wearing a lab coat like the other two.

"The classic double-slit experiment," Blackwell said. "Are you familiar with the observer effect?"

"No?" Garrett said.

Isabel decided to show off her knowledge of the subject. "It demonstrates the phenomenon in quantum physics where things like photons behave both as particles and waves. When unobserved, photons create an interference pattern when they pass through two slits, like we see now, acting as waves. Think of the slits like two pebbles dropped into the surface of calm water, and as the water waves spread out, they have peaks and troughs. Where those peaks and troughs intersect, they either cancel each other out, or double up. Which is what we're seeing on the screen when the photon waves from the slit interact.

"However, the act of observation collapses that wave function, forcing the photons to act as particles, so when we measure one of the slits to find out which photon is hitting the screen, for example with a photographic plate or a polarizing filter, we see two separate, distinct bands appearing on the screen, implying that the photons are now behaving as particles, and passing through either the left slit or the right one in a straight line, just like a particle would travel.

"That only means the act of measuring interferes with the particle, changing it so that it no longer interacts with itself before hitting the screen. It's like when you check the pressure of your tire, you cause some air to escape, and so you're changing the pressure in order to observe it."

Blackwell glanced at Garrett. "What she said is mostly correct. Though I would only clarify that, when particles like electrons or photons pass through the slits, they exist in a superposition of possible states. The interference pattern that appears on the wall represents the probability distribution of where these particles are likely to be detected.

"Bright regions on the wall indicate the higher probabilities, the dark regions the lower probabilities. This phenomenon illustrates that at the quantum level, we can only predict the likelihood of an unobserved particle's location, rather than its precise position, highlighting the fundamentally probabilistic nature of quantum physics.

"So for example, let's say you fire an electron at the slits one at a time, what do you think would appear on the other side over time?"

Garrett pursed his lips. "Well the electron would have to be lined up with either the first slit, or the second. Then you'd see a dot on one side or the other."

"Not true," Blackwell said. "The electron

launcher would actually have to be lined up with the center of both slits, and when fired, the electron will either pass through the first slit, *or* the second. Because electrons behave as waves, too."

"Oh, okay," Garrett said. "Then in that case, fifty percent will pass through the first slit, and the other fifty percent the second, so you'd get two dots on the other side."

"Again, incorrect," Blackwell told him. "Over time, you'll see a distribution pattern similar to what you're seeing on the wall right now: a series of light and dark bands of varying intensities. Because as each electron hits the plate and travels through one of the slits, it behaves like a wave, and follows the probability distribution of the bands you see on the wall. So the first electron might hit in the exact center. The next might hit in the region of the first band to the left, the third might hit in the next band, and so forth, with the probabilities declining the further out from the center we move."

"That doesn't make sense," Garrett said.

"Perhaps not, but then consider what happens when you measure the electron," Blackwell said. "Say with a SQUID, a superconducting quantum interference device. Then it makes even less sense, because all of a sudden fifty percent of the electrons on the other side line up with the first slit, and the other fifty percent line up with the second slit. Just as you originally predicted. So you see, the act of observation changes reality."

"Not true," Isabel interjected. "Again, that only means the act of measuring interfered with the particle, changing a fundamental property. Remember my tire pressure example?"

"My point is, we don't really understand why this

effect occurs," Blackwell told him. "Our current physics can't really explain it. That's why we've had string theory and brane theory and everything else since the general theory of relativity. But your brother has finally figured it out. The probability distributions are a byproduct of the way the dimensions stacked above our own are compacted and represented in our space and time. Anyway, I didn't bring you here to laud your brother's discoveries in physics. Keep watching the bands on that screen…"

As she watched, the intensity of the light and dark bands flickered ever so slightly.

"I see them flickering," she said. "A bit like a flame. That's it."

"That flickering you see is caused by the man seated next to the table," Blackwell explained. "He's a Kundalini adept. He's collapsing the wave function. With his mind. The flickering you see is the change in probabilities he's causing as his consciousness inter-feres with the slit."

"Doubtful," she said dismissively. "The flickering is because of inherit randomness in the light intensity."

"This is a single-mode laser," Blackwell coun-tered. "The wavelength is well-defined, with minimal divergence or frequency modulation. I'll prove it."

Blackwell knocked on the glass and the dark-skinned man opened his eyes. When he saw Black-well, his face cracked into a huge grin, and he waved happily.

Blackwell smiled and waved back. Without glancing at Isabel, he told her: "Look at the screen now. Notice, no flickering?"

Blackwell was right. The pattern on the wall had completely stabilized.

"Coincidence," Isabel said. "Or some other variable is at play. The only way I'll believe he's actually collapsing the wave function with his mind is if he closes his eyes and we see two separate beams, like you'd get if you actually placed a polarizing filter on one of the slits."

"No one is that powerful," Blackwell said quietly. "No one human, anyway. And he's not doing it with his mind. But his consciousness. There is a difference."

"What you're saying is impossible," Isabel said.

Blackwell finally looked at her. "Is it? You've heard of the Global Consciousness Project?"

"No... but the very name sounds suspect."

He smiled patiently. "A group of scientists set up sixty-five random number generators, or RNGs, distributed throughout the world. The point was to test whether global events and the impacts these events have on people could influence the behavior of these RNGs. The group constructed the RNGs to ensure the generated sequences were as random as possible, taking precautions to shield the devices from external interference.

"The group found that the devices exhibited completely random behavior during ordinary times—issuing a non-repeating, alternating set of 0s and 1s, but during major global events or crises, structure emerged from the data. Order, from chaos. A series of 0s or 1s repeated on the days of the events, when there should have only been random 0s and 1s. Strange deviations from the norm that could not be explained. After testing against five hundred formally defined events over twenty years, the odds against chance for such outcomes was above a trillion to one."

"But the experiment could have been tainted by subjectivity," Isabel scoffed. "A bunch of 0s and 1s in a row is not something unexpected when you're talking about random number generators. The experimenters could have biased the results: for example they saw a bunch of zeroes happening in a row on a certain day, and then they went off to look for any events that might line up with those deviations. Blindly selecting world events to 'explain away' the so-called lack of randomness, for example tracing it back to a world cup win in Argentina, or an Earthquake in Turkey."

"That's entirely possible," Blackwell conceded. "Or the physical world could indeed be affected by unusual moments of focused consciousness. Is it really so hard to believe that randomness can be influenced? Especially considering that randomness is really just the probability distribution of the wave function. All I'm asking you to do is keep an open mind. Humanity is capable of great things. We simply need to evolve a step further. Expand our consciousness. We're already at the early stages of this evolution in consciousness, and the only way to work our way out of this initial phase is to believe it's possible. To believe we're more than just the containers we call our minds and bodies."

She glanced at the four mercenaries who remained standing and at the ready beside Blackwell. "Is your boss always like this?"

They ignored her comment.

"He's claiming psychokinesis is real, courtesy of the untapped power of the human mind," Garrett quipped. "Next he's going to tell us that remote viewing is a thing!"

"It is," Blackwell replied. "Though it's accuracy

can vary wildly. But it's dirt cheap, and if we can get fifteen percent accuracy with an Intel gathering technique that barely costs us anything, of course we're going to use it. And remember, all of this is possible not because of the mind. No, this is beyond the mind. As I mentioned, it's done by consciousness. And while influencing randomness with one's consciousness is not particularly easy, it's not impossible, either. But it does require focus. And since we're still in the early stages of our evolution, some people are better at it than others, but we all have the seed, the germ... because we all have consciousness. Anyway, I digress. Let's move on."

Blackwell gestured for Isabel and Garrett to continue forward.

Before she moved on, she noted that the dark-skinned man inside the room had shut his eyes again, and the photon interference pattern on the screen had begun flickering once more.

31

I sabel and Garrett continued the tour through the brightly lit corridors of the underground facility, though there wasn't really much else to see. Most of the doors were closed, and there were no windows into these rooms. Sometimes a door was left ajar, but she spotted only people behind desks or scientists hunched next to computer screens connected to scanning electron microscopes, among other highlights.

One corridor did however have a particular long window embedded in the wall, providing a view of what must have been a bio-containment lab, judging from the researchers clad in full hazmat suits who worked diligently next to thick, transparent glass boxes housing test subjects, including mice and bats.

"Looks like you're developing bioweapons," she commented.

Blackwell glanced at his men. "Activate mute."

Almost as one, the four men touched the frames of the thick glasses they wore. Red lights appeared on the frames.

Isabel cocked her head. "Activate mute? As in, they can't hear us? Nice augmented reality glasses."

"Precisely," Blackwell replied. "These men aren't cleared for what I'm about to tell you."

"I guess I should be honored, or the very least flattered," she quipped.

Blackwell ignored the comment. "The men in the hazmat suits aren't developing a bioweapon, but a vaccine. A few weeks ago a mole in Jackson's compound revealed a plan to unleash a respiratory virus on the world. It proved to be a distraction, meant to muddy the time stream in an attempt to hide the true intent of the competing NHI faction. But we'd still like to create a vaccine, just in case."

"That's the second time you've mentioned the 'time stream,'" Garrett noted.

"Yes," Blackwell agreed. "The Entities experience time differently than us. How it's been explained to me is, they see past, present and future all at once. To them, time looks like a great tree. The branches of the future are the part of the tree above ground, while the divergences of the past are the roots buried underneath. The trunk, meanwhile, is the present moment, wherein all the previous branches converge *to*, and all the future branches converge *from*.

"Only one present is active at any given moment in our world. The many diverging branches of the future can be thought of as representations of the wave functions we talked about previously, wave functions that have not yet collapsed to form the present.

"The branches are probabilistic of course, but sometimes they align, converging so that only a few distinct possibilities present themselves rather than the usual infinite. These inflection points limit the possible futures, and one of those possibilities was the release of the virus. The other outcomes I mentioned —using a machine to rip apart the fabric of space time or to decimate the population—were obscured by that first inflection point, which is why I said it muddied the time stream. In any case, our Entity allies neutralized the threat of the virus. It took the teleportation of an entire airplane, but they did it."

"They took an entire airplane?" Isabel said in disbelief.

"Yes," Blackwell agreed. "It was messy to cover that one up, believe me. Our allies wouldn't tell us why they did it either—they aren't the most communicative bunch at the best of times. In any case, they prevented that disastrous inflection point from occurring. They've intervened similarly in the past, which is part of the reason why we call them the Verndari— which means the protector in Old Norse. Though sometimes their interventions are questionable... we're not sure if it was them who caused radar glitches at certain nuclear launch sites in the old USSR for example, in an attempt to trick the Soviet operators into launching a first strike against the United States."

"So if these Verndari didn't tell you about the virus, how did you figure out why they took the plane?" Garrett asked.

"The passenger and cargo manifests left a trail back to Jackson," Blackwell replied. "We did some digging, and found out one of the men on board the flight had previously worked for me. One Evan Fischer. He'd left my employment roughly six months after Jackson's fiery departure, no doubt to work for the traitor. Our channelers managed to figure out he was still alive after the plane vanished. I told you remote viewing success can vary wildly? This was one of the successes. They indicated we could expect him to return home shortly. So we set up a watch outside his house, and lo and behold, Evan Fischer showed up: sole survivor of the vanished flight."

"My men followed him and his wife when they departed for his lakeside cottage shortly after arrival, and they got to watch his wife kill him in the middle of the lake. We had reason to believe his wife had become an avatar for one of the opposing entities, who we call the Nesut. We captured and interrogated her and learned the truth.

"Unfortunately, we had to reveal some black technology we've developed that we didn't want the NHIs to know about," Blackwell said. "This includes our allies the Verndari, in addition to the Nesut."

"Wait, you said his wife became an avatar?" Isabel asked. "They can take over our bodies?"

Blackwell nodded. "Unfortunately, if we let our guard down or invite them in, they can."

She glanced at Garrett. "What a terrifying thought… assuming it's true."

But Garrett seemed to be more concerned about something else. "Why keep this black technology you mentioned from your inter-dimensional allies? Especially if they're sharing tech with you?"

"Let's just say, we're not entirely sure how long they plan to remain our allies," Blackwell replied. "We'd like to have some things up our sleeves, contingency plans in the event we ever need them. In any case, the virus plan was a distraction. Meant to send our remote viewers astray, as well as upend the predictive models of our entity allies. We, and they, knew a big inflection point was coming up, one that could impact our future as a species, and everything pointed to the release of that virus. But that event was meant only to sow confusion, to distract us from the other coming inflection point… their real plan."

"The device beneath the Alaskan mountains…" Isabel said.

Blackwell leaned against the wall. "That would be the one. While the Verndari weren't very forthcoming about the virus, they were about this. And adamant that you and Garrett help."

"I'm not sure how we can help you." Isabel truly meant it. "I'm just an out-of-work molecular biologist who lost her brother to the military industrial complex. I don't think I'm ever going to work for you guys again."

Blackwell seemed astounded. "Even if it means saving a billion lives? You have a role. I've already told you a lot, but I can tell you more. Much more. But first you must agree to help."

"We can't," Isabel said. "At least I can't."

"And I go where she goes," Garrett said stubbornly.

Blackwell exhaled in exasperation. "All right. Obviously you need more time. So I'll give you that time. But I'll need a positive response sooner rather than later."

Isabel was going to counter him, but then she thought of something that unraveled his whole story. "Wait, why don't your entity friends simply 'teleport' this base in Alaska you mentioned, the same way they took the airplane?"

"They can't," Blackwell explained patiently. "The Nesut have built the base upon one of the planet's lines of force, making it very difficult for the Verndari to intercede. At least without help."

"Very convenient of them. And that's where we come in, huh?" She glanced at Garrett. "Why do I get the impression this is all some sort of elaborate suicide mission?"

For some reason, Garrett seemed to wince when she said those last words.

"As I told you, I'll reveal more once you agree to provide assistance. But decide quickly. Time is short. They might be activating the device tomorrow, or the day after." Blackwell signaled the mercenaries to continue escorting them deeper.

The four men renewed the march, urging Isabel and Garrett forward. They'd kept their glasses on mute, at least she thought they did, because the red lights still appeared on the frames.

The loud clicks of Blackwell's heels echoed behind them as he kept pace.

She had a lot to think about. Competing Entity factions. A mission that could potentially save a billion lives. And whether or not any of it was actually true.

Finally the group stopped in front of one particular door at the end of a corridor.

"This is your room," Blackwell announced.

One of the mercenaries produced a key card and unlocked the door, revealing a modest room with two single beds. The walls were painted in muted gray, and the beds featured crisp white sheets and neatly folded blankets, with a small bedside table between them holding a utilitarian lamp. There was even an en suite bathroom on the far side, replete with sink, toilet, and shower. There was a mini-fridge set against one wall.

Blackwell offered Isabel a small two-way radio. "What's this?"

"Your direct line to me." He glanced at the ceiling, toward two antenna ears. "It taps into Wi-Fi points distributed throughout the compound. When you change your mind about joining me, give me a ping."

He turned to go.

"You say the Entities want us to join you?" Isabel blurted out. "The Vern… the Verndari?"

He glanced over his shoulder at her. "They do."

"I want to talk to them," she demanded.

He nodded slowly. "You may at your convenience." He reached into a pocket and handed her a set of ear buds and a portable music player, as if he'd expected this very question to come up.

Puzzled, she studied the items. "What's this?"

Blackwell grinned. "Binaural beats."

"Wha— why?"

He cocked an eyebrow. "Haven't you ever meditated?"

"Well, sure, but—"

"You said you wanted to talk to them. Then talk. Meditate. Listen to these beats. Open your heart, come from a place of love, and ask for guidance."

She stared at him incredulously. "You want me to ask for guidance from a place of love?"

"Yes," he said. "That will put your mind in the proper state. Eliminate all fear and negativity during your trance. Otherwise, you might reach the wrong entities."

"Wouldn't want that," she commented, shoving the portable music player into Garrett's hands, along with the Wi-Fi two-way radio. "All of this sounds so very woo."

Blackwell smiled patiently. "Most of how the universe works, at its core, is woo, at least in regards to our current understanding. Remember Clarke's third law: any sufficiently advanced technology is indistinguishable from magic."

"Sure." She entered the room and Garrett followed. One of the mercenaries shut the door behind them.

Garrett tried the door handle. "Locked. Though even if we could get out, they probably left a couple of men outside."

With a sigh, she sat on one of the beds. "Might as well be a prison cell."

Garrett perched beside her and rested the music player next to her thigh. "You're not buying any of this, are you?"

"I don't actually know, to be honest," she said. "It's a lot to digest. I think I'd need to see proof first. Beyond 'meditate and you'll talk to them.' Like show me a working avatar body, or a craft other than a big inanimate egg sitting on the floor like some abstract sculpture. And not some flickering double-slit experiment. Even better, let's see this inter-dimensional storage prototype that's supposedly working."

Garrett nodded. "It seems like a convoluted mess of lies, doesn't it?"

"It does," she agreed. "And yet, why is my gut telling me it's all true? You told me to always trust my gut, but in this case, I *know* it's wrong. I know it."

"What if it's not?" Garrett's eyes dropped.

She followed his gaze, and realized he was looking at the music player. "You don't really think I should do what he said, do you?"

Garrett shrugged. "It's worth a try. It's not any weirder than any of the other things he's told us. And, I didn't tell you this before, but I... remember when I told you I had a hunch that you were in trouble?"

"Wait," Isabel told him. "They're probably listening in on us."

He nodded, and then leaned in close to whisper in her ear. She felt his hot breath on her ear, and to be honest, she kind of liked it. But his somber words ruined the feeling.

"When I was sitting on my deck, the day I decided to check in on you, I was staring into the flames of my fire table, and I had a vision, a day dream. Of you. And I heard a voice in my head. 'She needs you,' it said. I don't know how to explain it. I've been trying to explain it every moment of every day since then, by conventional means, but I can't. Maybe it's time to try an unconventional explanation."

When he pulled away, she found herself missing just how close he had been. But she dismissed that thought, reminding herself he was just a friend. A good one, at that.

His words made her think once more of her own weird experiences with the glowing lights in the sky, and she wondered if she should share what she'd seen with him. But she decided not to, because despite the seeming earnestness in his explanation about the premonition, she had the unnerving feeling he had left something out.

"All right, I'll try meditating," she said. "If anything, at least I might be able to finally relax."

32

I sabel placed a towel from the bathroom on the floor. She sat cross-legged on it and let the ear buds fill her hearing with calming binaural beats.

She closed her eyes and thought of Virginia Beach, imagining the waves gently lapping against the white sand shores. She envisioned herself laughing as she danced across the wet sand in sandals. She focused on the love she felt as she did that. Love for the Earth, love for her fellow human beings. Thankful for being alive.

Unasked for, the exploding helicopter that had killed James intruded into her thoughts, and the love was replaced with fear, anger, frustration, and grief.

She tried to put the image into the mental box reserved for distractions, tried to visualize protective energy swirling around her body, shielding her from the helicopter, but she couldn't. Her legs, chest and abs were tense, too tense.

She couldn't relax.

Her seated pose likely wasn't helping... she decided to try lying down.

Meditating while supine was tricky, because she often unintentionally fell asleep, but she felt it was the only way she could relax her body completely at the moment.

So she got up and repositioned the towel so it covered the whole floor. She glanced at Garrett, but he was lying on the bed and not paying her any attention. He seemed to be staring at the ceiling, perhaps wrestling with demons of his own.

She lay back on the towel and closed her eyes. She remembered Blackwell's words.

Open your heart, come from a place of love, and ask for guidance.

She began the visualization anew. White sand. Love. Thankfulness.

She took several deep breaths, and with every exhale, produced a soft, gentle tone that caused her throat and lungs to resonate ever so slightly.

While she did that, she visualized a vortex of swirling energy around her body anew, and imagined drawing white light in the form of positive energy into it, and deflecting dark bands and mists of negative energy. She visualized Garrett on the bed beside her and redirected some of that light toward him, wanting to share the energy instead of keeping it all to herself. He'd looked like he could use the boost.

She stopped vocalizing the resonant tone, and forgot about her breathing. Instead, one by one, she loosened her muscles, starting with her toes, then calves, working her way up her midsection, and finally the face. When every muscle in her body was relaxed, she reminded herself of her intention: communication and guidance.

Communication. Guidance.

She began to count slowly, from one to ten.

1… 2… 3…

At ten, she told herself her mind would be completely clear and ready to receive guidance.

4… 5… 6…

She reached ten. Her mind was pristine, as promised. Occasionally thoughts and words bubbled up but she ignored them with ease and they soon dissipated. She had attained complete, mental silence —a rare thing for her.

She floated there for several moments, enjoying the quietude. But then she remembered her intent.

So into the silence, she made a request.

If anyone out there is listening, grant me guidance.

But in answer came only the blissful calm.

After several more moments, she saw herself in the desert and looking up at the night sky. The milky way was visible. She could see so many stars, and felt so small and infinitesimal among them. She was still surrounded by a protective sphere of light, but its intensity had faded into the background, allowing her to relish the beauty of the heavens.

She squinted, and saw a small, glowing dot moving amid the stars. Its movements were slow and deliberate as it made its way across the sky, just as if it were guiding her, like it had on two occasions before.

Guidance…

She followed, slogging barefoot across the dunes, pursuing the glowing dot. Her feet sunk deep into the sand with each step, the individual grains seeming to claw and pull at her as if to hold her back. She was moving too slowly… the dot was creeping ahead, slipping closer to the horizon with every passing moment, and if she didn't quicken her pace she'd soon lose it. But she couldn't go any faster, not with that thick sand bogging down every step.

Wait a second. I don't have to walk…

She stopped and focused all of her attention on the dot until it was all she could see. There was nothing but her, the dark sky, and that dot.

She suddenly zoomed up toward the heavens until the object of her desire hovered before her—a small, baseball-sized orb of pure light. Though feelings of love and awe filled her, she remembered her intent.

Grant me guidance.

And then she sensed it. A vague presence. As if something was watching her. The sensation wasn't coming from the orb, but somewhere behind her. She turned around, but there was nothing there.

She reinforced the protective vortex of swirling energy around her body, and told herself nothing could harm her, not while that vortex surrounded her.

Who are you? Show yourself.

She turned back toward the orb of pure light. It floated toward her resonating shield; instinctively she poured more energy into it, drawing from the positive flow of the universe around her. Doing so only seemed to attract the orb: it moved toward her even faster, as if it was made of the same positive energy. She didn't panic, instead trusting that nothing could harm her here. The glowing orb seemed to be emanating love and joy, which only further calmed her. A part of her thought it might be a trick. Another part of her fully embraced that love and bliss, and welcomed it.

The orb passed through her protective membrane and touched her core. She felt a warm sensation in her solar plexus, and then, just like that, the sphere entered her body, or the visualization of her body anyway, and the heat dissipated, as if she'd fully absorbed its light.

The vague presence was gone. Even so, she believed it had… tagged… her somehow, forming some link between itself and her consciousness, placing a marker so it could return and find her among the sea of consciousnesses that was humanity.

How did it find me before, then? When I was lost in the woods. Or hunted at the motel?

She didn't really know. She could only trust that she had done the right thing.

She began counting backwards from ten, with the intention to emerge from her meditative trance and back into waking consciousness.

When she reached the number one, her memory of everything that had happened after asking for guidance became vague, dissipating into the realm of the subconscious, so that by the time she opened her eyes, her first thought was:

What just happened?

Well, one thing was for certain: she felt completely at peace. Along with a strange sense of certainty that everything would be all right.

She knew then what she had to do.

She sat up and glanced at Garrett, who remained on the bed. He'd shut his eyes, but he opened them again when he sensed her moving.

"I'm going to help Blackwell," she announced.

Still lying down, Garrett turned his head toward her. The usual haunted look had momentarily left his eyes, and there was a peacefulness in them she hadn't seen in a long time.

"All right." Garrett didn't ask her if she'd succeeded in her communication attempt, and she was grateful for that.

She didn't want to second guess herself on this.

LIEUTENANT MITCHELL MADE his way through the underground compound and stopped when he arrived at the aptly named Office of Informatics. He used his key card to enter, and nodded at the lead computer science technician who worked near the entrance. He made his way through the cubicles until he found the one he was looking for.

"Oh hey, Marcus," the glasses-wearing techie named Abigail said, looking up from her keyboard.

"Did you make a copy of the LockKey yet?" the lieutenant asked.

"As requested." She handed over the stick. "Is all of that stuff on there real?"

"I can neither confirm nor deny any of it," he replied.

"Misinformation, then," she said. "Anything else I can do for you?"

"That was it." He pocketed the memory stick. "Thank you, as always."

She broke into a big goofy grin. "My pleasure."

"We'll have to go for lunch together sometime soon," Mitchell told her.

"I'd love that!" she said enthusiastically.

Mitchell flashed her an indulging smile and then made his way back to the entrance of the room. He was well aware of the dome camera in the ceiling watching and recording his every movement.

Eventually Blackwell would find out that Mitchell had made a copy of James Lockwood's research, of course.

But by then it would be too late.

33

I sabel awoke. Without windows or a clock, she'd lost track of any sense of time, and guessed it was morning. She rubbed her eyes and then sat up.

The motion-activated lights turned on, prompting Garrett to rise as well.

"What time is it?" she asked groggily.

He glanced at her, his face appearing just as weary as she felt. "I don't know."

Yesterday, after she'd agree to help, Blackwell had gathered her and Garrett into a conference room and briefed them on the planned mission. At first Isabel didn't agree with much of what was shared, but Blackwell could be very convincing. She had to admit that a part of her had volunteered solely so she could "explore" some of the new technology Blackwell had promised they'd get to play with.

Still, it had all happened so very fast. Now that she was sitting here and ready to begin, she almost couldn't believe she had agreed to do this in the first place.

Crash retrieval programs. Inter-dimensional storage tech. Non-human intelligences watching and pulling strings.

A few days ago, she would have never believed any of this even existed, let alone that she'd be a part of it.

But then her brother had died…

She went over to the table and grabbed the Wi-Fi two-way radio. She pressed the "transmit" button and said: "Hello?"

"Blackwell," a familiar voice came from the other end.

"Is it done?" she asked.

"Yes," he replied. "Everything is ready and going as planned."

"Should we be feeling this groggy?" she asked him.

"It's perfectly normal," Blackwell replied. "It will take a while for the drugs to completely kick in. By the time you reach Alaska you should be ready to go."

She smiled sardonically. "Assuming Jackson's men actually take us to Alaska…"

"They'll take you," Blackwell assured her. "Lieutenant Mitchell will be down to escort you shortly."

She set down the radio and rubbed her eyes once more between her thumb and index finger. She heard grunting from the floor beside her, and saw that Garrett was doing push-ups.

"Someone's already adapting," she commented.

"Exercise," he replied. "Best way to naturally boost serotonin."

"Uh huh." She got up, spread a blanket on the floor next to him. "I'm going to try making contact again."

They were both given a drug cocktail meant to

increase the activity of dopamine and norepinephrine, as well as triggering the release of additional neurotransmitters like serotonin and the synthesis of certain neuropeptides. Basically Adderall on steroids.

It was meant to enhance the mind-body connection and improve performance for the mission, and in theory would help her more easily connect with higher consciousness.

She wasn't entirely sure she bought it, however, given how she felt. She reminded herself that it was supposed to take some time to kick in.

She sat down on the blanket and closed her eyes. She had to fight the grogginess, which made it a constant battle to stay awake. She didn't dare lie down for this.

Once she focused, the meditation came relatively easy this morning. Before she even reached the count of ten, her mind had cleared.

And shortly thereafter, she sensed a presence.

Her eyes shot open. "It's here."

"Who's here?" Garret was doing sit-ups now.

The presence hadn't gone away. She couldn't quite place where it was in the room, but she knew it was there, as if it had latched on to her consciousness by means of the "tag" it had placed yesterday.

"One of the entities," she said distractedly.

Garrett stopped. "Where?"

But then it faded. "It's gone. *Something* was here, but I lost it. For all I know, it was one of the bad ones."

Garrett shrugged, then continued his sit-ups.

She clambered wearily to her feet, went to the mini-fridge and picked out a Red Bull. It was probably a bad idea to drink it, given the current drug cocktail she was on, but she supposed Blackwell wouldn't have allowed the staff to put it in her fridge if it wasn't safe.

Right?

She downed the Red Bull in one go. There, much better.

Not really.

Her gaze groggily drifted to the door, and she froze, becoming alert instantly. And not because of the Red Bull.

The hair stood up on the back of her neck, and she blinked several times in disbelief.

She saw a shadow outlined against the door, as if cast by a being her eyes could not see yet whose body still blocked light at the quantum level. The shadow seemed humanoid in shape.

"Uhhh," Isabel said.

Garrett was doing bicycle crunches; he followed her shocked gaze to the door and instantly froze.

The shadow seemed to sink into the wall next to the door, before vanishing entirely—to her shock and disbelief, the door unlocked and opened inward of its own accord. The creak those hinges made was the creepiest sound she'd heard in a while.

She exchanged a frightened glance with Garrett, and they both warily approached the doorway. Garrett took the lead.

There were no men standing on guard outside, which made some sense, she supposed, because they were all "on the same team" now. Still…

Garrett stepped outside and she followed. She gazed down the corridor, toward the T intersection ahead, but saw no one.

The shadow was gone.

"You saw it, didn't you?" she asked.

"I did," Garrett confirmed.

She grabbed onto his thick forearm. "Then where did it go?"

He didn't answer. Not at first. Then: "Could it be a side effect of the drugs?"

"I don't really think we'd have a shared hallucination…" she told him.

She heard the footfalls of heavy boots coming from around the bend ahead, and tensed.

A man dressed in black fatigues rounded the corner.

Isabel felt relieved, despite how menacing the man looked, because at least he wasn't a shadow.

"You," Garrett stated coldly.

"It's time," the man told him just as icily. "Are you ready?"

"You know him?" Isabel asked Garrett.

"He's the guy I captured outside Archer's home," Garrett explained. "Lieutenant Marcus Mitchell."

"I *let* you capture me," Mitchell corrected. "Stay close."

Mitchell led them through the twisting hallways.

She kind of liked the sudden tension in the air between the two men, because it helped her forget what she'd just witnessed.

Was it on our side? Or a member of the opposing faction? The… Nesut?

She wondered vaguely if she'd mistakenly allowed one of the wrong entities to latch onto her consciousness.

That would probably be bad…

They reached an elevator. When the doors opened, an armed guard waited inside.

"Good morning, sir," the guard told Mitchell.

Mitchell nodded absently. "Morning."

The three of them entered, and Mitchell pressed the topmost button.

She watched the floor indicator slowly decrease, dropping from ten all the way to one, at which point the elevator came to a halt.

As the doors silently slid open, Isabel stepped into a hangar of sorts. Her eyes widened in astonishment as she took in the vast, cavernous space, which seemed deceptively empty at first glance. Its metallic expanse stretched before her, with a glossy concrete floor that reflected the dim overhead lights.

The most curious aspect was the odd placement of numerous HVAC devices scattered across the hangar's floor, their metal frames and ductwork sprawling like some mechanical maze. The soft hum of the ventilation system filled the air, evidence of the vast underground complex that relied upon it. Meanwhile the large hangar doors at the far end remained firmly closed, but there were grills all along the west and east sides to allow air to circulate from outside.

It wouldn't be uncommon to find so many HVAC units positioned near the surface entrance of an underground structure like a parking garage, but she found it peculiar that the engineers had placed them inside the hangar itself. Until she realized they were doing it to completely obscure the presence of the underground base from the spy satellites of adversaries, because so many HVACs outside the building would be a dead giveaway.

Mitchell led them to a back entrance, where an SUV was waiting. He handed Garrett a key FOB, an ID card, and a Visitor Pass.

"Go. You'll have a five minute head start. Show this at the main gate and any other checkpoints along the way." He pointed at the ID and Visitor Pass.

"Also, you'll have to give me a shiner. So it's believable when the moles find out."

Smiling obligingly, Garrett punched him in the face.

Mitchell stumbled backward and Isabel rushed to support him. "Garrett! Did you have to hit him so hard?" She studied Mitchell's quickly swelling eye. "Are you all right?"

"What?" Garrett raised his hands defensively. "He asked for a shiner."

"I'm fine, I'm fine." Mitchell shoved her toward Garrett. "Go!"

She reluctantly left him and joined Garrett in the SUV. He drove toward the main gates of the Air Force base.

Using the ID and Visitor Pass, they crossed all the checkpoints and exited the gates without issue.

Then they headed north for the next thirty minutes until they reached the designated motel. They bought a room using the money Blackwell had given them and settled in for the wait.

Blackwell was supposed to leak to certain moles in his organization the news that Isabel and Garrett had refused his offer and escaped from his custody: there was a certain spy satellite operator who Blackwell would make certain was on duty when the SUV "theft" was reported by Mitchell.

"I'm still convinced Jackson's men are going to shoot us on sight when they arrive," Isabel told Garrett.

Garrett pursed his lips. "They may or may not."

She smiled sadly. "Assuming they actually come."

"Oh they will. I just wish Blackwell had let me keep my Glock."

They sat near the window with the curtains

closed; a crack in the middle allowed them to peer outside.

"You can sleep, if you want," Garrett offered.

She rubbed her forehead. "I wish. I'm actually starting to feel a bit better. I don't want to become groggy all over again."

Garrett chuckled softly. "The drugs are finally kicking in, are they?"

"Or the Red Bull worked." She stared at her hands. "Is this even real? I can't help but feel I'm living some sort of dream right now. Or nightmare, maybe. We're working for some shadowy organization, heading into a trap, hoping for help from interdimensional beings who reveal themselves to us as dark shapes."

Garrett exhaled with a loud huff. "It's real. Unfortunately. We're doing this. For good or for bad."

"You think it will work? That they'll actually help us?"

"No idea," he replied. "So far I haven't seen any evidence that the so-called Verndari or whatever they're called will help us."

"Well it *did* open the door for us…" Isabel quipped.

"Nice of it," Garrett agreed.

She shrugged. "Maybe it was just trying to show us that it was there and ready to offer assistance."

He grunted. "Like an employee at a mall kiosk."

"Yup!' She studied him a moment, her smile fading. "We didn't really get time to talk last night after the briefing. Everything was so rushed. I'm not sure when I'll get another chance, so I just wanted to say thank you. For everything."

He nodded slowly. "Thank you as well."

"Me?" She was a bit stunned. "Why? You've saved my life multiple times now."

"And you've saved mine," he countered quietly. He looked down at his hands, seeming suddenly emotional.

Her heart went out to him. "Garrett. What's wrong? Is there something you want to tell me?" She squeezed his hand, and when he met her gaze, there were tears in his eyes. "Oh Garrett."

"Nothing," he said. "Nothing's wrong. I'm just... glad I found you again."

"And I'm glad I found you." She gave him a hug right there while sitting next to him.

After a moment he broke free and told her gruffly: "Have to watch the parking lot."

She smiled sadly and looked away. With a sigh, she excused herself and went to the bathroom to freshen up.

After washing her face she stared at her reflection in the mirror. Her vision seemed particularly vibrant today, the colors of her body and clothes bright and lush, the details resplendent and sharp. Her skin was almost glowing—it wasn't from a sheen or anything like that, as she wasn't sweating at all.

Definitely had to be the drugs.

She finished up and rejoined Garrett at the table, but found herself fidgeting with nervous energy, so she sat in front of the TV instead, and put it on a random channel, not really paying attention.

It wasn't long before Garrett announced that vehicles were pulling up en masse in the parking lot just outside the unit.

"Men in black are emerging from the vehicles," he added. "And they're armed to the teeth."

She suppressed a sudden panic. "What should I do?"

He met her gaze coolly. "Stay calm. Remain where you are. When they kick the door open, don't react. When they tell you to put your hands in the air, do it."

His voice sounded so deadly calm. It worried her. "And what are you going to do?"

He shrugged. "Put my hands in the air."

True to his word, when the door exploded inward Garrett didn't react, and when told to raise his hands, he did so. Isabel followed his example, and they were searched, stripped of weapons, flexi-cuffed, and then herded outside into one of the SUVs.

Hoods were pulled over their heads and then they were on the move.

By now Isabel had lost track of how many times she'd been forcibly hauled into a SUV and kidnapped.

Apparently it's become a common thing for me.

She half expected there to be an attack on the vehicle so that the crazy time-loop she kept finding herself trapped within could repeat once more.

But no such attack came.

In about thirty minutes the vehicle came to a halt. She was escorted outside and up a flight of steps, then forced into a soft seat. Her flexicuffs were cut away, and someone pulled off her hood. She resided in the back of a private jet. Garrett sat on a couch across from her. The black clad men lurked nearby, the straps of their rifles still slung over their shoulders. She wondered what would happen to the cabin if they fired their guns in here.

Wouldn't be pretty.

The mercenaries weren't wearing balaclavas, and their eyes were visible behind the glasses they wore.

She met the gaze of one of her captors.

"Where are you taking us?" she tried.

The man looked away.

She gazed longingly out the window as the plane took off. If she and Garrett were being taken to Jackson's supposed base in Alaska, as Blackwell predicted, that meant their flight time would be close to six hours.

She closed her eyes, and didn't think she'd sleep at all, as the engines were rather loud for a private jet. But eventually she did fall in and out of sleep, and that helped pass the time. She did worry that the sleep would make her groggy again, though.

At one point, she thought they were getting close to arrival because the plane's engine hum had lowered in pitch, and outside they were descending over a large mountain range.

Several orbs, roughly the size of small cars, approached the private jet and began to chaperon it. Blackwell had told her about these, said they belonged to the opposing faction of Entities—the Nesut. Apparently, these small craft, as inconspicuous as they might seem, could disable any fighter jets or missiles Blackwell launched at Jackson's base. They could also vaporize any unauthorized vehicles that tried to approach via land routes.

Meanwhile Blackwell's allies, the Verndari, could not interface with our world at all here. Something about the "lines of force" where the base resided. But why the Nesut could, she had no idea.

Hence the need for Blackwell to try a more clandestine, unorthodox approach. And that's where Garrett and Isabel came in.

During the entire trip, the presence she'd felt in the room hadn't returned: she wondered if it had abandoned them. Perhaps the so-called "force lines" of this place prevented it from finding her consciousness, despite the tag.

I'm not sure I can do this alone.

She glanced at Garrett and when he met her eyes, she felt strength and determination filling her.

I'm not alone.

Yes, she could do this. As long as Garrett was with her.

She glanced through the window and watched as the private jet touched down at a remote airstrip next to the mountains.

The hood was pulled over her head again and she was flexicuffed, then hauled to her feet in darkness.

34

S till hooded, with his hands bound in front of him, Garrett felt the stomach-lurching motion of an elevator descent, followed by the characteristic pinging of floors. He counted twenty floors in total before the elevator slowed to a halt.

That was fairly deep.

When the doors opened, he was led forward. From the way the sound echoed around him, he had the impression he was walking inside an underground cave system. The floor was somewhat uneven beneath his feet, as if it had been carved directly into the rock.

He picked out Isabel's dainty footsteps among those of the booted men, along with her soft breathing beside him. He occasionally let his elbow glance her as he walked, mostly to reassure himself that their captives hadn't separated them.

A short time later the group came to halt. Someone slid his hood away, and after confirming Isabel was still at his side—her hood had also been removed—he surveyed the chamber.

Sharp angles in the rock implied that the place had been meticulously hewn into the stone. The low ceiling gave the chamber an air of heaviness—Garrett could almost feel the weight of the mountain pushing down on him from above. Dim ceiling lights with unknown power sources cast shadows that danced along the uneven stone walls.

Ornate shelves delved into the rock held thick tomes spanning the gamut from the geopolitical to the paranormal—such titles as *The Grand Chessboard: American Primacy and Its Geostrategic Imperatives* rubbed shoulders with *Penetration: The Question of Extraterrestrial and Human Telepathy*.

In the center of the room, an expansive holographic globe hovered above a rocky recess in the floor, its dynamic display illuminating the room with shifting data. It seemed to be tracking different aircraft across the world, given the flight numbers above most of the craft. But some of those craft had names that would belong to no such human flights, such as UAP 9982 and so forth.

On the far side of the chamber, a high-backed leather chair was situated behind a large rock whose top was shaved down to form a desk of sorts. Next to it, a man stood off to one side with his hands folded behind his back. His short-cropped hair, as dark as the shadows that danced on the stone walls, framed a cleanshaven face marked by the lines of late middle age. Dressed in a sleek suit devoid of a tie, he exuded a sense of casual confidence, having opted for a black T-shirt beneath his tailored blazer. His look was topped off by a pair of sunglasses. No… not sunglasses, but augmented reality glasses—the lenses had been tinted to prevent any outside light from disturbing whatever it was he was viewing.

"Sir," one of the men escorting Garrett and Isabel said.

The suited man raised his head and the tint dispersed from his lenses. When he saw Garrett and Isabel his eyes seemed to glint with a mixture of contempt and amusement.

"Ah. You've arrived." He stepped forward and walked to the holographic globe. His sharp, steely eyes darted across the map for a moment, as if distracted. Then he glanced at the mercenaries. "Leave us."

The dark-clad men departed and the door closed behind them.

"I'm Jackson Kane," the man said, returning his attention to the globe. "It's good to finally meet you in person. Our little phone call earlier was far too short. I trust Blackwell didn't treat you too badly? My former boss can be a bit... overzealous at times."

"He kept us as prisoners in his underground base," Isabel told him. "We escaped."

As during the encounter with Blackwell, Garrett had decided he would mostly assume the role of unassuming bystander. Watching, listening, learning. Ready to strike at a moment's notice.

Jackson smiled. "So I heard. But I think... Blackwell let you go." He still hadn't looked up from that globe.

"I don't care what you think," Isabel told him. "We're going to escape from you, too."

His smile deepened. "I doubt that."

She raised her chin defiantly. "We'll never help you. You might as well kill us now."

"If you insist." Jackson took a step back, then reached behind his back and grabbed something from the flat rock that served as his desk. A pistol.

Garrett was confused. He hadn't seen a weapon on the desk. Either it had been stowed in some secret compartment, or—

But he had no time to ponder. He immediately stepped in front of Isabel, shielding her with his body. He considered closing the gap with Jackson and attempting to wrestle the weapon from him, but he'd likely take a fatal shot to the chest before he reached the man. He preferred to stay alive a little bit longer than that.

Garrett spoke between gritted teeth. "You didn't fly us all the way up here just to kill us in person."

Jackson shrugged nonchalantly, then retreated behind the flat-topped rock. He sat in the chair, lay back, and placed his feet on the rock desk. He crossed his legs and let the pistol dangle casually from one hand.

Jackson's eyes momentarily defocused, as if he was reading a notification on his augmented reality glasses. "Come in."

Mitchell entered, replete with fresh black eye.

Garrett stared at him in disbelief. For a moment he thought Mitchell had been captured, too, but realized no one was escorting him.

"You." Isabel glanced at Garrett, evidently sharing his confusion. Then her eyes widened, and she said, softly: "He's a mole."

"Playing both sides, are you?" Garrett taunted Mitchell.

"Just the one." He slammed his fist into Garrett's eye, repaying him the favor.

Garrett keeled over in pain.

"No!" Isabel was crouched beside him, trying to look at his eye.

Garrett pushed her away with his bound hands. "I'm fine." His eye socket hurt like hell, and he could feel it swelling up. He just hoped this fresh shiner wouldn't interfere too much with his vision. Already the eyelid was involuntarily starting to close somewhat.

He stood up straight and did his best to hide the pain.

By then, Mitchell had walked forward to stand by Jackson's side.

"Blackwell seems to have some serious personnel retention problems," Garrett couldn't help but comment.

Play the unassuming bystander, he reminded himself.

Jackson smiled widely. "Indeed. Anyway, I told Mitchell here he might as well come in, since Blackwell's base won't exist after today." He glanced at the lieutenant. "Did you bring the LockKey?"

Mitchell retrieved a USB stick from his pocket and handed it to Jackson.

"Excellent work." Jackson admired it for a moment, then connected the device to a port on top of his glasses. He frowned. "I'm getting a password prompt. Do we know the password?"

"Sorry sir, we don't," Mitchell replied.

That took Garrett by surprise. Blackwell had bragged that his handpicked team had already unencrypted the data. Perhaps he hadn't shared that little tidbit with Mitchell.

Maybe Blackwell had already suspected Mitchell...

Either that, or Blackwell had lied about decoding the data.

"Would you like me to interrogate these two for the password?" Mitchell continued. "I'll start with her. I have a feeling our ex-SEAL will spill his guts fairly quickly when he sees what I do to her."

Garrett glowered at the lieutenant. He resisted the urge to plow into the man and start pummeling, well aware of the weapon that still dangled from Jackson's hand beside him.

"That's fine," Jackson said. "You can go."

Mitchell nodded.

When he walked past, Garrett feigned a sudden lunge, creating the illusion he was about to attack the man, and Mitchell jumped right back. He scowled at Garrett, and in turn Garrett merely smiled as Mitchell gave him a wide berth on the way out.

When the door shut, Isabel spoke. "I'm surprised your mole didn't get you a copy of the backup when he was on-site with Garrett's ex-CIA friend."

Jackson cocked his head. "Mitchell would've tipped his hand too early if he did that." Jackson rubbed the edge of the USB stick, which was still connected to his glasses. "You might as well give me the password and save me the trouble of running this through my data retrieval team. Not that I need it for my immediate plans anyway, but at some point soon it will become useful."

Jackson waited, but neither Isabel nor Garrett spoke. "No? Then I have no need of you and your SEAL boyfriend..."

Once more Garrett and Isabel held their tongues. Garrett kept his eyes on Jackson's pistol, and was ready to shield Isabel once more if the man opened fire.

Jackson tapped his lips with one finger. "We're all on the same side here now, you know. You'll see." When they still didn't reply, he focused on Isabel: "Would it help if I brought in your brother?"

Isabel visibly stiffened. "What are you talking about?"

Jackson smiled patiently and spoke as if to a child. "Your brother. James Lockwood. Would you like to see him?"

35

I sabel stared at him uncertainly. What game was this man playing?

Jackson's eyes momentarily defocused. "Bring him in."

The door opened and Jackson's lackeys hauled in… her brother?

Isabel gasped in disbelief. Unable to hide her shock and joy, she ran forward and would have given him a hug if she wasn't bound. "James!"

James was unbound and he *did* hug her. "Sis. I'm so glad you're all right. I've been worried sick about you these past few days."

"I thought you were dead!" she told him, tears streaming down her cheeks. "I saw you die in the helicopter explosion! I'm so relieved to see you."

"They—"

Jackson interrupted. "All right all right. That's enough. If there's anything I can't stand, it's mushy sentimentality. Take him away."

Isabel stepped toward the rock desk. "But you can't—"

Jackson gave her an amused smile. "I can. You'll have ample time to talk to him *after* you cooperate with me. If you cooperate, that is."

She watched the mercenaries haul James back outside.

"Bye sis," her brother said before the door shut.

She raised her bound hands to her cheeks and wiped away the tears as best as she was able. Then she spun on Jackson. "How is he alive? How did you do this? And more importantly, *why?*"

Jackson slid his feet off the rock desk and leaned forward. "Did Blackwell tell you I had complete, working versions of your brother's research already? Devices that scaled well beyond single particles?"

Isabel studied him uncertainly. "Yeah, he did actually."

Jackson shrugged. "There you go. That's how. I had two of my moles aboard the Blackhawk. They had a version of the storage device prototypes. They slid oxygen masks over their faces and your brother's and then activated the device, storing themselves in a pocket universe while other men we had hidden on the ground shot down the helicopter.

"In the confusion that followed we retrieved the storage device. It had a tracker and was relatively easy to find: apparently it had been blown well clear by the explosion. The only tricky part was retrieving it and extracting the three men in time. Thirty seconds doesn't leave much margin for error. But we did it."

She actually remembered someone aboard the helicopter shoving an oxygen mask over her brother's face. Now that she thought about it, ordinarily people don't wear oxygen masks on low-level helicopter flights, but her mind had glossed over that tidbit at the time, given the tragedy that followed immediately after.

He's been alive all this time… unbelievable.

Something still didn't quite make sense to her. "So okay, I get it, you want his research so you can extend the storage time past thirty seconds. But if you already have James, the physicist responsible for this very same research, why do you even *need* the memory stick?"

"Recollection."

She furrowed her brow. "Recollection?"

Jackson bobbed his head slowly up and down. "There are certain unwanted interactions between upper dimensions and organic matter at the moment, specifically the neurological circuits responsible for memory, such as the hippocampus. Who would have thought, when you move upward to a dimension where information is less compacted that you'd actually lose some of that information in the process?

"There are other unfortunate physiological side effects as well, but those are more treatable. No don't worry, don't worry, I see your face… your brother is doing fine. His body is healing well after the extensive molecular trauma he incurred, which was more akin to the microtears in muscle fibers one gets from working out at the gym than anything else. Of course, we did have to apply aggressive hydration to flush out the release of creatine kinase and myoglobin from his bloodstream, along with the monitoring and correction of electrolyte imbalances, but he's fine, as you saw.

"As for the neural trauma… his mind is healing, too. But the only problem is he can't remember the last two weeks of his life. So as you can imagine, we've had James trying to rediscover precisely what it

was he did to get the physics to work for storing particles indefinitely. And that is why we still need his
research."

Isabel stared at him, and her hands balled into
fists. "It sounds to me like you almost killed my
brother by storing him in that device of yours."

Jackson waved a dismissive hand. "You're over-
reacting. We've stored and retrieved many human
subjects. We were well prepared to handle any
outcomes. Including the memory loss." He sighed.
"In any case, he's proving quite useless to me at the
moment. Did you know, when I had him brought
here for you, I was going to hold a gun to his head?
But I figured we could do without the childish melo-
dramatics. We're all adults here. You know I have
him. Just tell me the password and I guarantee you
he'll live past the next minute."

"You'll never harm him," Isabel said, though she
wasn't entirely convinced. "You need his research."

"And there you hit upon it. I need his *research*. Not
necessarily him. As I told you, if you won't tell me,
my data retrieval team will crack the device eventually anyway."

"You're bluffing," Isabel pressed. "You wouldn't
kill a scientist as gifted as him. Not when he can
discover so many other things for you."

He pursed his lips. "I would prefer to keep him
around, yes. But I've ended men just as talented as
him for less. So…."

"And what about Garrett and I?" she pressed.
"Will you kill us after I give you the password?"

"Not at all," he said. "I'm not a monster. I'll let
you live. But you'll be working for me now. Both of
you. I have a use for both your skill sets, and I
always hate to see valuable skills go to waste.

Garrett can do security. And you can do molecular biology. You have quite a talent for working with non-human biologics I hear. Of course, I'll have to keep both of you confined for at least a week so I can arrange the necessary chemical brainwashing sessions."

Isabel swallowed. "Chemical brainwashing... so that's how you got so many of Blackwell's men to work for you."

He grinned widely. "Of course! You think they joined me of their own free will? Many of them were loyal to Blackwell to the core and would have died for him and what he believes in. Like Lieutenant Mitchell for example. Money only goes so far with people like that. Much like you two, I'm sure."

Isabel glanced at Garrett. He seemed confused. She'd seen the smug expression on his face when Mitchell had entered, as if he wasn't surprised that the man was a traitor. Now Garrett seemed as if he was unsure just what to think.

Isabel felt the same way. "Did you... chemical brainwash my brother?"

Jackson flashed a patient smile. "Not yet. I'm still arranging his sessions. They'll come soon enough. Assuming you don't make me kill him." He stretched for a moment. "So, what'll it be? Will you give me the password? Or will I give the order to have your brother executed? It's up to you."

He already admitted he didn't really need the password, as he had men who could crack the device. Maybe he was bluffing about that in some way. Still, if Garrett's friend Archer—a private individual— could do it, then someone with the resources Jackson had likely wouldn't have much difficulty. It seemed more likely that this was just a power play on Jackson's part. He merely wanted to exert his will over her.

She'd known people like that at her previous job, and had thoroughly disliked them.

She sighed. Was withholding the password really worth her brother's life? She'd only just gotten him back. She couldn't lose him again.

She could feel Garrett's eyes boring into her, reminding her of the potential consequences of her actions. Who could say what harm to humanity Jackson would cause with this research? But again, he had already built devices, and could already store people inside inter-dimensional space, among other technological feats—or nightmares, depending on one's point of view.

She would let him win his little power play. It wouldn't help him for very long anyway, if Isabel and Garrett succeeded in their mission.

"The password is Tridekeract." She spelled it, ignoring Garret's penetrating gaze. She knew he would understand. "Capital T, then everything else is lowercase: r- i- d- e- k- e- r- a- c- t."

Jackson typed at a seemingly invisible keyboard on his desk. "There. That wasn't so hard, was it?" He paused, his eyes defocusing. "Yes. Yes. This is perfect. Thank you."

He looked up suddenly. "Well, since you're going to work for me… did I ever tell you Noah Patel was one of my assets?" He paused for a moment, as if to absorb the shock on her face, then he smiled chillingly. "I had the real Noah Patel terminated at the same time as his colleague Liam Malcomn, but replaced him with an avatar so you wouldn't know the difference. If I couldn't capture you, I knew you'd find your way to him eventually. I could have replaced

Liam too, I suppose, but I wanted to funnel you to one of them… make things easier for my team."

Isabel stared, dumbfounded. Finally, she found the words to speak. "Noah was an avatar?"

"Indeed. Didn't Blackwell tell you I've made quite a few advancements with avatar tech? They're essentially full-blown biological robots. You've seen the movie Avatar, right? The concept is similar. Except instead of connecting to alien bodies, we connect to human bodies. We've advanced to the point where we can create a body for anyone from something as simple as a hair follicle. It's just a matter of splicing in certain genes and viola, we have a functional clone.

"To be fair, we're not entirely certain how the piloting process works… we inject a certain drug cocktail involving ample amounts of DMT and other goodies into the driver, and they focus their consciousness on the host, concentrating on the special neural receptors in the engineered brain that allow for the linkage, and in moments their consciousness is rerouted from their existing body to the avatar and they gain full control, piloting it as if it were their own flesh and blood.

"The process is similar to what the Entities do when they connect to their own avatars to experience our plane of existence. I admit they helped us a little bit on this one. I won't get into the details, but let's just say they were happy to lend a hand, as it were."

She was only half listening, still thinking of Noah. He had been dead long before his apparent "death" in the SUV. They'd replaced him. Assuming any of this was true, of course. "Who was piloting his avatar?"

"One of my scientists," Jackson explained.

She remembered when she and Garrett left Noah

alone to go to the bathroom and he had "blown up" the place... maybe he had disconnected from his avatar and informed his colleagues what was going on. And the same thing must have happened in the washroom at the coffee shop right before they were captured.

That also explained why Jackson's faction had timed their campus attack to coincide with Noah's kidnapping. It had seemed like a stroke of luck at the time, that Garrett and Isabel had intervened just before Noah would have otherwise been killed. But Jackson's team had only wanted to make it seem like they had been trying to kill him, to reinforce the illusion he was an innocent scientist on the run, and not a plant. It felt like an entirely unnecessary attack, however, given how real Noah had seemed to her and Garrett.

She nodded slowly. "So that's how he communicated our location to you... he wouldn't even need a phone. Just unplug from the avatar and debrief you directly. But if that's true, you could have brought us in whenever you wanted. We left Noah alone a few times, giving him ample opportunity to get in touch with you."

Jackson pressed his lips into a thin line. "Actually no... he contacted us only once, after you called me, when you let him use the coffee shop washroom. We were monitoring his brain wave patterns, and it seems there was some sort of unknown interference. I suspect Blackwell's Entity friends decided to get involved, as they often do. And they only allowed that final communication through because they wanted us to receive it."

"For what purpose?" Garrett chimed in.

"He speaks!" Jackson exclaimed. "And who can

say? Why does a whale swim north when it could swim south? In any case, thank you for the password, it's time for you to go to your rooms. You can sit out the end of the world there."

She exchanged a worried glance with Garrett. "What are you talking about? The end of the world…"

Jackson wore a thoughtful expression. "Blackwell didn't tell you? Oh, I suppose he doesn't know the full extent of my plans. We're going to turn on the device we're building underneath this mountain."

"Actually, he did mention something about a device that would decimate the population…" Isabel admitted.

Jackson raised a finger. "Ah ha! We were successful in muddying the time stream, then! Because you see, Blackwell has it wrong, the device won't *decimate* the population. Decimate means to reduce only by ten percent. My plan, *our* plan, is to reduce the population by ninety percent, *leaving only* ten percent behind.

"You see, once activated, the device will send out psychotronic waves across the world to automatically kill ninety percent of the population. Only ten percent who have a genetic adaptation will survive. Those ten percent are the next level of evolution, men and women who have some features of a higher consciousness but don't know it—the ability to easily remote view, interact with objects at a distance, and so forth. All humans can do it currently, but it takes a lot of effort and isn't reliable… for most it's hit and miss."

"What about everyone on this base?" Garrett asked. "Will they survive? What about you?"

"Everyone here will be safe, we're well-shielded underground."

Isabel folded her arms. "You're assuming it's actually going to work. Blackwell seemed to think there was a chance it would rip apart the fabric of space and time."

"It could do that, too," Jackson admitted. "The Nesut will be happy either way, I'm sure. Anyway, assuming it works and the universe isn't ripped apart, some time after the population is gone, we're going to replace all the remaining world leaders or those who succeed them with avatars. Some will be operated by my men, some the Nesut.

"We're currently the real government anyway, but after this plan executes, we'll be fully in charge of both the temporary governments and the real governments of the world. The technology you shared with us will be a key part of that plan. It will help us position our replacement assets and dispose of the original targets with utmost ease. Our avatars will help prime the world for the coming sea-change in consciousness." Jackson studied her a moment. "You don't seem impressed."

"You plan to destroy society and rule over the survivors with a one-world government led by you. Oh I'm impressed." Her tone was flat.

Jackson shrugged. "In any case, I'm turning on the device this afternoon. Lesser men and women worldwide will begin to die off immediately. It will take about a month before everyone from the unevolved portion of humanity is finally gone. Have you heard of Havana Syndrome? The symptoms will be similar, but stronger. It isn't the best way to go, but it's unavoidable. Anyway, we're done here."

He swiped at the air, as if dismissing a screen that only he could see.

The door opened behind Isabel and eight armed mercenaries entered. They led Garrett and Isabel outside, and then split into two groups, taking her and Garrett in separate directions.

"Garrett!" she said, unable to suppress a rising sense of panic. She didn't want to be separated from him. Not now.

The presence in her mind returned.

36

I sabel glanced over her shoulder at Garrett as they took him away. He returned her gaze and she could see the worry in his eyes, which was replaced by determination when one of the men shoved him forward.

Garrett gritted his teeth and then suddenly lashed out, slamming his bound hands upward into the chin of the man who'd pushed him, and then spinning to strike another merc in the ribs with an elbow.

Isabel's captors immediately threw her to the floor and raised their automatic rifles; they all spun to face the commotion.

She shielded her face with her bound hands before she hit the stone floor, and scraped her elbows against the abrasive surface. Ignoring the throbbing pain, she glanced toward the disturbance but the other group had already subdued Garrett, and were currently pinning him to the stone floor. Didn't look very pleasant, not to mention he had blood oozed from a gash on his forehead. Her heart went out to him.

"Get off him!" she shouted.

She was relieved that he hadn't been shot, at least.

Isabel's captors lowered their rifles and hauled her to her feet.

She struggled in vain against them, watching as the other men finally released Garrett and hauled him to his feet. He looked very weary—that blow to the head had taken a lot out of him, and she dearly hoped he didn't have a concussion.

When he met her eyes, she saw the pain there, mixed with shame, and she felt terrible: his pain wasn't because of the nasty gash on his forehead, but because he'd let her down.

She felt a sudden sense of indignation then, but it wasn't her. It was… the presence.

She ignored the feeling, not even sure if it was something real or imagined—courtesy of her earlier drug cocktail.

"Garrett," she said, raising her voice as she was hauled away. "I'm sorry."

He said something then, but she couldn't quite discern it. She thought it was: "I'll find you."

She rounded a bend, losing sight of him. She began to despair, and was hardly paying attention when one of her captors simply vanished in thin air.

The other men, shocked, immediately stepped back.

"Corporal?" a man said, the panic obvious in his voice. "Corporal!"

Isabel felt terror herself. Not just because of the vanishing man, but the sudden sense of pleasure she felt at the back of her mind, coming from the presence.

"Don't hurt him," she said softly.

The feeling instantly changed, as if rebuked, and Isabel felt a sense of calm and reassurance fill her.

At the same time, two of her escorts gave her a sharp look. "Where's the Corporal? What have you done?"

She recoiled from that angry pair. "I... I don't know!"

One of the men gave her an accusing look. "Then why did you say 'don't hurt him?'"

The vanished mercenary suddenly reappeared. He was gasping hard, as if he had run a marathon and was out of breath. He sported a particularly big scar on his right cheek—Isabel could have sworn that scar had been on his left cheek earlier.

"Brother, your scar," one of the others commented, echoing her own thoughts.

The scarred soldier touched his right cheek, then his left, and his eyes widened. Next he dropped a shaking hand to his chest, to his heart. He then slid the hand to the opposite side.

"My heart's on the wrong side," he said in disbelief.

Someone rammed a pistol into her cheek. "Put him back the way he was!"

Isabel defensively raised her hands. "I didn't do anything."

Wait... her hands... she looked from one well-spaced wrist to the other and realized, to her surprise, that she was no longer bound.

She swallowed, looking nervously between the pistol and the men around her. Her captors were starting to notice she was no longer restrained, and as they did, one by one their backs visibly straightened. Anger shone on those faces.

She still had that calm sense of reassurance filling

her, but it was vying against the fear and adrenalin pulsing through her veins.

She focused all of her intention on the pistol, hoping against hope that her Entity tagalong would help her jam that weapon somehow.

Please jam it, please jam it.

She imagined it jamming, putting all of her will into that thought, knowing that her life depended on the gun not working.

But then, her attacker simply lowered the weapon.

Not what I intended, but good enough.

Isabel exhaled in relief.

He was staring at something just behind her. His eyes had gone quite wide.

And then, just like that, all four men who escorted her popped out of existence.

She spun, trying to see what had frightened the first man, but there was nothing behind her except poorly lit rock.

She felt a renewed sense of urgency, as if something was pressing her on. She tried to visualize the map of the compound she'd memorize the night before, but was having difficulty concentrating, so instead she retreated back the way she'd come, hoping to find Garrett.

She heard several thuds behind her. Looking over her shoulder as she ran, she saw that the men had reappeared. They'd fallen to the floor, and were gasping for breath.

She rounded the bend and the mercenaries vanished from view.

She felt an anger coming from the presence in her head. Reality around her began to distort, and she felt something else… immediately she recognized it as a competing presence. One of the Nesut was trying to do to her what her unseen helper had done to the men.

As reality further began to bend and distort, she did her best to clamp down on the fear she felt, instead trying to imagine herself anchored in place by a huge weight tied around one foot.

You can't take me.

The distortions at the edge of her vision pulsed in and out, as if the Entity within was pushing back at this unwanted intrusion.

And then, just like that, reality snapped entirely back into place and the competing presence faded. A sense of triumph emanated from the remaining Entity.

She pressed on through the stone corridor. She had no time to think about what had just happened. Probably for the best, because thinking now would likely serve only to confuse and distract her.

As she neared the intersection ahead, Garrett suddenly ran into view. He'd tied off the gash over his head with a piece of fabric that looked like it might've been ripped from his shirt. He was also unbound, and carried a rifle slung over one shoulder.

"There you are!" he said. "Come on, the target shouldn't be far now."

"Wait!" she said. "We have to get James. We can't just leave him here."

"There's no time," Garrett told her. "The world—"

"Can wait," she said. "I won't lose my brother a second time. I won't!"

He studied her a moment, and took a deep breath. She could tell he was going to refuse.

"We can split up," she pleaded. "You continue to the target. I'll get James."

Garrett smiled patiently. "You don't even know where he is."

But Isabel refused to back down. "The Verndari are helping us. I can find him."

"Isabel—"

"No. I'm going, I don't care—"

"I'll go with you," he interrupted.

That surprised her. "You will? Oh."

He nodded. "We stay together."

The presence seemed to approve, judging from the sensation of glowing appreciation she felt.

"I looked out the door when they took him," Garrett explained. "They went down this corridor. It should be on the way to the weapons locker anyway."

He led the advance, and they reached an intersection shortly. He immediately went left. "Your brother is this way."

"How do you know?" she asked.

"I—" he paused. "I'm not sure. Maybe I'm wrong, but…"

From the presence she felt absolute approval.

"No, you're right," she said. "Let's move."

He nodded, leading the way. "We have to hurry... no doubt we've tripped a silent alarm by now. There are cameras everywhere."

She glanced at the ceiling and spotted one of the very same dome cameras he was referring to.

As Garrett led her down the corridor, her eyes lingered on the combat rifle slung over his shoulder.

"By the way, how did you get away?" she asked.

"Brute force and ingenuity." He spoke with a confidence that seemed forced somehow. "As always. And you?"

She wasn't sure how to explain it to him. "I don't actually know." Blackwell had told them to expect outside help. Just not help like... this.

He gave her a sidelong glance but said nothing.

After a moment they reached an intersection, and he paused briefly as if to orient himself. "Okay. I think I know where they're taking your brother. If the map we looked at yesterday is still accurate, there should be some guest rooms this way."

He started down one of the side passages, and she quickly followed.

Just then, more men appeared ahead.

Garrett held up his rifle to mow them down but the men winked out of existence.

"So it *was* real," she said softly.

Garrett looked at her in astonishment. "You did that?"

She dismissed the idea with a curt wave. "No. One of the Entities. It's tagging along with my consciousness, I think."

He gave her a concerned look. "Should I be worried?"

"Only for them." She nodded toward the spot where the men had disappeared. "Let's go."

They hurried on.

A few moments after they passed the area where the men had vanished, a flash came from behind, followed by the sound of bodies hitting the floor. A quick backward glance confirmed that the men had been returned to this reality. They gasped for breath, and when Garrett paused to finish them off with his rifle, she tugged at his arm.

"There's a reason why the Entity is taking them away like that," she told him. "To spare their lives! No one needs to die. As long as we keep going!"

Garrett hesitated only a moment more, then he turned away and continued the advance. Over his shoulder he told her: "You do realize that if we're successful a lot of people are going to die here anyway, right?"

She didn't answer. She knew he was right, but tried not to think about that too much.

First we have to save James.

She would worry about everything else once that was done.

Again reality began to distort around her. This time Garrett felt it too, judging from the way he held a hand against the rock wall to steady himself. She felt dizzy as well, because the distortions were a lot worse this time—the light warped around her in mesmerizing ripples, bending and refracting so that everything seemed elongated and elliptical around her.

For a moment she thought she was going to be crushed by what could only be described as some aberrant space-time bubble, but once again the distortions began to pulse outward. At the same time she sensed determination coming from the presence inside her.

In moments the bubble dissipated entirely and she and Garrett were able to stand straight.

"It seems we're not the only ones who have help…" Garrett commented.

"All the more reason to keep up the pace," she replied.

Twice more they encountered opposition in the form of Jackson's mercenaries, and twice more before Garrett could shoot or be shot, their attackers disappeared, only to reappear after she and Garrett had passed.

"We'll need to take a momentary detour," Garrett

announced shortly. "The weapons locker should be this way."

She glanced at him in wonder. "I don't know how you can still remember that map. You didn't look at it for longer than five minutes, whereas I spent half an hour with the thing, practicing and redrawing it from memory, and I can barely remember a thing."

"Call it a gift," he told her. "There's a reason why I was one of the best special operators during my duty tours. I live for this."

He detoured down a side passage and they came upon a weapons locker.

"Right where it was supposed to be." Garrett pointed the rifle at the entry pad and fired at point blank range. He breached the lock inside and the door swayed open. "Lucky shot."

Blackwell's ideas regarding randomness floated into her mind.

While influencing randomness with one's consciousness is not particularly easy, it's not impossible, either. But it does require focus.

Garrett pulled on a tactical vest and grabbed several demolition bricks, sliding them into various pouches on the vest. Apparently, normally this particular armory wouldn't have had any charges, but they had an inside man who had arranged for a bunch of C-4 to be left there.

But the C-4 was mostly incidental to what they had actually come for.

"Here it is." Isabel reached for one of the two metallic lighter-sized devices their mole had placed at the bottom of the rack beneath the rifles. These were variants of the inter-dimensional devices that Blackwell's group had developed, precursors to her brother's work that allowed for the storage of matter in an upper dimension for up to thirty seconds.

She pocketed one and gave the other to Garrett. Blackwell had shown them how to operate the devices during yesterday's briefing.

"You sure you remember how to use them?" Garrett teased.

She gave him a polite smile, then put on her own vest. She stared at the remaining demolition charges, hesitating.

If the storage devices don't work, we're going to need the C-4.

As much as she hated the thought of what that C-4 would do down here, she grabbed the charges, along with extra ammo, and shoved them into the vest's pouches.

Finally she retrieved one of the two remote detonators and attached it to her vest; she also took some of the smaller signal boosters that would need to be placed along the way. Blackwell had walked her over the detonator's usage during the briefing, so she knew that pressing the button would give them five seconds until the preprogrammed timer reached zero.

Not enough time to do much of anything, so they would have to be well away from the charges if they activated them.

Garrett reverently grabbed the second detonator and secured it to his own vest alongside the signal boosters he'd collected.

Then she chose a combat rifle. Garrett commented on her choice, something along the lines of "glad you're coming to your senses."

She frowned. "It's not for me. It's for James." She slung the rifle strap over her shoulder. "Where to now?"

He led her back the way they had come, and soon they reached an area where several closed doors lined the rock walls.

"All right, this is the guest housing area," Garrett announced. "If he's anywhere, he's here."

Isabel studied the different doors. "Which one?"

"Ordinarily, I'd tell you the door that had the guards out front," he replied. "But since there are none, I'd say we go with the locked ones."

She grinned sardonically, and pointed at the keypads next to each entrance. "They're *all* locked."

Garrett returned her grin. "Guess we start kicking in random doors."

37

I sabel tried one of the doors on the off chance that it would open. Locked of course.

So much for consciousness influencing randomness.

Garrett lined up his rifle with the door. "Maybe your Entity friend can give us a hint?"

As if on cue, behind Garrett a small flash came from the gap beneath the third door on the right.

Isabel pointed at it. "That one."

Garrett had been about to fire on the current door, but then looked over his shoulder to where she was pointing and went to that one instead. He aimed at the lock.

She rested a hand on his arm before he could fire. "Careful. We don't know how much space is inside. James could be right up against the door for all we know."

Garrett angled the rifle downward and laid into the lock. Then he kicked in the door and narrowly dodged to the side as a pistol blast erupted from within.

A guard rushed outside, weapon in hand, but then he winked out of existence.

Garrett approached the entrance and aimed inside; he immediately lowered the weapon and spoke over his shoulder: "Isabel."

She rushed forward. James was inside, cowering on a bed. The room could best be described as a cramped prison cell carved into the rock. There was a toilet next to a sink—she wasn't sure how they'd managed to set up plumbing in here. Beside the bed resided a desk set, along with some shelves. A hanging light fixture in the ceiling provided dim illumination.

Her brother's face brightened when he saw her.

She dashed to him. "James!" She was finally able to give him a hug of her own. "We're getting you out of here!"

She couldn't help the tears that once again flowed down her cheeks. She felt a bit embarrassed because of all the crying she'd been doing lately, and hoped the pair didn't think less of her for it.

James pulled away and to her surprise his cheeks were wet, too. "It's good to see you, sis. It really is." He wiped his face with one hand. "The last couple of days have been… trying, to say the least."

She pointed at Garrett behind her. "You remember Garrett, don't you?"

James ignored the question. He was staring at the corridor beyond Garrett. "What happened to that man?"

"Your guard?" Isabel replied. "He won't be bothering you anymore."

"What did you do?" He looked at her, and she wasn't sure if she saw confusion in his eyes, or fear. Probably a little of both.

"It wasn't me," she said softly.

Garrett offered a hand. "Come on, we don't have much time. You may not believe this but we've got other work to do here besides rescuing you."

James tentatively reached for the offered hand.

But then outside the guard abruptly reappeared.

James started and withdrew his hand as if burned. He fell backward onto the bed.

Meanwhile the guard collapsed and, like the others, held his throat, gasping for breath.

Garrett leaped outside and instantly scooped up the fallen man's pistol, followed by a good kick to the ribs.

"Garrett!" Isabel scolded him.

"What?" Garrett shot her a wry smile. "Just helping him get some more air into his lungs. Can't you see how hard he's breathing?"

"Uh huh." She pulled her brother off the bed and the jolt seemed to recover him somewhat, because he was actually moving and seemed less afraid.

But before she got very far James reached toward the desk. There was an open journal on it that she hadn't noticed before. "Wait. My research! I've almost cracked the code to inter-dimensional storage."

"You already did it," she explained slowly. "We have your research."

He seemed confused. "You do?"

"We do." She gently nudged him toward the exit, but he scooped up the journal anyway. Finally she was able to draw him from the cramped room.

James gave the rasping guard another kick to the ribs as he passed.

"James!" Isabel said in shock.

Her brother shrugged. "He's an asshole."

The presence in her head brimmed with amusement.

Isabel turned toward Garrett but he was already retracing his steps. She and James followed. She glanced over her shoulder one last time at the unarmed man on the floor and then rounded the bend.

"What are you doing here anyway?" James asked her softly. "This is certainly an unconventional rescue."

"Unconventional times," she explained. "We're here to destroy a certain world-ending device. And apparently, Garrett and I are the only ones who can do it."

"I see. Just a world-ending device. Nothing big, right? And... uh... do I want to know what the happened to that guard back there?"

"Probably not," Isabel told him.

"Was it my research?" he asked worriedly. "The discovery I made, that I can't remember? Is that what caused him to vanish? And is that what's going to end the world?"

"No," she assured him. "To both questions. I'm not sure how I can explain this, but all I can say is: we're not alone in this world. And we're not at the top of the food chain, either. There are forces out there beyond our understanding and control, forces that are vying to change humanity's destiny. Some want to help us. Others don't."

"And which side are we on?" James asked.

She gave her brother's hand a consoling squeeze. "If you want my honest answer, I'm not entirely sure. The forces of good, I hope."

"But you don't know. That's not very comforting"

"It's the best I have." She increased her pace so she could get closer to Garrett. "We have to get him to the surface hangar."

"We'll do that after the charges are set," Garrett promised.

She sighed. "We never planned for this. Never hoped we'd find him alive again."

"We didn't plan for any of this," Garrett agreed. "But changing circumstances require changing plans. One way or another I'll get your brother out of here. I promise."

There could be no denying his tone. And when he met her gaze, those solemn eyes told her he meant every word.

Ahead, four soldiers rushed into view; immediately they winked out of existence.

Her team hurried past.

"Again!" James said. "Is it... an alien race doing this?"

"You could say that," Isabel agreed. "Some call them the Entities. Apparently they've been on our world for a very long time."

"Cryptoterrestrials," James said breathlessly.

"Something like that," she agreed.

The mercenaries reappeared behind them and toppled, incapacitated, to the floor.

"These Entities are handy companions to have in a pinch," James remarked.

No more men bothered to block their path the rest of the way. Apparently they, or Jackson, had finally wisened up.

At last Garrett came upon a set of thick, metallic double doors that towered over the three of them. There was no obvious means of entry: no lock, no keypad.

"Okay, this is it," Garrett said. "We're going to have to rely on our Entity friend to open this door, because the C-4 isn't going to cut it. We need that for the target, anyway."

Isabel waited, and while she still felt the presence in her mind, she sensed no emotion whatsoever from it at the moment.

Can you open the door for us?

Nothing.

She exchanged a glance with James and Garrett. "It's not listening to me."

"What do you mean?" James asked. "How are you communicating with them? Telepathically?"

She sighed. "I just… I don't know. I do try to visualize things, and yes, ask for help in my head. But it just seems to *know* when we need help, so I'm not sure what's wrong here. We were injected with a drug cocktail before we left, maybe it's finally starting to wear off."

"Or maybe it never fully kicked in," Garrett countered.

"Could be," she agreed. "Still, I can feel the presence of the Entity, but otherwise…"

"Then focus on it," Garrett encouraged her.

She pressed her lips together, then nodded. She focused on the presence, and then the door.

Open.

She visualized the door opening in her mind.

Open. Please.

She imagined an ax breaking the door into splinters.

Open!

No good.

Time and space seemed to collapse around her in what could have only been another Nesut attack, and she felt the panic rising within her.

Stay calm. The Entity will help us.

The distortion continued to press in around her.

Stay calm…

To prevent herself from panicking, she closed her eyes and visualized the beach she loved. She imagined all the good times she'd spent there with James. And Garrett. She envisioned a glowing ball of light surrounding her, filled with love and joy, its swirling beams sourced from the top of her head and reentering her body at her feet. She imagined it surrounding her, James, and Garrett, and let it press outward against the invisible force that threatened to crush them all from existence.

And then, just like that, time and space returned to normal.

The presence in her head overflowed with approval and pride.

"What just happened?" James asked.

"That would be the bad ones," Garrett replied. "If it weren't for our invisible friend protecting us, I'm not sure we would have survived."

Isabel wasn't entirely sure what had just happened. Had she repelled that attack, or had the Verndari with her done it? If the latter, why did it exude such feelings of approval? Merely because she'd tried?

The double doors abruptly telescoped open.

Well, that definitely hadn't been her.

"Okay, let's go." Rifle raised, Garrett led the way into the expansive chamber beyond. As Isabel followed, the presence in her mind suddenly felt… busy.

Inside, the vaulted steel room was brilliantly illuminated, bathed as it was in a cascade of light from spotlights suspended high in the arched ceiling.

On the far side, the gleaming surfaces of three

large steel doors polished to a sheen reflected the intense illumination.

The spotlights created a sense of both openness and scrutiny, exposing every detail of the chamber's harsh, industrial beauty. Their footsteps resonated vibrantly in the well-lit expanse, adding an auditory dimension to the vast, steel-encased space.

When they had all stepped inside, the telescoping door sealed shut loudly behind them. There was a certain unnerving finality to its thud.

"Is this where you wanted to be?" James asked.

Garrett exchanged a confused glance with Isabel. "According to the map, this was the destination."

"Our target is behind one of these doors," Isabel said with certainty. "The question is, which one, and how do we open it? I'll try asking—" She paused. "Wait. It's gone."

Her brother snapped his head toward her. "What's gone?"

"The presence. In my head." She blinked and rubbed her eyes, hoping it would come back, but it didn't. "Entering this chamber has somehow cut me off from the Entity. It's shielded in some way. I don't think Entities from either faction will be able to interact with us here on out."

Garrett was pivoting in place as if expecting an attack to come at any time, from any direction. "That's both good and bad."

"Yes." She walked toward the central door in front of them.

James joined her. When they reached the door, he slid a finger across the metal. "There doesn't seem to be an obvious way to open it. No seams, just like the door outside."

Isabel tried touching the door, hoping she'd get

some sensation or clue from it, but she felt only cold metal.

She sat down in front of it, crossed her legs, and closed her eyes.

Garrett joined them. "What are you doing?"

"Trying to put all those expensive drugs they gave us to use," she replied.

38

Garrett paced back and forth nervously while Isabel sat on the floor meditating.

"Can you stop making so much noise?" she finally asked.

Garrett halted. "Sorry." He stared at the three doors, and sighed. Blackwell had seemed convinced that the Verndari or whatever they were called would help them surpass all obstacles on the way to the core of the underground base.

And now, apparently, he and Isabel were cut off from them. If their unseen helpers couldn't open these doors, they were royally screwed.

"I was able to... reconnect," Isabel announced after a few tense minutes. She opened her eyes and looked up at him. "I had to... leave my body." She must have seen the questioning look on his face, because she quickly added: "It's hard to explain. Anyway, the Entity is no longer here with me. It can't enter this room. The entire underground base is partially shielded from it in some way, but things are especially bad here... its consciousness can't reach inside at all. It's only barely hanging on to the tether in my mind."

Garrett harrumphed. "Assuming it's telling you the truth."

James spoke up. "We don't trust them? These... cryptoterrestrials?"

"Would you?" Garrett asked. "Creatures you can't see that can wink humans into and out of existence?"

"Good point." James cocked his head slightly. "Wait, I'm not understanding something. You said the entire underground base is partially shielded? Then how has this creature been helping us up until now?"

"It tagged my consciousness," Isabel explained. "And tethered itself to me. But now... it's up to us. Before the door shut behind us, the entity was able to analyze the chamber, which was previously shielded from its view. Apparently, those three doors ahead of us operate on randomness. As in: ten minutes after the entrance behind us seals, the mechanism picks which of the three door to open based on a random number generator. Behind each door is a known quantity. The middle one leads to our target. The first door opens to death by drowning, and the third to all-consuming flames. Randomness. Only those who can influence randomness with their consciousness can open the correct door."

Garrett paced in frustration. "What a ridiculous concept. What, it's supposed to prevent normal people from entering?"

She gave him an uncertain look. "Apparently it was designed for the Nesut themselves, to allow only them. But then they decided that it was too risky, because a Verndari would be able to bypass it as well. So a week ago they shielded the chamber from *all* Entities, both Nesut and Verndari, and other factions, so none could get through. Apparently Jackson is the only one who can enter anymore."

"Jackson?" Garrett found that interesting. "Does that mean he's attained some form of higher consciousness?"

She raised her shoulders in a shrug. "I don't know. But he's beyond the middle door right now. With guards."

Garrett lifted an eyebrow. "The Entity told you all that?"

She lowered her gaze to her hands. "Not in so many words... the exchange was mostly... images. Feelings."

"Well, if Jackson really is there, we'll deal with him when we actually get through." He took a deep breath. "Okay. So. We have to focus on the middle door." Garrett glanced at James. "All of us. As crazy as it sounds, we need to influence randomness with our consciousness."

"I've seen some pretty crazy stuff today," James commented. "So believing this isn't much more of a leap."

Garrett nodded. To be honest, he wasn't really sure about this himself. But he would try. "Concentrate on the middle door. Imagine it opening. We can do this."

He couldn't shake a lingering sense of doubt.

I don't really believe it. And because of that, we won't open it.

He forced the thought away and closed his eyes. He visualized the three doors in front of him. Ten minutes. Ten minutes until one of those doors opened. And he had to somehow influence which door that was. Actually, it was more like seven minutes. Or five minutes, since Isabel had spent a good portion at the beginning looking for her Entity friend.

Focus.

He imagined reaching down toward the three doors and latching onto the middle one with a large hairy arm and ripping it open like a giant ape. He visualized a wrecking ball smashing into the steel and tearing the door off its hinges. He let several more images fill his head, each one grander and more outrageous than the last.

But his mind quickly wandered, and he thought of Jackson, that self-important, posing prick, threatening to hurt Isabel and her brother again. Garrett had never felt so enraged as in that moment. If Jackson had harmed her or her brother, Garrett would've lost control. He would've—

Focus.

He tried to concentrate on the door, he really did, but now he kept seeing himself seated in front of his fire table, Glock in hand and pointed at his temple, ready to blow his brains out.

He felt so ashamed of that moment. If he'd done it, Isabel would've faced all of this alone. She might have never saved her brother. But the entities had intervened, apparently.

Or had they? And if so, which side? The Verndari? The Nesut? Or something else?

He couldn't even be sure if it wasn't his own subconscious mind that had arisen in that moment to save him.

He sighed.

Can't focus.

Ten minutes. There had been ten minutes available. How much time was left now? Three minutes? One?

He couldn't do this until he got something off his chest. He needed to talk to Isabel. It would use up precious time, but there was nothing for it. Did he really want to risk disturbing her own concentration, though? If anyone could do this, it was her. He sighed, then made up his mind. It would only take a moment.

She was still seated cross-legged on the floor, her expression calm and serene. James sat not far from her, his eyes closed and his lips pressed together as if in intense concentration.

Garrett sat next to her.

She sensed his presence and opened her eyes. "What's wrong?"

"I have to talk to you," he said.

She glanced nervously at the doors. "Is now really the time? We're minutes away from certain death… I won't let this be the end of us. And James."

"I can't concentrate. I need to get something off my chest."

She regarded him uncertainly. "Okay…"

"I'm not sure how to tell you this." He swallowed nervously. "I have a confession to make. I told you that the day I decided to check in on you, I'd been sitting at my deck, staring at my fire table, when I had a vision about you and heard a voice."

"I remember…"

He swallowed. Damn this was hard. "Well, I left out something. I was also holding a gun to my head."

Her brows furrowed. "A gun? Whatever for?" Her expression abruptly softened, and her eyes glistened. "Oh Garrett. I'm sorry I wasn't there for you when you needed me the most. You were always here for me when I needed you, and I… forgot you… left you for the wolves."

"It's not your fault. I had some things to work out. My last… best friend… had shot himself a few days before. I just couldn't take it anymore. I couldn't reintegrate with society. At least that's what I told myself. Checking out seemed like the logical choice. An end. A relief. But I realize now it was the easy way. Giving up. Abandoning everything and everyone. Including you. When I look back now, I can see how selfish I was being, and I'm ashamed, so ashamed I was even considering what I did.

"I guess what I'm trying to say is… I was purposeless, directionless… like a boat floating downstream without a rudder. And finally I have a purpose again. You are that purpose, Isabel. *You*. You've given me a reason to live. To fight. To never give up. You've shown me the man I can be. The man I was meant to be. You've unleashed my best self. And I'll never forget that. You say I've saved your life, but you're wrong. When I tell you that you've saved *mine*, I truly mean it. So thank you, Isabel. For everything."

He realized his cheeks were wet. Odd. He was never one to weep. It must have been perspiration.

"Oh Garrett." She blinked, and tears flowed down her own face. She wiped a finger underneath her nose, and quickly rubbed her cheeks. "I love you, you know."

Those words unlocked something inside him. He didn't quite know what, but something was… different.

He lowered his chin, then rested his palms on either side of her head and gently leaned in until their foreheads touched. He blocked out everything. The room. Her brother. The world. There was only him and Isabel. "I love you, too. Always have. Had a crush on you in grade school, you know."

She giggled softly. "So did I. Why did we never…"

"You know why," he said softly. "We drifted apart. Followed our own paths. Tried to defy the pull of fate and love, only to be led right back together again. We were meant to be here, in this moment, together. Whatever happens here today, win or lose, we will always know that we stood together, and we gave it our best. And we didn't give up. That's all that can be asked of anyone. Whether any of this is real about Entities or consciousness, I don't know. This could all be some vast dream. Life itself could be. But all I know is, you and I are real." He gave her a gentle kiss on the lips, and felt the electricity flowing between them.

He wanted to stay locked against her sweet lips for so much longer, but he couldn't: not while the clock was ticking.

So he pulled away. "I want to take you on a proper date when this is done."

"Oh you do, do you?" She gazed with obvious longing at his mouth before finally lifting her eyes to his. "I haven't been completely forthright with you as well. You don't know this, but the Entities protected me and guided me. When I was in the woods after the first attack, Jackson's men walked right past me, even though I was crouched in plain sight next to a tree trunk. One of them looked directly at me, but his eyes simply swept by, moving on.

"I also saw a light in the sky after, when I got lost, a moving dot that led me to the road. I saw the same light again when I was alone in the motel, and it led me outside to the woods right before the SUVs and men-in-black raided our unit. This is why I believe. This is why I know all of this is true, and not a dream. It must be. Because if it *is* a dream, and we're merely imagining all of this, then please let me know where I can buy more of those fancy drugs they injected us with."

He guffawed softly at that and the spell broke: he became aware of the rest of the world again. He realized James was looking at them. He gave her brother a brief smile, and then returned his gaze to Isabel.

"Together," he told her, gripping her hand.

"Together," she agreed, squeezing tightly. She glanced at James and extended her other palm toward him.

Her brother glanced at her hand, then grabbed it, so that Isabel gripped them both. It seemed somehow appropriate.

Garrett turned to face the three doors, not letting go of her. He never wanted to let go.

Now he could concentrate. Finally. Already it felt like his consciousness was attuned to a higher level. She'd definitely unlocked something inside him, he still wasn't sure what. The protector within, maybe, because he knew he'd do anything to save her and her brother.

I love her.

He cleared his mind and focused on the door. This time, no other thoughts intruded—he had full control of which mental images he allowed. His confession had utterly cleansed him. As had the kiss.

Yes, she was right. This wasn't a dream. They were really doing this. Deep inside an underground mountain base, using their consciousness to influence which of three randomly triggered doors would open.

He could feel a certain electricity flowing from her hand, similar to what had come from her lips, as if she was attempting to give him energy somehow.

He wasn't sure how to reciprocate, but he was thankful, and swore to put that energy to good use.

The doors. The middle door. The middle door will open. It obeys me. I am the door. The door is me.

The logical part of him was vaguely aware of how ludicrous those thoughts were, while the rest of him continued focusing on that door.

He glanced at Isabel. Again her face had become peaceful, and as usual James wore an intense look of concentration. Isabel's approach was probably closer to what they needed. Blackwell had mentioned as much during the briefing. What was it he'd said? Come from a place of love and an open mind?

He thought about the double slit experiment Blackwell had showed them, and how Blackwell believed consciousness could reach into space and time and somehow interact with matter, influencing randomness and probability on the "quantum scale." What did he call it? Something about the wave function collapse.

That thought triggered certain memories from his tours of duty. In Afghanistan and Iraq, Garrett had an odd knack of surviving dangerous situations. He used his "gut" to avoid stepping on or driving over IEDs, identifying suicide bombers, and steering clear of ambushes.

In Afghanistan Archer had called him Froggie, not just because he was a Frogman—a SEAL—but because he was the "luckiest man alive," like a frog crossing a busy road. In Iraq, meanwhile, his team members had nicknamed him Spidey because of his "spidey senses"—they often followed his lead in life-or-death situations were there was little room for error. The two times when he hadn't followed his gut, he'd lost good friends. He'd never forgiven himself for those incidents, and he'd left the military shortly after the second deadly event.

He'd forgotten about all that. It had seemed so very long ago. Oh, he remembered the deaths of his friends quite well, and the blame he'd put on himself. At the time, he'd assumed his so-called "spidey senses" and "gut" were responsible for their deaths, but he realized now that his mind had somehow reframed those incidents, and he had misremembered. He had *ignored* his gut, and that was what had led to the horrible outcomes.

I ignore my gut at my peril.

But weren't they all just coincidences? Perhaps. But Garrett believed there were more to these than mere luck. He had to have some sort of extrasensory perception. He had to.

And he would use it to save Isabel and her brother.

He *would*.

So he took the energy Isabel gave him and funneled it toward the middle door. He cleared his mind and imagined three doors, side by side, with the middle one lying open. Always the middle one.

A deep hum resonated throughout the steel-encased chamber.

We're doing it!

But then the undersides of his crossed legs felt wet and he heard the flow of rushing water...

He opened his eyes. The leftmost door was creeping upward.

And from beyond it, water was surging inside.

The wrong door had opened.

So everything he'd done, all the lucky times he'd survive in Iraq and Afghanistan, it all boiled down to coincidence after all.

He really thought something had changed. He really thought something inside of him had unlocked.

But he was wrong.

Garrett exchanged a sorrowful glance with Isabel. "I'm sorry."

39

The water level rose rapidly as the door lifted higher and higher and more liquid rushed inside. Garret was already submerged up to his neck, and in moments he could no longer feel the bottom as he was lifted off the floor by the ever-rising levels. He let go of Isabel as the three of them were pushed to the far side of the chamber by the flow. They treaded water to stay afloat.

As the water continued to flood inside, the ceiling quickly approached.

"What do we do?" Isabel shouted his way.

Garrett looked between her and James. The fear and desperation on their faces was evident.

Garrett turned away. He didn't have an answer.

He'd failed them.

It was coincidence, all these years.

His head was already bobbing up against the ceiling, and there were only three or four inches of breathable air in the gap between water and steel.

"Garrett!" Isabel pleaded.

But he had nothing. He couldn't think beyond surviving the current moment. Fear, uncertainty, and regret filled him.

"What about the inter-dimensional storage devices?" Isabel shouted.

"The what?" James asked.

A flicker of hope welled inside Garrett, but quickly faded. He met Isabel's eyes. "Instead of drowning in water, we'll suffocate inside a dimensional pocket. Even if we don't, when we return after thirty seconds, we'll drown anyway. Plus it will wipe our memories and we'll have no idea where we are or what we're doing."

"But we have to try something!" Her voice sounded so desperate... it hurt him to hear her like that.

He tilted his head back as the liquid rose past his head, so that his mouth and nose resided just above the water level against the ceiling. He inhaled as deep of a breath as he could, because a moment later even that small gap of air was gone and he was completely submerged.

He opened his eyes. The spotlights in the chamber were still active, so he could see clearly. His rifle bobbed up and down beside him, still slung over one shoulder. He gazed at Isabel and James floating underwater beside him. They were holding their respective breaths, and their eyes were filled with fear. Bubbles occasionally floated from their nostrils.

As a Navy SEAL, Garrett knew a thing or two about water, having trained and operated extensively in its depths over the years. The chamber had flooded too quickly: there had to be air pockets somewhere.

He ran his gaze across the ceiling, searching... there. A large pocket stood out, looking like a dollop of liquid mercury thanks to its mirrored sheen; its boundaries waved to and fro, reflecting the spotlights in a mesmerizing dance as it clung to the overhead surface.

Using hand gestures, Garrett caught the attention of his companions and then pointed at the precious air. With large sweeping motions, he pulled himself through the water to the pocket, then pressed his lips to it and inhaled deeply.

Isabel and James crowded in beside him, their faces touching his own.

Garrett took only as much as he needed for that one moment, and then shoved away from the ceiling so that James and Isabel could share the rest.

As he slowly descended, watching the two of them struggle to stay alive above him, his own survival instincts began to ebb away, replaced by acceptance, and almost… peace?

He had done his best. That was all anyone could have asked of him. He'd failed, yes, but he'd tried. He'd been close to giving up a few times, but he'd managed to see this one through. His only regret was that Isabel and her brother would go with him.

Death would come momentarily. When he could no longer suppress the urge to breathe, his final inhale would be agonizing as his lungs flooded with water—it would feel like his insides burned away.

But it would be over mercifully quickly.

Wasn't that what he wanted?

The death he had long sought would be his at last.

No.

He didn't want the peace of death anymore. Not yet.

But what could he do? He'd done everything possible. *Everything*.

Or had he?

Have to save Isabel. Have to save Isabel no matter what.

He didn't care if he died. But he had to save her. And her brother.

He wouldn't give up. Not until every last bit of air was used up inside of him.

There had to be a way to do this. During the briefing, Blackwell had spoken of achieving their true potential. He had said the drugs might help them unlock some amazing abilities. Well, in that moment of utmost need, everything that Blackwell had told them they might be able to do, Garrett would do.

He *would*.

His spidey senses in Iraq were *not* coincidence. *Not* imagined. He had a power inside of him, a power all humans shared but kept buried deep within.

A power that he would fucking unleash.

He closed his eyes and visualized the center door. All other thoughts faded away.

He felt someone grasp his hand. Without opening his eyes, he knew it was Isabel. He could feel the electricity flowing from her touch.

He squeezed her hand tight.

The door will open.

His lungs began to burn in their need for oxygen. He ignored it.

The door will open.

As oxygen continued to ebb away inside of him, depriving his brain of that most crucial element necessary to function, something odd happened.

The drug cocktail must have finally kicked in. Either that, or he'd found the once-in-a-lifetime focus that came with utter need. Because though his eyes were closed, he could *see*. And around him, he saw blue lines of force emerge from his energy centers. They appeared as long, thin lines tethering him to his surroundings and joining him to the doors, walls, ceiling, and floor—some even terminated inside the water itself—altogether forming an intricate web of energy.

He was also linked to Isabel and to a lesser extent James, the tendrils of energy intertwining between them like the roots of a tree. He was still holding her hand, and the lines of force swirled around the exterior of his arm to hers, where they wrapped around the blue tendrils coming from her own body.

He focused his attention on the middle door, and visualized a giant sledgehammer slamming down upon it, shattering the metal door into a thousand pieces. The tendrils of energy that connected his energy centers to the door flared brighter for a moment, but the door did not move.

He slammed the sledgehammer again, this time upward, striking at the door from underneath, and imagined the impact ramming the metal up into its frame.

At the same time he focused on his handhold with Isabel, concentrating on the threads of energy from his arm that intermingled with hers.

Give me strength.

All at once energy seemed to flow into him from her, and once again the lines of force connecting him to the middle door intensified. Other tendrils from his body entered the steel wall just above the door, and they too flashed with an almost blinding amount of energy.

And then, incredibly, the middle door began to slide upward.

But was it all only in his imagination?

He opened his eyes.

His view remained the same: the door was opening. The water level receding. Wispy tendrils connected him to everything.

The burning sensation in his lungs reached a fever pitch: he knew he would inhale any second and fill his lungs with water.

He glanced at Isabel, who floated above him and still gripped his hand. He saw that her head was already above the water line, as was her brother's, so Garrett wouldn't have to worry about hauling them to the surface with him.

He wrenched his hand free of Isabel's, severing their connection. He quickly sliced his arms through the water and kicked his feet. As he approached the surface he inhaled a second too soon and breathed in a good mouthful of water, burning his throat before he emerged into the growing gap between surface and ceiling. He continued that frantic, rasping inhale for a good five seconds, and then coughed for the next five seconds before inhaling again.

And so he continued coughing and breathing in turns like that as the room drained. He had the presence of mind to search for Isabel and James during all that: he saw that they were all right, treading water beside him. Isabel gazed at him, and she had a strange expression on her face. It seemed to be some mixture of concern for him, and... bliss?

The levels continued to fall as the chamber drained through the opening door, and Garrett, Isabel and James were quickly sucked into the new room and deposited sprawling across another steel floor. The water was venting out through grills situated all along the outer edges of the room.

Garrett lay there for several moments, collapsed, alternately gasping for air and coughing uncontrollably. The lines of force had vanished so that he vaguely wondered if he had seen them at all.

While he was coughing there on the floor, rough hands rudely slid the rifle down from his shoulder and took away the weapon. He didn't resist—he had no fight in him at the moment.

Finally, when he had expelled most of the water and was coughing only sporadically, he pushed his upper body upright.

Only to find Jackson standing before him, wearing a wide smirk. Jackson had several armed men with him. The dark fatigues covering their lower bodies were wet.

Garrett surveyed the chamber beyond. They resided in a vaulted room similar to the last, except instead this time the walls were made of gold, not steel. At first he'd mistakenly thought the floor here was steel, but it proved to be gold as well, polished to a sheen.

On the far side was a rotating cube of some kind, also crafted of gold. Subtly humming, it floated four feet in the air and seemed to grow and shrink in size as Garrett watched, as if rotating in some higher dimension at the same time. It also alternately flattened and elongated. It was actually quite unsettling to watch.

That was their target.

"A tesseract," James said in awe. "It's beautiful."

"I see the look of triumph on your face," Jackson told Garrett. "You think you beat the trap? I'm the one who allowed you to enter."

Garrett was disappointed for a moment, until he saw the momentary flicker of doubt on Jackson's face.

Garrett immediately understood that Jackson was only saying that to save face in front of his men, and to sow uncertainty in Garrett's mind about what he'd just done.

"I wanted you to bear witness to the activation of the greatest machine humanity has ever seen," Jackson continued. "A machine that will simultaneously destroy man and yet elevate him. Welcome to the future of all that is, and all that will be."

Garrett gauged the distance between himself and Jackson. He was certain he'd be able to tackle the man before any of his lackeys could get a shot off.

Garrett attempted to leap to his feet, but instead only managed a weary clamber. He'd underestimated the toll almost drowning had taken on him. Not to mention the effort of manipulating those lines of force to open the door.

Assuming he had actually done the latter...

Jackson had already taken a step back. At the same time, his men had lifted their assault rifles so that every last one of them was pointed at Garrett.

Damn. He wasn't going to reach Jackson now, at least not do it and survive. He gave Isabel one last glance, but she wasn't even looking at him. She appeared lost in her own world as she knelt there on the floor with her eyes defocused. She had to be in shock.

James, meanwhile, seemed to understand what Garrett intended, because when their eyes met, James subtly shook his head.

Garrett ignored her brother. He'd made up his mind.

He gathered his strength...

But before Garrett could leap at Jackson, all of

the rifle barrels pointed at him twisted into corkscrews at the same time, as if subjected to unseen forces.

Jackson stared at the ruined weapons in surprise. "How—"

"Don't point guns at my friends," Isabel said calmly.

40

I sabel stared at the vivid scene before her. She saw everything in raw, incredible detail. The colors around her were sharp, vibrant. Every sound seemed somehow enhanced. But most beautiful of all were the tendrils of blue light connecting her energy centers to everything in the room: to the rifles, the golden walls, the rotating cube, and even the other men. And though the colors were sharp and vibrant, everything seemed semi-transparent, somehow, as did the gold walls themselves. She could look right through the men to the gold walls behind them, and beyond those walls to the rock past them.

She probably should have been afraid, but she felt only joy, oddly enough. It was obvious to her she'd somehow attained some altered state of consciousness.

Something had happened the moment before the doors had opened. What exactly, she wasn't quite sure. But it was something…. extraordinary.

She had been close to drowning, and in a last ditch effort, she'd tried to fill her mind with love for her brother and for Garrett. She was willing to sacrifice herself for them in body, spirit and soul. She let go of all fear of dying, of all fear period, and thanked the world for allowing her to exist up until she had.

In that state, she suddenly *felt* Garrett asking for strength, through the bond of touch they shared. That's the only way to describe it.

So she offered him her energy. All of it. She had envisioned a resonant sphere around her, drawing in all the positive forces of the world, and she'd redirected it to Garrett through their touch. She'd also given her own, internal energy to him, wanting him to have it all, even if it meant she had none left for herself.

That act of sacrifice had somehow changed her. Or changed reality. Because just like that she'd spontaneously attuned to a higher state. Her mind had cleared, her thoughts replaced by absolute clarity and bliss, so that she felt only oneness and connection to the Source.

And she could see the *real* reality. A reality of blue, interlinked energy, showing how each and every one of us was inexorably linked to the other. A reality that existed regardless of whether her eyes were opened or closed.

She had watched Garrett redirect this energy to open the door, and when she washed up on the golden floor of the adjacent room, she had suddenly understood how to manipulate the force lines that connected her to everything. It had been a trivial matter to twist the barrels of those weapons. Child's play, really.

She turned her attention toward the rotating gold cube, their target. Like everything else, it too had tendrils of energy emerging from it. Some of those connected it to the floor, others to her and everyone else. It was hard to believe something so seemingly innocuous could destroy so many. She wouldn't allow it. She refused to.

Garrett suddenly leaped at Jackson and wrestled him to the floor. Other men tossed aside their ruined rifles and instead drew backup pistols; Isabel immediately twirled the threads of energy that connected her to those pistols, corkscrewing the barrels just like she'd done to their previous weapons.

Two of the men suddenly piled on top of Garrett in an effort to aid Jackson. Another two ran straight for her.

"No," Isabel pronounced.

She sent her intent down the strands connecting her to the men, along with positive energy. The pair that ran toward her froze in their tracks. The other two who had leaped onto Garrett broke away.

Garrett had been choking Jackson, but he released his hold and looked down at his hands as if he didn't recognize them. He stood up, stepping away from Jackson. When he met Isabel's gaze, he seemed... relaxed, and content.

Isabel approached Jackson. Garrett had broken Jackson's wrist in the struggle—everything still appeared translucent to her, including human bodies, and she could see right through his flesh to the bones underneath, and the broken part of his wrist was obvious, at least to her.

Jackson winced as she held up his hand to give the break a closer look. She focused her consciousness on it.

Heal.

Her human mind had no idea how to set and heal a bone, but her higher consciousness did. Strands of energy from her fingertips intertwined around the broken bone and gently positioned it back into place. The tendrils flared around the break, and when she withdrew them the severed bone was whole.

She surveyed his body, and saw other ailments that needed tending; she further directed healing tendrils across his being and in moments cured him of every bodily sickness. This, for the man who wanted to destroy her and so much of humanity. Perhaps by showing him love and the path of healing, he would come to understand the folly of his ways. Everyone deserved a second chance, no matter who they were.

When it was done, she withdrew her energy and looked directly into Jackson's eyes, through his cornea and brain, and into the depths of who he really was.

"Turn the machine off," she instructed him.

Jackson shook his head sadly. "I can't. Once it's activated, there's no way to turn it off."

She smiled. "There's always a way."

She turned from him and headed toward the gold cube. The mercenaries standing in her way instantly side-stepped so that she had a clear path to the device.

SHE MUST PREVAIL.

She didn't so much hear that voice, but rather felt it. From somewhere deep inside her consciousness.

She didn't slow, and the words didn't faze or otherwise influence her in any way. She refused fear, doubt, and confusion, and only allowed joy to fill her as she approached that cube.

As it rotated, the gold structure alternately shrank and grew and stretched in periodic spurts as its four-dimensional structure interacted with our three-dimensional realm.

Slowly, methodologically, as if in a trance, she retrieved the inter-dimensional storage device from a vest pocket and held it beneath the floating machine.

"What are you doing?" Jackson asked urgently from somewhere behind her.

She ignored him, knowing that Garrett would ensure he didn't interfere.

Plan A called for capturing the machine via the inter-dimensional storage device. Every thirty seconds when the storage time limit was exceeded and the cube returned to our reality, she would simply move it back into the pocket dimension. In that manner she would proceed to carry the device outside of the mountain base. Once they reached the surface, the Entity with her was supposed to guide her to an appropriate vehicle, either a van or preferably a helicopter, while other Verndari would protect her and her companions from attack by the Nesut.

She activated the tracking component of the device as Blackwell had taught her, but it proved unable to latch onto the inter-dimensional cube. A lock was required to select and transport an object into the pocket universe of the device, but the only valid lock displayed on the miniature screen was herself.

Worried that her body might be interfering with the tracking, she set the device down directly underneath the floating cube and activated the tracking component again. This time she stepped back.

As soon as she was three feet distant, her signature vanished from the tiny display entirely so that the storage device had no objects eligible for a lock at all.

She attempted several more configurations and positions, even trying Garrett's device—which he tossed to her—but couldn't get a lock. The trackers embedded in the storage devices were simply unable to detect the cube machine, probably because of its higher dimension status.

Plan B, then.

She carefully unfastened a demolition brick from her vest, unwrapped the protective covering that had shielded it from the water, removed the backing, and attached it to one of the ever-changing faces of the cube as it slowly rotated past. She was careful to place the brick in the center of the face, well within the boundary of the cube's smallest size, so that the charge wouldn't be cut off at any point during the growing and shrinking cycle.

She repeated the process and placed three more charges on the rotating surface, choosing a different face for each one.

When she was done, she took a step back to admire her handiwork. She suspected these charges, powerful as they were, wouldn't be enough to destroy the machine. It existed in multiple dimensions: detonating the charges would only cause a metaphorical scratch on the surface. Even Blackwell had hinted as much during the briefing, having told her Plan B was a long shot, but they had to try.

Still, if she was right, and they couldn't destroy it, most of humanity was doomed. Space and time itself might collapse.

There had to be another way.

A better way.

I need to get a broader view.

She glanced up and ran her gaze along the energy tendrils that connected her to the ceiling. She focused on the top of the chamber, and just like that she was viewing the room from that particular vantage point.

It wasn't so much as if she had left her body, but simply transferred her viewpoint.

She looked down on herself and the others in the room, then concentrated on the cube. From this height, she saw that there were far more tendrils of energy emerging from it than she originally realized —the strands only coalesced into existence several feet above the cube—but it was clear the machine was the source.

She zoomed out even farther, past the hundreds of feet of rock and minerals to the surface, and then a mile beyond that, so that her consciousness was looking down on the mountainside that housed the device. She could see a thick blue line emerging from the planet there—she was fairly certain it didn't come from the cube, but the Earth itself. When she zoomed out even further, she realized more such lines emerged at regular intervals across the world, folding back upon themselves and entering the planet on the sides directly opposite, somewhat like the unseen cords of a magnetic field.

Blackwell had told her the base had been built upon one of the planet's lines of force, but she hadn't quite known what he'd meant at the time. She did now.

She zoomed back in to the mountainside and focused on where the force line emerged from the surface. Within that energy, she spotted the generated strands that came from the machine—the thin, dark, tendrils were a deeper blue that stood out against the planetary line of force they piggybacked on. When that major line reentered the planet, the tendrils from the machine would in turn spread to the other planetary centers: the machine was using the force lines to redistribute the generated energy across the rest of the world.

That energy was psychotronic in nature. Meant to interfere with the human mind, which acted as both a sender and receiver of consciousness, and that interference would prove deadly to those who hadn't developed the particular set of psychic adaptations Jackson was looking for.

She had a thought then.

What if we don't have to destroy the machine? What if it could be… repurposed?

She noticed a very faint, translucent, infinitely long blue cylinder passed through the site just above where the energy from the machine emerged and joined with the planetary force line. It reached all the way to the heavens.

Without knowing how she knew, she realized the cylinder was what shielded the inner chamber from the Entities. She spotted an even smaller cylinder inside that one, coinciding almost precisely with the machine's emergent energy beam but vibrating at a different frequency; again, somehow she knew that the smaller beam gave the Nesut direct access to the cube in humanity's realm.

Previously her Verndari contact had indicated the machine was shielded from *all* Entities, and only Jackson had access to the inner chamber. But either her contact hadn't been entirely forthright with her, or it didn't know that the Nesut had left themselves a back door.

Either way, it would not do to allow the Nesut unfettered access to the machine. Not when she wanted to make some… modifications.

Acting on instinct, letting her consciousness guide her, she redirected some of the energy coming from the planetary line of force toward the twin translucent cylinders. She allowed the energy to pass through the outer cylinder unharmed, but when it reached the inner, she used it to tie off the smaller cylinder, severing the connection the Nesut had with the golden cube and denying them any further access to the device.

When that was done, she enlarged the outer cylinder, expanding it so that it covered the entire mountain, preventing all Entities from coming close to the site, and the planetary line of force in that location, ever again. The Entities could still reach the site in their upper dimensions, just not in the three-dimensional reality humans experienced, which was all that mattered.

Again, she wasn't really sure how she did any of this, because it was more her consciousness... her higher self... that performed the work. She was merely a conduit... a vessel for that consciousness.

She returned her attention to the rotating cube. She was back inside the chamber, floating just above the golden machine, watching it ever growing and shrinking.

"I can't let you destroy the machine," she distantly heard Jackson say.

She felt a moment of odd disorientation. A strange... severing, or recoiling, as if she had been cut off from the energy that anchored her to the Earth somehow, and now floated free.

She focused on the main area of the room, and saw Jackson sprawled on the floor, with a pistol lying on the reflective surface several feet away—he must have produced a previously hidden weapon while she was distracted by the cube.

In seeming agony, Garrett was on his knees beside

someone else, cradling their lifeless body. Blood oozed from a gaping hole in their forehead, and the energy centers on that one's body had become pitch black.

Oh.

The body was her own.

But her death barely registered: she wouldn't let it. She felt a slight pang for the pain of loss Garrett was obviously enduring, but quickly buried it, refusing to allow anything but bliss to influence her in that moment. She couldn't be distracted from her work.

She returned her attention to the cube, and the outward moving lines of energy it produced that were barely visible this close to the device. The vibrations from the emergent field seemed somehow counter to the vibrations emanating from the planetary line of force it piggybacked on, as if it was slightly out of phase and thus partially canceling or negating the planetary beam somehow.

That gave her an idea.

She reached inside with the tendrils of conscious energy that were all that remained of what she was, and imagined changing the vibration so that it was no longer out of phase but rather more in phase, so as to boost the vibratory power of that particular planetary force line. She envisioned it to be just powerful enough to emanate well along the line, but not so much that it would spread to other lines of force across the world.

Her consciousness understood her intent, and it made the change inside the gold cube. Or perhaps it made the change in the higher dimension that she could not see…

If she focused, maybe she *could* see it.

And just like that, the world as she knew it fell away, replaced by a confusing cornucopia of images, past, present and future overlapping and overwriting one another, with every object now become a plural, and the golden machine this massive, geometrically intense thing composed of symmetrical cubes abutting one another in multiple dimensions. She saw tesseracts, penteracts, hexeracts…

She quickly filtered her perception of reality back to the three-dimensional, as the higher dimensions were too much for her to comprehend at the moment.

In front of her, the cube now released tendrils of energy that were more in-phase, just as she had intended. It was now adding to humanity's strength and power, not taking away from it. At least in the immediate area of the mountain base.

She saw Garrett leading the mercenaries out of the room with James at his side. Garrett held the pistol he'd confiscated from Jackson in one hand, and in the other he held the detonator—with that he could activate the charges she'd attached to the machine. At least he was being true to his word and getting James out of there. Unfortunately, he'd left Jackson on the floor.

Isabel wanted to save the man, but like her own body, his was now beyond healing. At least he would soon know the same joy she did, if he did not know it already. Perhaps she would seek him out at some point in the higher realms.

Garrett and the others left the room. She wanted to tell him not to detonate the charges, but he was unreachable—in his current state, filled with hurt and pain, she had no way of getting to him. His energy centers had all but sealed up. James was no better. She considered connecting with one of other men with him, but quickly realized the charges would do no harm to the machine anyway, so she let it slide.

She waited patiently for the detonation, wanting to confirm that the machine would not be harmed. But then she realized there was no need to experience time the same way human bodies did.

She switched to a higher dimension; after some moments of disorientation, she managed to jump ahead a few minutes. Then she returned to the 3D realm.

Just like that, the charges detonated.

When the dust had cleared, she realized several small chunks were missing from the golden cube, but the machine continued to operate unhindered. As she had already understood, the machine's representation in this realm was but a small subsection of the entire device, and the explosion had merely grazed the outer layer.

She zoomed out and ensured that no further men bothered Garrett and James, and saw the pair safely to the hangar bay on the top floor. She watched them escape inside a helicopter.

Her work there was done. The machine would no longer kill those who could not attune to its frequencies. Instead, she had weakened the veil between the realm of humanity and the upper dimensions in this particular area. It would make it easier for people to expand their consciousnesses and connect with the Source here.

Perhaps one day, when humanity was ready, she could return here and increase the radius of effect, allowing it to spread to the other lines of force across the planet.

One day.

Or perhaps it would be better to simply allow

humanity to evolve naturally, with their minds—those great senders and receivers of consciousness—becoming able to more easily connect to the Source on their own.

Either way, she had a new universe of possibility to explore. There were some planets she had been meaning to visit...

She turned toward the sky above, and with a grin etched onto the psychic representation of her face, she blasted through the air toward the stars.

41

Garrett and James retreated through the corridors, which were refreshingly vacant. Garrett had the detonator turned on, and kept an eye on the signal quality light as they proceeded: he attached signal boosters to the walls along the way to make sure the light remained green.

He ran out of the boosters near the elevator, but the signal remained in the yellow range, which was good enough for his purposes.

When they were inside the elevator, Garrett kept the doors open with one foot. He slid a finger over the detonator but hesitated. According to Blackwell, there was a slight possibility the explosion would knock out the base's power, but Garrett needed to be sure the charges activated and he wasn't confident he'd be able to feel the blast while the elevator ascended.

If the power *did* go out, located next to the elevator was a tunnel with a ladder that led straight to the surface. He and James would simply have to climb it if that happened. Truthfully, he was probably more worried that the detonator wouldn't activate and he'd have to go all the way back to reset the charges.

He went ahead and pressed the detonator. Five seconds later the corridor shook violently from the explosion in the distant chamber room.

Definitely would've been able to feel that…

The power remained up and running. He removed his foot so the elevator door could shut, and they began the ascent.

After nearly drowning, he'd lost his ability to see the lines of force and influence reality. But something was happening… ever since leaving the room that harbored the golden cube, he'd been feeling a growing sense of joy. He'd resisted at first, because he didn't want to feel any sort of happiness after what had happened to Isabel, but as the elevator ascended, the joy became impossible to hold back. It was like trying to keep the floodgates of a dam closed against a tsunami.

And the dam just broke.

Joy, mixed with guilt, filled him. But so too could he see his energy centers once more, with thin lines connecting him to everything else, including James. Those lines weren't as bright as he'd seen them earlier, but they were definitely present.

James seemed to feel the change, too, because like him, he was looking down at himself and examining his body. "What's going on?"

"Detonating the charges did something," Garrett told him. "Either that, or it was Isabel. I don't know."

Her brother smiled sadly. "Isabel. It was her. I know it."

Either way, it seemed obvious the machine hadn't been destroyed. Even so, Garrett had done everything that was required. He'd come here, detonated the charges as Blackwell had asked, and it was time to go. He would get James out of here, fulfilling his last duty to Isabel.

At the top floor, three men armed with rifles were waiting. Garrett was holding his pistol, but opted not to use it. Instead, he twisted the tendrils of energy connecting him to the rifles, yanking the weapons right out of the hands of the men. The rifles smashed into the rock wall and landed in a clutter on the stone floor.

"What's happening to us?" one of the men asked, looking at his open palms.

Garrett kept his pistol raised and at the ready, though he doubted he'd need to sever these men from their bodies. "You see them, too. The lines of force connecting all things. You don't have to live this way anymore. Living in pain, in fear. You're free now, all of you. Let go. Embrace joy."

The three men exchanged looks of awe, and cleared from his path.

Garrett and James walked past. Behind him, one of the mercenaries said: "Where are you going?"

"The hangar bay."

"I'll escort you," the man said.

"As will I," a second chimed in.

Garrett nodded. "Lead the way."

The third man stayed behind. He was holding a hand above one of the rifles that had landed on the floor, as if trying to lift it with his consciousness. By the way the barrel was bobbing up and down of its own accord, it looked like he was succeeding.

They encountered no further trouble. All of the remaining mercenaries seemed either too shocked by what was happening, or too busy experimenting with their newfound expanded consciousnesses to care about a pair of escaped prisoners. The original guards at the top of the elevator proved to be an aberration, the change in consciousness too soon for them to understand what was truly happening.

When they reached the hangar, their escort found them a pilot.

"You're Garrett Bennett?" the pilot asked.

"That would be me," Garrett agreed.

"You're in luck," the pilot replied. "I'm the mole Blackwell sent to meet you."

"You're a mole?" one of the men escorting Garrett and James asked. "No way. Well, I guess sides don't matter any more do they? We're all the same, now." He indicated the tendrils of energy connecting himself to the pilot.

"That we are," the man agreed.

The pilot led Garrett and James toward a Blackhawk, and when they loaded into the cabin he gave them a pair of David Clark headsets. These used noise-canceling tech and would allow them to communicate during the flight.

"Keep your mind blank," Garrett instructed the pilot and James. "Don't let any thoughts about crashing the helo or anything like that enter your mind." He was worried one of them might disable the helicopter by accidentally manifesting reality, silly as that might sound. But it seemed a valid concern at the moment.

The pilot, grinning widely, nodded his head. "No worries about that, Cap! To be honest, I feel more peppy than a badger on cocaine, than anything else. Minus the jitters!"

Garrett felt the positive vibes, which intersected well with his own joy in that moment, and he couldn't help but laugh even though he was putting his life in the man's hands. He still felt a distant guilt as well, as if he shouldn't be laughing after what had happened to Isabel.

In moments they were in the air and headed toward the closest city. The roar of the helicopter blades easily penetrated the noise-canceling tech of the headphones, providing for a noisy ride.

Thankfully, the Blackhawk seemed to have no problem staying airborne. Even so, Garrett was ready to intervene with consciousness if necessary. He wasn't sure how he'd keep the helicopter aloft if it came to it, but he'd find a way, somehow. He owed Isabel that much.

As they moved away from the mountain, the joy he felt, and his ability to see lines of force and therefore influence reality, diminished, until he lost the power entirely.

The sense of overwhelming loss returned. He thought of the final kiss he'd shared with Isabel and reverently touched his lips.

I love you. I always have.

He heard a whimpering coming over the headsets. He glanced at James: Isabel's brother was weeping.

Garrett couldn't console him. He had nothing. No emotions left.

Instead, he lay his head back against the vibrating hull of the Blackhawk and closed his eyes, sinking into a deep sleep of utter weariness that neither the noise of the helicopter nor its vibrations could stave off.

ISABEL BLINKED.

Garrett, James, and Blackwell hovered above her. The soft hum of machinery resonated faintly in the background. The air smelled vaguely of antiseptic.

"Sis." James squeezed her hand gently.

She met Garrett's eyes, and he cupped her cheek tenderly with one palm.

"What happened?" she asked.

"You managed to destroy a billion dollar body, is what happened," Blackwell commented coldly.

Garrett ignored him. "I wasn't sure you were going to find your way back."

She sat up. Momentarily disoriented, she realized she was in the avatar room, inside one of the pod chambers. That meant she was back at Blackwell's base. Around her lay an array of gleaming pods, all currently open.

The linkage ring was still wrapped around her head. She touched it. "I wasn't sure, either."

Blackwell flicked a switch at the base of the pod and delicate electrodes retracted into the ring around her head. Blackwell removed the device and set it down.

She swung her legs over the edge of the pod and dangled them above the floor. She felt a little queasy, and wasn't quite ready to stand, not yet.

"What happened after you were shot?" Blackwell inquired.

During the briefing, Blackwell had warned them he wasn't sure what would transpire if either of them died while operating their avatars. It wasn't something that any of the other operators had had the misfortune to experience, at least up until then. And there hadn't been any real experiments to that end, given the insane production costs associated with each avatar body.

She blinked groggily. "I'm not entirely sure... I was..." She searched for the appropriate word. "Uncompacted."

Blackwell pursed his lips. "I think I know what you mean. You know, it's interesting... I've heard some chatter from the channelers... the Nesut fear us even more, now that we—you—have cordoned off one of the planet's lines of force from them, along with the very machine they built to destroy us. Then again, they live on fear. It's their frequency of choice. I'm not sure what you did, but you changed everything. How you managed to alter their machine, repurposing it to magnify our innate abilities in the immediate vicinity of the base... just incredible. "

"I'm not sure what I did either," she admitted. "My memories of what happened in that chamber are vague, to say the least. It's as if I unlocked all the secrets of humanity and consciousness, the secrets of everything, but forgot it all the moment I returned here to my body. It's almost like there's no way to represent the information I experienced within the compacted confines of the human mind."

Blackwell guffawed softly. "I know the feeling, believe me. Well at least we have a place where humans can go now to study and train. With Jackson out of the way, and the mountain apparently abandoned by the Nesut—and all Entities, for that matter—we were able to take control of the Alaskan facility in short order. It helped that everyone at the base was essentially high as a kite."

Isabel crossed her arms. "I hope you're not planning to weaponize it."

Blackwell seemed puzzled. "What, the Nesut machine?"

"No, consciousness."

"Of course they are," Garrett answered. "They already have. Remote viewing. Psychotronic attacks."

Blackwell shrugged. "Weaponize is too harsh of a word. We'll study the effects of the machine, yes. See if the consciousness enhancements in the immediate vicinity of the mountain can offer us any advantages over our adversaries. Early results are promising, to say the least."

"Why do we have to keep thinking of each other as adversaries?" Isabel asked Blackwell. "You're talking about the Russians and Chinese, right? We're all part of the same species."

Blackwell grinned. "It would be nice if we could all get along, wouldn't it? And yes, I would lump the Russians and Chinese into the adversary category, along with certain Entities, like the Nesut."

Isabel had one question still on her mind. "What ever happened to Lieutenant Mitchell?"

Blackwell's expression darkened. "The defector?"

"I didn't see him on the way out," Garrett told her.

Blackwell pressed his lips together. "He surrendered when we assumed control of the base. Like everyone else there, he was high on consciousness. I still haven't decided what I'm going to do with him. You know, I always suspected he was a turncoat, but I simply wasn't sure. I actually managed to hide the entire existence of our avatar program from Mitchell and the other moles: the wonders of compartmentalization. He had no idea you two were using avatars. Good thing I erred on the side of caution."

She exchanged a glance with Garrett. "Jackson admitted to chemically brainwashing Mitchell and others."

"During the debriefing Garrett told me as much,"

Blackwell acknowledged. "And there might be some truth to that. I'd heard Jackson might be experimenting with different mind-altering substances and psychological conditioning techniques to control thoughts and behaviors, but I didn't think he'd come very far along. That's too bad, because I've lost a lot of good men to him, and I'm not quite sure how to reverse it, at least not yet. Though I have teams pouring through the troves of data we recovered from the facility."

"You found Jackson's body?" Isabel pressed.

Blackwell pursed his lips. "Actually, we didn't, but he was presumed incinerated in the detonation."

"I shot him after he killed your avatar," Garrett told her. "I highly doubt he survived."

She inclined her head slowly. "Unless he was operating an avatar, like we were."

"I suppose it's possible," Blackwell agreed. "In any case, it's not something you need to worry about. We scoured the base and there was no sign of him. And he has nowhere to hide, not with our QUASAR system monitoring cameras worldwide 24/7. If he's still alive, we'll find him. But enough of that: I want to congratulate you on successfully completing your mission."

She regarded him dubiously. "I thought you were angry I lost a billion dollar body?"

He waved a dismissive hand. "I was half joking. Because let's be honest, it's worth spending a billion dollars if it means saving the world. That's only one-twentieth of our budget this year anyway."

Her eyes widened. Garrett had told her as much, but she hadn't really believed it. Or was it Jackson who'd told her? She wasn't sure anymore—it was all becoming a blur. "Nice."

"In any case, I'm looking forward to your continued service," Blackwell continued. "I can't promise that you'll always be doing such exciting work for me, but I'll certainly try to keep things interesting. Does a molecular biologist position interest you at all? It may or may not include the occasional flights in reverse engineered craft."

She was taken aback. "You're asking me what I want to do for you?"

Blackwell grinned patiently. "You've certainly earned that right... if it helps, Garrett and your brother have already agreed to work for me going forward. They, and you, will be compensated more than generously, believe me."

Isabel didn't answer right away. She gave Garrett a curious look. "His offer was that good, was it?"

Garrett didn't back down. "It was. I feel I can be useful here. That I can make a difference. So can you."

She returned her attention to Blackwell, and thought for a moment. "The Alaskan base... I want you to set aside a portion of the facility to use as a school for the gifted, and for those who would like to learn about consciousness. Civilians, not military personnel."

Blackwell cocked his head. "We're all civilians here in case you hadn't noticed."

"I don't want any ex-military invited, for now," she clarified.

"Ah. And let me guess, you'd like to be a teacher at this school for the gifted?"

She smiled ironically. "How'd you guess?"

Blackwell returned her smile. "I'll see what I can do. We owe you. All of humanity does. In any case,

I'll leave you three… I believe you have some catching up to do."

With that, Blackwell departed.

Isabel finally felt confident enough to attempt standing, She tentatively put weight first on her left foot, then the right, and slid off the pod. She was relieved when she didn't collapse.

She stepped forward and promptly gave Garrett a hug, kissing him on the lips. "Come on, it's time to go on that proper date you promised me." She reached out and grabbed her brother's hand behind her. "You come, too."

"I don't want to be a third wheel," James told her.

"You're never a third wheel," she said. "Besides, things aren't going to get too mushy or touchy feely, at least until the end. I think."

"If they do, you have my permission to eject," Garrett joked.

James laughed, and then joined Garrett and Isabel as they left the chamber and headed for the main elevator.

She leaned toward Garrett and whispered, "I love you."

In answer, he only nodded. His eyes were glistening, and his lips quivered, like he couldn't speak.

He didn't have to.

She squeezed his hand and he returned her touch. It was gentle, yet also somehow fervent.

She felt the presence in her mind then, one last time, as if the Entity was saying farewell but also hinting that this might not be the last time they interacted. One way or another, the presence seemed to promise, they would meet again.

She hoped it wasn't anytime soon.

AUTHOR'S NOTES & RESOURCES

One of the fun things about being a science fiction and technothriller author is that people in high places occasionally write in, sometimes anonymously, offering their expertise on everything from how a Blackhawk helicopter behaves during vortex ring state, to all the strange things they've seen in the sky during their stint in the Air Force.

Of course just because someone sends an email my way doesn't necessarily mean the contents of the message are true, which is why it's always important to follow up any leads with extensive research. That said, even if something turns out to be false, that doesn't necessarily mean I won't use it, especially if it's something I want to explore or feel will add value to the story. For example, the Airline Abduction video (mentioned below).

What follow are some of the resources I used while researching this book. While by no means an exhaustive list, I've tried to cover the most engaging and controversial topics, even if those subjects were mentioned only in passing, so that you will have at least a few interesting suggestions for further reading and viewing.

Lastly, if you're an author yourself, you'll find lots of fodder for your own writing here.

—Isaac

Using a Thermo Tarp to hide from thermal imaging

https://youtu.be/redhD3P7xrA?
si=xTgrWpGwU7gTlCGE&t=235 (Can These Materials Hide You From Thermal Devices?)

Off-the-shelf tarps can be purchased that will completely hide one's signature from thermal imaging. While it does work for short periods of time, in real life it would be difficult to keep the exterior of the material cool enough to outwit any thermal imaging drones for prolonged periods, as all that body heat has to go somewhere...

QUASAR & Zero-Day Exploits

https://en.wikipedia.org/wiki/PRISM (PRISM)
    https://wikileaks.org/ciav7p1/ (Vault 7: CIA Hacking Tools Revealed)
    https://en.wikipedia.org/wiki/Vault_7 (Vault 7)

QUASAR, the massive AI system Blackwell's team created to monitor the Internet 24/7 is based on PRISM, the codename for the clandestine mass electronic surveillance data mining program operated by the NSA.

Whistleblower Edward Snowden revealed the existence of the program in 2013. PRISM allows the NSA to access user data held by major technology companies, including Microsoft, Google, Apple, Facebook, and others, and collects a wide range of information, such as emails, chat logs, photos, and videos, in its efforts to track and analyze communication for national security purposes.

In theory, PRISM cannot be used on domestic targets without a warrant. However, the FISA Amendments Act of 2008, which has been consistently renewed, "specifically authorizes intelligence agencies to monitor the phone, email, and other communications of U.S. citizens for up to a week without obtaining a warrant" when one of the parties is outside the United States. The courts have upheld that the U.S. government may collect information about U.S. citizens without obtaining a warrant even if the information is gathered inadvertently while carrying out surveillance of non-nationals abroad.

The hoarding of zero-day exploits to obtain intel is also real. As detailed in Wikileaks Vault 7's documentation, many of these security weaknesses and attacks were directly discovered by CIA employees/hackers, and kept under wraps so that the companies who developed the vulnerable hardware and software could not issue fixes for the exploits. Other exploits were purchased directly from private companies, who also concealed the vulnerabilities from the creators of the technology.

It is entirely possible—even likely—that private companies or defense contractors have developed their own PRISM equivalents and, in combination with zero-day exploits, are using them to spy upon Internet users and competitors worldwide. One can only imagine how effective the software would be when combined with modern AI to filter data based on patterns and keywords, giving a strategic advantage against competitors and enabling everything from corporate blackmail to espionage.

Air Force Enhanced Use Lease Playbook

https://www.afcec.af.mil/Portals/17/documents/EUL/AF%20EUL%20Playbook%20-%2020160829.pdf?ver=2016-10-06-110839-517 (Air Force Enhanced Use Lease (EUL) Playbook)

    https://sgp.fas.org/crs/natsec/IF11309.pdf (Department of Defense Outleasing and Enhanced Use Leases)

Pursuant to Title 10 United States Code, Section 2667, the Secretary of Defense and the Secretaries of the Military Departments (including the Secretary of the Air Force) are authorized to lease out department-owned property. This is done via two types of contracts. The first is for short-term (five years or less) activities such as farming and grazing. The second, more complex leases are called Enhanced Use Leases (EULs), and typically have leasing periods from five to fifty-five years, and may include unique development terms that can benefit military installations.

In Blackwell's case, the terms of his lease involved the development of an extensive underground facility beneath an Air Force base, which he would return to the military after thirty years when his private sector lease expired. He built it to facilitate the transfer of crash retrievals, so his company could jump to the top of the queue among defense contractors competing for access to the same materials. If you were the Air Force, and had the choice of shipping a craft across the country to another facility or sending it across the street to a hangar on the same base where you'd already delivered the materials, logistics-wise you'd probably pick the latter. Of course, there may be other reasons for choosing to send the material to external locations (plausible deniability among them).

This arrangement of Blackwell's is considered mutually beneficial, because it fulfills the types of in-kind consideration named in Title 10 United States Code, Section 2667 (10 U.S.C. §2667): Construction of new facilities for the Secretary concerned.

Crash Retrieval & Reverse Engineering Programs

https://thedebrief.org/intelligence-officials-say-u-s-has-retrieved-non-human-craft/ (INTELLIGENCE OFFICIALS SAY U.S. HAS RETRIEVED CRAFT OF NON-HUMAN ORIGIN)

https://www.youtube.com/watch?v=JLZzDhDYMcw (We are not alone - David Grusch Interview - NewsNation)

https://www.aaro.mil/Portals/136/PDFs/FY23_Consolidated_Annual_Report_on_UAP-Oct_2023.pdf (Fiscal Year 2023 Consolidated Annual Report on UAP Oct 2023)

https://www.dodig.mil/Portals/48/Presidential%20Policy%20Directive%2019_update.pdf (Whistleblower Protections: Presidential Policy Directive) *https://www.dailymail.co.uk/news/article-12796167/CIA-secret-office-UFO-retrieval-missions-whistleblowers.html* (**CIA's** secret office has conducted UFO retrieval missions on at least **NINE** crash sites around the world, whistleblowers reveal)

Former intelligence official and decorated Afghanistan war veteran David Charles Grusch has provided Congress and the Intelligence Community Inspector General with extensive classified information regarding covert programs, alleging that these programs have retrieved intact and partially intact craft of non-human origin, asserting that such information has been illegally withheld from Congress.

Meanwhile AARO, the All-domain Anomaly Resolution Office set up by the DOD to "standardize collection and reporting" related to UAP, confirms on their website that UAP patrol our airspace with relative impunity. While 99% can be explained away as mundane objects such as air balloons or drones, there is a 1% that defy all explanation and exhibit flight characteristics beyond our known physics.

One will notice that AARO, NASA, and all official Pentagon statements as of November 2023 claim that there is "no evidence UAPs are extraterrestrial in nature." While that may be true, it should be noted that their particular wording is intentional, and specifically (purposely?) leaves out other interpretations, including that UAPs may be intraterrestrial, interdimensional, or achronal.

Many in the Ufology world/twitter regard AARO as a DOD puppet organization whose sole purpose is to spread disinformation, along with acting as a honeypot to protect some very specific CIA, DOE, Air Force and NGO programs from exposure by would-be whistleblowers. Because of this, many whistleblowers bypass AARO entirely and report directly to the Intelligence Community Inspector General, especially if facing reprisals (as per the second last link above).

Interestingly enough, despite all this, in the AARO annual report's glossary, the following terms are defined:

UAP Incursion: *Any UAP incident in, on, or near U.S. military installations, operating areas, training areas, special use airspace, proximity operations, and/or other national security areas of interest. Other areas of interest include but are not limited to U.S. critical infrastructure, IC installations and platforms, and national defense equities of Allied military and intelligence coalitions (e.g., Five Eyes).*

UAP Engagement: *Bringing UAP under kinetic or non-kinetic fire, to deny, disrupt, or destroy the phenomenon and/or its object(s).*

UAP Interrogation: *The elicitation of UAP location, capabilities, characteristics, and/or intent using passive and/or active sensing capabilities-including but not limited to electro- optical/imagery, infrared/thermal, radio frequency/radar, light/laser/lidar/ladar, electromagnetic, gravitational, and radioactive means.*

UAP Attribution: *The assessed natural or artificial source of the phenomenon and includes solar, weather, tidal events; U.S. Government, scientific, industry, and private activities; and foreign (allied or adversary) government, scientific, industry, and private activities.*

Lastly, according to the DailyMail (admittedly somewhat of a tabloid organization, though the reporters involved in the linked story are reputable) the CIA's Office of Global Access (OGA) has reportedly coordinated the retrieval of crashed UFOs globally for two decades, recovering at least nine "non-human craft" according to three anonymous sources briefed on these operations. That number—nine—is in reference to the craft recovered since the OGA was launched in 2003, and does not include any recoveries the CIA's Special Activities Center may have facilitated and obfuscated before that date.

These claims definitely contribute to the mounting evidence suggesting the U.S. government and private defense contractors may be concealing technologically advanced non-human vehicles.

2004 Nimitz Incident AATIP Report

https://www.handprint.com/UFO/2004Nimitz_AATIP.pdf (2004 Nimitz Incident AATIP Report)

https://s3.documentcloud.org/documents/20743466/nimitz-unredacted.pdf (alternate copy of the above report)

https://www.ncbi.nlm.nih.gov/pmc/articles/PMC7514271/ (Estimating Flight Characteristics of Anomalous Unidentified Aerial Vehicles)

https://www.navair.navy.mil/foia/sites/g/files/jejdrs566/files/2020-04/1%20-%20FLIR.mp4 (NAVAIR - FOIA: Unresolved Case: FLIR Video)

https://www.navair.navy.mil/foia/sites/g/files/jejdrs566/files/2020-04/2%20-%20GIMBAL.wmv (NAVAIR - FOIA: Unresolved Case: GIMBAL Video)

https://www.abovetopsecret.com/forum/thread265835/pg1 (the FLIR video was first posted on abovetopsecret.com in 2007, and was originally believed by many forum posters to be fake, until the video was declassified ten years later and revealed to be actual fighter jet footage)

One of the most well-documented UAP encounters. In November 2004, during preparations for the Nimitz Carrier Strike Group's upcoming deployment to the Arabian Sea in the Southern California Operating Area, the USS Princeton detected multiple anomalous aerial vehicles rapidly descending from 60,000 feet to 50 feet and hovering briefly before quickly departing with extreme velocities and turn rates. The VFA-41 Black Aces were finally sent out and recorded what is documented in the links above.

Note that the strike group was seeing these objects on radar for two weeks prior to the documented incident.

US Congressional Hearing

https://www.youtube.com/live/SNgoul4vyDM?si=yHRDrqy2cn18Gonm (House holds hearing on UFOs, government transparency)
https://www.youtube.com/watch?v=JLZzDhDYMcw (We are not alone - David Grusch Interview - NewsNation)

In July 2023, former Navy pilots (one from the Nimitz incident) and a former intelligence officer (David Charles Grusch) gave dramatic testimony before Congress about their personal encounters with unidentified aerial phenomena. David Grusch's NewsNation interview precipitated the hearing (linked here and in the Crash Retrieval & Reverse Engineering Programs section).

U.S. Navy Range Fouler Reports

https://www.theblackvault.com/documentarchive/range-fouler-debrief-forms-and-reports/ (Range Fouler Debrief Forms and Reports)

In U.S. Navy parlance, a "range fouler" is any activity or object that interrupts pre-planned training or other military activities operating in restricted airspace. John Greenewald of The Black Vault has published several of these range fouler reports that he obtained from the U.S. Navy via the Freedom of Information Act (FOIA) process, the latest of which is "Range Fouler Reports, Unknown timeframe, Released December 2023."

While much of the contents of these reports are redacted, there are some inclusions that make it obvious Naval Aviators are seeing objects they can't explain, again and again, usually by multiple people and in the same locations, operating with impunity in restricted airspace. These observations are sometimes made visually, other times detected by radar, and in some cases recorded on multiple sensor systems with several eyewitness accounts.

Some notable examples from the released documents:

- "reported 2 separate UFO sighting in [REDACTED] by 2 different ACFT with a total of 6 UFO's seen."

- "observed a [REDACTED] UFO in [REDACTED]."

- "This is a reoccurring issue and has been previously reported on [REDACTED] in the same location."

- "reported additional sightings in [REDACTED

] at previous location now with 8-10 objects between [REDACTED]."

- "solid white, smooth, with no edges."

- "uniformly colored with no nacelles, pylons, or wings."

- "approximately 46 feet in length."

- "the entire bridge team had eyes on the contacts,"

- "multiple sUAS continued to be reported on both port and STBD side. At one point 3x UAS were visually spotted"

- "we merged with the object low to high with about 350 kts of airspeed."

- "[REDACTED] showed a drastic drop in altitude to sea."

- "I (pilot) noticed 6-8 small [REDACTED] objects stable in the field of view"

- "encountered multiple 10-15 small UAVs"

- "Upon...getting closer to the object, the pilot and WSO both became [REDACTED]."

The Schumer-Rounds 2023 NDAA Amendment

https://www.democrats.senate.gov/newsroom/press-releases/schumer-rounds-introduce-new-legislation-to-declassify-government-records-related-to-unidentified-anomalous-phenomena-and-ufos_modeled-after-jfk-assassination-records-collection-act--as-an-amendment-to-ndaa (Schumer, Rounds Introduce New Legislation To Declassify Government Records Related To Unidentified Anomalous Phenomena & UFOs)

https://www.democrats.senate.gov/imo/media/doc/uap_amendment.pdf - (full text of the amendment) *https://docs.house.gov/billsthisweek/20231211/FY24 %20NDAA%20Conference%20Report%20- %20%20FINAL.pdf* - (final version of the full NDAA)

The Schumer-Rounds 2023 National Defense Authorization Act (NDAA) amendment, titled the *Unidentified Anomalous Phenomena (UAP) Disclosure Act of 2023*, came in response to all the closed-door testimony the senate was receiving from whistleblowers. The Act mentioned the word Non-Human Intelligence (NHI) nineteen times, and called for the creation of a UAP Records Review Board, an independent 10-person panel that would have been required to include at least one sociologist, one economist, and one historian to review all UAP records and assess the potential impact and/or ontological shock disclosure of said records would have upon society. It also would have given the federal government eminent domain over any and all recovered Technologies of Unknown Origin (TUO) and biological evidence of NHI that may have been controlled by private persons or entities. For each formal determination concerning public disclosure or postponement the Review Board would have made, the President would have had the sole ability to overturn or concur that determination.

The House stripped the review board and eminent domain sections from the final bill, and instead added new provisions to exempt disclosure if it poses threats to national defense or intelligence— meaning the DOD can ask for an exception to *every* record on the grounds of national security. In the final version of the full NDAA linked above, refer to *SEC. 1843. GROUNDS FOR POSTPONEMENT OF PUBLIC DISCLOSURE OF UNIDENTIFIED ANOMALOUS PHENOMENA RECORDS.* Also it should be noted that the nineteen mentions of NHI were cut to two in the final bill.

Those changes in and of themselves are a form of disclosure, because one has to ask, if there is nothing to hide, why the resistance? Again, this only contributes to the mounting evidence suggesting the U.S. government and private defense contractors may be concealing advanced technologies of unknown origin.

Holographic Universe Theory

https://www.wired.co.uk/article/our-universe-is-a-hologram (Theory claims to offer the first 'evidence' our Universe is a hologram)

https://www.scientificamerican.com/article/is-our-universe-a-hologram-physicists-debate-famous-idea-on-its-25th-anniversary1/ (Is Our Universe a Hologram?)

https://www.brandeis.edu/now/2018/november/thetake-podcast-hologram.html (The theory that the universe is a hologram explained in under 5 minutes)

The holographic universe theory postulates that everything we experience may actually be a holographic projection from a two-dimensional boundary. In other words, our 3D reality could just be an illusion, like a hologram, projected from a 2D surface that contains all the information needed to recreate the experience of a 3D world.

Some physicists theorize that the surface area of a black hole's event horizon, for example, represents the two-dimensional boundary for the holographic projection of all the information swallowed by the black hole.

The Observer Effect and the Double Slit Experiment

https://www.youtube.com/watch?v=A9tKncAdlHQ
(Double Slit Experiment explained! by Jim Al-Khalili)
   https://www.youtube.com/watch?v=NsVcVW9GI60
(How Physicists Created the Double Slit Experiment In Time)

For those interested in a visual explanation of the weirdness behind the double slit experiment, which was only briefly touched upon in the novel. Note that I've also linked to the most recent study, which confirms that the unexpected results from the double slit experiment also apply to the time dimension, not just space.

Consciousness and the Double Slit Experiment

https://noetic.org/publication/consciousness-and-the-double-slit-interference-pattern-six-experiments/   (Consciousness and the Double-Slit Interference Pattern)
   https://www.dropbox.com/s/dm44eobt0qi2zra/Radin2012doubleslit.pdf (document associated with above link)
   https://www.researchgate.net/publication/258707222_Consciousness_and_the_double-slit_interference_pattern_Six_experiments   (Consciousness and the double-slit interference pattern: Six experiments)

https://journals.lub.lu.se/jaex/article/view/24054
(Psychophysical Effects on an Interference Pattern in a Double-Slit Optical System)

The results suggest that consciousness/psychophysical effects can *slightly* influence the spectral ratios produced by the double slit experiment. In this novel, the influence of consciousness was exaggerated for effect—the light wouldn't visibly flicker, and the changes would only be detectable via sensitive equipment.

Global Consciousness Project

https://noosphere.princeton.edu/results.html (Formal Results: Testing the GCP Hypothesis)
https://noetic.org/research/global-consciousness-project/ (Global Consciousness Project)
http://www.jsasoc.com/docs/Sep1101.pdf (Global Consciousness Project: An Independent Analysis of The 11 September 2001 Events)

The results point to the influence of global consciousness on random data, but some of the data points have been disputed, with assertions similar to Isabel's objection of experimenter bias (see the pdf link at the bottom).

Airline Abduction Video

https://web.archive.org/web/20140525100932/http://w ww.youtube.com/watch?v=5Ok1A1fSzxY (Satellite Video: Airliner and UFOs — 2014 video deleted from Youtube, but available on web.archive.org)

https://www.youtube.com/watch? v=o5BNiduJwnM&t=2s (Follow-up debunk video from the creator of the background textures used in the video)

https://twitter.com/KimDotcom/status/172853215739 4714739 (Kim Dotcom offers $100K reward for debunking the video)

https://dr.reddit.com/r/AirlinerAbduction2014/comment s/18dbnwy/first_satellite_video_fully_debunked_source_for/ (Reddit debunk post)

https://twitter.com/KimDotcom/status/173319894952 2293158 (Kim Dotcom accepts the debunk video and agrees to pay the award)

The first link is footage of an airliner apparently being abducted by UAPs that was first posted in 2014 but only really drew any public attention in the summer of 2023. Several months later, Kim Dotcom offered a $100k reward to anyone who could debunk that video. Lo and behold, after 12 days, the cloud background was found on textures.com and posted on Reddit by someone looking to claim the reward. A day later, the creator of the textures posted a video showing how someone had manipulated his 2012 images to form the background in the video by mirroring and pasting the clouds together. Kim Dotcom made a final tweet instructing the creator to get in touch for his reward.

While the video is debunked, science fiction

authors love this sort of thing—we're always running "what if" scenarios through our heads—so of course I had to incorporate it into the plot.

Also, something to keep in mind: if an advanced alien race (or races) were visiting us or cohabiting this world, it's likely they'd possess the technological means to take any plane they desired on a whim.

Remote Viewing

https://www.cia.gov/readingroom/docs/CIA-RDP96-00791R000200180005-5.pdf (An Evaluation of the Remote Viewing Program: Research and Operational Applications - 1995 declassified CIA document)
https://www.cia.gov/readingroom/docs/CIA-RDP96-00788R001700210016-5.pdf (Analysis and Assessment of Gateway Process - 1983 declassified CIA document)
https://www.youtube.com/watch?v=Uq1lwrqWZ2I (STARGATE Physicist Unmasks The Pentagon's Most Disturbing BLACK Project | David Morehouse)

The CIA has dabbled in remote viewing with some (limited) success. Blackwell wasn't wrong when he said the hit rate can be abysmal. That said, it's relatively cheap to implement, as such even if the results often give a low success rate, it's still worth utilizing as a secondary intelligence gathering source.

Various CIA programs also experimented with telekinesis, and had some results but they were inconsistent and unpredictable.

It could be that consciousness is reluctant to allow itself to be used as a weapon.

Or it could simply be that we have not yet evolved as a species to a state where we can readily tap into consciousness to view remote times and places with one-hundred percent accuracy one-hundred percent of the time. But when we do eventually evolve such capabilities (some would say we're well on the road already), there will be no need to utilize consciousness as a weapon. When everyone knows everything about everyone else, there can be no secrets—a thought that is both scary and comforting at the same time.

Munroe Institute

https://www.monroeinstitute.org/products/starlines-I (Starlines I—Explore the vastness of your universe in this multi-dimensional journey through deep space)

https://www.monroeinstitute.org/products/starlines-reunion (Starlines Reunion—Explore your role and our collective human role in facilitating extra-terrestrial contact and human/planetary development)

https://www.monroeinstitute.org/products/gateway-experience (Gateway Experience—Enter the Gateway of higher consciousness in this 8-week online course to explore beyond the physical realm)

https://www.monroeinstitute.org/blogs/blog/discovery-combining-research-and-consciousness-exploration-at-tmi (Discovery: Combining Research and Consciousness Exploration at TMI)

The Munroe Institute founded by Robert A. Munroe.

Offers courses on such esoteric topics as out-of-body travel, NHI communication, and remote viewing.

This is the same Munroe Institute mentioned in the 1983 declassified CIA document, "An Evaluation of the Remote Viewing Program: Research and Operational Applications" (see the Remote Viewing section above).

Most people get their start with the Gateway Tapes, a recorded course combining binaural beats, guided meditation, and some light self-hypnosis.

As with any meditation-based course, it can be difficult to stay awake long enough to achieve any progress. That's because most of the courses attempt to induce a Theta wave state in the brain—a state most often associated with sleep.

Because of this relationship with sleep, it can be hard to tell if what is seen or viewed during these sessions is something based in actual reality, or something dreamed. Many people experience audiovisual hallucinations and feelings of a "presence" during ordinary sleep paralysis, for example.

That said, apparently researchers at Munroe have hooked up people to an electroencephalogram (EEG) to measure brain activity during vivid guided meditations (as per the last link above). From the article: …*it was preceded by an EEG that briefly showed a significant reduction in brain activity in the cerebral cortex, almost a flat-line… …the participant's report was of a profound experience, not what one would expect from a flatlined brain.*

If true, it would imply that what the participant experienced was something outside of the brain, taking place instead within consciousness.

ABOUT THE AUTHOR

 Million-copy, *USA Today* bestselling author and Kindle All Star Isaac Hooke has been publishing books since 2013. Get in touch with him through any of the following means:

isaachooke.com
isaac@isaachooke.com

Join his mailing list:
Isaac's Mailing List

Join his VIP Facebook group:
facebook.com/groups/746265619213922

As always, more sensitive information can be confidentially sent to isaachooke@protonmail.com (remember, ProtonMail is most secure when both parties are using it)

Made in the USA
Las Vegas, NV
08 January 2024

84071247R00277